Ken Cameron

EDDIE PIKE IN PARIS

or

THE LOST PICASSO

Also by Ken Cameron

THE PROVENANCE OF MADAME REY
LOST IN FRANCE

Order LOST IN FRANCE online at www.trafford.com
or email orders@trafford.com

Most Trafford titles are also available at major online book retailers.

Printed in Victoria, BC, Canada.

ISBN: 978-1-4269-0651-0 (sc)
ISBN: 978-1-4269-0652-7 (dj)

Our mission is to efficiently provide the world's finest, most comprehensive book publishing service, enabling every author to experience success. To find out how to publish your book, your way, and have it available worldwide, visit us online at www.trafford.com

Trafford rev. 2/9/2010

www.trafford.com

North America & international
toll-free: 1 888 232 4444 (USA & Canada)
phone: 250 383 6864 • fax: 812 355 4082

Ken Cameron

Born in Tenterfield, Australia, Ken Cameron has worked as a director of film and television in Australia and the USA.

He is the author of the novels THE PROVENANCE OF MADAME REY and LOST IN FRANCE, and the director of the feature films MONKEY GRIP and THE GOOD WIFE.

His television credits include the mini-series BANGKOK HILTON, BRIDES OF CHRIST, THE OLDEST LIVING CONFEDERATE WIDOW TELLS ALL, BORDERTOWN and MY BROTHER JACK.

He has won both Australian Film Institute and Australian Writers' Guild awards for his work.

He lives in Sydney and also spends time in a village in Quercy, South-West France.

For Sibyl and Selina

1

Tuesday, August 4: Paris, Rue Des Martyrs

Luc Pellegrin was awake, his arms wrapped around his lover, Catherine, when the ringing began.

'Tu dois le répondre,' she said, in a voice languid with post-coital torpor. *'Peût être il y a d'urgence.'*

'Non – ça m'est égal. Ils peuvent laisser un message.'

The ringing soon ended, but thirty seconds later, the caller dialed again.

'Quel con appele à vingt-onze heures?' he protested, as he detached his arm from around her waist and flung back the sheet. For a few moments, he sat on the edge of the bed, hoping for the caller to ring off. He was in no state of mind for urgencies or demands. He stared at the curve of Catherine's bare hip, her skin tinted a silvery blue in the moonlight. While he had lain beside her, a fog of depression had descended. This was to be

their last possible night of lovemaking, and the knowledge that their intimacy could not continue was crushing.

'S'il te plait,' she murmured, *'je veux me rendormir.'*

He launched himself towards the bedroom door and padded unsteadily through the apartment. The parquet crackled beneath his bare feet. Without switching on a light, he retrieved the glowing *portable* from the kitchen table.

He uttered a terse *'allô,'* followed by *'un instant, s'il vous plait,'* then stumbled through the cluttered *salle de séjour* towards the open doors of his balcony. It was a soft, warm night in early August and it was perversely calming to stand naked and exposed high above the silent street.

'Je voudrais parler à Monsieur Luc Pellegrin.'

'Oui – c'est moi.'

'Ah – *pardon pour appeler à l'heure qu'il est. Vous parlez anglais?'*

'Yes,' he said, warily.

'Then do you mind if we do?'

'But not for too long, no?'

'I tried to call you at your gallery, but – '

'Yes, I was out all day.'

'Finally, I tracked down this number.'

The voice at the end of the line was unfamiliar. A woman, mature and commanding: an American. She told him she was calling from the south of France - wouldn't specify where - and that she needed some advice on the sale of a Picasso. Although she revealed almost nothing about herself apart from her name, he was picturing a wealthy, educated New Yorker in her mid-forties, and from the lush drift of her smoky voice, imagined Alana Daniels to be a Lauren Bacall type: a sharp woman with a cigarette and a dry vermouth.

'Why call me?' Luc wanted to know. 'Why aren't you talking to Christie's or Sotheby's?'

'Because I don't like the way they talk back.'

'So you want an evaluation *plus bien disposé?'*

'I want an independent evaluation.'

'But naturally, in the end, you will go to them to get the highest price.'

'Let's just say, I don't want to approach them uninformed.'

'I'm sure whoever you choose to handle the sale would act in your best interest. *Toujours le meilleur pour la cliente. C'est normale.*'

This seemed to amuse her enormously. 'Listen,' she said, 'even I don't know what my own best interest is.'

At around that point in the conversation he realized that nothing was going to discourage her, short of an admission of total unsuitability.

'Didn't they tell you that my gallery is very small? I'm not in the business of conducting major auctions.'

It wasn't exactly the truth, but he suspected the woman was a misguided amateur, someone in possession of a worthless and unconvincing copy of the kind sold in Los Angeles decorator-galleries.

'Yes, of course I know you're small,' she said sharply, 'but I also know you once worked at the Musée Picasso and were the curator of a wonderful exhibition devoted to his war years.'

'A long time ago, I'm afraid.'

'But I'm sure you can still tell a Picasso from a Matisse.'

'Only just. But those Picassos that look like Braques – they fool me every time.'

It made her laugh. 'I like your approach,' she said in her husky, provocative voice, 'your confidence is immensely reassuring. I think I want your advice right now.'

She had the familiar impatience and cheek of the moneyed. He assumed she was a woman well used to having her needs attended to without opposition.

'Why don't we make an appointment? You can come to my gallery and we can talk about your painting properly.'

'I'm afraid I can't,' she said. 'I'm a long way away, and I need some help urgently.'

He realized that she wasn't going to be easily escaped, and he couldn't press his luck by remaining naked on his balcony for too long. Catherine was already beckoning him from the bedroom, wanting reassurance that the call was nothing serious. But he decided to ignore her and instead settled himself on a wrought iron balcony chair. The metal was surprisingly cold against his bare skin, but at least he was better concealed. From where he sat he could see the floodlit façade of Sacré Coeur peeping above the phosphorescent foam of his neighbour's petunias.

'Okay. Tell me about your Picasso,' he said.

'Oh, it's an oil painting of one of his women,' she said, dismissively, her pressing tone suggesting that the artist's name alone should have been sufficient to secure his interest.

'Well, there were quite a few of them. Which one?'

'Dora Maar.'

The mere mention of that extraordinary woman caused him to catch his breath. 'Does your painting have a name?'

'Oh, sure,' she said, in a tone of perfect deadpan, *'Portrait of Dora Maar.'*

'Do you have a reproduction you could fax or e-mail me? From memory, Picasso painted Dora Maar in so many different ways, it would help if I knew exactly which painting we're talking about. And I'd need you to fax me the accompanying papers as well.'

'Look - if you don't mind, I'd rather you saw the painting itself.'

'Where is it?'

'With me, at my home near St-Paul de Vence.'

'Oh...Provence. That's a very long way from here.'

Luc thought she must have caught the note of displeasure in his response, because she quickly came back with, 'I'll fly you down here, at least to Nice, and pay all your expenses, if that suits you.'

'You are serious. But it's not possible, unfortunately. I'm very involved with another curatorial obligation.'

'I can make it worth your while to fit this in,' she said, persuasively. It sounded as uncomplicated as having a coffee around the corner.

'I'm contracted for quite a long time. Can it wait?'

'No. Do you have a colleague whose opinion you trust? A talented substitute you might persuade?'

'No – not at the moment,' he said. It was too late at night, and his thoughts too troubled, for him to think clearly on the matter. 'Perhaps if you leave me a number…'

'No, I don't think so. How about if I call you late tomorrow morning? Will you be at your gallery?'

'Yes, I will.'

'Then it's *bon soir,* Monsieur Pellegrin.'

'Bon soir, madame.'

Somehow he had been manoeuvred into an arrangement. But did her proposition make any sense? He was hardly likely to press any of his colleagues into making the futile trip. But he had no sooner closed his *portable* and wandered back into the kitchen for a nightcap of Calvados than his thoughts strayed to the realities of his precarious business.

It had been a desperately lean year for him at the Gallery Claude Pellegrin. He had inherited the gallery seven years ago, after working alongside his father for most of the previous twenty. It had always specialized, with great success, in the early twentieth-century French Moderns: Matisse, Bonnard, Braque, Leger, Dufy, and of course, Picasso. Now he had problems.

Unlike in his father's era, the boom years of the modern art trade, there were now very few important (and affordable) paintings coming onto the market. All of the best works were on the walls, or in the vaults, of the major galleries around the world, where they were bound to stay forever. Private sellers expected astronomical prices and usually went straight to the large international auction houses. Luc's business was largely reduced to the trade in oil sketches, engravings, lithographs, and other works on paper.

And now there was the financial crash of '08 to contend with, the global recession that had effectively slowed the market to a standstill. Of course there were now hordes of would-be sellers, but they were on the whole too nervous, too greedy and too desperate, to contemplate lowering their expectations. While the few frustrated buyers had no real confidence and no painless lines of credit. The rental on his gallery, meanwhile, had remained absurdly high.

The contract with the Musée Picasso had effectively saved him. It was for several month's work, assisting in the preparation of a major exhibition focused on Picasso's years on the Côte d'Azur, to be held the following summer at the Picasso museum in Antibes. It had been a financial lifeline, but how long could he make the money last?

Now he was turning down a woman who might be sitting on a gold mine. He would have to sleep on it. Already, he had to admit - before pouring a second glass of Calvados - he found the woman dangerously intriguing. Balzac's roguish formula for happiness leapt to mind. To be content a man needed three women in his erotic life: the mistress he was tiring of; the one he was in lust with; and the one he was lining up.

Naked in the dark kitchen, with the echo of that siren's song still whispering in his ear, Luc imagined that he might already be in lust – and here he was passing up the possibility of any future. He laughed aloud at his preposterous, chauvinistic turn of mind. But there was certainly no future for his relationship with Catherine – now blissfully asleep in his bedroom – although he wasn't in the least tired of her.

Catherine was precariously married to André, an ambitious photo-journalist, currently on assignment in New York. She and Luc had met at the Maison Européenne de la Photographie where André had a selection of his work on show. It had only taken five minutes of chance conversation for Catherine to reveal to Luc her erotic discontent. They met for lunch on the following day, and a week later they were lovers.

For the month and a half that André had been away, Luc and Catherine had pursued their affair without their customary furtiveness. They had enjoyed the freedom of the city for the first time; spent entire nights together without the strain of 3:00 a.m. departures and covering lies. But André was returning in several days, and Luc believed that Catherine was resolved to repair the relationship. Luc's own marriage – his second, to an insecure Danish painter called Hanne – had ended many years ago in recriminations and the finality of safe distance. Fortunately, there were no children, and in spite of her substantial claim on his assets, no lingering regrets. Now he was about to be on his own again, and the prospect unnerved him.

He padded back to the bedroom and stood at the doorway for almost a minute, looking at Catherine asleep. Relieved by the small, slow movements of her breathing. The exposed triangle of her pale back was as perfect as an Ingres.

Finally, he lowered himself gently onto the bed alongside her. He lay on his back, eyes open for a long time. The air was warm and stale, without a whisper of breeze from the open window. He was dreading the dawn light and her inevitable departure.

2

Wednesday, August 5: Bangkok

'Forget Manila. We're going to have this meeting in Bangkok.'

That's what they had told him. Their terms or forget it.

And so Eddie Pike had flown in late Friday night. Tail end of a typhoon. The whole planeload terrified. All along the aisle, that look in their eyes. Toilet floor slippery with vomit. All of them, wanting to kiss the tiles in the arrival hall.

They were picking up the tab for two nights at the Royal Orchid. Room on the tenth floor with a nice view along the river. But the meeting was going to be in the Bussaracum, downstairs at the Dusit Thani hotel. Had to be Royal Thai cuisine. You're going to fly all this way for a meeting, you're going to at least eat right. That's how they put it to him. They were going to lay out their whole proposal between the courses of the best Royal Thai banquet he'd ever had. Who could tell where these guys were coming from?

Eddie liked hotels. Beat the hell out of the old days in Bangkok, when he'd rented a dump of an apartment off Rajadamri. Had a good view of Lumpini Park, but that was all there was to recommend it. Eddie took a long shower, made himself a vodka over ice, scooped up a handful of complementary lychees, then stepped out onto the balcony in the bathrobe-that-he-might-choose-to-purchase. He liked the warm breath of the river air on his damp skin. It was five years since he'd lived in Bangkok, but it still felt like home. He cracked the horny skin of a lychee with his teeth, separated the pulp with his tongue, then spat the smooth seed over the railing. Heard it bounce off the steel roof of a moored river ferry. Complaining Thai voices floated up to him. That kind of silly shit could still make him laugh.

Later, he unpacked his case. Hung up his shirts and trousers, spread his toiletries along the bathroom shelf, and stored his weapon, a Beretta 92 Fs 9mm, in the room safe.

He took an air conditioned taxi up to the Dusit Thani. It was a short ride. He could easily have walked up Silom, but why break a sweat. They were paying.

Eddie was there first, watching from a bar stool as they came down the carpeted stairs. Calm looking pricks was his first impression. Here to instruct the tradesman. They all mumbled greetings and shook hands. Just like business associates, if anyone happened to be observing. Mister Piers Toop and Mister Dom Gornik. Toop introduced himself as a company director, and Gornik claimed to be a financier. Both had their businesses in Melbourne. Both had recently been burned by the global financial meltdown. That much needed no explanation.

A slender, doll-like waitress ushered them to a table at the back of the hushed, sparsely occupied room. Eddie knew he should have been scrutinizing Toop and Gornik, but he couldn't take his eyes off her. She was beautiful. Rosebud lips, almond eyes, perfect honey skin. He was prepared to string out the ordering all evening if it meant he could stare at that long neck and bare shoulders.

She triggered a sudden picture of his daughter, Shelly – Michelle, twenty-two years old on the 2nd of July, living who knew where, last heard from in early '06, a postcard from the Barossa, five lousy lines, *'screw nursing,'* now living with an itinerant grape picker called Trig. She had those same lips, skin that tanned easily, eyes to get lost in. Last seen, aged sixteen. He still fired off the occasional card, but nothing ever came back. That was the price he'd paid.

He took in the Thai girl. She was nothing like those country rough-heads you saw down on Patpong. The ones he'd seen night after night in neon-lit joints. Sliding towards you on a wet bar top. Firing ice cubes from their twats. This one was refined, educated, probably promised to some slick young banker with family connections. Nothing about her you could ever buy. For a few silly moments, he tried to imagine her undressing in the bedroom of his hotel room above the Chao Phya. Bad idea. Not possible.

Gornik and Toop ordered the full course banquet for three, and blew a wad of baht on an expensive bottle of *Châteauneuf-du-Pape*. They also attempted to flirt with the waitress. Asking unnecessary questions - it was all there on the menu - and plying her for recommendations. She reminded Eddie of one of those Singapore Airlines hostesses. All titillation and professional distance. On a flight out of Sydney one time he'd made the mistake of touching one in the wrong place. Rested an unsteady hand on her tit as he made his way back to his seat during turbulence. Easy mistake to make, but she'd called the steward, who threatened arrest upon disembarkation. Eddie had faked an apology, doing a fine impersonation of a man who'd just come to his senses. Strangely, they had upgraded him on the spot, but not before sedating him with sleeping pills. Nearly lost a foot from numbness. By the time they landed, the offended hostess had vanished - hiding up the back of the plane, he guessed. Never to be seen again. Eddie, meanwhile, had staggered off into the night with his head full of dark expectations. Things happened to you in Asia.

When he had first come here, back in the early nineties, he couldn't help himself. There had been some nights. But in Bangkok, he soon learned, an unchecked appetite could kill you. They turn you into skeletons, an old hand had once told him. He was far more discriminating these days, The only ones who ever aroused his interest were unattainable. Safer that way. Their exotic bloom was an affront to the middle aged.

Eddie transferred his attention to his dinner companions. It was Gornik that had him worried. He reminded Eddie of a tennis star from the eighties: a suntanned Ivan Lendl. Gornik had that same central European, long-faced smugness. The same vain air of fitness and self preservation. And Eddie could read intolerance and calculating superiority, and possibly even a dangerous mendacity in the man's tiny blue eyes. Of Toop, he could discern very little. Second generation Dutch, he guessed - whatever conclusions you could draw from that. It seemed the man was determined to remain unmemorable. However, he certainly looked aggrieved, as though the shame of being fiscally undone was still eating at him. The man's every word and gesture was masked by an insufferable civility, and it was just as well he allowed Gornik to do all the talking.

If the meal had not begun to arrive so promptly, Eddie might not have gone the distance. But as if their only problem had been acute hunger, Gornik and Toop seemed to relax at the appearance of the first steaming dish. Another bottle of the *Châteauneuf-du-Pape* was ordered - not that you could taste anything but alcohol under all those spicy sauces - and every new platter was all but licked clean.

There had been a time when Eddie, too, had considered Royal Thai to be the ultimate dining experience. Bangkok was his number one place for ultimate experiences. Nowadays his palate was more jaded - too many red curries, too much coriander. His dining pals had no such reservations. They appraised each new dish with a kind of phoney gourmandizing zeal. Gornik's only recognizably human reaction all evening came in the form of a blazing chili flush. His eyes teared up and his face ran with sweat. In a panic he grabbed the bottle, poured, and swilled his mouth with wine.

'Stuff your mouth with rice,' Eddie advised, but Gornik ignored him and croaked a request to the ever-solicitous waitress for a jug of iced water.

Once Gornik's crisis had been dealt with, Toop signaled that business was to commence by pushing aside a few of the plates. He took a piece of folded paper from his pocket and spread it open in front of Eddie. It was a digitally printed reproduction of a mid twentieth-century painting, a portrait of a glamorous looking woman, rendered in bright colours, with all her facial features distorted. The photograph also included the ornate gilt frame, and revealed a portion of the bare ochre wall on which the painting was hung.

It didn't do a thing for Eddie. He wasn't entirely ignorant when it came to modern art, but his tastes were very narrow. He liked Pop Art - bright, simple things, visual jokes, stuff that you could get straight away. But he also liked that painter Balthus - all those mysterious young girls, standing around in tense, erotic postures. And he liked Klee, too - colour and geometry, he could appreciate work like that.

'Know what you're looking at, Eddie?' Gornik said.

'Art,' he answered, with a dead, supercilious grin.

'It's painted by Pablo Picasso, and it's called *Portrait of Dora Maar*. And it could be worth anything up to twenty million U.S. That's what these things fetch today.'

Picasso? Eddie wouldn't have picked it as a Picasso. He had only ever associated the name with sad looking harlequins, chopped up guitars, and buxom women cavorting on beaches.

'So who was this woman?' Eddie asked.

'Old girlfriend of Picasso's, back around World War Two.'

Gornik said. 'He painted her a lot of times. This is one of his more attractive attempts.'

'And this is what you want me to repossess?'

'That – and a few others.'

'So where are they?'

'Somewhere in France,' Gornik said, with straight-faced amusement.

'Should be easy then.'

They're wherever Michael McGraw is hiding out,' Toop offered. 'They might be on a wall in some *château*, might be boxed up in a cellar some place, or even in the boot of his fucking car. We don't know...exactly.'

Eddie smiled. 'Not at all, in fact.'

'But you know who we're talking about?' Gornik said.

'Sure.'

Eddie had heard a lot about Michael McGraw. Everybody had. He had been Australia's largest hedge fund manager until the crash of '08; until over a billion dollars of Australian investors' money had mysteriously evaporated – vanished, as the media had speculated, into McGraw's vast offshore holdings in Europe and Asia. Now McGraw, too, had disappeared, pursued by the Australian Federal Police, the Attorney-General's Department, and the Australian Securities and Investments Commission. Not a week went by without newspaper reports of the hunt for Michael McGraw.

Toop took several other folded sheets of paper from his pocket, then laid them flat in a row alongside the *Portrait of Dora Maar*. He explained that they were all photographs of works painted by Picasso in the decade before World War Two.

The first was of an anguished woman's face, constructed from flattened geometric shapes and painted in clashing primary colours. Next was a small picture of what appeared to be a terrified dying bull, drawn with misplaced horns, rump, hooves and testicles. The last was of a gigantic, ungainly couple, playing on a beach, painted to give the illusion of being a sculptural assemblage of massive orange stones.

'He owns other paintings,' Toop said, 'but we don't know anything about them. These four are the money. Together worth anything from a hundred to a hundred-and-twenty million US – maybe even more.'

Eddie was more curious about the setting in which the pictures had been taken. 'Who took these photographs?' he asked.

'Not sure,' Gornik said. 'Probably somebody working for McGraw. Most likely taken for insurance purposes. But I don't know how Leon got hold of them.'

'Who's Leon?'

'Leon Meyer – he's the client.'

'Right. I already had the impression it wasn't you two.'

'So who is this Leon Meyer?'

He's an American investment banker who used to work with McGraw. He ran a similar, associated hedge fund out of New York.'

'So now he's trying to steal his old partner's assets?'

Gornik and Toop both looked at him vacantly, clearly moral issues weren't their concern.

'So what's your connection with Leon Meyer?' Eddie asked. He had the impression they were trying to side track him.

'Leon? We're in business together,' Gornik said. 'He looks after Europe and the US for us.'

'This is since McGraw disappeared?'

'Yeah – whenever,' said Toop, dismissively. 'We're all owed by McGraw.'

'And that's where we come in,' Gornik interjected. 'My friend here,' he continued, giving Toop a consoling pat on the shoulder, 'lost seventeen million to that prick.'

'Believe me, that hurt,' said Toop.

'And you're trying to get some of it back before the vultures from ASIC and the Australian Tax Office move in?'

'Something like that.'

They went on to tell him some of McGraw's history. The man was clearly trying to salvage as much of his personal fortune as possible. Most of it appeared to be tied up in Asian real estate – resorts and high-rise residential developments in several countries – but he had diverse holdings in Europe as well. And that was where they believed he was living at present. They explained how the process of trying to extradite him, and then attempt a recovery of his assets, might take many months. Toop and Gornik claimed to be frustrated with the rate of progress, and were skeptical of the outcome. Australia didn't even have a direct agreement with France when it came to legal proceedings in civil and commercial matters, but had to operate under an outdated and unwieldy 1922 convention between the UK and France. They had good reason for believing that most of McGraw's readily liquidated assets – besides works of art, they were talking about US Treasury Bonds, stock options, and a mountain of cash – were, in the meantime, being squirreled away in France. And so 'alternative' and immediate reimbursement was what they were seeking.

'But the government investigators – surely they must know about these paintings,' Eddie said.

Toop shrugged. 'Maybe they do. Maybe they don't. They certainly never refer to them in their press releases when they list all his other assets.'

'So why do they overlook them?'

'Probably because they're not even legitimately McGraw's property. Well – at least the *Portrait of Dora Maar* isn't. From what Meyer tells us, McGraw bought that one from a crooked dealer in Switzerland. The painting had been out of circulation for years. Apparently someone stole it way back in the forties, and it's been in criminal hands ever since. But then, who knows the real story? All I'm told is, it's never seen in public - always kept under wraps. My guess is, most people aren't even sure if it still exists.'

'Maybe you should explain the deal to me, ' Eddie said.

'Five hundred thousand euros – a million Australian, give or take - to deliver these painting,' Gornik said. 'Simple as that.'

But explaining what was simple about it had taken the pair another two hours. Eddie would receive the first installment of his fee - one hundred thousand euros - upon arrival in Paris. It would be waiting for him in a bank account, under whatever name he chose. The remainder, he'd get in cash at the airport, once the paintings had been handed over and positively identified. He could hire whomever he liked. They didn't appear to want involvement. But Leon, they assured him, would be prepared to make some recommendations. Naturally, he would prefer Eddie to use locals. Men with no records, people you could walk away from.

'So the only problem is finding McGraw,' Eddie said, with quiet sarcasm.

'Leon tells us that he moves around a lot,' was all Gornik had to offer.

'That's a big fucking help.'

They tried to reassure him that Leon would be taking care of that small detail.

'I'll be meeting this Leon guy in Paris, is that it?'

Toop shrugged. 'Who knows what the arrangement will be? But you'll hear from him one way or another.'

'And how does Leon know so much about what McGraw has done with his paintings?'

'Believe me, he'll know where they are, and how to get to them,' Gornik said. He was the blunt instrument, ever vigilant, ready to head off any awkward questions.

'How does Leon know they aren't in some bank vault? Thing's are worth that much, you'd expect the man to lock them away.'

'McGraw can't risk letting them out of his hands,' Gornik said. 'If the legal challenge by the Australian Attorney-General's Department succeeds, then the bank would simply hand them over.'

"That's if they're even in a French bank.'

Gornik ignored the complication. 'Besides, McGraw would be wanting to sell the works any way he could - he'd have to keep them close at hand.'

'Sounds like this Leon guy's got it covered,' Eddie said, making no attempt to hide his cynicism. 'So why does he need me?'

'You're a professional,' Gornik said smoothly, helping himself to the last of the *Châteauneuf-du-Pape*. 'He likes your work.'

'He knows fuck all about me,' Eddie challenged.

'Don't you believe it. The man does his research.'

Eddie had to admit that it was possible they knew it all. It wouldn't have been hard to track down his recent history. He was getting a reputation out east: asset recovery; all difficulties surmounted. He had once lifted a Rolls from a walled estate in Manila, right under the noses of armed bodyguards, no complications. Eddie had the pedigree, and he had the mystique. Cost you a bundle, but you got your result.

'What kind of approach is he expecting?'

'What have you got?' Gornik asked.

'There's slow and there's fast.'

'I'd say, give us fast.'

'Okay - there's also clean and there's messy.'

'You're gonna tell me that fast is messy, right?'

'Can be. One way, I take my time, look into it from all directions. Make a plan. Plans take up time. Other way – given I can ever find this prick - I walk straight in and lift them off the wall. Anything can happen. You get your paintings, but you also get all the shit that generally comes with it.'

Gornik was beginning to look concerned. 'Okay, okay. Clean and untraceable will be just fine,' he said. 'But it better not be too slow.'

'Your choice.'

'I hope so,' said Toop, with a none too subtle note of warning.

'Sounds to me like Leon should be around to run this himself.'

'Oh, he'll be around,' Gornik said, shooting an amused look at Toop. 'He won't be over your shoulder, but he'll be around.'

Getting to McGraw, that was Leon's responsibility. He would steer Eddie in the right direction, give him enough play money. Their main concern was that there were to be no loose ends. Nothing and no one to bite them on the arse once news of the deed broke. As it inevitably would. And as for Eddie Pike? He was to simply melt away and lie low for as long as it took. That was the arrangement. He didn't like it, he could leave the table before the coffee and dessert.

And what if McGraw got hurt in the process, Eddie wanted to know. Evidently it wasn't regarded as his concern. Mr Toop and Mr Gornik remained stone-faced and evasive.

'We realize that asset recovery is a complicated, risky business,' Gornik said blandly.

'So you don't give a fuck if it ends in the man's death?'

'Just so long as it ends in our satisfaction,' was all Gornik added

'Speak any French, Eddie?' Toop asked, in what Eddie realized was his habitual patronizing manner.

'Even my English is rudimentary.' It was the answer Toop deserved.

He'd take care of the language problem the same way he always did. Buy a Lonely Planet phrase book and a nine dollar ninety-five pocket dictionary. Only problem was, there were never any entries for *'Look at me when I'm talking to you, arsehole!'* or *'Drop the gun! Right fuckin' now!'* He'd have to set aside a little study time. Figure out how to tack a few new phrases together. End up with a language anyone could understand.

Eddie wasn't sure he trusted these guys. They seemed all too easy to read. Claimed to be Melbourne businessmen, but offered no details. Private school manners, Eddie thought. Arrogant and smooth, but maybe not as smart as they imagined. Of course, it was all about reimbursement - at least he knew that. But these guys were too ineffectual, too cautious, to go after it personally.

And there were curious hints of rancour beneath their veneer of civility. They'd turn their backs on him when the time came, he knew at least that much. And as for Leon Meyer - there was no comfort there, he'd have to wait until he met the man.

All that was clear was that Eddie was being hired to perpetrate a serious theft. If he fucked up, the French police would descend upon him, and the consequences of the operation would be his alone. After the job had been completed, these guys expected him to fade back to Asia. There would be no other links.

Eddie tried to explain to them that of all risky criminal undertakings, major armed theft was the most unmanageable. Right up there with kidnapping and murder. Things had a tendency to unravel, no matter how well planned. But nothing seemed to faze these guys. They encouraged Eddie to think of it in that favourite phrase of theirs: simple asset recovery. Professional all the way.

There was no rushing into this, they reassured him. They wanted him to sleep on it. They'd all meet again tomorrow at noon - terrace restaurant of the Oriental.

Mr Gornik and Mr Toop rose from the table at ten, pleading jet lag. Early nights were necessary in the tropics. They each shook Eddie's hand and departed, leaving behind a pile of baht for the bill.

And leaving Eddie wondering whether the waitress with the neck would come to collect it.

3

Wednesday, August 5: Paris, Rue des Martyrs

Luc Pellegrin woke to the sound of movement in his apartment. A curtain flapping in the breeze. An empty bed. Discarded pillows. Catherine's clothing and cosmetics heaped on a chair by the window. He rose and shuffled to the bathroom. Rinsed his face and studied himself in the mirror. This was the morning of her leaving, and there was nothing he could do to prevent it.

He went out for croissants, coffee beans and a copy of *Le Monde.* By then she was dressed and almost packed. He found her in the *salle de séjour*, gathering up the last of her possessions: a boxed set of Schubert's piano sonatas (she seemed to never tire of the melancholy last one in B flat major), the discs scattered like drink coasters on the low table near the stereo; a DVD of *Don Giovanni* that they had intended to watch together; a Stieg

Larsson thriller that she had been reading alongside him every night, now destined to be finished in her husband's bed.

'Here – you should keep the Don Giovanni,' she said.

'And watch it alone? No thanks.'

'But you must at least find an occasion to open the Taittinger Réserve.'

'Oh, sure.'

It had been meant for oysters on the balcony on their final night, but they had argued and eaten out late, instead.

'Can I at least walk you to the métro?'

'No. It'll be too hard. Let's say it here.'

And so they embraced on the stairs for the last time. He watched her descend. Heard the dull click of the security door. Listened for her diminishing footfalls.

He considered going to the balcony in the hope that he might glimpse her in the street before she vanished into the crowd. But he resisted the impulse. Instead, he returned to the kitchen, where he tore open the packet of coffee beans and filled the reservoir of his grinder. The whine of the machine was solace enough.

It was only much later in the morning, while taking the *métro* trip to his gallery in the eighth, that he recalled the arrangement with Alana Daniels. Soon after emerging from the Métro Alma-Marceau onto the Avenue Montaigne he dialled a colleague at the Musée Picasso. This was Mitchell Jameson, a young Australian post-graduate research student, who was working with him as an assistant curator on the exhibition devoted to Picasso's time on the Côte d'Azur.

Luc explained Alana Daniels's proposition to Mitchell, and he immediately expressed enthusiasm. Of course it would depend upon them giving him leave from his curatorial duties for several days, but Luc thought it hardly a problem since his position was unpaid. There might also be a way, Luc suggested, for him to combine the trip with a useful side excursion to the museum in Antibes. Luc made no promises, other than that he would commend Mitchell's expertise and enthusiasm to Alana Daniels when she telephoned. He did, however, propose that they meet at 1:00 p.m. for lunch at a restaurant in the Place de Thorigny, just around the corner from the Musée Picasso. By then, Luc expected he would have heard back from the woman.

It wasn't their habitual dining place – an unpretentious local haunt in a well-concealed, scruffy courtyard, unfortunately closed for all of August – but a simple tourist restaurant serving uncomplicated traditional fare. They were lucky to get a table, the place being crowded with English and Americans, who, judging from their poster tubes, guides and postcards, had just stumbled out of the Musée.

They both ordered the inexpensive *menu à prix fixe (entrecôte grillée avec sauce au bleu)* and shared a carafe of cheap Bordeaux.

For a few minutes they caught up on museum business. Mitchell explained that he had spent the morning drafting e-mails of enquiry to several regional museums that were holding pictures they were hoping to secure for the exhibition, but he was soon keen to shift the topic to the American woman's proposal of a trip to Provence.

At twenty-seven, Mitchell was almost exactly half Luc's age. Seated opposite one another, they would have looked like father and son. Both were olive-complexioned and long-boned, with piercing grey-green eyes and assertive noses. A pair of sombre El Grecos, Luc might have observed. But Mitchell wore his black hair in a spiky mop, while Luc's glossy pepper-and-salt was immaculately trimmed *en brosse.*

Over the months of their collaboration on the Picasso exhibition, their relationship had developed a relaxed, avuncular quality. Their conversations were mostly conducted in English, but Mitchell occasionally sought the opportunity to practise his shaky French. Mitchell had many questions about museum protocols and the Parisian art market and Luc was happy to impart advice without being the least bit patronizing.

'Do you reckon this Alana Daniels will be disappointed if an ignorant young Australian shows up to appraise her Picasso?'

'Disappointed with you? She'll be thrilled. You just relax, listen to her spiel, then seduce her into bringing her painting up to Paris.'

'I guess I'll need to read what I can about Dora Maar. Ah – but I'm getting ahead of myself. First I've got to persuade Henri to let me go.'

'Forget Henri – I'll talk to him. All you'll need to think about is how to charm a huge fee out of this woman. I'm sure she's loaded.'

In spite of displaying his familiar, lightly-worn cynicism, Luc struck Mitchell as being somewhat morose.

'You'd rather be going yourself?' Mitchell asked.

'No, no.'

'Something else bothering you?'

'Oui. j'ai d'autres soucis,' Luc said quietly, while looking away. He took a pack of cigarettes from his shirt pocket, then sighed when he recalled the no-smoking regulation.

'Nothing you want to talk about?

'No - let's eat.'

Their meals arrived, and they finished all three courses in companionable near silence. Afterwards, Luc ordered coffees and *l'addition.* In the brutal afternoon heat they strolled back to the Musée.

4

August 7: Saint-Paul-de-Vence, Provence

On the following day, Mitchell took the early morning Air France flight to Nice.

There hadn't been much time beforehand to adequately prepare for the meeting with Alana Daniels. Earlier he had visited the research library in the Musée to consult their copy of the thirty-four volume Christian Zevros catalogue of Picasso's works. He wanted to have at least some knowledge of the range of Dora Maar portraits before confronting Alana Daniels's example. He also spent an hour sitting before the Musée's vibrant *Portrait of Dora Maar Seated*, trying to commit to memory as much detail as possible of the composition, colour and brushwork. (In their single, brief conversation, Alana Daniels had told him very little about her painting, being more concerned with establishing a venue for their rendezvous.) The only work of reference he packed for the trip was a paperback copy of Pierre Daix's biography of Picasso, a work he had read many years ago, but whose particulars he had largely forgotten. On the short plane trip he read the chapters devoted to Picasso's affair with Dora Maar.

She was a twenty-eight year old photographer involved with the Paris Surrealists when the fifty-four year old Picasso first met her. Dora's mother was French and her father Croatian - hence her actual surname, Markovich. She had grown up in Argentina and spoke Spanish fluently, which was to afford her an intimacy with Picasso denied his current lover, Marie-Thérèse.

Their first significant encounter took place in early 1936 at the Café de Deux Magots, and it foretold everything. Dora had arrived with mutual friends, and was soon intriguing Picasso with her performance at the neighbouring table. She had spread her gloved hand on the table in front of her, and with a small knife proceeded to stab the spaces between her fingers, jabbing with increasing tempo and recklessness, until she had drawn blood. How could Picasso have failed to be aroused by this exquisite and mysterious woman, willing to flirt with pain in a mad game of chance? He sought an introduction, and requested the bloodied glove as a keepsake. Within a very short time they became lovers, remaining in a frequently tormented relationship until the early years of the war. Never living together, since Picasso was not prepared to give up the other women in his life, the serene, almost bovine, Marie-Thérèse, with whom he had a daughter, Maya.

Dora had been his ally and mentor during the difficult creation of *Guernica* . She had found him a studio on the left bank at 7 rue des Grande-Augustins, and it was there that she extensively documented his work. But still Picasso kept her in a 'permanent state of availability' without commitment. The end came in 1944 when Picasso encountered the beautiful young painter, Françoise Gilot. And when he finally abandoned Dora completely, her decline and collapse was almost tragic.

At 11:00 a.m. Mitchell walked out of the terminal at Nice and searched for his hire car in a lot full of gleaming bubble-shaped Renaults. The clear sky, streaked with wisps of high cloud, was the intense blue that often signalled the arrival of the mistral. But on that morning, the exposed sun was merciless and the air completely still. The temperature had already climbed to around thirty degrees.

He was in a vague, unsettled mood composed of lightness and disorientation, one that travel to unfamiliar places so often engenders.

After studying the map, he took the coast road, the N7, west towards Antibes, which he planned to visit on his return trip. The holiday traffic was worse than Paris at peak hour. Ten kilometres out of Nice, he turned with relief onto the less frantic D2, and headed north into the hills towards Saint-Paul-de-Vence. It was there, she had decided, they would meet.

Saint-Paul-de-Vence was a well-preserved, *bastide* village, surrounded by ramparts that commanded views across the surrounding countryside. It had once been a military stronghold, but now the only threat appeared to come from the hordes of summer tourists. Fastidious restoration work had turned the place into a museum.

Every steep, cobble-stoned street was lined with inessential souvenir boutiques - at least fifteen of them art galleries - selling strident contemporary renderings of typical Provençal landscapes. Wandering in search of his hotel in that touristic mono culture, he felt neither in the presence of the past, nor in the here and now; just adrift in some kind of anodyne medievaland.

Not surprisingly, Alana Daniels had booked him overnight into the legendary Colombe d'Or. Maybe she was trying to impress him, or perhaps seduce him with a little luxury. Either way, he didn't mind. He could never have afforded to stay there himself. In the nineteen-twenties and thirties, he discovered, it had been patronized by artists. Matisse, Picasso, Léger, Braque and Bonnard had all dined there, and paid their restaurant bills with paintings, which were still kept on display. After the war, the hotel had been a favourite with movie stars visiting the Cannes festival. Now, it seemed, the glamorous days were over – all it took to get a table was sufficient money.

Alana Daniels had arranged to meet him at the hotel bar upon his arrival. He didn't know what to expect from the encounter. On the telephone, in spite of her charm, she had seemed slightly overbearing, and also, he suspected, a little too desperate to unload her Picasso. No doubt she would attempt to manoeuvre him into doing her bidding, whatever it might turn out to be.

In the dark bar of the Colombe d'Or, a striking young woman cast a glance, put down her brandy glass, then turned towards him with a look of recognition. He remembered thinking that she couldn't possibly have been Alana Daniels. She was far too young to have possessed that voice on the telephone.

'Mitchell Jameson?' she inquired, with a smile.

'Alana Daniels? Pleased to meet you,' he said, awkwardly, still not quite believing this was the woman he had come there to meet.

'Wonderful,' she said, languidly extending her hand, at the same time flicking aside a stray wisp of her shoulder-length chestnut hair. 'Shall we stay here? Or maybe take a table on the terrace? Is it too early for you? Have you had lunch?' It was then that he recognized the low, silky voice. But surely this woman was at least fifteen years younger than the one he had been imagining. She was wearing a low-cut Bordeaux-coloured cotton top that beautifully exposed the milky contours of her bare throat, and several pieces of elegantly simple silver jewellery. And as she uncurled herself from the bar stool, she revealed her tight black mini-skirt and a flash of pale thigh. She could have been an actress, or an ex-model, such was her poise and effortless charm. In spite of knowing better, Mitchell felt flattered by the performance.

'Lunch?' he said, in a daze. 'Sure - whatever. Wherever you'd prefer,'

'Good,' she said, then led the way through the bar and out onto the terrace, where a dozen or more people - wealthy tourists, Germans and Dutch mostly - were already dining in the dappled, filtered sunlight provided by carefully manicured small trees.

'You know this place?' she asked.

'No. I rode a scooter along the coast road to Italy five or six years ago, but that's about it.'

A young waitress greeted them and with a mere hand gesture, suggested a table by the balustrade.

They took their seats at the table. The light reflecting from the pure white tablecloth gently illuminated her pale, oval face. There was something of a classical hauteur about her elegant profile and broad, sensual mouth, and her way of holding her head high and meeting his gaze whenever she spoke gave her a disconcerting strength. She was intense and she was beautiful. Her unsettling half-smile, however, was pure New York. It conveyed the impression that she already had the goods on him, but wasn't about to make a fuss. While her extraordinary eyebrows, two graceful half-moon sweeps of a fine black brush, had an ironic language all of their own. And for the first time, he saw that her large possessing eyes were not brown, but a deep, bronze green.

Mitchell found it hard to detach himself from the fascination her presence was arousing. For a while, it was an effort to begin a conversation.

'So - you're living nearby?' he asked, lamely.

'Yes. If this terrace were on the other side of the village, you'd be able to see my villa. I could have walked here.'

'Villa, huh? Your *maison secondaire?'* It felt good to try a little French with her.

'Good God, no. It's not even *ma maison.* I've just borrowed the place for a few months. In the off season, of course. It belongs to a good friend in New York.'

'And the portrait? Do you have it with you?'

'Yes. It's always lived in Europe. It's difficult to explain simply.

But it was a wedding present from my late husband. And now I'd like to sell it.'

From the casual way she had tossed a reference to her 'late husband' into the conversation - with no greater weight than she might have given 'old boyfriend' - he had to wonder whether she was being deliberately perverse.

'And after we've eaten, you're going to show it to me?'

'Of course.'

Over lunch (*crevettes assaisonnées à l'estragon*, for her*; carré d'agneau du Triscatin*, for him; and a modest bottle of *Côtes du Lubéron*, which they hardly dared touch in the languid heat of the afternoon) Alana Daniels won him completely. She appeared to trust him from the outset, and showed no signs of the arrogance and impatience that he had seen earlier. Instead, she was buoyant, amusing, and eager to learn as much about his view on the market for Picassos as he was prepared to bluff.

'How much did the last one to go up to auction fetch?' she wanted to know.

'Twenty-five million US,' he plucked out of thin air - until he remembered having heard the figure in a conversation with Luc. 'But that wouldn't mean much in relation to your *Portrait of Dora Maar*.' That was quite a famous work, and from a more sought after period.'

'I understand,' she said, parodying a reaction of mild insult.

She took a digital colour snapshot of the painting from her bag and passed it to him. 'It's a terrible photograph,' she said, blushing slightly. 'I took it myself. But at least it won't upstage the real thing.'

Unfortunately, she had taken it in poor light, too low for a good exposure, and so had ever so slightly blurred the image. Apart from the fact that it seemed to be almost certainly a portrait of Dora Maar from the mid to late 1930's, very little about the physical state of the painting could be discerned. Mitchell was sure of one thing: he had never seen the painting before. It certainly wasn't in Christian Zevros's catalogue. He was about to return the photograph to her, when it dawned on him - the very reason why Alana Daniels was the owner of this painting - or more accurately, the reason why her 'late husband' had made her a present of it. Her resemblance to Dora Maar was unmistakable. It was a matter of subtle correspondences, but once having been suspected, was ever after inescapable. Alana Daniels' hair wasn't the same colour as Dora Maar's and she wore it very differently. It also appeared, from a closer look at the painting, that she used far less make-up. But the presence of Dora Maar was there, vaguely echoed in her every feature. However, Mitchell didn't want her to think he had observed the resemblance.

'Yours is one of the early portraits of Dora,' he said.

'Yes, I know. It was painted in 1936, I believe. You can see what a forceful beauty she was,' she added, without irony. 'No amount of Picasso's distortion can hide that.'

'Have you seen many of his later portraits?'

'Sure, yes - but mostly only in books. Though I did see the *Picasso and Portraiture* exhibition in New York in '96. Some of them were hideous. Painting her as that tortured weeping woman. Using his abuse of her as inspiration. There was a dark side to it all.'

'Yes, they're unsettling. First he paints her as a crazy melancholic, and then he paints her as a monster. Sometimes she's a harpy with talons and claws, and a huge beak, imprisoned in a birdcage. Then she's a bizarre spider at the centre of a mad web of lines. And have you seen the late portraits of her with a dog's muzzle, or as a carcass with a skeleton's mouth?'

Mitchell was recalling his hour spent looking at Dora Maar reproductions in the Christian Zevros catalogue. It was clear that they had evolved over the course of Picasso's relationship with her, in much the same pattern as they had with every other woman who entered his life. In the early stages of the affair the sketches he made of her were sensual and adoring, products of an obvious infatuation. Soon after came a period of almost classical portraits, in which Dora's beauty is weighed down with melancholy and the coded signs of neurosis: dilated eyes, contorted poses, extravagant gestures. Then came the extreme post-cubist experiments in distortion: the split frontal and profile perspectives, the displaced features, the reduction of Dora's physignomy to a few recognizable signs - the wide eyes, the enlarged nose and flared nostrils, the fullsome scarlet lips, the elongated hands, and the claw-like painted nails. And then, in the final dying days of the relationship, he painted her as a grotesque caricature, half-human, half-beast, a deranged and pathetic monster.

'Obviously, he was afraid of her power. He couldn't stand the fact that she was his equal, an intellectual and a talented artist. So he had to put her in her place. Finish her off. Vanquish her.'

'Well, I can see why you want to get rid of the painting,' he said.

'Are you theorizing about *my* marriage now, Mitchell?'

'No. Just agreeing with you. The Dora Maar paintings aren't one of the high points in the history of male-female relations.'

'Oh? There are high points?' she said, with a flash of mockery in her eyes.

'But, still - you haven't told me about your husband. What did he think of the painting?'

She looked away for a moment, out across the balustrade towards the far hillside, where a veil of smoky heat haze the shapes of the distant farmhouses. When she turned back, her face had clouded. He could see that he had upset her.

'I'm sorry,' he said.

'That's Okay. It's not much of a story, but it's one I need to forget.'

Mitchell supposed that he should have ignored the evasive tactic and seized the opportunity to press her further about the terms of the 'wedding present', but he didn't, which only left him wondering about the cause of the man's death, and the possible discrepancy in their ages. Nothing in her demeanour suggested widowhood. He knew she had decided to withhold something from him, and he couldn't help but wonder about its significance.

She reached for her bag from beside her chair. 'I've brought a document I want to show you,' she said with surprising brightness, as though aware that the subject needed changing.

'Now, or after?' he questioned, while taking a sip of the *Côtes du Lubéron.*

'Okay, after.'

'Do you have a special affection for Picasso's work?' she asked, in the coy, cajoling way one might extract commitment from a wavering lover.

'That's a delicate way of putting it,' he said. 'I'd just say he's unavoidable.'

'Like a wall you can't see around?'

'More like a natural phenomenon, someone that's way bcyond the reach of criticism, if that doesn't sound too pretentious.'

'It does – but don't worry,' she teased.

'Okay. You asked for it. For me, his work doesn't seem to be a matter of individual masterpieces. I think of it more as this inexhaustible source of visual play, or just plain creativity. Or maybe, just a lifelong experiment, one that comes with an invitation for us to see the world that way, too. That's what I admire about his work; but on the other hand, I can just as easily see it as a man's lifelong attempt to live up to – '

'Or get past the bullshit,' she interjected.

'Right – the bullshit - of his own extraordinary myth. Creation for its own obsessive sake. As if the work has no significance outside the fact that the great Picasso is doing it. ' He paused to take in her amused reaction, aware that he might have said far more than the situation required. 'I'm losing you?'

'Completely,' she said, with an ironic smile. 'That sounded more like a college lecture than a passionate defence.'

'Once you've decided not to try to judge an artist's work, something has to lie down and cool off.'

'But I thought that's what you did for a living – at least

that's the story Luc told me. You study paintings and you make judgments, or attributions, or whatever you call them. At least that's what I'm paying you for.'

'Only on questions of authenticity. Never on taste.' He knew he was pushing his luck, but now that he realized Luc had oversold his services, he believed he had little choice.

'Now you *are* beginning to worry me.'

Mitchell suspected she might have been more than half serious, but still, he was enjoying her playfulness.

Their waiter returned to see if they wanted dessert. This led to a long and complicated conversation in French, in which the merits of the various offerings were explained in excessive detail. Mitchell did his best to translate: *Tarte aux clafoutis framboises, Charlotte aux myrtilles et aux framboises* and *Galtette aux pommes et noix,* but he could see that Alana was either wasn't following or wasn't particularly interested. He took the hint and ordered coffee for them both. She did, however, seem impressed by his ability to sustain a conversation in French with the waiter.

'You seem at home over here,' she said. 'Have you spent a lot of time in France?'

'Only a few months. But I worked hard studying the language before I arrived. I can struggle through a menu like this without ending up with calves' brains, but I can't hold up my end of a conversation about anything more complicated than the weather.'

After the remains of lunch were taken away, and the coffee had arrived, Alana produced a piece of yellowed paper from her voluminous, soft leather bag. It was an *expertise,* written in 1965, by someone claiming an association with the Jeu de Paume - on the occasion of a sale of the painting, through a Swiss gallery, to an unnamed buyer - guaranteeing the painting's authenticity.

'This is interesting,' Mitchell said, 'but do you have any documentary proof of your *husband's* purchase of the painting?'

'His executors have it, I suppose. But I'm sure I have some

evidence that he gave it to me as a wedding present. It must be lying around somewhere.'

'Not quite the same thing,' he said. 'It wouldn't mean anything. What you need to find are the papers supplied by the gallery he purchased it from.'

She looked at Mitchell blankly. 'So what is the point of this paper, then?' she said, indicating the *expertise*.

'It can't hurt, I suppose - provided you have the other documents. But it's a bit like me writing you a note pronouncing your painting genuine. It means nothing unless you have absolute faith in the judgement of Mitchell Jameson. And who knows who this gentleman is,' he added, pointing to the signature on the document.

'You're very encouraging,' she said. She sipped her coffee for a while, appearing to think over what he had told her.

'Look at it this way - if I were a potential buyer, I'd want to know everything about the painting's history: from the day Picasso sold it, to the day your husband took possession.'

'Sixty years,' she said after a moment's calculation. 'That's a lot of time to account for.'

'Do you have any idea who might have owned it previously?'

'Some gallery in Switzerland, obviously,' she said, pointing to the *expertise*. 'They must have given this to my husband. Is there anything suspicious about that?'

'No. Not in itself. But some of Picasso's paintings from that era are known to have a strange history of ownership.'

'What do you mean?'

'Well, a lot went missing during the war. Picasso's dealer was a man called Paul Rosenberg. He ran a prominent gallery in Paris, and owned a large personal collection of contemporary art, including many Picassos. But he was also Jewish, and after the fall of France in 1940, all his property was confiscated by the Nazis.'

'Yes, I know a little bit about that,' she said.

'They classified Picassos paintings as "decadent", but those thieves weren't so ideologically pure as to burn them. Instead, they traded them, along with a lot of other extraordinary modern works, for the kind of classical Germanic stuff they admired. The exchange rate was probably about ten "decadent" paintings for one classical masterpiece. They did business with corrupt French dealers, but also with a number of Swiss galleries.'

'Well, that was sixty years ago,' she said. 'Anything might have happened back then. How could you ever tell?'

'You probably couldn't. It may have been a confiscated work, or it may have been sold internationally and have a perfectly legitimate history. I'd only be guessing to suggest anything. But there might be ways of finding out - if you're prepared to come to Paris with me and bring your Picasso.'

'What? And have Monsieur Rosenberg's heirs turn up and claim my painting?'

'Well, yes. I guess there is a degree of risk once an attractive colour reproduction of the portrait appears in the Sotheby's spring catalogue – if that's where you end up trying to sell it.'

'And why wouldn't some curious people make the same deduction as you did - that the painting had once been confiscated by the Nazis?'

'Yes, I agree. It's a possibility. They might try something - a moral claim, maybe. It's also a substantial detraction, a possible turn-off for bidders. It's definitely a taint that you don't need. But I think you knew all this already. And that's why you didn't want to go to a major auction house in the first place. It's why you approached Luc Pellegrin.'

'Of course,' she said, with a troubled expression. 'All of those things were on my mind. I just wasn't sure of anything.'

Again she fell silent. When she spoke again, it was to change the subject entirely.

'You must think I'm in an awful hurry to sell this painting.'

'No more than most people, I suppose with tens of millions tied up in a couple of square metres of oil and canvas.'

'Oh - you think it's worth as much as that?'

'Probably. Picasso still excites people in all sorts of unpredictable ways. It isn't always the painting that they want, it's a slice of the reputation. So who knows what some corporate high roller might be prepared to pay on impulse at an auction?'

'But you'll know more when you see it?'

'Not really, I'm not that skilled. For that sort of certainty you'll have to show it to Luc, and maybe a few other experts. But if you're in a hurry for an answer, you should pick up the phone to Sotheby's.'

'No, we've dealt with that one already,' she said soberly, giving him a pointed look to let him know that the subject was closed.

But Mitchell didn't think they had actually dealt decisively with anything. He couldn't be sure whether her shifts between deflection and deference were the consequence of her being genuinely undecided about what to do with the painting, or whether it was a clever deception, a strategy to exhaust his objections and bind him to her purpose.

She went on to tell him that, as much as she loved the work, it was going to be necessary to sell it in order to maintain what she ironically termed her 'lifestyle'. What this lifestyle might have been, she didn't explain, but Mitchell immediately pictured houses in California and the south of France, expensive European cars, and first class travel all the way. Alana Daniels made no pretense of being an educated connoisseur, but she did seem to like the *Portrait of Dora Maar* for what it was, as opposed to what it represented; and she did reveal that she had a sensitive appreciation of Picasso's significance. He even thought he could detect a measure of sadness over the decision to part with *Dora.*

When he asked her when he could view the portrait, she tossed down the serviette that she had been dabbing her lips with and smiled. 'It's waiting for us back at the villa.

5

August 7: Saint-Paul-de-Vence, Provence

The ride out of town in her silver Mercedes coupé took only five minutes. The house was impressive beyond all Mitchell's expectations. It was a formidable three-storey *maison de maître,* built from stone the colour of camel hide, sited with its back against a hillside, and flanked with broad terraces on three sides. A nearby grove of olive trees partly shielded the house from the roadway. As they pulled up, he caught a glimpse beyond the wooded hills, of an azure strip of the distant Mediterranean.

They walked together up a dry-stone walled driveway lined with tall pines. The terraces were bordered with gigantic urns, all overflowing with scarlet and yellow flowers. Down the slope, a small *pigeonnier* was almost concealed by the wisteria that festooned its columns. Sunlight danced across the ice-blue surface of the oval swimming pool, barely visible behind a hedge of manicured lavender. Glancing upwards, he was puzzled to see that most of the olive green shutters of the top storey were closed against the heat, but not those at ground level.

'Bit of a heap, huh?' she said.

'Well – I guess if you have the money,' he trailed off, never quite sure of how to respond to the lavish lifestyles of foreigners. He worried that he liked what he saw far too much.

Alana apologized for the absurd indulgence of being the sole occupant of such an excessive piece of real estate, but once again she assured him that it had been borrowed - under duress - from a friend in New York. Mitchell liked the fact that she didn't take herself too seriously, and in spite of his initial wariness, found himself enjoying her company.

The interior of the house had been imaginatively restored to its original rustic simplicity. Most of the walls were bare sandblasted stone. Others were roughly plastered and painted a chalk-white. A subtle patina of soot surrounded the large open fireplaces. The ground level floors were laid throughout with large uneven tiles, worn in places by a couple of centuries of use, and coated with wax the colour of dark honey. The furniture was an eclectic mix of chic, but unpretentious, contemporary sofas and lounge chairs, and the kinds of antique oddities that might have belonged to the original owners. There were worm-eaten, crudely constructed *placards* and *coffres* - pieces that usually sold for several thousand dollars or more in Australia. Most impressive was a refectory sized dining table made from uneven planks of aged oak that gave off the dull glow of beeswax. It was surrounded by an assortment of turn-of-the-century rush-bottomed chairs with frail legs and curved backs, buffed to a sheen by long use. There were no paintings on the walls - although there was a faded parchment map of the old *domaine* mounted above the largest fireplace - and the only ornaments were a few antique Mediterranean stone vases, a collection of blue Clérissy *faïence* plates and dishes, and some casually displayed shards of Roman statuary. Mitchell couldn't imagine who these friends of hers in

New York might have been. They clearly had an appreciation for French rural living, but the place was too idiosyncratic and impractical to be a summer rental.

'Too much, or something quite special?' she asked, aware of his divided reaction to the place.

'I can't blame the furniture.'

'Okay - it's upstairs,' was all she said.

What struck Mitchell as odd - considering she was keeping a Picasso under wraps - was just how vulnerable to burglary the house appeared to be. The shutters on the downstairs windows were weathered and insubstantial, and could have been prised open in a minute. It was no wonder that she hadn't bothered to close them. Or was it that she didn't realize the chance she was taking? Perhaps she was the kind of person who considered everything in life a risk, and hence, all consequences unavoidable. Then again, quite possibly she believed that nobody knew about the Picasso.

He followed her up a curved flight of oak stairs and along a dim, narrow corridor lined with books - Michael Connelly, Elmore Leonard, Henning Mankell - summer reading mostly, many with torn or faded jackets and sun-buckled bindings. They came to a window with a half-open shutter creaking in the breeze. There was a view beyond the hillside to a distant mountain capped with pale grey granite. Opposite the window was a heavy wooden doorway studded with huge brass nails. He saw that it was listing badly on its antique hinges. Alana inserted an unwieldy cast iron key into the lock, and after a great deal of mechanical difficulty, which required her to crouch to keyhole level, she finally managed to spring the latch and force open the door.

The precaution of locking such a cantankerous thing each time she left the house seemed absurd, but he supposed it to be her one concession to having a Picasso lying around.

'*Voila!*' she exclaimed with an ironic show of exhaustion.

He was surprised to see that they were actually standing in

her bedroom. But Alana saw nothing odd about inviting him to enter.

Dominating the room was her vast bed: a mahogany stained monstrosity, with an ornately carved headboard featuring religious symbols intertwined with birds of prey, tormented beast and sinuous vines. It looked more like an altar than a place for a good night's sleep. Her duvet was flung back to expose suggestively rumpled sheets. One of her plump feather pillows was still indented from her sleeping head. An embroidered linen nightdress was draped, inside-out across the foot of the bed, along with two long woollen bed socks. And beneath the bed, a turquoise rubber hot water bottle lay alongside a tumbler, a bottle of what appeared to be sleeping pills, a quart of Scotch, and a splayed copy of *Vanity Fair.* The door of her *armoire* had been left open, revealing a rack of jumbled clothes and a pile of shoes. A drawer stuffed with cosmetics was pulled out so far that it tilted precariously towards the parquet floor. Mitchell's obvious fascination with this intimate portrayal of her frantic morning didn't seem to faze her at all.

'Messy girl,' she said, with a self-deprecatory giggle. 'You can see the rush I was in to make our meeting. Get it together, girl.'

'I'm wondering - did we open the right door?'

'Oh! You're thinking, why did she bring me up here? Well...I thought I had a Picasso lying around somewhere.'

She crossed to the *armoire,* on the way flicking a pair of errant shoes out of her path with her toe, sending them clattering out of sight under the bed. From the space between the *armoire* and the wall she carefully drew out a large rectangular object wrapped in a white linen sheet.

'Not how they store them in the Pompidou - but here it is.'

She unwound the sheet, and lifted the framed painting clear. Then, being careful to keep the back of the canvas faced towards him, she carried it across to the window.

'Come and take a look at Dora,' she said.

Mitchell thought he must have approached like a nervous lover, tingling with anxiety and heightened anticipation.

'May I?' he said, taking the painting from her, in order to angle it more suitably to the light.

The portrait was both flattering in its erotic particularity and brilliantly cruel. It was as mesmerizing as any Picasso he could recall. He was absolutely certain that he had never seen it before – not that his limited experience counted for much. But even if he had been exposed to the work for less than a minute, he was sure he would have remembered it all his life.

'So - the *Portrait of Dora Maar*'

It was a modest-sized canvas (about 90 x 60 cms), typical in dimension of the portraits of that period. Mitchell had memorized that fact. Dora Maar had been posed staring directly at the artist, reclining her head at an anatomically impossible angle across the back of a lounge chair. The perspectives of her face were split between frontal and profile: her enlarged eyes, one emerald green and one crimson, were set at right angles; only her swollen lips and exaggerated nostrils oriented her face towards the viewer with any certainty. Her skin was rendered in clashing tones of chrome yellow, pale green and rose pink. Her garments were predominantly black. The room in which she was seated was minimally sketched; the oppressively close walls and ceiling were of a radiantly hot orange.

Dora was neither in a state of surrender nor repose, and in spite of the degree of distortion, it was possible to see something of the madness and rigidity Picasso had claimed of her: *'she carried herself like the holy sacrament'.* The overall effect was of psychic disturbance.

'What do you think?' Alana Daniels demanded. 'Do you like it?'

'Yes, I do. It's an extraordinary painting.'

'Oh, you're easily seduced,' she said, teasing, but with an edge of sarcasm.

'Seriously, I do. It's similar to one I've just been studying that's in the Musée Picasso. You must have seen it. It's often reproduced.'

'I don't know anything about that portrait,' she said unenthusiastically.

'Well, in that one he gave her a similar haughty expression, and these same mad, differently coloured eyes. But that painting has an underlying bird imagery: Dora Maar has shoulders that look like black wings, claw-like hands; and she's seated in a confined space that looks like a bird cage. I think in your painting she's just as tortured, it's certainly a telling portrait of her - but it's also a little less cruel, a bit less obvious.'

But she wasn't interested in a dissertation. All that mattered to Alana Daniels was whether Mitchell thought the painting was genuine.

'Are you convinced? Are you sure?' she kept on repeating, like a mantra, while he did his best to make a hasty examination of the work. There was no time to do much more than see whether the obvious physical properties of the canvas, the oil paint, and the techniques employed, matched what little he knew about Picasso's work in that period. His scrutiny was unavoidably superficial and hardly professional, but he knew she would be expecting him to display some evidence of serious attention. His let his eyes linger on the painting's surface for several minutes, but no revelations came.

She wanted a verdict immediately. 'Can't you at least tell me whether my Picasso is genuine?' she implored.

Luc had warned him to be careful on this question. Arousing hopes – just as much as dashing them – could lead to trouble.

'Is there any good reason to doubt it?' he said, already weary of the pressure.

'No - I don't think so...not at all. But now that you've looked it over, can you write me an *expertise* to say that it's authentic? That's all I need. Can't you at least do that?'

Mitchell hesitated before replying. He suspected that she had a concealed reason for doubting the authenticity of her painting, but he couldn't bring himself to confront her directly.

'Well, as I said, I'm hardly qualified to write an *expertise.* It would be next to worthless.'

His reply seemed to infuriate her. 'But what do you actually *think?* Here it is! You've seen it! So what's your opinion?'

'All I can say is that it looks good to me,' he said quietly. 'But then, Picasso wasn't exactly like Cézanne – he used so many different styles and techniques. Some were painted hastily and are little more than sketches, others were more considered, more worked. If you had all of his Dora Maar portraits lined up around the room, you'd probably think that two thirds of them looked 'wrong.' So, common sense tells me that it's the real thing – unless you have a good reason to think it isn't.'

'Common fucking sense?' she protested. 'That's like some doctor telling me I've either got a headache or a brain tumor. What use is advice like that? I don't know why your boss bothered to send you down here?' Her tone remained light in spite of her evident fury.

'Luc's not my boss – he's a friend, and a vastly more experienced colleague. Alana, we're going around in circles here. I've really only come to encourage you to take your painting up to Paris.'

'Oh, that's right. We've already discussed that one.'

'I'm sorry I'm no help to you.'

She searched amidst the mess until she found a packet of cigarettes. It was empty and she discarded it in frustration. 'Do you know anything at all about fake Picassos?' she demanded.

'Only the little I've learned since working at the Musée.' He was determined not to establish any further false expectations.

'Which was?'

'That there have been several well-known cases over the years of people with the skill to paint Picassos capable of fooling experts. He certainly wouldn't be the most difficult artist to fake.'

'Exactly. That's why I want an answer.'

'There've been other cases where wealthy people have

commissioned brilliant copies of paintings, simply because they were too afraid to hang the originals on their walls. But you don't imagine that's the case with your painting, do you?'

'I have no idea.'

'Unfortunately, it's going to take time to get an answer.'

'More time? I don't *have* much time, Mitchell. I need an opinion right now.'

He was amazed at how rapidly her easy sophistication had been shed, replaced by an unreasonable vehemence.

'In reality you're not going to be able to sell the painting tomorrow,' he told her calmly, 'so why the urgency? What I'd like to do is take a photograph of *Dora,* at a better resolution than the picture you have already, and also make a photocopy of your document - you have a fax or scanner here I hope - then go back and consult Luc and some other experts at the Musée.' He was attempting to placate her by overlooking her rising panic and offering a plan of action, but it was evidently the wrong approach.

'And how long would that take?' she snapped. At one moment she was vigorously scratching the back of her hand, the next, stroking her throat in agitation. It was like witnessing an attack of some kind.

'A few days - a week at the most. Look, I do assume it's the real thing. But if any *expertise* is going to be worth anything - and, after all, you're going to need to supply a pretty convincing one when you try to sell the work – then it will have to be backed up with further research, as well as some sound opinions from solid sources. It's in your interest, too.'

'Don't you understand?' she said, coolly. 'I need to find a buyer right *now.*'

'Sure - and maybe you could unload it on E-Bay tomorrow, if you were lucky enough to find a buyer stupid or trusting enough.'

'Please don't get cute about this. This is a huge problem for me, and I can't be messed around - I won't be. And I'm sure not waiting for some bunch of experts to tell me what should be obvious.'

'I'm sorry, but these things are never obvious.'

'Doesn't Luc Pellegrin have and seriously rich clients? People who might want to buy my Picasso?'

'Not waiting in the wings, exactly. But maybe he'd know one or two people you might approach - serious collectors, foreign museums, perhaps, with the wherewithal. But they'd need to know a hell of a lot more than you're telling me. And it wouldn't be a matter of a quick sale.'

'Forget it.'

'You know something? I'm starting to get the idea that you already have a buyer. I know you absolutely have to sell. But maybe someone's already made you an offer and you're not too happy with it. You're afraid to close the deal and you desperately want some competition. Am I close?'

It was more than provocative – it was insulting and probably cruel. But it was an appropriate challenge, and she had no intention of meeting it. In the space of a few minutes she had lost all confidence and become more petulant and unreasonable than an anxious child. He was certain that nothing he could say would reassure her. Some stubborn streak caused him to persist with the questions he wanted answered.

'Or maybe there's some potential buyer who's not totally convinced that *Dora* is genuine? Someone whose money can't hang around? Or is it the other way around? Maybe you're the one who needs a fire sale, but you're afraid you might be throwing away a fortune? Is that it?'

'Why are you putting me through this? I thought we'd made a straightforward deal.'

'We did. But you didn't tell me everything.'

'No, I'm sorry, I couldn't...' she said, her voice trailing away to silence.

She crossed to the edge of the bed and sat down carefully, remaining almost motionless for a time, staring at the floor in glum silence. Mitchell watched as the strength drained from her body, her shoulders becoming rounded as she sank forward, her elbows pressing into her thighs. Her breathing quickened, each intake becoming a small gulp of panic.

He had no idea what exactly had caused such an extreme reaction. 'Alana, can't you tell me what is it? What's happened to cause you to...?'

'No, it's nothing you've said.'

'Then, what?'

'It's what I haven't told you,' she said flatly.

Had there been a chair in the room, he would have sat down himself. He felt the kind of lightness in the head that usually precedes a terrible announcement. But still he resisted placing himself at a disadvantage. As much as he wanted to meet her eyes, he wasn't going to kneel at her feet.

When, at last she spoke again, it was in a voice of utter resignation.

'You see...my name isn't Alana Daniels.'

'Of course it isn't,' he said. She had given him too much time to think the worst, and he had already arrived at cynicism.

'Would you like a Scotch?' she asked, distractedly. 'I sure need one - if I can find us a glass.' She reached down and groped around in the debris beneath her bed, looking for a tumbler and the bottle of Scotch. She retrieved the only tumbler and held it up to the light, squinted while she examined the residue of dried liquor and dust, then gave the inside a wipe with the corner of the bed sheet. For a moment he had the image of himself as Pip, visiting Miss Havisham.

'Is that it?' he said, when her attention returned. 'You're not Alana Daniels?'

She merely nodded, while she poured a Scotch and passed it to him. 'I like you, Mitchell. And I trust you, too. And I'm sorry I lost my cool. Not the sophisticated dame you came in with, huh? Sorry about that, too. But at least I think we look at things in a similar way, don't you? We've got some common ground.'

'But I don't own a Picasso.'

She uttered a burst of raucous laughter. 'No - you don't!'

'And maybe you don't, either.'

'Oh, no, no - that's not it.'

'Then let's get back to who you are again.'

She took a short sip from the Scotch bottle, then said in a voice one usually reserves for customs officials, 'My name's Marlo McGraw.'

'Marlo? That's M-A-R-L-O? I thought they only had Marlos out in Hollywood.'

She ignored the crack, fixed her eyes on his, and said, 'Doesn't the name mean anything to you?'

He shook his head. 'You're my first Marlo.'

'I mean McGraw. You still don't know who I am?'

'Look - I'm sorry. I don't keep up with who's who in the USA. I read *Art in America*, the odd *New Yorker*, and I occasionally pick up *Time* in waiting rooms, but that's about it.'

'I'm taking about Australia,' she said.

'Australia? Sorry - I'm still not getting this.'

'My husband's name is McGraw, Mike McGraw. The name still mean nothing to you?'

Of course Mitchell knew that name, ever since the global financial meltdown, every Australian did. But the man he was thinking of wasn't dead - at least not to his knowledge.' Your *late* husband?' he asked.

'No, no - he's alive. That was just part of my story, too.'

'So it was all a story? You don't even own the painting?'

'No - the painting's mine. It was a wedding present from Mike.'

'Who isn't dead - just missing?'

'That's right. And I don't know where he is. You see, we're separated - our marriage is finished.'

'And I seem to remember reading it had just begun.' He wasn't being deliberately funny. He did vaguely recall that there were reports earlier in the year of McGraw leaving his first wife and marrying again in California. But if he had been asked to name his new wife, he would have probably said Maria Moore, or Mira Moore, or Marissa Moore. He was close, her maiden name had been Moore. The wedding had been kept a secret from the media. He was no longer a man who courted celebrity. There had been rumors rather than reports, and no photographs at all. Such was her anonymity, almost any beautiful young woman - and to be convincing, she would have needed to be both young and beautiful - could have fooled him into believing she was the new Mrs. Mike McGraw.

'We were together for six months,' she said, with a trace of sadness. 'That's long enough for any couple to get on one another's nerves.'

'So - are you divorcing him?'

'Or is he divorcing me? It's complicated. His lawyers are sorting it out.'

'Or maybe cleaning you out?'

'Most probably. I haven't seen him in months.'

'That's not part of the story, too?'

'No - I really don't know where he is.'

'You're not on the run from the Tax Office or the Australian Federal Police, or anything like that?'

Mitchell knew enough of McGraw's recent history to get the picture. He had read about the collapse of McGraw's hedge fund, the vast losses incurred by his investors, his flight from Australia, and the hunt for the missing hundreds of millions.

'I'm not on any charges,' she said, innocently. 'They have no claim on me. And the portrait of *Dora* is absolutely my property.'

'But do they know where to find you?'

'You had no trouble.'

'Really? You came to Luc under a false name.'

At that she laughed loudly, putting an end to his inquisition. He was pleased, at least, that her fragile, volatile mood of some minutes ago had completely passed.

'You're probably going to have to tell me everything,' he said. 'I don't remember very much of the Mike McGraw story. I've had my head stuck in art books for an entire decade.'

Marlo brought Mitchell downstairs and made espresso coffee for them both. She served it with almond *biscotti* and luscious, powdery slivers of Turkish delight. Over the course of the next half hour she told him her version of the Mike McGraw story. He didn't mind hearing things that he already knew; it was revealing to get her perspective on McGraw's life, and amusing to see just how much spin she was prepared to put on his appalling behaviour. She called him Mike, just as the journalists - even the most hostile – had called him Mike. He had never been Michael, except perhaps in the legal documents drawn up against him.

Some aspects of the story were familiar to Mitchell, in the way that most newsworthy personalities leave their traces, but much of it was a revelation. McGraw's arrival into the financial pantheon had been legendary. Already a multi-millionaire in his late-twenties, he made the cover of the now defunct *Bulletin* when he was appointed chairman of the Antipodes Group investment bank at the age of thirty-five. Five years later, he established his own hedge fund, McGraw Securities, the cornerstone of a financial empire that stretched from New York to Hong Kong.

Whether you admired or despised him, however you tried to sum up the financial world of the previous decade, Mike McGraw had to be in the picture somewhere. At its height, in late 2007, McGraw Securities was responsible for international investments of over fifteen billion dollars, and the posted returns of 10-12% were regarded as phenomenal by industry standards. His own investments included world class luxury resorts, towering residential projects and futuristic business parks in Singapore, Malaysia and Thailand; a budget airline flying out of Spain; a multi-award winning organic Margaret River winery; a twentieth-century art collection, in scope and quality, said to be worthy of its own museum; and several ambitious, forward-looking co-ventures in Australian tourism.

Some said he fashioned himself on the Kennedy brothers in his pursuit of power, glamorous women, and the recreations of the rich. But somehow he eluded everyone, managing to seem both an instinctive and uncompromising capitalist as well as a passionate and surprisingly enlightened man of ideas. He had made – or, some said, plundered - a fortune, but he also espoused the many causes of environmental protection both in Australia and globally. Of course he didn't charm everybody. And in the end, it seems as though he convinced nobody.

If you conjured an image of him from those heady days, it would probably have been of the jaded celebrity in a dinner suit, striding arm in arm with the glowing model to the waiting Rolls. But it might just as easily have been of the down-to-earth businessman in the bush hat, talking with conservationists in the heart of the Tasmanian wilderness; or of the suntanned millionaire in the wet suit, off the coast of some Queensland tropical island, swimming in the company of dolphins. He was a man of limitless mystery. An illusionist, forever attracting extravagant speculation. And when he disappeared, it seemed as though he had single-handedly ended an era. It wasn't that Australians mourned Mike McGraw, as they might the fall of a once popular government, or the defeat of an invincible cricket team; it was more that some notion of our former selves – or the fantasy of our bad-boy, bushranging, risk-it-all selves - had gone missing, slid away into the irrecoverable past.

Ten years on, after the financial tsunami of '08, the legend had soured, and the romance had been exposed for the confidence trick it had always been. Now Michael Dylan McGraw was just a man notorious for having fled Australia owing international investors – including some of the world's biggest banks - over fifteen billion dollars, all of it vanished somewhere into what was now exposed as an elaborate Ponzi fraud.

Marlo didn't tell Mitchell, but he could remember that before anyone could calculate the extent of the illegality behind the collapse of McGraw Securities, there were reports that Mike McGraw had secreted much of the capital in various international tax havens, and had fled to who knew where? Menton was often mentioned – he owned a sumptuous villa on the Cap-Martin peninsula - but nobody had reported seeing him there. It was also common knowledge that, before leaving Australia, McGraw had erased all traces of the complex chain of his personal holdings, and had divested himself of all former friends, and business associates. That included his estranged wife, Katherine. She had remained in Australia, stripped of all connection to McGraw's businesses, a target of speculation, but in fact herself as much a victim as McGraw's hapless creditors.

The way Marlo told the story, McGraw had been a victim of the greedy corporate investors and opportunistic bankers, but she didn't argue that version too strenuously.

'During the good times, he made them all a fortune,' she said, 'and if they took a fall during the inevitable downturn, then *tant pis* – so did everybody else.'

Assuming Mitchell's ignorance, she didn't comment on the fraudulence of what had widely been reported as McGraw's elaborate Ponzi scheme. She could easily guess Mitchell's political and ethical views. It wasn't that she denied her husband had been a fugitive from Australian justice, it was rather that she saw McGraw as corporate descendant of Ned Kelly - a man whose expansive vision of life's possibilities clashed with the narrowness of the law. She didn't offer much detail of her own entry into the story. He supposed she thought he was more interested in McGraw's connection with the painting than in his connection with her.

'I met him at a party in California,' she said, her eyes glazing a little, as though she realized she was embarking on a long tale that would leave her with a measure of sadness. 'He was renting a house on the beach in Malibu. It belonged to some movie producer - I don't remember who. I was far more interested in Mike. He didn't seem much interested in the producer, either. That's what I instantly liked about him. He didn't take anything in L.A. seriously. He came there to do business, and then he left. He was amused by the ambience, and the cult excess, but the rest of it bored him. He was really only interested in Europe. I remember him saying: 'The more I see of L.A., the more I miss France.' And of course, he was a very exciting man to be around. Mike seduced everyone without trying. I mean, people just fell at his feet. Women - my God. He really was the missing Kennedy brother. Impossibly good looking, but not at all like a self-involved model. Just warm and solid.'

Mitchell could see that she was somewhere else. Maybe back on the beach at Malibu, back there in the days when everything had been going right.

'Well - he was a wanted man, even then,' he said. 'That must have helped.'

'He was always glancing past your shoulder. Not because he was bored - just watchful. You always had the feeling with Mike, that if you looked away for even a minute, he'd be gone, slipped out the door. It made you want to take care of him...love him. Maybe that was just his ultimate trick.'

He wasn't going to ask her about their affair. He was already feeling a twinge of jealousy. 'And so you married him? On the spot?'

'I would have married him right there on the carpet,' she said, with a husky laugh that acknowledged the unseemly haste of their decision. 'Right after our first time. Oh, yes - wow! He'd already left Katherine. That was over. But don't ask me about the details, I have to be in the mood. And then - there we were on Santa Catalina. Married.'

But something in her memory of the event had caught up with her, and her expression abruptly altered. Her animation faded and her eyes drifted, betraying regret.

'He wanted a second chance,' she said with a sigh, 'but he

didn't think he was going to get one. He used to joke: "The world's a very small place when you owe a few billion dollars."

'Fifteen billion,' Mitchell corrected.

'Well - he stopped counting, and started running.'

'And then you came to France?'

'Followed by investigators from the ASIC and smart-arse lawyers from the Attorney General's Department,' she said with ironic contempt. 'No doubt soon to be joined by goons from the AFP, backed up by a horde of supercilious *gendarmes*.'

She didn't tell Mitchell how their relationship had deteriorated. But he supposed their happiness had lasted only as long as their false pictures of one another.

'Why do you think he risked coming to France?'

'He hadn't broken any law here – as far as I know. So I guess he thought he'd be safe for a while. At least until he'd secured all of his most important assets in this country.'

'Right. That villa at Cap-Martin must be worth a bit.'

'I guess so,' she sighed. 'It's been beautifully restored.'

'And protected by a very big wall, no doubt.'

'Oh, yes – but I'm sure he knows just how long he can ward off any Australian government attempts to extradite him.'

'Do you know much about the rest of his art collection?'

'He had other Picassos. None as nice as mine, though. And he has a Matisse still life that's probably very valuable, as well as a small Bonnard domestic interior. He has quite a lot of lesser items, too – drawings, pastels, that sort of thing. But the truth is, I've never been involved in his collecting. And I've only visited the Cap-Martin villa once, straight after our marriage.'

As he considered what she was telling him, he realized that he still had no clear idea of what she might be expecting him to do with the *Portrait of Dora Maar.* She had resisted his advice so far, but he knew she must have had something else in mind.

'Are you absolutely sure that your Picasso won't be among the assets your husband's creditors might attempt to seize?' It was a crude attempt to unsettle her, but one thought he needed to try.

'Absolutely,' she bristled, 'it's mine and mine alone.'

Still, Mitchell couldn't help being concerned about being implicated in helping a criminal - or criminal's wife - to conceal assets from legally entitled creditors, particularly assets as valuable as *Dora.*

'Sure,' he said, 'but there's no telling how these ASIC people will see it.'

'I suppose not. But my divorce proceedings are already underway. It'd be pretty outrageous for anyone – no matter who they were – to claim than my business affairs were any longer bound up with Mike's.'

Mitchell thought that her objection sounded unconvincing, but wasn't prepared to antagonize her any further.

'Where do you imagine he might be now?'

'Who knows? Taking care of business. That's my best guess.'

He wasn't sure that he believed her on this; for that matter, he wasn't sure he trusted anything she had told him.

'Lucky he gave you the Picasso before the divorce was settled.'

'No matter what's gone down, Mike's never stopped being generous.'

'Doesn't sound like the way he made his fortune. Will he still be generous now that he's landed in this kind of trouble?'

'He's not vindictive, either.'

'Anyway, you know that Luc can't help you unless you bring *Dora* up to Paris.'

'Weren't you talking about only needing a better photo of the painting and a photocopy of the documents at this stage?'

Mitchell smiled at her evasiveness. 'Sure – if that's all you're prepared to do at this stage. But the best that will do is arouse Luc's curiosity. I thought you were in a bigger hurry than that. Besides, once Luc finds out that you're married to a man running from his creditors, you might find that he'll just say: forget it, too hard, I don't want to know.'

She sat in silent, anguished contemplation of her dilemma, until at last Mitchell spoke again.

'Show him the painting – he'll be as intrigued as I am.'

'But it's not exactly a sound exercise, is it? Lugging a Picasso through the streets of Paris?

'You wouldn't be the first to ever do that. I can call Luc now, make some appointments for tomorrow afternoon, and we could fly up in the morning.'

Cornered by her own need, she continued to protest the inconvenience and lack of security. But Mitchell knew she was wavering. Finally, she agreed, almost apologetically, to take the trip with him.

By then it was almost dusk, and the room they were sitting in was being briefly illuminated by the last rays from the low sun. Shadow patterns of leafy branches and window frames were cast against the stone wall behind them, turning it a shimmering gold. In that rare light she seemed even more fragile, and her allure struck Mitchell as something illusory, a trick of his own arousal. But he could easily see why Mike McGraw had loved her, if only for a brief while. She was complex and she was troubled, in a way that would sooner or later demand everything you could possibly give. It was more than that, though. As he watched the sunlight die down and return her face to shadow, he had the sense that the mark of time was on her. She wasn't strong, and things were slipping from her grip. McGraw must have seen that in rescuing her - and there would have always been some crisis in Marlo's life - he might have redeemed some part of himself.

Mitchell also felt that pull. It was what made him take on the burden of her suspect Picasso. She had probably known all along that he wouldn't - couldn't - turn away from her. He suspected that she had an unerring instinct for the kind of men who couldn't bear to let her down. That was her dangerous strength.

She took his hand lightly in hers and thanked him. 'You've done so much already.' she said. 'Now I'm taking you back to the Colombe d'Or.'

As he took a last look at the house, Mitchell thought again of how the place might be in mellow, perfect autumn, when she was long gone, and the New York owners had returned, bringing with them the clamour of parties and house guests and good times. She had, after all, told him nothing about her plans beyond that afternoon. Who was she seeing now that Mike McGraw was gone? Where was she headed to once she left Saint-Paul-de-Vence? He didn't feel that he had the right to ask, and she volunteered nothing in the brief interval before she dropped him at the entrance to the hotel.

'You're a very persuasive guy, Mitchell,' she said with a teasing smile, 'but that's okay. I forgive you.'

'You're going to like Luc,' he said, to deflect his embarrassment.

As he stepped out of the car he turned back to briefly take her hand. 'So - 8:00 a.m. tomorrow at Nice,'

'Don't worry – I won't change my mind.'

6

August 7 - 8: Nice and Saint-Paul-de-Vence

At dusk, in a pool that he had entirely to himself, Mitchell swam a dozen lengths, then stretched out on a canvas lounge chair with a glass of white Bandol. Marlo McGraw had prepaid his bill and urged him to enjoy everything the hotel had to offer; and as unused as he was to that kind of pampering, he was pleased to comply.

The encounter with her had shaken and disturbed him in ways that weren't entirely negative. Her allure, her quixotic moods, the contradictory web of stories she had spun, and the excitement of seeing her fabulous painting, had all contributed to his feverish state.

Until that day, he had imagined a future – a not too extravagant fantasy, he admitted - as a curator in some Australian regional art gallery. Because he had no taste for commerce, promotion, or deal making – and no prospects of adequate financial backing - he could never imagine himself as a private gallery owner. It was the fate his studies – Art History Honours followed by a Master of Art Curatorship at Melbourne University - had prepared him for. The only contest had come from his own painting, which he kept at fitfully, whenever his work schedule allowed. He was still in thrall to many of the first American abstract expressionists: de Koonig, Kline, Motherwell and Rothko. He had chosen a tough path, a cul de sac almost, and wondered whether he would ever have the confidence to explore beyond its narrow constraints. As for ever exhibiting his work, he barely allowed the idea the light of day.

But the brief time spent with Marlo had truly upended his thinking He had discovered how easily he could be lured into the challenging world of attribution and authentication. It had been thrilling to stand in front an extraordinary painting and not be at all sure whether it was the real thing. Instantly, he had found himself playing a game that tested the limits of everything he had learned. He was fascinated by the idea that, behind the seduction of the painted surface, there might possibly lurk a mind intent upon deception. Forced to question everything about the painting, he wondered whether he could ever look at a Picasso again with innocent eyes. The walls of the Musée would be forever altered for him. From now on he would be skeptical of everything.

But in this game, he knew he was a junior partner. Keener eyes and minds than his were soon to cast their judgement.

From his suffocatingly Provençal room – faux-mediaeval troubadour mural, farmhouse four-poster, and overpowering bowls of pot-pourri on every surface - he telephoned Luc in Paris. He reported the meeting with Alana-Marlo in all its improbable detail. Although amused by the tale, Luc wasn't prepared to make pronouncements about the authenticity or otherwise of the Picasso. He merely congratulated Mitchell on being able to coax

Marlo to Paris, and protested when Mitchell volunteered to split her generous fee.

At daybreak on the following morning, Mitchell drove to the airport, expecting to rendezvous with her in good time for the 9:00 a.m. flight to Paris. She didn't show up. As the deadline for flight-closure approached, he telephoned her mobile several times and left a series of increasingly terse messages. He also unsuccessfully tried the landline in the villa at Saint-Paul-de-Vence, but found it was not even connected to an answering machine.

Finally, in frustration, he left a message for her at the airline desk, then returned to the car hire booth. After enduring the rigmarole of rehiring the Renault, he drove back up the *autoroute* to her villa.

The place was now completely shuttered, and there was no sign of her Mercedes. He entered the property and rang the front door bell, then listened as the loud chimes echoed through the rooms. Afterwards he navigated a path that took him via a series of terraces to the rear of the house. He thumped on the back door, called her name loudly, and tried peering through a narrow gap in one of the shutters. There were no signs of her presence.

He considered the possibility that something had happened to her on the way to the airport, but believed it far more likely that she had changed her mind and departed elsewhere.

He could only guess at the actual reason for her behaviour. There were too many conceivable explanations. Perhaps, after weighing up all that he had said, she still didn't trust him sufficiently, and had wanted to put herself out of reach of persuasion. Possibly she feared that either he or Luc might betray her to the lawyers from ASIC, the Australian Federal Police, the *gendarmes*, or whoever else was on her husband's trail. Why would she take the risk of arrest and the loss of her property?

But the most reasonable assumption was that her panicked flight - if that was what it was - had been triggered by his expressions of uncertainty about the portrait's authenticity. It was probably as he had at first thought: she had been merely using him to discover whether the *Portrait of Dora Maar* might pass muster if it were put up for auction in London or New York. Now she probably feared that it wouldn't. Not that she would have doubted his denial of being an expert. But she knew he was a representative of someone who was – and that would have been enough to shake her confidence.

Did it mean that the painting was a fake, or only that she *thought* it might be? He had only his first impressions to rely upon, and they were ambivalent at best.

The experience had been disorienting and upsetting, the kind that exposes the shaky foundations of confidence. Enough anticipation had been allowed to develop around both Alana Daniels - or Marlo McGraw, or whoever she was - and her painting, for Mitchell to feel a terrible disappointment at her disappearance. It had to be admitted that the first sighting of the *Portrait of Dora Maar* had aroused a certain fantasy in him: it had seemed for a moment, that here was an opportunity to be associated with the rediscovery of a major stolen painting. A trap of his own making.

His final reaction was a slow-developing, diffuse anger. He had been conned and used by this woman. It wasn't that he hadn't been paid. The experience, while it lasted, had been exhilarating, and there was a cheque for a thousand euros on his dresser. It was like being jilted after a thrilling first date. He had been having one kind of experience – she, another. He had been naïve and foolish. And worst of all, he didn't believe he would ever see her again.

7

August 8: Manila to Paris

On the long night flight over the subcontinent, with the cabin in darkness and most of the passengers masked and wedged, in their comfortless attempts to sleep, Eddie, unable to switch off, stood by the emergency door at the rear.

He gazed down at the galaxy of lights that was Dehli; another place he would never visit. Too late for tourism, he thought, now that terrorism and conflict had turned everywhere to shit. Travel set him adrift, gave him too much time to think about the trail of mess in his life: his broken marriage; his estranged kids; the sudden unravelling of his police career; his own inexorable drift towards criminality.

There had been no word from Darren, his youngest at nineteen, for at least three months. Shelly, he had already given up on – three years out of touch, lost to him altogether. Back in early June, Darren had written to him asking for money for a second-hand ute. Claimed he needed it for some mowing business he was starting with a mate. Eddie had been quick to send a cheque – probably far too small, too mean – but had heard nothing in reply. Better in future, he supposed, to send any money straight to their mother. Let Dee slug it out with them. Unbidden thoughts of his children's contempt slashed at his heart. He would send them postcards from Paris. It was becoming a sad habit. Not that he believed they gave a damn where he was in the world.

It was the Wood Royal Commission into Police Corruption – he could sheet it all home to that fucking inquisition. Five years a detective senior-constable, not a single demerit, all plain sailing, until that debacle. Then in October '97 he was arrested, along with seven other members of Task Force Bolivia, accused of being too closely associated with the drug dealers they were supposed to be hunting.

Eddie's charge was more serious. He had been working undercover for four months on an operation designed to crack a drug distribution network operating across the Queensland-N.S.W. border. Twelve-thousand dollars in used fifties – Police Department money allocated as bait for a proposed drug buy - had gone missing from his hotel room in Surfers. Eddie was charged with misappropriation, but in truth he had been cunningly scammed – possibly by some of his own team. His case had quickly gone to trial, but he was acquitted because of insufficient evidence. Dismissal from the force was automatic. Out on his arse at thirty-seven. Worst of all, it had coincided with the collapse of his marriage. Lost his job and his family at the same time. All his own fault, he believed. Undercover work was relentless and ultimately damaging. A loner's life. Domestic intimacy was the first casualty. That was what the occupational health and safety pamphlet had warned. But no one had forced him into it. Dee, who said she'd had a gutful, had taken off back to her mother's place in Melbourne with the kids. Sure, he drank and gambled and didn't give a shit. But the funny thing was, he hadn't even been fucking anyone on the side.

Fortunately, an ex-copper mate called Marty Royce offered him a job – and a chance to fuck off out the country - with his security firm in Manila. It was only freelance muscle work, flatfoot stuff, but back then the hours and pay had suited him. Now he had moved up to high-end asset recovery. Sometimes it was dirty, but mostly just straight lucrative. If you could live with the occasional confusion about who actually owned what, it was a tolerable occupation. The money kept him in the Philippines. He had upgraded from a flea-bag hotel down on the Manila waterfront to a three bedroom air-conditioned bunker with a kidney pool, out in Quezon City. These days he had no plans for moving on.

Eddie's plane arrived in Charles de Gaulle at dawn. He picked up a Paris guidebook at the airport and telephoned a few of the cheaper hotels in the Marais. Gornik and Toop had already mentioned a couple on the Left Bank that might have suited him, but Eddie made it a policy to always make his own arrangements. When the business was finished, the fewer remaining points of contact, the better.

A friend who travelled a lot - an old Chinese thug who owned a restaurant-casino down on Manila Bay - had told him about the Marais. That was the place to stay, the old Jewish quarter, with its warren of narrow streets, where trendy boutiques and shoe salons were found right next to shabby kosher delicatessens and dingy *bar-tabacs.* According to Eddie's guidebook, it had once been the most fashionable residential district in Paris. But that was back in the seventeenth century. Eddie soon discovered that, as with most things in Paris, its best days were over. The tourists had moved in and the locals now shopped elsewhere. But it was lively enough and he'd probably be less conspicuous there than most other places in Paris.

The hotel he chose, sight unseen, had a couple of stars and was reasonably cheap. It was in a side street that connected the Rue de Rivoli to the Place des Voges. For a man seeking inaccessibility, the fact that the woman who picked up the telephone could barely be understood, was an immediate recommendation. Eddie couldn't penetrate her accented French, and she had the greatest difficulty in comprehending even his simple phrase book request for a room. It was just the way Eddie liked things. The more reduced the communication, the safer he felt.

His taxi driver, a silent young Vietnamese, required a complete circumnavigation - possibly gratuitous - of the Place des Voges before being able to locate the hotel. Eddie considered challenging him over the fare, but lacked the necessary vocabulary, and after a thirteen hour flight, wasn't exactly in the mood for a brawl. Fortunately, he liked the look of the hotel. The street was a backwater, and the place was inconspicuous. So unimpressive looking that you could pass it without even realizing that it was a hotel. The entrance was just a doorway beneath a faded sign.

The small, overheated lobby was hotter than an afternoon in Manila. The walls were grey stone. Heavy, dark-stained oak beams supported the low ceiling. A cracked leather lounge and pair of club chairs took up most of the available space, but were difficult to reach because of a pile of some departing guest's luggage. A plump woman, in a black woollen dress, sat behind the huge antique reception desk.

Eddie introduced himself and surrendered to the torture of signing in. Five minutes passed like half an hour. The woman stared up at him from time to time through her thick-framed glasses while she made the necessary entries. His passport, which was in his own name, seemed to arouse her curiosity. She leafed through it with a fat forefinger, and made some amusing comment, which Eddie failed to comprehend, before cracking it wide open and copying down his particulars. Finally, she requested his credit card in order to take an imprint. All the while he practiced a smile that might seem appropriate for a man enjoying his first day in Paris. Finally, with a sigh that suggested she was acceding to something ill advised, she handed him his room access card.

The stairs were steep and narrow, and the rickety old cage lift took forever. It was no place to find oneself cornered, but Eddie had no intentions of ever letting things come to that. His second floor room was ridiculously small with a view onto a damp air well. The decor, you wouldn't have been able to describe five minutes after departure.

He had brought one large, nondescript suitcase, and a slim bag for his notebook computer and essential documents. He had also brought weapons. These days he didn't like going anywhere without the goods: his Beretta 92 Fs 9mm, and a nasty item he called "Mister-Kiss-My-Arse." MKMA was a customized .30 calibre M2 Winchester U.S. military carbine that had been shorn of its bulky stock. Selective-fire, fifteen-round magazine, one previous owner, less than eighteen-inches tip to tail. Picked up from a dealer in Manila for five hundred dollars. Eddie was no marksman. He knew how everyone got the jitters once the covers came off. He'd rather spray the scenery than take his chances on a lucky shot. One in the slot, and fourteen more in the rack suited him just fine. Perfect drinking man's armament.

Never bothered him to come through customs with these items in his check-in luggage. Wrapped in an oil-soaked flannel rags and tucked into a flat Black and Decker steel tool box, what was an X-ray machine going to see?

Whatever else he owned back in Quezon City would soon be forgotten. If he never saw any of it again it would be of no account.

For the next hour, he did what he always did upon arriving in a strange city. He showered and changed, hung up his clothes in the musty closet, then lay on the bed and studied the street map. Afterwards, he took a watchful stroll around the neighbourhood, bought a pack of beer, a sack of roasted nuts, a block of dark chocolate, a dozen oranges, and a bag of exotic Tunisian dates. He located the *métros* at Bastille and St. Paul, bought a copy of the previous day's *Herald Tribune*, and drew 250 euros from an automatic teller at a Credit Lyonnais. For an hour or two he became a tourist. He allowed himself to forget his mission. In the early evening he would select a restaurant from the guidebook, and try to do a little more forgetting. But first he had to make some phone calls.

8

August 8: Nice

It was dark by the time Mitchell returned the hire car for the second time. A cold wind was blowing in off the ocean as he hurried across the desolate concourse carrying his overnight bag, heading in the direction of the airport terminal. He was far too preoccupied with all that had gone wrong to take much notice of a black Mercedes that was slowing to intercept him.

From behind, a man called to him in an urgent tone of voice. When he turned to see what it was about he was given a violent shove from the opposite direction. He toppled sideways onto the concrete. While trying to break his fall, the heel of his right palm struck the concrete, sending a bolt of pain up through his neck and shoulders. As he began to react, a powerful hand was clamped over his mouth.

Two men stood over him. Before Mitchell could even grasp

what was happening, they had taken hold of his arms and dragged him, dazed and unresisting, onto his feet. One of them retrieved his bag, then clamped his fingers onto the back of Mitchell's neck and hissed at him to 'move!' Spasms of muscle pain tore at his back as they frog marched him towards the open back door of the Mercedes. He could recall thrashing against his attackers, trying to whip his arms from their grasp, but couldn't summon either the strength or co-ordination to break free. At the last moment, his head was forced down and he was given a powerful shove to propel him into the back seat of the car. His collision with the stiff leather upholstery was like a fist blow to the forehead. Within moments, both men were inside the car, trapping him between them. As the unseen driver accelerated away, he was hauled upright, and his arms were pinned against the back seat.

Mitchell had the overwhelming sense that this was all some grotesque mistake. Whatever this attack was about, he couldn't possibly be their intended victim.

'What the fuck is this?' he shouted. 'Why are you doing this to me?'

None of them responded to his protests. Nor was there any further violence, and he soon gave up the idea of struggling. He was being driven at great speed into the centre of Nice, where he trusted everything would be made clear. His hope was that they were plainclothes police of some kind, whose error would soon be realized. His fear was that they were not.

They took a main route that followed the course of the bay, but he was too shocked and disoriented to keep track of where they were heading. His body ached all over and wanted only the opportunity to sort out the mistake. Soon they were rounding a headland, where he glimpsed a signboard for the Old Port.

A squall had sprung up, spitting rain on the seaward side of the car, blurring visibility out the side windows. After a few more minutes of driving into the storm, one of the men alongside him said something in an indecipherable patois to the driver, who soon slowed and pulled over.

'I don't mean to be uncooperative,' Mitchell said, 'but I have a plane to catch back there.'

'I think you goin' be too late,' said the man sitting on his right. 'But what this matter, huh? They have plane every day - tomorrow, next week. No problem for you.' He spoke English with a stilted American accent, but Mitchell followed him perfectly. It was the intent behind his insinuating casualness that he couldn't fathom. 'You give us your name,' the man said.

'Mike McGraw,' he said, without considering the consequences. 'Name mean anything to you?'

The men on either side of him looked at one another. They knew he was talking garbage.

'Okay, mister smart man. We take look in you bag. Where you keep passport?'

'Wait a minute,' Mitchell demanded. 'Who exactly am I dealing with? Are you guys with the French Police? Are you undercover *gendarmes?* Is that it?'

This produced smiles all round.

'Do you have some good reason for all this?'

While the driver sifted through the contents of Mitchell's overnight bag, the silent man on his left frisked his jacket until he discovered a wallet and passport. He passed them across to the English speaking one on Mitchell's right.

'So - Mr Mitchell Jameson?' he said, reading from the passport, 'What you business here? Why you make this visit with Mrs McGraw?'

'Is there any good reason why I should answer these questions?'

'Because you in my car,' he said. 'You want get out - you answer.'

Mitchell had no idea where 'out' was anymore. He couldn't see through the windows, the condensation from their hot breaths had fogged them up completely. The coercion that was about to take place would be entirely hidden from the street.

'How you know Mrs McGraw?' the one who spoke English

asked. He was a formidable presence, at least six inches taller than Mitchell, with huge shoulders and a massive head capped with a mop of uncombed curly hair. His protuberant eyes, which hardly seemed to belong in his pale, unshaven face, were the colour of liquid chocolate. But his mouth was his most remarkable feature. It was entirely lipless, no more than a broad slit, so that in profile his lower face, with it's steeply receding chin, reminded Mitchell of a toad.

'I don't really know her,' Mitchell said, tempting the man's irritation.

'We know you go to her house.'

'Well, listen,' he said, 'since you probably know more about her than me, I'll just shut up and let you do the talking.'

'You see her at the hotel in St-Paul,' the man said calmly. 'You do business with her. We know. So - what she want?'

Mitchell presumed that they had been following him ever since he had arrived in Nice, and had witnessed his meeting with Marlo. But it was also possible - assuming they hadn't also been tapping her phone conversations - that they had no idea of what their business was about. He decided to offer them a thin version of the truth.

'Look – I'm an Australian research student. I've been working up in Paris. I came down here to see my friend, Marlo McGraw.' Having no idea of who they were or what they wanted, he had instinctively lied about the purpose of his visit. He knew it was inviting trouble.

Toadmouth showed no sign of interest in the story. 'You work for the Australian Federal Police,' he suggested bluntly.

'Sorry...that's ridiculous,' Mitchell said.

The man on his left, who looked like an emaciated version of Daniel Auteuil, said something in his thick patois. He had a long thin face and restless, foxy eyes. Even in the claustrophobic confines of the back seat, he kept a cigarette going the whole time, He gave out a dangerous nervous energy. Although his accent eluded Mitchell (in recollection he christened him 'Patois'), the man was making it clear that he was frustrated with the lack of progress his inquisitor was making. In fact, all three men appeared disgruntled, short-fused, hungover. They looked as though they had been on a stakeout that had gone on far too long.

'Okay, ' said Toadmouth, carefully returning Mitchell's wallet to his coat pocket, a gesture of absurd solicitousness. 'We stay here, and we have little talk until the sun come. And pretty soon - if you smart - you tell us everything we want. Or we can drive, take you my place - you don't know where - and you stay there two, three days - a week if you like. Until you tell us. Or anything will happen. Who knows?'

'Anything, huh?' Mitchell said, attempting nonchalance. 'Then what do you want to know? Whatever it is - I'm yours.'

He was expecting a nasty reaction to his facetiousness, but instead they continued with their dogged questioning.

'You represent Australian Government?'

'No – I've already told you. I'm a research student – an art historian.' He immediately regretted giving them a clue to the real purpose of his visit.

For a few moments, the two on either side of him conversed in rapid, cryptic French. Then they seemed to be questioning the driver, who had all the while been making a patient search of Mitchell's belongings. Without turning his head, the driver answered with a shrug. He was a dark complexioned, somewhat mysterious man - a North African, most probably. He had shoulder length, wavy hair, thick with oil, wore a tight fitting black leather jacket, and sported many silver rings on both hands. All that Mitchell could see of his face was a sliver in the rear view mirror.

'After you have business – where do Mrs McGraw go?'

'I have no idea.'

'You know.'

'I hardly know the woman. She didn't tell me her plans.'

'You lie.'

Listen – this is crazy. I've already told you the truth.'

In reply, Patois stepped abruptly from the car and stood for a moment in the rain looking around. Mitchell felt a sudden panic, thinking the man's next move would be to haul him out into the gutter. Instead, he slid back in alongside Mitchell, and while Toadmouth secured both his arms, Patois deftly unfolded a barber's razor. Through half-averted eyes, Mitchell watched as Patois took his time, testing the edge with his thumb, turning the bone handle a little in his palm so that the blade caught the cold blue light from the car window.

In fear of the slash, Mitchell shrank back against the seat, automatically pressing his chin against his chest - a futile effort to protect his throat. His breathing gagged on a sudden intake.

'All right,' Mitchell stammered. 'What's this…?'

'He don't like way you told story,' Toadmouth said. 'He want you do it better this time.'

'What does he want to know?'

'He want to know the truth this time.'

Patois reached into Mitchell's lap and plucked at the gathered fabric of his trouser fly. He yanked it upwards, then with neither a hint of threat nor amusement, began to slice away at the corduroy. With two swift strokes of the blade he had opened a vent that exposed Mitchell's underpants. Then he reached in, and as though robbing a bird's nest, grasped a handful of the stretch fabric. He tugged it out through the opening, extending it as far as possible. Then he cut again, this time tenderly sawing the razor. The fabric sprung apart. Mitchell's genitals were now absurdly displayed at the centre of his slashed lap. He saw his exposed cock, as pale and vulnerable as a peeled mushroom.

Toadmouth also took a disdainful look at the damage. With great care, Patois eased the long blade of his razor beneath the head of Mitchell's penis. There was some observable shrinkage. This amused Patois, who made some joke in his indecipherable French.

'He think it be better for you if you don't laugh too much,'

Toadmouth said, while demonstrating a dangerous, exaggerated giggling motion.

'What does he want to know?' Mitchell asked in a strained voice.

'He want to know about a painting – a painting by Picasso. He think that why you go see her.'

Mitchell knew there was no chance of holding back under such duress. He took a deep breath, then began to tell them an uncomplicated version of the reason for his visit. In the course of his account he revealed nothing of Marlo's other identity, nor anything about her state of panic and indecision. Nor did he stray onto the subject of her husband and his financial and legal problems. He made the relationship with Marlo McGraw sound like a straightforward appraisal on behalf of a gallery in Paris, but he was careful to offer no opinion about the authenticity of the Picasso.

They continued to insist that he knew where she had gone, but after many consistent denials, they finally accepted Mitchell's protestation of ignorance. Once they believed they had extracted everything else he knew about the woman and her painting, they were suddenly keen to be rid of him. They opened the door and dumped him face first into the wet gutter. A moment later his half opened overnight bag went skittering across the cobbled footpath.

'Bonsoir, con!' Toadmouth yelled back at him, as their car sped away.

It took him several minutes to realize that his ordeal was over. He staggered to his feet and retrieved his bag, still too confused to form any kind of plan. He was cold and still fearful that his attackers might change their minds and reappear.The rain squall had abated, but the persistent drizzle soon soaked him to the skin. There was nothing protective in his overnight bag - no dry shirt and no spare trousers; just some clean underwear, a couple of books, a diary, a road map of Provence, and an apple.

When he finally was able to think clearly, he decided to

make for the centre of Old Nice. It was a matter of heading in a vaguely northerly direction while keeping the Cathédrale de St-Réparate in sight when possible. Half an hour later, sodden and demoralized, he arrived in the almost deserted Place Rossetti. The glistening facade of the Cathédrale loomed over him. He found an open bar nearby and sought shelter, all the while holding the overnight bag so as to conceal his gaping trousers. The bagman eyed him suspiciously at first, but then seemed indifferent to the presence of a drowned rat with slicked wet hair and dripping clothes. In the warmth of its smoky interior Mitchell consulted a telephone directory. It was past 10:00 p.m. and he had long ago abandoned the idea of getting a night flight to Paris. He scoured the listings for a nearby budget hotel and found what he was after in the vicinity of the Gare Routière. At least it would simplify tomorrow's trip to the airport.

An hour later he had checked in to the dismal little hotel and was standing under a lukewarm shower, trying to erase the absurdities of the evening. Tomorrow he would try to make sense of the event, try to figure out whom they could possibly have been. But tonight he would put it all out of mind.

Before turning in, he managed to make a reservation for an 11:00 a.m. flight to Orly, and put through a futile call to Luc's message bank. Later, he drifted towards sleep with his water logged paperback copy of Pierre Daix's Picasso biography. He had barely been able to separate the pages of the sodden wad, and the miserly glow from the low wattage bedside lamp made it a struggle to focus on the words. He did wonder for a while why he was bothering, but then had to admit that the mysterious disappearance of Alana - or was it Marlo? – had actually fuelled his interest in the Dora Maar - Picasso relationship.

9

August 9: The Marais, Paris

Eddie had followed Gornik's instructions, and on the previous day telephoned the Australian Consulate, where he asked to speak to a Mr Roger Knight. He was a lawyer working for the Attorney General's Department, a member of the team working on the extradition of Mike McGraw. A secretary told him, in a reassuring honest Australian accent, that Mr Knight was still at lunch. Eddie declined her suggestion that he leave a message.

At 3:00 p.m. he telephoned again and was put straight through to Knight. The man was immediately on guard. He had clearly been expecting Eddie's call, and was affecting a tone of official politeness. What did he know about this business? Somehow Gornik and Toop had got to the man, found out that he was amenable. But what had they told him? That McGraw owed them money? That they had certain negotiations to transact with the fugitive? You could be sure they had omitted any hint of their plan to steal his Picasso. But whatever he knew, it soon became clear that the man was going to feign ignorance and let Eddie make the running. Knight talked about Gornik and Toop as though he barely knew them, giving the impression that they had come to him for the kind of routine assistance that his position had obliged him to render. What else could the man do? The name Leon Meyer drew a complete blank. Whatever they were paying him, he was taking an enormous risk. Quite possibly, he was prejudicing the outcome of the entire extradition process.

From the man's light, cultivated voice and his tendency to upwardly inflect the endings of every sentence, Eddie judged him to be in his mid-thirties, and definitely from Melbourne. Eddie had developed an immediate distaste for the man. He sensed that Knight was the kind of lawyer who habitually patronized older cops, and had nothing but contempt for those who had retired to the dubious shadow lands of police work.

They arranged to meet for lunch on the following day, a Sunday, at a restaurant in the Places des Voges called Ma Bourgogne, some place that Eddie had picked straight out of the guidebook. This was a choice made as a strategy rather than a culinary adventure. He wanted something nearby so that he'd be able to take a closer look at it before the appointment, most probably an unnecessary precaution, but one that he took by habit.

Half an hour before his lunch appointment with Knight, Eddie took a walk in the Places des Voges. He circumnavigated the Place via the broad stone arcades, then crossed diagonally through the gardens. Even at the hour of the sacred Sunday *déjeuner*, it was crowded with families There were small children everywhere, romping on the grass, chasing one another beneath the shadowy box-cut lime trees, weaving dangerously on pint-sized bicycles as they shouted to one another. He observed the young parents watching from the nearby benches. A tiny girl let out a squeal of delight as she ran into her mother's embrace. A young father, taking the opportunity to laze in the sun with a paperback, looked up anxiously to locate his own child.

For a brief, unexpected moment, Eddie was back in his own days of parenthood. Surfing holidays at Coffs Harbour. Camping trips to the Blue Mountains. Family boating on the Hawkesbury. All far behind him now. But the fleeting reflections soon passed, and he walked on.

Ma Bourgogne looked as though it had been there forever. It was exposed on three sides. Diners could be watched from the gardens or from either end of the arcade. But did it matter? There was no reason to anticipate a set up. Knight had no motivation to cross him, especially since he was already on the payroll.

Eddie entered the restaurant, stumbled his way through the initial contact with the headwaiter, and was shown to an indoor table by the windows.

There was no mistaking Roger Knight. Eddie identified him even before he reached the restaurant door. He had caught sight of him through the trees, walking along a gravel pathway in the gardens. A short, stocky man, wearing a pink polo shirt and grey chinos, but incongruously carrying a lawyer's black brief case. He raised his sunglasses and gazed about with serious apprehension He looked as though he had strayed in from the wrong end of town.

Eddie, raised a hand in greeting. Knight smiled back, then lumbered across to Eddie's table and extended a damp, pudgy hand.

'Hello, I'm Roger Knight.'

'Pleased to meet you. Eddie Pike.'

Knight covered the awkwardness of their stilted greeting by taking a long time to settle himself in a chair that seemed far too small for his liking.

'Good choice,' he said. I've dined here two or three times before. I like the food. Very traditional, of course. A little too conservative to be truly interesting, but nicely done all the same. Marvellous cellar, though.' The man was probably no more than thirty-five, but had the stuffy, patrician manner of a fifty year old.

'You'd better take care of the ordering, then.'

'Oh, no. Each to his own, poison, so to speak.'

For a long time they avoided talking about their real business. Knight ordered the house specialty, the spicy steak tartare - nothing but a mound of raw mince, as far as Eddie could see - while Eddie was guided towards the Auvergne sausage. To the irritation of the waiter, Knight fussed for ages over the wine list, before settling on an expensive Burgundy. The man was already beginning to grate on Eddie. With his furrowed brow and oracular manner of saying even the simplest things, he struck Eddie as a pretentious dill. He had the same private school veneer and lawyer's smugness as Gornik. It was the assumption of control and the effortless dispensing of phony wisdom that Eddie couldn't stand. They regarded men like Eddie as gullible plebs. None of them were to be trusted.

While they waited for their entrées, Knight peeled the crust from his bread roll, absently depositing the crumbs into a pile beside his plate. He appeared anxious to impart his information and be on his way. He had already committed his crime. This was the grubby aftermath.

'You have something for me?' Knight asked.

Eddie placed a thin envelope on the table in front of him. He knew what it contained: five thousand euros in clean hundreds. Knight lifted the flap and peered inside, but didn't count the contents. He awkwardly stuffed the envelope into his back trouser- pocket.

'And what do you have for me?' Eddie asked.

'What did they say I'd have?'

'An address, maybe. A telephone number or two. Some idea of what the man is up to these days.'

Knight took a thin folder out of his briefcase and sifted through an assortment of papers. He selected a document and passed it to Eddie. It was a typewritten list of addresses, four in all.

'These are McGraw's known French addresses dating back five years. The bottom one – on Cap-Martin, near Menton - is current, as far as I know. He owns that place, and it's been his French home for the last couple of years. Or *was,* to be more accurate. McGraw doesn't exactly appear to have a home these days.'

'So where is he?'

Knight shrugged.

'You're no more help than the clowns who hired me.'

'Well – we know he arrived in the country twenty-seven days ago, and hasn't yet left.'

'Did he visit this place at Cap-Martin?'

'We believe so. But it's locked up and abandoned at the moment.'

'What – the Attorney Generals Department organized a raid?'

'Not so simple. French detectives paid a visit on our behalf.'

'Broke in and took a good look at the contents?'

'Possibly, but not officially. I haven't yet been shown a report, so I don't know exactly what they did at Cap-Martin, or indeed what they found.'

'But you know for sure there was no sign of McGraw.'

'That's right. And until the extradition process has been completed, we can't make a move. Obviously, an attempt is being made to locate McGraw, even though he can't yet be apprehended.'

'Your crowd doesn't seem to move too fast.'

'French bureaucracy,' Knight said, with an open-palmed gesture of hopelessness he had learned from the Parisians. They both laughed. It was perhaps the only moment in which they shared an emotion.

'Can I ask about the nature of the business you have with Mr McGraw?' It was a bold question, but obliquely put. Knight also had the revealing habit of making frequent unnecessary adjustments to the position of his wire-framed glasses. Not surprising that the man was so jumpy, Eddie thought, given how far his arse was hanging out. The fool had made the mistake of selling information to Toop and Gornik, and was now dealing with the prospect of dire consequences.

'I'm going to invite him to pay some of his bills.' It wasn't the answer that Gornik and Toop might have recommended, but Eddie was seeking a reaction.

Knight gave a nervous laugh that caused his Burgundy to take a wrong path. He spent a few moments coughing into his serviette before speaking. 'Is there a plane load of you, then?'

'Only me.'

Eddie could see that Knight wasn't at all reassured.

'Is McGraw aware that you've been tracking his every move?' Eddie asked.

'Of course. Well – I mean, I assume he is.'

'And it doesn't bother him?'

'I'm sure it bothers him, but what can he do about it? He'd like us to disappear altogether, but then he's not sure whether or not we'll succeed with the extradition. So, right now, it doesn't pay for him to be acting like a fugitive. I'm sure – when and if we manage to confront him - he'd claim he was a legitimate investment broker in the process of re-scheduling a few irritating debts. Meanwhile, no doubt, he's making plans to squirrel away his liquid assets as quickly as possible. Oh, he has companies in Luxembourg and Malta, and no doubt accounts in the Cayman Islands and other tax havens. We may be too late – you included.'

Eddie reached across the table to take possession of the document. Knight withdrew it sharply. 'It's on our letterhead. You'll have to make your own copy.'

He handed Eddie a ballpoint pen and a page torn from a small notebook. He also showed Eddie a map of the Côte d'Azur and pointed out the location of McGraw's villa on Cap-Martin.

'Nice part of the world. You'd love it down there.'

'What makes you think I'm paying a visit?' Eddie said with quiet contempt.

"Oh – sorry. Really more a comment on the charms of the place.'

Having no picture of that part of Provence, the endorsement meant little to Eddie. He copied down McGraw's address and handed the papers back to Knight.

The rest of their meal was mostly given over to small talk. Knight recommended some other restaurants in the area, and advised Eddie of a few Parisian pleasures he should experience. They didn't bother with dessert, or the cheese plate, or coffee. Both were in a hurry to get away.

Eddie took the bill. Afterwards, they shook hands and walked away in opposite directions.

10

August 9 - 10: Rue des Martyrs & Avenue Montaigne

'You can't just forget about it, you're going to have to report this incident,' Luc insisted.

'No – my French isn't good enough to handle complicated questions from police officers. Besides, these guys didn't exactly beat me up. They just encouraged me to talk, then threw me out.'

'With a hole in your trousers,' Luc said with a smile.

'But no nick in my dick. I'm just happy to be here.'

Mitchell was sitting with Luc Pellegrin on his shaded balcony with a view of the Basilique du Sacré Coeur, having just finished an improvised lunch of salmon bagels and salad, washed down with a couple of glasses of Sancerre. He could tell from the chaotic state of Luc's apartment that all was not well. His friend was obviously unhappy and distracted; his familiar weekend good humour had given way to a nervy insistence.

Before lunch, they had discussed the abduction in Nice and the possible motivation of his attackers, but had been unable to come up with anything beyond the simple and obvious fact that the men were after the Picasso. On whose behalf they were acting, neither had a clue. Luc thought they didn't sound like French undercover police, and Mitchell knew they certainly weren't Australians.

As for Marlo's Picasso, and the question of whether it might be a fake, they had both already exhausted their theories. Besides, nothing that Mitchell could recount from his careful observation was of any real help. Luc told Mitchell he would have needed to see the painting himself to draw any conclusions. But given what he had been told about Marlo, he was prepared to believe either possibility.

Luc didn't appear to want their discussion to end, having found the entire scenario both bizarre and threatening but Mitchell was utterly depleted by so much bottomless speculation. He had recovered somewhat from the shock of his experience, and was now keen to put it all out of mind.

'Okay - I'll go to the police with you,' Luc said. 'I know a senior man in the *commissariat* over by the Grand Palais. If you like, I'll be the one who does all the talking. And don't give me that look – we're doing this.'

Luc, who possessed the most animated language of cigarette gestures Mitchell had ever witnessed, was becoming agitated. His smouldering Gaulois was now being wafted and passed with a conjuror's sleight of hand from mouth to hairline to table height and back again.

'But what's the point? What'll come of it? A new pair of trousers?'

'I'll tell them the bare facts. Of course, they'll do absolutely nothing, they're French policemen, but at least we'll have a clear conscience. If anything happened to that woman, we'd regret it. Bad for business.'

'Sure, I understand. But judging by the frustration of those thugs, I'm positive she made a clean getaway.'

As far as Luc was concerned the matter had already been settled. He would telephone his friend at the *commissariat* for an appointment first thing in the morning.

Mitchell acquiesced. He wanted to return their conversation to the puzzling matter of Marlo's failure to show up at Nice airport.

'I still don't get why she bothered to make the arrangement in the first place,' Mitchell said.

'She obviously thought more deeply about the consequences of exposing the painting to any scrutiny.'

'But she agreed to allow me to take a better photograph – which surely would have amounted to a preliminary kind of exposure.'

'But then you didn't actually get to take one.'

'Right.'

'Then maybe she made the arrangement to get rid of you while she made plans to escape.'

'Why would she bother going to that trouble, when all she needed to do was say "no" and show me the door?'

Luke shrugged. 'I'm in no shape to understand women,' he said ruefully. 'But you've met her. Spent the whole day with her. What do you think?'

Mitchell had no explanation either. If he hadn't been so fascinated by Marlo and her painting, he would have been happy to forget the entire demeaning experience.

'There's a person who used to work at the Musée that I want you to talk to. Her name is Paulette Berg. She wrote a very good article about the fate of Paul Rosenberg's gallery during the war. Turning it into a book, I think. Paulette knows more about Picasso's work from that period than almost anybody.'

'Why should we follow this up? The woman's gone, and we'll never see her or that portrait of Dora Maar ever again.'

'Ah – but you're still curious. And so am I.'

'Maybe if you tell Paulette everything you can remember – describe the painting to her in minute detail – she might be able to surprise you.'

'Tell if it's genuine?'

'Of course not. But maybe tell you if such a painting ever existed.'

The following morning, at his gallery in the rue de Montaigne, Luc introduced Mitchell to Paulette Berg. Anticipating a visit from a client, he urged them to retire to a neighbouring *tabac* to continue their conversation.

She was a plump, owlish woman in her late forties, with Gertrude Stein style cropped grey hair, and bright blue eyes magnified by a heavy pair of red circular framed glasses. Being only half-French, and having lived and studied in New York for many years, her English was excellent. She told Mitchell that she lived nearby and welcomed the mid-morning break from her writing.

He showed her the photograph of the *Portrait of Dora Maar* originally given to him by Marlo McGraw. Paulette's delight struck him as excessive. She pored over it like a dealer in the presence of a rare stamp.

'My God! I've never seen this before. Marvellous,' she exclaimed. 'How on earth did you come by this?'

He told her the story of his meeting with Marlo Shanahan, leaving out the Alana Daniels subterfuge, and explained his professional interest in knowing its provenance. 'Can you put a date on it?' he asked.

'Only the obvious one - 1937. I'm sure you know this already – but since it's so similar to the portrait in the Musée Picasso, I could only assume that they were painted at much the same time.'

None of which surprised Mitchell. He feared it was going to be a long morning.

'And what about it's history of ownership?'

'Almost certainly it would have been sold through Paul Rosenberg's gallery in Paris. Everything of that era was, as you no doubt already know. That had been the standing deal with Picasso since 1918. But to whom? Much more difficult to answer. Rosenberg had a pretty large international clientele. He sold all over Europe and spent a couple of months each year travelling to America selling to museums and private collectors. His was the leading gallery in the world capital of art. They used to call his gallery at Rue de la Boétie the "French Florence" - it was where all the most important modern collections of the day were born. So, as to whom he might have sold your Dora Maar: without documentation, who could guess?'

'Did Paul Rosenberg keep good records of all his sales?'

'Yes, he did - every painting was photographed and placed in an inventory book.'

'Which you've studied closely?'

'No, unfortunately. No longer possible. When the Wermacht arrived in Paris in 1940, and the looting of Jewish property began - Rosenberg had by then fled to America - a loyal friend managed to burn his inventory book before it fell into Nazi hands.'

'So you've been unable to find out what happened to most of the Picassos he owned?'

'Only with a lot of painstaking cross checking. A great many of them spent the war years in America. In November 1939 Rosenberg helped organize a big retrospective of Picassos at the Museum of Modern Art in New York. Of course I have that catalogue, and I can account for all of those works. I'm afraid your painting wasn't one of them.'

'Which suggests - what? That it had been sold at some earlier date?'

'Most probably. Or that it had remained for some time in his private collection. I'll sift through all my records and see if I can find anything that matches the description of your portrait.'

'I didn't mean to put you to any such trouble - '

She removed her glasses and gave him a smile that signalled nothing more clearly than the utter loneliness of her days. 'Please,' she said, 'it's become my obsession now, too. Now I'm going to leave you to go home and consult my references. With any luck, I'll be able to telephone you with some answers this evening.'

As Mitchell anticipated, the session at the *commissariat de police* with Luc's friend, an Inspector Maurice Sylvain, proved tedious and uninformative. While Luc re-enacted the details of the abduction/mugging/kidnapping – however it was defined under French law - Mitchell's attention drifted to the view of the park available through the Inspector's grimy barred window. In the end, after enduring half an hour of barely understood exchanges, Mitchell was left no wiser about his situation. The interview, which had been taken down in shorthand, was typed into a computer, and Mitchell was handed a copy for his approval. There appeared to be nothing contentious in the document, and so he signed it, shook the Inspector's hand, and departed with Luc. He expected to hear nothing more about the event. In fact, as he walked away from the man's office, he even thought he heard the sound of a sheet of paper being balled and binned.

That same evening, he received an excited call from Paulette Berg.

'The bad news, I'm afraid, is that I can't find any reference to your painting of Dora. Nothing at least by that name.'

'I thought you said the list, whatever it was, had been burned.'

'The original itinerary, yes, but naturally Rosenberg tried to reconstruct it once he learned that the Nazis had confiscated his collection.'

So, are you about to tell me some good news?'

'I think so. The closest match to your painting that I could find was one called *Portrait of a Young Woman.* An unpromising title, I'll admit. But in every other respect it sounds like your work. The canvas size matches, it was painted in the same year, 1937, and the brief description conjures your painting remarkably.'

'What else do you know about it?'

'That it was sold by Rosenberg in July 1938 to a Parisian collector called David Kaufman.'

'A Jewish name, right?'

'One would presume.'

'The title of this painting bothers me,' Mitchell said. 'Surely - since Rosenberg would have known Dora Maar personally - any portrait of her would have been described as such.'

'Not necessarily,' she said. 'Picasso may have requested that it remain a generic portrait of a young woman. The anonymity of the sitter may have been a part of the deal. After all, it's a little odd to be selling off a portrait of your current lover.'

'I suppose so,' Mitchell conceded. 'Then, do you know anything else about this David Kaufman?'

'Only that he was a wealthy senior banker right up until the German invasion. After that - I have no idea what happened to him. He may have successfully fled the country - many did. Or he may have eventually been rounded up and sent to his death. There's certainly no further mention of him in any of Rosenberg's documents.'

'So, there's a possibility that Kaufman's Picasso was confiscated by the Nazis?'

'A really strong possibility. It would explain why it's been out of circulation for over sixty years. And the fact that it eventually turned up in a dubious Swiss gallery also makes me suspect that's what happened.'

Mitchell understood perfectly. He knew enough about the Nazi policy towards the 'decadent' art of painters like Picasso and Matisse to imagine the scenario.

'After the war, the Swiss would have simply claimed ownership.

They enacted a law to protect all this ill-gotten bounty. Their new legislation in effect put a five-year statute of limitations on claims that any given work of art was stolen. If a person or gallery had possession of Kaufman's Picasso for a period of over five years, and could prove that they had obtained it in "good faith" – however they liked to interpret that loaded little phrase - then no claims by Kaufman or his heirs could be made against it.'

'So possession became ownership?'

'Maybe you could find out more about this David Kaufman through the records of his employers,' she said. 'He worked for the Banque Nationale de Commerce et Industrie.'

'Worth a try, I suppose' he said without commitment, not imagining that he would ever go to such lengths. She had already answered his prime question with uncertainty, and that was how things were bound to stay. The David Kaufman story sounded as likely as any other he expected to hear. It certainly provided an explanation for the painting's 'outlaw' status. But since the *Portrait of Dora Maar* had vanished along with its owner, there was nothing to be done about such speculation.

11

August 10: The Marais

Leon Meyer summoned Eddie to a lunch at Georges, the swank brasserie on the rooftop of the Pompidou Centre. Impossible to anticipate what was on the man's mind, but there was no mistaking his attitude. Eddie needed to circle the entire building to find the entrance: a discreet stainless steel doorway into an elevator guarded by a muscular, supercilious doorman. Without even a nod of acknowledgement, Eddie strode straight past the man and rode up to the sixth floor.

He had no difficulty in placing Meyer, there being no other short, balding, Jewish New Yorkers in sight. The man was sitting alone at a high table, perusing a diary while one arm nursed a glass of white wine. Behind and below him lay all of Paris: a panoramic view of the Left Bank all the way to the Tour Eiffel. He shook Eddie's hand firmly and gave him an unconvincing white-dentured smile. Meyer's left hand came to rest on Eddie's shoulder as he guided him onto a chrome stool. A technique, maybe, that conveyed the impression that he had known you in some former life.

'Now, you're not going to fuck this up on me, are you?' Meyer asked with brutal directness, his dead fish stare fixed on Eddie.

'Not planning to - not unless you've set me up,' Eddie said, giving back some of the same.

'Well that gives me confidence,' Meyer said quietly. There was a hint of amusement at the edges of his wet mouth. He slid a menu towards Eddie. 'Go ahead - I already know what I want. My advice is, keep it simple. Nobody comes here for the food.' Meyer ordered a plate of oysters, which he was soon to wash down with an expensive Chablis. Eddie saw nothing on the menu that made any sense apart from a gourmet club sandwich.

'Why did you want this meeting?' Eddie said flatly. The question was blunt but his mode was dispassionate. 'Don't you trust what Knight tells you?'

'You're working for me. That's enough reason.'

'So what do you want to know?'

'Nothing more. We didn't hire you out of the phone book.'

'Good.'

'But maybe there are some things about McGraw you'll need to know.'

'What have you got? His current silent telephone numbers? A cut of his latest front door key?'

'There's a history that might interest you.'

'Probably not. I don't work backwards. The less I know of the personal stuff, the easier it is.'

'I'm talking about my business relationship with McGraw.'

'That's your concern.'

'Don't you want to know who you're dealing with?'

'I wasn't planning on a long conversation. Not with McGraw, and not with you.'

Meyer smiled. He was getting to like Eddie.

'So what exactly did Knight tell you?'

'Fuck all. He showed me a place on the map. That was it. What do these clowns from the Attorney General's Department think you're up to?'

'They think I'm co-operating with their inquiries. Which, to a certain extent, I am. About ninety-five percent.'

'What do they think you're getting out of it?'

'Excuse me?' Meyer interjected, with quiet amusement. 'What-the-fuck is this? You're working for me. This isn't your concern.'

'I'm not working for you till I'm working for you.'

They stared at one another in silence. Finally Meyer broke it by loudly drumming his fingers on the bar top.

'You're not drinking anything,' Meyer said in a conciliatory voice. He splashed a dash of the Chablis into a second glass and pushed it towards Eddie. 'Sorry, I lost my cool there, ' he said. 'Have an oyster. Naturally, the deal is – whatever goes down - I get immunity from prosecution.'

Eddie declined the oyster and held Meyer's gaze.

'Do they know about this art collection of McGraw's?'

Meyer shrugged. 'Who knows what these fuckers know? But I don't believe so. They're behaving with uncharacteristic tactical finesse if they do.'

'That's comforting.'

'Believe me, you've got nothing to worry about.'

At that moment Eddie thought Meyer looked like nothing more than a jumped up salesman, a pushy little Woody Allen look-alike with an angle on everything.

'So what happens when I take possession of these paintings?'

'You call me, and I'll give you delivery instructions.'

Meyer took a stubby Mont Blanc fountain pen from his breast pocket and wrote a number on a page of a small spiral notebook. He tore out the leaf and handed it to Eddie.

'I don't answer the number, ever, but the woman you reach will know how to find me.'

'So - no final instructions?'

'Just one thing. Don't hesitate to use your connections to hire some local assistance. In the wrap up, it'd be very useful to have someone to lay all this onto.'

'Who says I have any?'

'I'm talking about your old pal, Didier. Name ring a bell?'

'How do you know that name?'

'Eddie - that's why we've got you on this job. I just hope you still know how to find him.'

'He's around.'

'I hope so. He sounds perfect.'

'Though I wouldn't recommend you trying to fuck up Didier's day.'

Eddie knew what this was all about. The same thing used to happen when he worked undercover. Some uniform with rank would always show up to lay down the terms of involvement, let you know just how powerless you were in the set up. It was why you had to get out in the end. The certainty that those pricks would hang you out to dry when the time came. The closer you got to a criminal organization, the less they trusted you. Same thing with Meyer. He needed Eddie to do the job, but he didn't trust him out of his sight. And he surely wasn't going to need him around when it was over.

'So, I trust you have a sound methodology, Eddie. I'm relying on you to be able to find McGraw and his cache of goodies.'

'Trawling the French countryside – should be easy,' Eddie said, facetiously. 'But it sure beats the backstreets of Manila.'

'I can always get our Roger Knight to supply dossiers on the AFP officers the Attorney General's Department has put on the case.'

'You think I ought to just follow in their footsteps?'

'It might be the easiest way.'

'If I'm behind them, I'm already too late.'

'So, how?'

'I have his old address. That's enough for a start. He must have left a trail. Most people do.'

'Once a policemen, huh? I can see you like to surprise your employers, Eddie.'

'Yeah. I also like them to fuck off and leave me to it.'

They wrapped up their lunch meeting soon after, and Eddie took a solitary walk around the Forum at Les Halles. He was hoping to find somewhere to buy a pair of soft soled shoes, but gave up in the maze of escalators and passageways that led nowhere. He was too distracted to shop. His mind was on the dangerous deal he'd made with a man he didn't trust.

Eddie had been through it all before, back in '95. He had been working undercover with the AFP - seconded for six months from the N.S.W. Police Force - on a joint operation targeting a gang of cocaine importers. They had inserted him as a front man for a Melbourne syndicate of buyers, and given him thirty thousand in play money.

His first contact had been a meeting with a half-wit poser called Ray Hickey in a bar in Coogee. Hickey boasted of having a foolproof system for getting any amount through Australian customs, but declined to explain exactly how. His partner, Terry Gaines, was already over in Colombia. Gaines had the connections. The money would be wired to his account and he would buy the cocaine at the best price, directly from a cartel in Bogota. As instructed, Eddie dropped some big names and handed over fifteen thousand for a first taste. If that went smoothly, he told Hickey, bigger orders would follow.

Three weeks later, Hickey requested an urgent meeting in a bar at Randwick Racecourse. He had the gall to report that the news from Bogota was not good. Gaines had struck some complications. Eddie warned Hickey that his Italian mates in Melbourne wouldn't appreciate being fucked around. Was this a money back situation or what? Hickey pleaded for more time. Eddie was called in for a session with his AFP minder, a senior man called Rick Scholes, who suggested Eddie show some appropriate concern for their money. Scholes wanted him to fly to Bogota and kick Terry Gaines's arse.

Three days later, Eddie flew economy class to Bogota, via L.A. and Miami. After a little legwork, he found Terry Gaines holed up in a resort hotel with a melon-faced eighteen-year old Colombian prostitute. Gaines was talking shit and drinking heavily, and claimed his people were telling him to lay low and be patient. Some line about being too risky at that moment for a foreigner with a suitcase full of money. In Eddie's judgment, the man had simply lost his nerve. Why the AFP bothered going after such amateurs, he had no idea. But they were impatient for this to work, and Eddie had been instructed to insist on a meeting with the suppliers. It turned out this was easily arranged, and took place the following day in a dusty car park at the edge of the city. Three men - one, the boss, wearing a crushed yellow sports coat and green slacks; the other two in bright orange acrylic running gear - stepped out of a small grey delivery van. Eddie knew it was all heading south the moment Gaines lifted the suitcase from the boot of his car. The man in the sports coat was an informer, the other two were drug squad detectives. It was a US funded DEA set up.

Eddie and Gaines spent a week in a high security Bogota jail while the AFP took their time looking into matters. Finally, Rick Scholes flew in, checked into the best down town hotel, and later secured a private interview with Eddie. He wanted Eddie to stick with the scenario in order to protect the operation, give the AFP back in Australia time to arrest the other principals. If this meant a few weeks in a Colombian prison, so be it. Since there now wasn't going to be any cocaine arriving in Australia, Eddie couldn't see how his being in jail in Bogota was going to facilitate operations back in Sydney. But Scholes gave him no real choice in the matter.

In the end, there were no arrests back in Australia and the operation was quietly dropped. When questions were raised in

Parliament, Scholes had been all too ready to sell Eddie out, attributing the fiasco to his incompetence, and even trying to hold him accountable for the money Gaines had pocketed. Eddie wrote his resignation from the AFP on the plane out of Bogota to Miami. If he hadn't had good mates at N.S.W. he'd have been rooted.

Eddie knew that Leon Meyer was out of the same mould as Rick Scholes. He would have to watch his arse every step of the way and plan his exit from the scene with extreme care.

12

August 11: Paris, rue de L'Amiral de Coligny

The rendezvous was for 6:00 p.m. at Le Fumoir, a café and wine bar on a side street at the eastern end of the Louvre.

Marlo had telephoned him that morning at the Musée Picasso. She didn't offer a word of explanation for her failure to show up at Nice airport. Nor did she give any hint of what she wanted from another meeting. Her voice was lighter than he remembered, and her manner veiled, terse even. She gave him no opportunity for questions, ringing off the moment the arrangement had been made.

While he wasn't sure of what he now thought of her, at least his curiosity remained intact, and so desperate was he to understand what had gone wrong, he would have agreed to see her again on any terms.

No doubt her hasty disappearance was connected with the shakedown at Nice airport. Somehow she had been alerted to the plans of these French lunatics, and had acted quickly to gather the painting and vanish. That much was obvious. Still, he believed she owed him an explanation, since she obviously knew that they had been on her trail. The disturbing thing was, she had given him no warning. Had she been pleased to let him take the fall? Had that been the plan all along?

And now she had sought him out again. Why him and not Luc? What was that about? Perhaps her need to confess was as strong as his need to understand. Did that mean she had successfully eluded her pursuers? Or was this a move out of desperation? Most probably she was taking a huge risk in resurfacing.

As much as Mitchell wanted to see her again - he had to admit he was still fascinated by the memory of her erotic manipulations of that afternoon in Saint-Paul-de-Vence - he also seriously doubted the wisdom of further involvement.

Le Fumoir was crowded at that hour. The sidewalk tables were all occupied and an animated party of attractively louche thirty-year olds had taken over the bar.

Mitchell walked through to the reading room at the rear of the café, taking in faces as he passed, but Marlo wasn't among them. Even if she were to arrive at that moment, they wouldn't have been able to find a spare table.

As he made his way back to the entrance, he noticed that a young woman appeared to be following his progress. She was sitting alone at a side table in the sallow light cast by one of the tall yellow window shades.

'Maybe you're looking for me?' she brazenly enquired as they passed her table. 'Are you Mitchell?'

'Yes – but I don't think…' he stammered, completely puzzled as to who this brash person might be.

'Well, hi,' she beamed. 'My name's Marlo.'

She certainly wasn't the woman he had met in France, but her insistent welcome demanded an equally effusive response. 'I'm

Mitchell Jameson,' he said, equally brightly, 'but I know you're not Marlo McGraw.'

'Oh, but I am.'

Mitchell stared at her with a silly, fixed smile. He was waiting for the joke to be explained.

'Sit down,' she said. 'Join me. It's a complicated story, but I'll bet you knew that already.'

Mitchell did as he was instructed and took the seat opposite her, doing his best to overlook her slightly calculating smile. At last he was able to see her clearly. She didn't look very much like the Marlo McGraw he had met in France. Maybe across a crowded room, or in a poor photograph, one might have confused them. There was a passing resemblance. They both styled their shoulder length chestnut hair in a similar way. Both women wore clothes that were suggestive of a comparable level of poise, taste and money, and both were women that one could describe, without risk of flattery, as highly attractive. But there the similarity ended. The woman he had met in Saint-Paul-de-Vence had a beauty of a more conventional, media-influenced kind. She had the classical profile, the sensual mouth, and the icy hauteur of a photographic model, as well as the studied languor of a woman used to making an impact with the minimum of effort. It was altogether, unmistakably, an effect that she strived for. The new Marlo McGraw - if that was who she was - wasn't trying nearly so hard. Her attractiveness - although he didn't quite know how he knew this, since barely a word had been exchanged - seemed to be more an authentic expression of personality. Perhaps she was a year or two older, but that was difficult to judge. It was only her voice that threw him: it had the same low, husky timbre as the other woman's.

'Are you the one who telephoned me last night?'

'Sure - I'm the one you arranged to meet.'

'But you're not the woman I saw in Vence.'

'I'm surely not.'

'So who was she?'

'I'm hoping you'll tell me.'

'Maybe there's a slight resemblance.'

This made her smile, but it wasn't the dimpled transformation of the other Marlo. Nor was it a spontaneous smile. Her lips tightened and her head tilted back a little, like a subtle warning. No irony. Nothing going on in the eyes. No pleasure transacted at all.

'But you know the woman I'm talking about?'

'I know a little about her.'

'Was she impersonating you? Or are you impersonating her?'

'Oh, no,' she said, this time with a nicely timed flicker of a smile, 'I'm the real thing. She's just a poor copy.'

'What do you know about my business with her?'

'I know you're a research student, working at the Musée Picasso. And I know that an associate of yours, a gallery owner called Luc Pellegrin, sent you down to Saint-Paul-de-Vence to offer her an opinion about a painting.' She spoke with such assurance and cool authority, it took Mitchell a moment or two to summon the impertinence needed to ask her how she knew all this.

'Hey - I *am* Marlo McGraw, remember.'

'Convince me,' he said, immediately wishing he had added a 'would you mind?'

Without hesitation, she produced from her handbag an American passport bearing a recent photograph and a French driver's licence displaying her address in Cap-Martin, Provence. She also showed him a well-travelled snapshot of herself, arm in arm with Mike McGraw.

'Taken at our villa in Cap-Martin, last Spring. Happier times.'

'Now I'm wondering how much of your story she got right.'

'So am I. You'd better tell me what she told you.'

It took Mitchell ten minutes to recount in detail his recollections of the meeting with the other Marlo McGraw. He left out any reference to the sexual frisson that she had stirred – knowing that no woman ever wanted to hear that kind of detail - as well as the ugly incident at Nice airport, curious to see whether she would refer to it herself. The woman - he continued to have difficulty calling her Marlo McGraw - appeared to follow his account with an almost exaggerated attention, betraying irritation when a waiter arrived to take their order.

'That woman's got my Picasso.'

'How did she manage that."

'Stolen from our villa at Cap-Martin. You're Australian - surely you know about my husband's financial difficulties at the moment. Well, he's obviously been somewhat distracted of late. The villa had been left unoccupied for too long.'

'Left unoccupied with a twenty-million dollar Picasso on the wall?'

'Obviously we had security, but…' She wafted her hand in a gesture of futility. 'Even if I do ever see it again - I don't know how I'd ever be able to prove it's mine.'

'If the woman I met was fronting for thieves, trying to line up a sale, then the painting might turn up sooner than you think.'

For the first time he heard her laugh, a thrilling low chuckle of disdain. He was stuck by how similar it was to the other Marlo McGraw's laughter.

'She managed to impersonate your laugh perfectly. How could she have known?'

Marlo ignored the question. 'Might turn up sooner than I think? Really? How can you be so reassuring?'

'Just like you, she was very plausible.' Said in his own defence, it sounded pathetic. 'I believed her when she said she needed to sell the painting.'

'Sorry - I'm not blaming you for anything.'

'But I'm also deeply curious about why anyone would go to such elaborate lengths to stage such a hoax. After all, the woman – and whoever else conspired in the theft - has already got the Picasso. Claiming to be Mike McGraw's wife wasn't going to get her very far with anyone looking to buy it. Why would she risk that?'

'She obviously thought she had no choice. She knew that the documentation inevitably linked the painting to Mike McGraw.'

'But the document she showed me didn't. She had nothing that proved McGraw was the owner.'

Marlo pondered Mitchell's meaning for a while. 'Well, who can figure how a criminal thinks?'

'She went to a lot of trouble to achieve very little.'

'Maybe she thought you'd bring a lot more to the party.'

'I could have helped, but she didn't want to risk following through.'

'Something spooked her?'

'Maybe she thought she'd be exposed in Paris,' Mitchell said, attempting to give the impression he was considering the idea for the first time.

Marlo gazed into his eyes. Mitchell was sure she could see the evidence of the fascination that the first woman had held for him.

'Who do you think she was?' he asked.

Marlo shrugged and tried to look perplexed. He was certain she knew something about the other woman's identity, but had decided to withhold the truth.

'She really excited you, huh?'

Mitchell tried to shrug it off with an unconvincing laugh.

'And now you're sitting here with the woman herself and the meter's hardly registering.'

She had caught him out and it made him laugh. She was far more relaxing company than the woman in France.

'A glass of good wine on the terrace of the Colombe d'Or...'

'With a gorgeous woman...'

'And who can be responsible for what they feel?'

'So, you fell for her, made a fool of yourself' she joked.

'Maybe. But she truly did look a little like you.'

'Just lacked a certain *je ne sais quoi,* right?'

'Right.'

'No - I think she was probably just some talented, out of work, L.A. actress, chosen for her looks and her ability to stick to a script. She's not in this on her own, you realize. She's just a minor player.'

'She would have needed a bit more ambition than that.'

'Not to mention nerve.' He could have also added that she had been counting on his not having ever seen a photograph of the 'real' Marlo McGraw; but then it occurred to him, unsettlingly, that his companion might have also been counting on the same thing.

'But you don't know her name?' he asked. 'No clue as to who she was?'

'No. But forget her, she doesn't really figure.'

So vehement was she on the subject, Mitchell was sure there was far more to it.

'Do you think she was a party to the raid on your villa in Cap-Martin?'

'Probably not. I'm certain that she was just hired for the job that she did on you. As for Cap-Martin, I don't know what version she told you, but - '

'Just that lawyers from the Australian Securities and Investment Commission and the Attorney General's Department were in France petitioning to extradite Mike McGraw and claim his assets. They were poised to make a move, but that was all she knew, as far as I can recall.'

'They weren't the only ones after Michael's assets. Did she tell you about the others?'

'No.'

'Michael had creditors everywhere. 'Enemies on four continents,' he used to say. And most of them weren't working for governments. These were hungry people, ruthless operators, trying to take whatever they could.'

Michael? She called him Michael he noticed, while everyone

else - including the woman in France – seemed to call him Mike.

'Maybe you should tell me about it.'

'Why?'

'Presumably there's some service you're going to ask me to perform.'

'Oh, you're itching to perform, are you, Mister Wilder?'

'Shall I request the bill?'

'Shall-I-request-the-fucking-bill?' You're as funny as the English. No. Stay seated. We'll order more coffee, and I'll tell you the lot.'

With barely a pause, she served up an intriguing version of McGraw's financial débacle and the events following his flight from Australia. She was far more convincing than the 'Marlo McGraw' he had met in France, and afterwards seemed untroubled by the range of his questions. The other woman had a tendency to resort to, what he could now see had been, an exaggerated emotional distress whenever she was faced with any questions outside the scope of her prepared script. In hindsight, it had been like witnessing a polished, but nevertheless brittle, acting performance. The facts of the story were all in place, but the confidence to embellish had been missing.

Among the many things she told him, all recounted in persuasive personal detail, was that she and Mike McGraw were soon to be divorced. But it was her elaborate telling of the events surrounding the theft of the painting that finally convinced Mitchell of her case.

'Michael flew to Paris,' she said, 'when he heard they were about to make a move on his assets over here. I'm sure it didn't exactly surprise him. He'd already been cleaned out in Australia.'

'So you were in regular contact with him?'

'Now and then,' she said, with a sigh of exasperations recalled. 'But it all got messy at the end.'

'Did he travel down to Cap-Martin himself?'

'He didn't tell me any of his plans. But knowing Michael,

his first priority would have been to get into a huddle with his attorney down there, and together they would have found a way to hide all the peas under a whole new lot of walnut shells. Michael loved that part of the game.

'Who was this attorney?'

'You really are interested in this story, Mister Jameson.'

'Do you know?'

'Of course I do - but why do you want to know?'

'Naturally, I'm interested - but, obviously, it's entirely your business. So tell me nothing, or tell me everything. It's all the same to me.'

'But it isn't really all the same, is it?' she said with irritation.

'Say no more.' Mitchell raised both hands in mock surrender.

'Oh, there's more,' she said, obviously enjoying the combat. 'He's called Maître Pierre Lavalle. He has his office in Menton. He's one of those Frenchmen who imagines he's immensely charming, but who's actually a transparently sleazy little operator. Not a guy you'd want to know.'

'And what about your Picasso? Weren't you concerned enough to want to retrieve it personally?'

'Yes, but I knew that wasn't an option.'

'So you trusted McGraw to recover it, and at some point in the future, to hand it over?'

'I didn't trust anything. I guess I kissed it goodbye.'

'What was in the house that he might have wanted to salvage?'

'As you can imagine, there were quite a few other paintings - nothing as valuable as my Picasso, but still, Michael had some wonderful things. He had a striking Matisse, a small Bonnard, an absolutely beautiful Dufy, and several other lesser Picassos. And as well, he owned lots of drawings and lithographs by these same artists that he loved. And of course, the house was full of magnificent French antiques. When he bought the villa, he spent a staggering amount of money furnishing it. All in all, I'd say there could have easily been ten, even twenty million dollars' worth in the house.'

'And where do you think it all ended up?'

She answered with a derisive head shake. 'Of course, there must have been a robbery – but beyond that, I don't even have the vaguest idea. Does Michael know everything? I don't know. By that stage he wasn't confiding anything in me.'

'And you didn't ever question him about the fate of your Picasso?'

'Of course I would have - if I'd ever managed to speak to him again. But the oleaginous Maître Lavalle is the only one I've been able to contact.'

She said nothing more for a while, leaving Mitchell to pick at his slice of fruitcake and finish his coffee. And then something - he had no idea what - persuaded her to tell him some additional things about the raid on their villa in Cap-Martin.

'Michael told me that another bunch of so-called creditors had found out about the Attorney General's Department's plans. He was afraid that these people would move quickly to get in before the legitimate creditors. And then later, Lavalle told me that his office in Menton had been broken into, and that all Michael's files and financial documents had been stolen. He wouldn't have lost any of his cache of money - but I'm sure there were share certificates, US Government Bonds, and, I suppose - '

'The papers of authentication belonging to your Picasso?'

'Yes, I'm positive that's where they were kept.'

'But you haven't spoken to Mike...Michael, so you don't know this for certain?'

She shook her head.

'Lavalle told me everything was gone.'

'Did he know much about the raid on the villa at Cap-Martin?'

'He didn't know anything for certain. By then he was a wanted man too, and keeping well out of sight.'

'I suppose you'd only be interested in stealing the papers of authentication if you also had plans to steal the painting itself. You'd need them if you were trying to offer it for auction or whatever. But you could also use them to give legitimacy to an existing fake version of the painting. Or even, later on, once the fuss had died down, you could commission a fake version. But even as I describe them, I don't quite buy those last theories.'

'Not when there's such an obvious explanation.'

'Yes – a woman trying to sell a Picasso, in need of some authenticating documents.'

'Trying to sell *my* Picasso.'

'So how can I help you?'

'Do you know how to find this woman again?'

'No idea, I'm afraid. As I'm imagining you already know, she was supposed to come with me up to Paris. But she missed the flight, fled the place she was staying in, and hasn't made contact since. Unless she calls me again, I have no way of finding her.'

'Then that's how you can help. You'll be well rewarded.' She took a blank card from her purse and wrote a telephone number on it. 'Please leave me a message if you hear anything from her. I know it's highly unlikely that you will, and I'm guessing you'll probably want no further involvement in the matter. I'd understand that completely. But I guarantee, she'll never know that it was you who informed on her.'

There was a moment when Mitchell might have declined the suspect proposition, but instead he took the card from her.

'Thanks for the coffee,' he said, rising from his chair. 'And also for the shattering revelations. I can now walk home along the Seine in the knowledge that nothing makes sense and that my judgement is well and truly faulty.'

She took it rightly as phony self-effacement and nailed it with one of her tight smiles.

'Just live with it. At least you haven't lost twenty million. Good meeting you at last, Mitchell. And if we don't meet again – good luck.'

As he walked from the café, out into the miraculous evening

light, he had the pleasant feeling that he wouldn't be seeing this Marlo again, either.

13

August 11: Paris, the Marais & Blvd. Saint-Denis

Eddie gave some serious thought to the journey he was about to make down to Cap-Martin. Tomorrow, he'd take the TGV south to Marseille, then connect with the first train heading east. In Menton he'd hire a nondescript car and take it from there. He'd book nothing. Leave no traces.

Before leaving, he wanted to outfit himself appropriately. He was still walking the streets of Paris dressed like a middle-aged sex tourist in Phukett. The obtuse woman on the hotel desk (by now Eddie had charmed her completely) had advised him to try BHV, a nearby department store on the Rue de Rivoli.

Menswear was on the ground floor. At first glance it looked like the arse end of Myers in Bondi Junction. Acres of cheap middle-of-the-road synthetic stuff. Plenty of famous brands, but bugger all real choice of styles. He had also had the bad luck to fluke it on an end of season sale day. He was going to have to elbow his way past swarms of hefty *madames*, picking through all that crap. At least he would find shirts that would fit - never mind the fact that they were mostly in colours only the French would wear - something he had never managed to achieve in Bangkok, where Eddie was several sizes larger than their XXL.

It took him half an hour to find everything he needed: a pair of summer weight khaki slacks; a simple navy windbreaker, cut loosely enough around the shoulders to accommodate a holstered weapon; a couple of plain cotton shirts; and a brown cap of the kind worn by middle aged English tourists. Last thing he wanted was to look like a man who had just stepped off a plane from Bangkok.

In the book section on the floor above he found an English language Michelin Green Guide to Provence and a large-scale map of the Alpes-Maritimes *département*. It was the kind of one stop shopping Eddie favoured. Trawling the streets drove him to distraction. Upstairs in the camping department he purchased a small daypack and a serious looking German made retractable hiker's stick. Eddie was hoping to appear - at least at first glance - like a man who had left his hire car in the parking area and set off to explore the woods. He wasn't planning for anyone to be given a second glance.

He had lunch in a dingy back street pizza parlour, where he found himself sharing the experience with a sad bunch of disenchanted tourists. Not having put much effort into studying the phrasebook, Eddie wasn't prepared to take his chances with a French menu. It wasn't worth the risk of ending up with a pile of inedible raw meat of the kind he'd seen on Roger Knight's plate.

But when the medium ham and mushroom arrived, he was disturbed to see a barely-cooked egg floating mid-pond. He wasn't sure how that misunderstanding had arisen. He was only able to avoid a total gastronomic *débacle* by sawing at it around the crusty perimeter and washing down the doughy mess with a *pichet* of watery red.

Later, sitting in a *tabac* nursing a cold coffee, he tried to compose a postcard to Dee in Melbourne. He'd chosen something artistic by a photographer called Henri Cartier-Bresson: a black and white shot of two small dogs humping in the street, being watched by another pair of curious mutts. Dee would spend ages wondering just what sort of insult he was intending. He'd have to stick it in an envelope to avoid stirring her elderly mother.

It often took him many attempts to get his message straight. No room on a card for more than fifty words, but he always had a hard time getting it right. He was roughing it out with a biro on the table napkin he'd saved from the pizza joint. So far he hadn't got past: *'Dear Dee, No doubt you'll be wondering how I've ended up in Paris.'*

Of course, he knew she wouldn't give a rat's how he'd ended up in Paris. She'd just be shaking the envelope hoping another cheque would flutter out. He felt foolish making the effort.

The alienation he felt on these streets was already getting to him. It was the fact that he couldn't speak the language as much as anything. He could memorize words on the page, but had no talent for pronunciation. Same thing with Spanish: all that time in Manila and he could barely say 'good morning' and good night'. He stuffed the unfinished postcard into his jacket pocket and walked out.

It didn't help to concentrate on the details of his mission. The ugly brutality of the enterprise was part of the problem – maybe even the whole problem. He couldn't rid himself of the thought that it was all going to come down to force. This wasn't going to be like lifting a BMW from some gutless Filipino playboy who'd got behind on his payments. McGraw was like a wounded lion, and he knew this jungle better than Eddie. He was no doubt well protected. A man like that would know you were coming and be ready Eddie could see he was on a path to destruction, but somehow his will was paralysed, and he couldn't get off it. Or maybe the sense of futility that was gnawing at him was really nothing but cold fear. The weightless drop before the elevator hits.

It was a familiar feeling, this tightness below the gut, and he knew where the solution lay. He needed to take up Gornik's suggestion of a special experience on the Boulevard Saint-Denis.

The recommendation of a night at this dive on the Boulevard Saint-Denis had come up back in Bangkok, at Eddie's second meeting with Gornik and Toop. This was over a late brunch on the Oriental terrace. The McGraw deal had been struck and all three were in the kind of relaxed and vaguely decadent mood that Bangkok induces.

'Are you partial to African girls, Eddie?' Gornik asked, spooning a sliver of papaya into his mouth. 'We know you like Chinese.'

'Depends on their personality,' Eddie said. 'They've got too much of that, it can ruin everything.'

At least he could make them laugh. Toop chuckled to himself, while Gornik sprayed the tablecloth with papaya juice and had to clutch at a bunch of serviettes.

'I'm talking about Paris, Eddie,' Gornik said, emerging from behind a scrunched serviette with an unpleasant leer. 'You'll take one look around those streets and your nuts'll tense up faster than a swift finger up the arse.'

'Please, please,' Toop protested. 'I'm having breakfast.'

'You've got the time, you'll want to get laid.'

'Maybe,' said Eddie, watching a stream of sugar trickle into his coffee.

'You're going to Paris to look at the paintings, are you? Huh?'

Eddie knew Gornik was just the taking the piss, and he wasn't interest in playing.

'I've just got one word for you, Eddie: Mar-tin-ique. Ohhh, fuck me,

Mar-tin-ique.' Gornik and Toop both laughed, Gornik looking to Toop to silently corroborate some extraordinary shared experience. 'Here, I'll give you this address, man of adventure - and the rest is up to you.' Gornik took out a gold pen and one of his business cards, flipped it over, and wrote down the name of the establishment on Boulevard Saint-Denis.

'Believe me, you'll thank us - if you ever make it back,' Gornik said, as he passed it to Eddie. It was the kind of two-edged remark he'd learned to expect from the clown.

That evening, Eddie rode the *métro* to Strasbourg-St-Denis, then strolled back along the length of the Boulevard before making his move. It certainly didn't look like Patpong Road in Bangkok. It didn't look at all like a place for classy erotic adventure. As far as he could see the whores working the street were mostly hard faced, hungry looking Eastern Europeans. A quick blowjob in the back of some parked van - that was about all you'd get for your fifty euros. The men on the street looked equally desperate. Shifty looking North Africans in tight jeans and shiny leather jackets. Pasty faced German tourists getting worked up on just the atmosphere. A six-foot tall potato faced blonde caught Eddie's eye and dogged him for a few metres along the footpath, offering her full range of services first in garbled French, then in fractured Russian English. Eddie didn't go for it at all - not with that huge purple mouth full of bad teeth.

Eddie like his vice to be more explicit. He liked the come on. The smell of perfume on warm skin, the tight, revealing clothes, the smiles and the cajoling voices. He liked the moral barricades all demolished before he arrived. Here, you could be anywhere. He was starting to think that Gornik had played him for a fool.

This address they had given him, a modern building on a corner block, it could belong to a dentist or a tax accountant. Although it was only six o'clock, far too early to be looking for a woman, he pressed the buzzer anyway. It had been a fortnight since he had slept with anyone, and the tension was turning him sour. The grand dame who answered the door was dressed like a real estate saleswoman, but with a little too much make up and gold jewellery hanging off everything. Eddie had come prepared for a conversation in stilted French, but she immediately recognized where he was from and spoke to him in English. In an accent borrowed from Marlene Dietrich, and with a hand planted on one hip, she invited him to come in. He followed her trail of perfume and her broad arse up a narrow flight of stairs. From a CD player, somewhere above, David Bowie was purring about *'Young Americans'*. At the landing she ushered him into a tiny, red-walled bar, lit like the ninth circle of hell. The fittings were all surfaced with reflective black glass, except for the spindly bar stools, which were padded in matte black vinyl. Eddie almost tripped up in trying to perch on one. He saw his face reflected in the black mirror behind the bar, and recognized for the first time in a long while the killer he knew he was supposed to be.

The woman called out to someone through a curtain of glittering jade beads, and then turned to Eddie.

'You're very early. Some of our girls haven't come in yet.'

'My Australian friends, Mister Toop and Mister Gornik, told me that you were open twenty-four hours.'

She looked at him with incomprehension. Clearly the names of Toop and Gornik weren't going to open any doors.

'Yes,' she said, wearily, 'Twenty four hours a night, not day.'

Eddie glanced down at his watch, letting her know that he was on the point of walking out, but he couldn't read the dial in the gloom. The woman appeared to relent a little.

'Si on buvait quelque chose?' she asked, momentarily forgetting whom she was talking to.

Eddie gave her the cold stare he thought she deserved.

She quickly corrected herself with a 'What'll it be? 'spoken in a clumsy accent meant to sound somewhere South of the Mason-Dixon line.

Eddie realized that he was still being courted and eased up on the hostility. 'Gin and tonic with one ice cube, and a slice of lime, if you've got it.' He liked the taste of gin and tonic on a woman's breath. Maybe they liked it on his.

A young gypsy-faced girl in her early twenties, with an abundant mane of sable black hair, appeared through the wall of beads. She was dressed like a roller-blader, in a skimpy white halter-top, skin tight pink shorts, and pointy black boots that must have elevated her a good nine inches, and a gold neck choker. Maybe it was a popular fantasy in this part of town. She smiled coquettishly and greeted Eddie with a breathy *'Bon soir, monsieur.'* The grand dame shot her a fierce, instructive look, and then left the bar.

Without further palaver, the gypsy girl set about making his gin and tonic, a drawn out process in which she never once made eye contact. The gin was spilled, some ice cubes clattered to the floor, and she experienced enormous difficulty in gnawing open a metallic pack of salted cashews. Eddie squirmed on his squeaky vinyl barstool. Toop and Gornik were going to need to do some explaining. From upstairs, beneath the soulful uplift of Stevie Wonder's *'Higher Ground'* Eddie could hear alternating bouts of uncontrollable laughter and muffled abuse. The overfilled gin and tonic was finally maneuvered by a shaky hand onto his allotted bar coaster. He tried smiling at the girl, but she had turned away to deal with the mess on the bar.

At that point, Eddie felt the pressure of a gentle hand on his shoulder. It was the grand dame, who had returned carrying a bulky ring binder covered in crimson plastic. She slithered onto the bar stool alongside Eddie, and invited him to peruse the book with her. It contained about fifty laminated file cards, each one devoted to a different girl and featuring, as well as a deceptively air brushed close up, at least one provocative half-nude pose. Beneath the photographs were some poorly typed essential recommendations and statistics, none of which Eddie was able to interpret. It was like selecting a gelato in a cheap Italian restaurant. You had to hope that the dish tasted as good as the picture. Some looked to Eddie like schoolgirls made up to appear adult, others looked like they'd been on the game too long. Most, unfortunately, were for more specialized tastes. Very big girls, obscenely skinny girls, girls with huge breasts, vacant eyes and pouting liver lips. They did nothing for him. They only made him reflect appreciatively on the discreet Thai waifs he had known. And where were these fabled women from Martinique, he wondered? He kept turning the greasy pages. More voluptuous Mediterraneans striking poses that wouldn't turn on a light bulb, unreadable Algerians, skinny looking English waifs, and Vietnamese tramps. Nothing he hadn't seen before.

'Vous avez des femmes de Martinique?' he asked. Somehow the phrase he had been practising down on the Boulevard Saint-Denis seemed to have come out properly. It worked.

The grand dame gave him a pinched look of surprise and then quietly closed the crimson binder. *'Oui. Bien sûr,'* she said.

Maybe some unpleasant memory of Messieurs Toop and Gornik was at last returning. Whatever was going on, she wasn't about to explain. She slid off the bar stool with a great huff of effort, and left him alone with his tepid gin and tonic and the sullen gypsy roller-blader. When she returned, after an agonizing three-minute's absence, it was to offer another ring binder for his perusal. This one was bound in glossy black leather. Right away Eddie knew that his journey had not been futile.

14

August 12: Paris, 11th Arrondissement

Since moving to Paris, Mitchell had lived in a tiny third-floor studio apartment, a short walk from Métro Voltaire in the eleventh. It comprised only two rooms: a fifteen-square metre bedroom with a closet-sized built-in bathroom, and a twenty-five square metre kitchen-living room. It was clean, stark, and anonymous – depressing if his purpose in the city hadn't been so compelling. He had been too busy to bother acquiring anything more than the bare minimum of furniture and appliances. Besides, all of it would have to be disposed of when he returned to Australia in several months' time.

His narrow work desk, his laptop, his Ikea bookcase (filled mostly with borrowed volumes on twentieth-century French art) and his miniature CD player: these were his most important possessions. There were no indoor plants, and no blinds or curtains to filter the light from the two tall windows. He owned a simple wardrobe of work clothes, bothered with few cooking implements, and kept a minimally stocked larder. He was a man in transit.

He liked living in the eleventh, and had grown accustomed to eating out alone several nights a week in many of the cheap restaurants (Vietnamese, Moroccan and traditional French) nearby on rue de Charonne. To his constant disappointment, he had no close friends in Paris. His colleagues at the Musée Picasso were his only contacts, but at least he was on friendly, small talk terms with some of the other tenants in his building. However, none so far had invited him into their apartments.

His chief fascination was with the anonymous young couple who lived in the third-floor apartment right across the street. He knew their habits intimately: when they dined - alone or with friends; when they slept and when they rose; when they argued and when they made love. He recognized their voices and their music, could even smell their cooking on hot summer nights. These things were played out in silhouette, etched against subdued warm light, transmitted through their narrow blinds. He didn't ever need to spy on them from a darkened room; he was constantly aware of them without effort or attention. And it wasn't that he ever actually saw more than fragments of either of them. They could have passed, unrecognized, in the street. It was as though their mysterious story ran parallel to his. It didn't make him lonely or sad, quite the contrary: it placed him securely in their world.

The only true loneliness he felt arose from the relationship he had left unresolved back in Australia. At his lowest, his thoughts returned to the confusing final phase of his time with a woman called Sophie. The memory of their recent months together, then apart, was almost unbearable. They had been lovers for almost a year - that is, if casual fucking and occasional furtive dinners constituted being lovers in any but the most tawdry sense. She was unhappily married to Adam, a young university tutor in English literature. Adam, in the inevitable way of these chains of betrayal, was in turn involved in a protracted affair with one of his students, an unstable, doe-eyed, nineteen-year-old manipulator (these were Sophie's words) called Bree. A clichéd enough occurrence in academic circles, but uniquely appalling when one had to live with the consequences.

Nothing about the arrangement between Adam and his two women was simple. Adam had never expressed any intention of leaving Sophie. And quite possibly, Bree herself had no desire for anything more than a casual affair. Bree and Adam spent the occasional weekend together; and there were many fraught weeknights when he would fail to come home.

Mitchell would learn of Sophie's anguish by telephone, but would be discouraged from coming around in case Adam should unexpectedly return. He was her "friend" only, to be kept at an appropriate distance, never a substitute husband. And through it all, Adam professed an unwavering need for Sophie. The marriage, as far as Mitchell could see, appeared to be held together by habit, convenience, a hefty mortgage, and a self confessed passivity on Sophie's side. She had developed an accommodation to the dismal prospect of settling for less, of concealing pain, of playing mummy to an emotional adolescent.

None of it had made much sense to Mitchell. But if he had wanted an involvement with Sophie he had to ignore the absurdities of the arrangement, Sophie knew that she ought to leave Adam, but could never seem to summon the resolve. Ultimately, her acquiescing to Adam's perverse needs had inflicted damage on the affair with Mitchell. Refusal of risk, of commitment, bred resentment. And once Adam knew about her affair, the pressure was on Sophie to declare an ending. Adam's ego could never tolerate a rival, and Sophie had no defence against his rage. Events were soon driven towards a conclusion.

Mitchell had understood the situation perfectly. By that stage, his planned study in Paris had emerged as a solution. Sophie came to visit one last time, not to take a lover's farewell, but merely to return some borrowed things: a set of Beethoven's Late Quartets, played by the Lindsays; a copy of a Cézanne biography; and a paperback of a new translation of *Anna Karenin*. Perhaps he might want to take them with him to Paris, she had suggested.

She had handed him the books and CDs in the doorway to his apartment. Anticipating only a farewell kiss. The invitation to stay for a drink had been Mitchell's idea. The embrace in the dark hallway had happened spontaneously, as perhaps they had both hoped it would. Both had been yearning for more than a blunt farewell.

The lovemaking had been unbearably sad. Sophie had wept in his arms. No question of release. Afterwards, they had lain naked, side-by-side on the cold sheet, both too overcome for conversation. Both too numb to concede the finality of the encounter. Their sleep, when it came, was a kind of inertia, a refusal to face what lay ahead. Broken finally by the ringing telephone: Adam, anxious about her failure to return.

When she woke he brewed coffee for her. She liked it strong, with just a little milk and sugar. He helped her to dress, overcome by the unfamiliarity of the black bra he had never seen her wear before. They talked in stilted tones about his proposed time in Paris. The comic "what if" of a possible last minute change of plans. But neither had such resolve. Perhaps she might meet him over there if things with Adam deteriorated. Leave it at that. They kissed goodbye. Far easier than words. Calmer than resolution.

Although he knew he ought to forget about the *Portrait of Dora Maar* – it wasn't any longer his business, and he was certain he'd never see it again – he couldn't manage to put the two Marlos out of mind. Who were these women? Why had one of them – perhaps both of them – gone to such lengths to deceive him? And why was he having such difficulty dismissing either as an absolute fraud? And what did he understand of the long, gothic shadow cast by Michael McGraw? Without having any compelling interest in his financial transgressions, Mitchell wanted to understand the personality of the man behind these tales of greed and chicanery.

He Googled the name MICHAEL McGRAW and was offered 179,352 references. Most were hysterical tabloid responses to the fraudulence that lay behind the collapse of McGraw's hedge fund. Slightly older ones hinted at rocky times ahead. Others, written in more benign and optimistic times, celebrated the range of his acquisitions, and marvelled at the consistently high returns McGraw Securities was able to guarantee its ever-expanding client base. But Mitchell was looking for far more intimate insights. He continued to refine the search, until he found what he was after: a lengthy article in the *Weekend Australian* from several weeks earlier.

The article was a chapter from a forthcoming book by an investigative journalist called Ilena Vadas. It wasn't just her impressive research and persuasive command of the McGraw investigation that fascinated Mitchell, it was the unapologetic way in which her writing drew upon some apparent, but unexplained, direct contact with the man.

Vadas not only quoted McGraw liberally, she dissected his fastidious dining preferences, his taste for exclusive Italian tailoring, and his amusing intellectual pretensions, with the lightly wielded irony of a trusted, but critical friend. However, the impression her piece made on him went beyond the racy surface detail. Her ear for McGraw's mordant witticisms, all flatteringly rendered, led Mitchell to think that she admired, even actually liked, the man.

As was often his way while on the internet, Mitchell soon found himself sidetracked. His interest in Mike McGraw was soon subtly overtaken by a fascination with Ilena Vadas. He remembered the woman very well from her time as a current affairs journalist for SBS. But because he had rarely watched television in recent years, his impression of her was somewhat sketchy. He had, somehow, retained the idea that her celebrity owed more to her extraordinary looks than to her intellect.

It took no time at all on the net to modify his prejudices.

In one article it was reported that her unnerving, feline presence had been used to boost the network's hitherto marginal evening current affairs programme. Viewers who had never normally tuned to SBS were catching Ilena at 7:30 p.m., if only to gaze at her mysterious raven-haired, Eastern European perfection. The author, however, rated her rather more highly. He claimed Ilena's interviews were always edgy encounters, threatening to break into open warfare at any moment, and revealed a predator's delight in running humbug to ground. What had amazed him was the way she gave out no sense of having rehearsed or having been fed her sharply intelligent questions and lethal rejoinders. Nor did she attempt to conceal her cynical view of the contemporary political game, or her disdain for even the subtlest displays of greed or vanity. She was always volatile, engaged, and immensely entertaining - but also in danger of alienating pompous egos. Unfortunately, even with her European credibility, she proved too self-possessed and glamorous for that minority network. The rules of television stardom demanded that she move on. But it seemed she hadn't progressed to bigger things.

Mitchell recalled that, just around the time that he was preparing to leave Australia, she had in fact left SBS. He wasn't sure of the circumstances. Quite possibly she had been shafted.

Soon he was back on Google, seeking references to ILENA VADAS.

He began by trying to track down the reasons for her departure from SBS. None of the articles he consulted was able to be specific about what had gone wrong. *"Rumours of creative differences." "Rumblings at SBS." "News revamp – time for change."* All the familiar evasions. Ilena Vadas had simply disappeared off air. *"Taking a long break from television,"* was how most of the television industry journalists had played her sacking. Or was it her resignation?

When she did finally re-emerge after many months, it was as a newspaper journalist, reporting on economic affairs in an occasional column for the *Australian*. The move - on the face of it, a terrible fall in status - didn't surprise a lot of people. She had always been an enigma. Nobody was too sure where she stood, but her opinions on most issues hinted at left wing sympathies. Perhaps credibility had been what she had craved more than anything. Possibly the switch to print was an acknowledgement of her only real future in the media.

What added to the mystery surrounding her departure from television was the repeated rumour of her easy access to a surprising number of media proprietors. There seemed to be a widespread belief that she could have had any on-air job she wanted on commercial TV.

The more Mitchell learned about Ilena Vadas's life, post-SBS, the more fascinated he became. In the early days after her departure, it was as though she was progressively screening herself from all scrutiny. There was no shortage of news items about her possible plans, but they were all mere speculation, raising questions without answers.

And then he began finding articles containing rumours that she had been given a lucrative contract with Seven. According to the most convincing of the pieces, she had been offered a twelve-month development deal for her own late-night current affairs show. The budget was reputedly huge, and the network was maintaining a respectful distance, allowing the show to evolve on her timetable. In the meantime, they were planning her exposure very carefully. Limiting her on-air appearances to twice a week, three-minute, financial report after the late news. The idea that she might have sold out appealed enormously to her detractors.

But the most extraordinary piece of all was a brief article in the *Sydney Morning Herald*, dated two days earlier, that claimed she was currently continuing to work on her book about Mike

McGraw, while at the same time, developing the format for her forthcoming current-affairs show. Her plan was to include early segments about the collapse of McGraw Securities and the search for the missing millions. The filming, it was reported, would take her to South-East Asia, New York, London and various destinations in France. She was presumed to be already in Paris, filming a segment about the Australian Government's attempts to extradite McGraw.

Far from being able to put the McGraw story safely out of mind, Mitchell was left needing to know more. He hoped that Ilena Vadas would want to talk to him.

15

August 12 - 13: Paris to Menton & Cap-Martin

Eddie had booked himself a one-way ticket on the early morning TGV to Nice. The second-class compartment was almost full by the time he boarded. He found himself seated next to a nervous elderly man who was in the process of obsessively checking his travel documents.

The train pulled out of the Gare de Lyon at twenty past eight. Eddie felt unaccountably anxious. He tried to distract himself with study of his phrase book, but nothing stuck. He leaned against the window and stared out at the endless railway yards. He was adrift again in the world, with no picture of what lay ahead.

The bare plains to the south of Paris gave way to wheat fields and the skylines of distant towns. Pine forests that splintered the hot white sunlight. Within half an hour he was dozing.

He dreamt, or maybe he remembered, his hour with the

girl from Martinique. Peeling her lime green g-string down her long chocolate thighs. The kinky bush of pubic hair, shaved like a Mohawk. The pink insides of her huge, laughing mouth. Clapping her hands in encouragement for his incomplete erection. Chanting some kind of French equivalent of *'Make him big!'* as far as Eddie could figure. Slapping him on the ribs while she spread her legs and furiously cycle-kicked, like an athlete warming up. All that wet pink flesh. He was out of his depth and drowning. Inside and coming in four or five quick thrusts. It was his money - so what the hell. More slapping. More urging. Eddie, losing control. The lime green g-string stuffed in her mouth. Nothing could shut her up.

He woke somewhere south of Lyon to a headlong rush of green. Low altitude chopper flight. The carriage swaying into the bends. The dramatic perspective shifts of river gorges. Tunnel bursts of sudden blackness. Villages, the colour of honey, perched on hillsides. Vines on dry sunny slopes. Far below, a sunny bend in the tea-coloured river. Stones visible in the shallows. Children swimming. Tents and caravans beneath the trees. Barbecue smoke. The past. Extinguished by another tunnel.

They passed Avignon and Arles, and before midday arrived at the vast hall of the Gare St.-Charles in Marseille.

West of Cannes, he saw the Mediterranean. Pure blue, dissolved in mist at the horizon. An old movie, hypnotically flickering between the tunnel pillars. Stale fantasies from his youth, of yachts and villas and beautiful women. James Bond, risking it all in a casino on the Riviera. Grace Kelly and Cary Grant, speeding in an open car on the *corniche*. Yellowing Cézanne prints on his high school wall.

The train pulled into Nice at 2:25 p.m.. He felt as though he had hardly travelled. In the air-conditioned chill of the railway restaurant he ate an indigestive *croque-monsieur*, washed down with a strong black coffee. Then, at 3:30 p.m. he took one of the quaint local trains, for the thirty-minute trip to Menton.

At an Avis depot opposite the station he hired a small grey

Renault, using a false passport and credit card he had brought with him from Manila. They were in the name of Wayne Geoffrey Marshall, a deceased friend from high school days.

Before driving anywhere, he sat for a few minutes in the shade of a dusty palm tree, studying the tourist map he had bought at the station.

He chose a hotel neat the sea: the Royal Wentworth on the Promenade du Soleil. It was a nondescript modern heap, with minimal atmosphere, but large rooms. The blandly courteous staff promised anonymity. In the evening he took a stroll over to the nearby old town. He liked the ochre walls of the old buildings, the narrow alleyways and steep staircases. It was the Riviera of his imagination. David Niven on a terrace in the moonlight. Later he stumbled into a cheerful Moroccan restaurant, where he was the only unaccompanied diner.

At midnight he stood on his hotel balcony, smoking a cheap cigar. A faint breeze was coming off the silver ocean. Tomorrow, he would have to get started.

At dawn, next morning, dressed like a summer tourist in baggy khaki shorts and turquoise polo top, Eddie drove west to Cap-Martin. As Leon Meyer had warned, cars were not permitted at the exclusive end of the peninsula. He left the Renault in a car park and set off on foot, carrying the equipment he would need in a beach bag.

The enormous luxury villas could only be approached by footpath. Most were hidden behind screens of flowering hedge and palms. Little was visible other than an occasional glimpse of pillared balcony or ornate tower.

McGraw's villa, called Le Rêve, was on the rugged, southern-most tip of Cap-Martin, with views across the Ligurian Sea to the mountainous Italian coast. It was protected on three sides by a pink, scallop-patterned masonry wall at least five metres high that descended to the shoreline and extended a long way into the sea. Security cameras were mounted on both front corners of the wall and above the driveway. A notice fixed alongside the massive barred gates warned that trespassers would be prosecuted. To see the place properly, it was necessary to view it obliquely from a knoll further up the pathway.

It was an impressive, but typical, multi-storied, pink-stuccoed Italianate wedding cake, surrounded by tall palms, cacti and cascading vines. Nothing about it suggested it was owned by an Australian billionaire.

Eddie beat his way through thick shrubbery, down to the lower end of the wall on the southern side. He was well out of sight of the footpath and other villas, but visible to anyone out at sea. On that morning, there were two yachts and several small powerboats cruising offshore. He would have to take his chances.

From his first study of the photographs Leon Meyer had given him, Eddie knew that he was going to require some special equipment. At a mountaineering shop in the Tenth, he had bought fifteen metres of 10mm climbing rope, a lightweight grappling hook, and spiked rock-climbing shoes. At BHV he had already purchased all the tools needed for efficient housebreaking.

He made a loop from the rope and experimented with the arc required to pitch the grappling hook. It took him several attempts before he was able to snag it on the high lip of the wall. He took another look at the distant activity out on the water before slinging the beach bag over his shoulder and digging his spiked toe into the masonry. The climb itself was easy. With a little straining of muscles he hadn't used in a while, he was soon straddling the wall.

He surveyed the grounds of the villa. There were no vehicles in the driveway. The dark green shutters were all closed. The paths were dusty and strewn with palm droppings. The lawns had not been mown in a long time. In the flower gardens, one species had grown unruly with cabbage-sized seed heads.

He looked over his shoulder. Out at sea, the crew of the nearest yacht was manning winches, changing tack, oblivious to his house-breaking. He dropped out of sight, landing in a garden bed of weeds.

Using a diamond-blade angle grinder with an auxiliary power pack, he cut a hand hole in one of the wooden shutters, then reached in and unhitched the steel crochet that locked the boards in place. In a similar way, he cut through a double-glazed windowpane and unlocked the frames.

He stepped through into the gloomy opulence of a large ground-floor reception room. It was now empty of all but the largest pieces of furniture: a long table and two enormous carved bookcases. The décor was just as Leon Meyer had described. The floor was an Arab-patterned marble mosaic, and the walls were lined with a continuous classical frieze of Roman figures and their hounds, hunting deer and wild boar in a stylised wood. The coffered ceiling was adorned with what looked like gold leaf. Whose taste was this, Eddie wondered? It would have cost McGraw a fortune.

Away from the open window, visibility dropped off badly. The only illumination came from the light leaking from the edges of the shutters. He took a torch from his bag and made a hasty search of the ground floor. It was the same in every room: only a few marooned pieces of furniture remained. There were hardly any chairs, no vases or rugs, no soft furnishings, and no paintings or sculptures.

In the kitchen he found evidence of what had taken place; an unused, flat packing carton and folds of protective foam. But there was no branding on the carton.

He spent another twenty minutes searching the rooms upstairs. Same story – only double beds and wardrobes remained. Judging from the amount of missing furniture, the removal operation had been formidable.

Retracing his steps in the gloom, he returned to the ground floor and located a doorway leading down to a chain of basement rooms. In a converted, barrel-vaulted *cave* at the far end of the building, he found what he had been searching for: the security system. It consisted of a bank of twelve monitors, digital recording devices, and a computer that controlled the entire network.

Eddie had seen a lot of security systems in the course of his "re-possession" activities, but it would take some time to fathom the workings of this one.

From an operating manual that he discovered in one of the desk drawers, he learned that McGraw's system was movement activated and could run uninterrupted for weeks. It recorded the findings from all cameras directly onto a single hard disc, with burnt-in time and date coding.

The system, however, was presently shut down, and the house power was also switched off. It took another ten minutes of searching for him to locate the power board for the basement. Fortunately, EDF had not disconnected the electricity at the mains.

To his relief, the computer booted up successfully and didn't demand an entry code, but it took Eddie another half an hour to learn how to access the hard disc recordings.

The last recordings were made on Monday, July 6th, the day on which the removals had taken place. The cameras placed above the front door and entrance gates recorded a steady stream of shrouded furniture items being handled by at least six different removalists.

Eddie though, if he had taken the time, he could have even calculated the number of paintings in McGraw's collection – though none of them was unwrapped.

The removalists themselves were of no consequence to him, he was more interested in seeing the signage on their van. But when their van was captured on camera, reversing out of the entrance gates, no markings of any kind were visible. All Eddie could see clearly was a licence plate. But that, he hoped, would be all he needed.

16

August 13: Paris, the Faubourg St.-Honoré

Mitchell arranged to meet Ilena Vadas at Willi's Wine Bar on the rue de Petits-Champs. It was her choice, having discovered in the brief time she had been in Paris, that it was popular with journalists and a lively media crowd.

During their initial phone conversation, he had explained his interest in Mike McGraw. He had given her a sketchy account of his business with the *Portrait of Dora Maar* down in Provence, and she had expressed an immediate desire to hear more.

And so, at 6:00 p.m. on a wet Paris evening, they were sitting side-by-side in a quiet corner of the bar. His glass was Bordeaux; hers was Bourgogne.

'I appreciate your taking the time to meet me,' Mitchell said. 'My first blind date in Paris.'

'I remember you well from your SBS days.'

'You're not here to offer me *another* television job, I hope?'

'I always used to enjoy your spot,' he said. It was an awkward start.

'Spot? Like something you'd get on the front of your trousers?'

She was in the kind of dangerous and playfully cynical mood that he had been told were the hallmark of her best television appearances. Maybe those moods, too, had been achieved with the help of a glass of red in the make up chair.

'Well - I thought you were great.'

'Minority opinion, I'm sorry. I had a very low female approval rating. They believed what I said, but they didn't like the way I said it.'

'I can't imagine that.'

'Too bolshie. The Ice Queen. Didn't smile enough.'

'Never bothered me. I liked my financial reports straight up. Anyway, I read that you've been offered another television job.'

'Yes. I've improved my smile – see.' She narrowed her eyes and gave him a facetious, slinky look. 'Now that I'm going to be working for a commercial network, I have to practise constantly.'

'I read a little about the show on the net. I gather that's why you're over here.'

'Yes. They've sent me here to do some interviews.'

'On the McGraw business?'

'Can't really say much about any of it.'

'Sure.'

'But I can say, they'd *absolutely love* me to get an interview with Sarkozy - can you believe the clowns I'm working for?'

'I'm sure he'd fit you in.'

'Not to talk about French politics, of course. Just to chat about his love affairs.'

'Life with Cecilia and Carla?'

'And the slappers, and the 4:00 a.m. disco parties.'

'Cool.'

'Fat chance. What an irony: they send me to Paris, but stick me with that. But, hey - my wine's very good. How's yours? Shall we order something light to go with it?'

She took a pause in the helter-skelter conversation to peruse the menu. It was the first chance he'd had to really take her in.

He was surprised to see that, at close quarters, her physical presence was not so formidable. She wasn't quite as tall as one might have assumed from her appearance on the television screen. She wore her clothing with casual aplomb: a svelte charcoal suit with a perilously short skirt, the coat unbuttoned over an oyster linen blouse. He couldn't so much as glance at the floor without his eyes straying to the exposed upper curves of her legs. In the play of warm amber light from the bar, she still struck him as a remarkably beautiful woman, but her face seemed slightly smaller, her features less assertive. And without her television make-up, the familiar graphic perfection was somehow blurred. Only the trademark cool gaze identified her unmistakably. The look that ambushed you at odd turns in the conversation, and met you with, what? Incredulity? A kind of eroticized disdain? He was all too aware of staring like a fan. He desperately wanted to resume their conversation.

'Sorry – what am I doing?' she said, discarding the menu. 'I probably haven't got time to eat right now. Do you mind?'

'Not at all?'

'Where were we?'

'Straying into confidential territory, I suspect. Maybe I should have opened by telling you I was very impressed by your article in the *Australian* on Mike McGraw.'

'Ah - my other life,' she sighed.

'I thought I already had a pretty good idea of what Mike McGraw was about - until I read your piece.'

The clumsiness of the compliment discomforted her, but she was in a mood to make allowances.

'Empty flattery. But do you trust what you read?'

'In your case, yes. I'm really intrigued by how you got so close to the guy.'

'Which is why you wanted to see me, right? Because of your encounter with his crazy wife?'

'Yes. More or less.'

'I'm sorry I rattled on about my ridiculous television career. I think it's being in this bar. I feel invisible here. I don't exist. I can say anything.'

There seemed to be something deeply sad about her, something she was making no effort to conceal. Possibly it was just the draining effects of international travel and jetlag. Or maybe it was simply stress; the humiliating pressures of an unstable career. Sacked one week; back on air the next. Knowing nothing else about her, he had to put it down to that – the ironies of an occupation that promised so much and yet (assuming she wasn't a complete narcissist) remained so insubstantial. Not wishing to reinforce her dark mood, he returned the conversation to what she knew of McGraw.

'I was asking you how you knew him so well?'

'Yes, you were,' she said, with the added suggestion that Mitchell was in danger of trespassing.

'Well – I'm sure you know I've spent a lot of time researching everything about that man.'

'I've read about your book.'

'Yes – my book.' She made the very idea of it sound burdensome.

'Is it going well?' he asked, tentatively.

'Of course it isn't going well. Books never go well.'

'Where are you with it? Do you mind my asking?'

'Oh, no – it's the perfect question,' she said, with amusement. 'I like the way you're homing in, appealing to the self-absorbed journalist in me.'

'Hey – backing off.'

'No - I'm the smart-arse who's being rude. I've written probably three quarters of a book - not *the* book - but *a* book. About one-hundred-and-twenty-thousand words – not all *good* words, but words, if that means anything.'

'So what's the problem? Are you having difficulty finishing it?'

'Not exactly - it's more that I've lost faith in my *capacity* to see it through. Obviously, it conflicts with my crazy television career.'

'Why does it have to?' he asked, genuinely unaware of the answer.

'Are you kidding? That work is relentless. It invades your every hour. Never let's you go. I doubt if I'll be able to summon the concentration, let alone find the spare time, to ever get back to the book.'

'But maybe by being in Paris, you'll find fresh inspiration.'

'*J'espère,*' as they say here.

'You may even get to meet McGraw.'

'In handcuffs – refusing to speak? That sort of meeting?'

'But you did know him once, didn't you?'

'Were we close? Is that what you're asking?'

'I think so. But if you don't like -'

'Oh, I don't mind. Yes – I believed I had gotten to know him very well. But now I think it was an illusion.'

'That you ever got near the man?'

'He's not so straightforward. I think you've guessed that already.'

'But you had some kind of relationship with him?'

'I met him more than a few times. Obviously this was in his pre-fugitive days. I was a finance reporter and he liked to talk about the business of making money.'

'So he was just a source?'

'Yes, that's it. A source. He had a lot of good stories about the way things were done in this town. But what's your great interest in the man?'

And so Mitchell told her in detail about his experience in Provence. Told her about the approach from Marlo McGraw, the trip to Saint-Paul-de-Vence, his introduction to the *Portrait of Dora Maar,* the woman's subsequent disappearance, and his abduction at Nice airport. He spent the best part of an hour recounting his story, and she seemed to stay with it all the way, in spite of the swelling noise from the crowded bar.

'She's a mysterious figure, this new wife,' Ilena said. 'As difficult as it is to believe, nobody seems to have ever been able to take a photograph of the woman. You won't find her picture anywhere - I've scoured the American gossip magazines and the tabloids. The marriage was kept a complete secret. And then McGraw disappeared.'

About McGraw's time on the run, not surprisingly, there was little, at least in the general sense, that Ilena didn't already know. She had a good source in the Australian Attorney General's Department. Although she had never been to Cap-Martin, she had a fairly clear picture of McGraw's movements, motivations and likely financial dealings since he had fled from Australia. About the marriage split, however, she knew next to nothing. Rumours, mostly. She had also heard little more than a whisper about the valuable collection of paintings and sculptures. And she certainly knew nothing about the *Portrait of Dora Maar*.

Ilena also didn't know about the 'other' Marlo McGraw. When Mitchell reached the point in his story at which it might have been natural to tell her about the recent meeting at Le Fumoir, he had hesitated. Would she find the notion of a double preposterous? How could he possibly tell it with any credibility when he barely understood the import of it himself? But on the other hand, would the omission of any mention of that meeting be a serious breech of faith? After some silent debate, he decided it wasn't the occasion.

They talked for a while longer, speculating about McGraw's likely moves in France, then at 9:30 p.m. she glanced at her watch and told him that she would have to be leaving.

'I have some calls I absolutely need to make back to Australia,' she said.

'Early risers?'

'Network stuff.

She scavenged in her purse to find some euro notes. Mitchell beat her to the bill.

'Get out of it,' she said. 'I'm on a network junket.'

Mitchell acquiesced.

'Do you think we could meet again?' she asked, when she had finished sifting through the unfamiliar banknotes. 'There seemed to be a lot we didn't get around to talking about. You came wanting to talk about McGraw, and I feel I've diverted things somewhat.'

'Pleasant diversion, though,' he said. 'But, sure - I'd like that. I'm working at the Musée Picasso till seven, every day this week. But evening's are usually okay.'

She consulted a scrappy Filofax. 'The rest of this week's difficult. So, could we meet next Monday evening?'

'Fine.'

Mitchell knew that she was far more interested in hearing his McGraw stories than she was in him, but in a foolish, adolescent way, he felt flattered by her proposal. She probably saw the arrangement as an interview, while he was already fantasizing about a date.

She stood to leave and offered Mitchell her hand.

'I'm sorry you have to have to rush away.'

At that she simply smiled. It was probably nothing personal, just the unique Ilena Vadas sign-off smile - and Mitchell, the only Australian male who wouldn't have recognized it for certain.

'Well, I have the compensation of an unfinished Margaux,' he said, raising the half-empty glass.

And then she walked away, squeezed herself between the broad shoulders of two huge men in suits, and disappeared into the night.

17

August 14 – 16: Menton to Montauban

Back at the Hôtel Royal Westminster, Eddie telephoned Leon Meyer in Paris. With a studied indifference, he reported on the state of McGraw's villa - including the evidence of the recent removal of its contents. None of the news seemed to surprise Meyer.

'So, we have no way of knowing where he's taken all these things?'

'I might be able to track down the removalist, if you can help me with a licence plate search.'

'How did you get that?'

'Don't worry about how I found it,' Eddie said, not wanting to give Meyer any more than the bare minimum. 'Can you get onto someone in the French police who can find the name of the owner?'

'Who exactly do you think I am?'

'You told me you were co-operating with the investigation. You just tell them this might help get to McGraw's assets a little faster.'

'Are you crazy? Why would I want to give them a head start on that?'

'Haven't they got their hands tied until they complete the legal process?'

'That may be so, but -'

'Then they're not going to bother investigating some van owner they've never heard of – just so long as you don't over-explain the connection.'

'All right,' Meyer said, reluctantly. 'Fuck you. I'll see what I can do.'

'Tell them it's urgent. I'm sitting down here in a high-end hotel I can't afford.'

'Sure, sure. I'll call you back this evening.'

Eddie passed the time by taking a walk over to the old port, where he had a leisurely seafood lunch and drank a couple of Italian beers at a restaurant on the esplanade. Afterwards, he went for a swim at the Plage de Sablettes. He hated shingle beaches, and the water was colder than Bondi in June, but he needed the exercise. In the late afternoon he slept soundly in his hotel room.

At 6:00 p.m. he was woken by Leon Meyer's call.

'Okay – the name is Paul Rigal. He has a removal business based in a town called Montauban. It's under the name of Paul Rigal et Frères.' Meyer gave him the address. It was a three-digit number on the N20, in the direction of a town called Cahors.

'Where is this place?'

'Which one? Montauban? How the fuck would I know? You've got a map, haven't you?'

'Okay – here's what I need from you.' Eddie proceeded to explain that he wanted Meyer to fax him a French translation of a number of questions that he wanted to ask the removalist. He had been giving them careful thought. They would have to be short and uncomplicated, since pronunciation was going to be a problem. He patiently dictated to Meyer from the notes that he had already made. 'I want a translation sitting in the hotel fax machine before dawn, understand?'

Meyer agreed without protest

Later, when he studied the map, he saw that Montauban was in the south-west, near Toulouse, at least five or six hours' drive from Menton.

Early next morning he checked out of the hotel. Leon Meyer's fax was handed to him at the desk. It was all there, just as he had instructed. He liked the fact that Meyer had even gone to the trouble of supplying a crude phonetic guide to pronunciation.

On the way out of town, he stopped off at the Avis depot and extended his car rental for another week.

For four hours, he hammered the little Renault west along the *autoroutes* of Provence. Weary with the monotony, he stopped at a *routier* for a hearty lunch of *cassoulet* and *pommes rôti.* Between mouthfuls, he studied the list of questions. He saw he was going to sound like an arse trying to get his tongue around the French. Maybe he would just hand the man the list and a biro. As he mopped up the last of the beans and sausage, he wondered whether a second mini-bottle of Bordeaux would spike his driving. No, he thought - he couldn't afford an unplanned nap in the car park.

He found the driving easier on a full stomach. The nondescript landscape no longer distracted him. He sang to himself – Rolling Stones and Al Green songs from the seventies, mostly - and he looked for road signs.

The A61, from Narbonne to Toulouse, became the A62, which in turn connected to the A20 to Montauban. And a few kilometres north of the town, he saw a turnoff to the N20 to Cahors. Ten minutes later, he was parked outside the ugly terra-cotta brick warehouse of Paul Rigal et Frères.

The pretty young girl in the front office took a long,

uncomprehending look at the fake Australian Federal Police badge Eddie had gently placed in her hand

'Bonjour,' he said. *'Je suis un gendarme d'Australie.'*

The unfamiliar badge was clearly troubling her. Like his other forms of ID, it was in the name of Wayne Marshall. She responded with a barrage of rapid, indecipherable French. The only words he recognized were *'monsieur'* and *'Marshall'*. That was the problem with speaking rote phrases, Eddie reflected – you got back nothing you could understand.

'Je voudrais parle avec Monsieur Paul Rigal,' he said, trying another of the sentences he had practised in the car park.

'D'accord,' she said, standing up from her desk with a smile, clearly pleased to be able to hand the matter over to her boss.

When she returned, it was with a lean, well-muscled, balding man in his mid-fifties. He greeted Eddie with a wary smile and tentative handshake. Paul Regal was no more impressed with Eddie's AFP badge than was his secretary, but he made no attempt to challenge its authority.

Eddie tried another of his prepared requests: *'J'ai plusieurs des questions, s'il vous plaît.'*

Paul Rigal nodded. He had the co-operative reticence police encounters usually instill.

'Je cherche un homme d'Australie qui a disparu.'

'Qui?'

'Monsieur Michael McGraw.'

Eddie didn't know how to ask: *'do you know him?'* Instead, he handed the list of questions to Paul Rigal. *'Vous écrivez,'* he said, handing him a biro. His phrasebook French was working better than he could have hoped. He was also counting on the probability that Paul Rigal's company had been hired on a purely professional basis. Most likely, the man would have had no idea who Michael McGraw was, or know that he was the subject of extradition proceedings. Paul Rigal et Frères would have been chosen for no other reason than their proximity to the intended destination of the furniture. Eddie was depending on the man's total indifference.

Paul Rigal glanced down the list of questions and uttered a sigh of irritation at the imposition. Eddie met his eyes and, while pointing at the first question, persuaded him to co-operate with a look of stern encouragement.

The first question was: *Can you confirm that on the 6th of July, 2009, you supervised the removal of furniture and art works from a villa called Le Rêve on Avenue Winston Churchill at Cap-Martin in Provence?*

It was intentionally expressed in the language of a police interrogation. Eddie watched, delighted, as Paul Rigal wrote: *oui*.

The key question was a request for the destination address.

In order to answer accurately Paul Rigal needed to consult a file kept in one of the metal cabinets behind his secretary's desk. He carefully printed the details onto Eddie's list.

'Is this a town?' Eddie asked.

'Un village? Non. C'est une ferme.'

'A farm?'

'Oui. La Serre. C'est le nom de la ferme.'

Eddie was surprised at the man's comprehension of English. It annoyed him that he had been wasting time committing so many phrases to memory.

'So, who's the owner of this place?'

'Pardon?' the man said, making a facial expression of utter incomprehension.

Eddie flipped through the pages of his mini-dictionary.

'Propriétaire?' he said, struggling with the number of syllables.

'Ah, non. Je ne sais. Mais, je pense il est la même personne.' He pointed to Michael McGraw's name on Eddie's list.

One of the final questions had been: *Where was the furniture finally unpacked?* Paul Rigal had written a response, but Eddie couldn't understand it. Eddie pointed to the question and gave the man a questioning look.

'Nous avons mis toutes les boîtes dans la grange,' Rigal said, merely repeating what he had written. Seeing the look of confusion on Eddie's face, he took out a pen and began to draw a diagram: a child's sketch of a van, a pile of boxes, and a building that was unmistakably a barn.

'And can you show me where this place is?' Eddie said. He took the Michelin map that he had bought at the *routie*r from his pocket and spread it on the desk in front of Paul Rigal.

'*Voilà,'* Rigal said, pointing to a densely-contoured, green-shaded area, accessed by a minor road. He marked the location of La Serre with a cross.

La Serre was in the hills to the east of a village called Brunquel. The farm buildings were sited on a level clearing, halfway up a steep, south-facing hillside, dense with scrub oak. The farm comprised a two storey stone house, of no particular distinction, two derelict sheds, and large barn with substantial oak doors. Eddie was amused to see how accurately the barn had been represented in Paul Rigal's sketch.

It wasn't clear from the rugged terrain just what the owner had farmed. Nor did it look like any kind of property that McGraw might have owned. The place looked like a tired, abused victim of rural poverty.

Eddie took a good look at the mailbox. There had once been a name written on its face, but weather and rust had obliterated most of the lettering. He rattled the box until he was convinced it was empty.

The house shutters were all closed, and there were no vehicles on the property. The place might have been abandoned for a few days or many weeks. There was no way of telling accurately

Eddie scouted around each of the buildings, taking pictures from various perspectives with his tiny digital camera. Then he returned to the house. He tested the shutters, but all of them were snugly fitted and locked. He searched, but couldn't find a light gap anywhere, no means whatsoever of seeing what was inside. The property was too close to neighbouring farms to risk breaking in with power tools. The sound would carry for miles.

The barn doors, too, were securely bolted, but around the back he found a loose shutter, something he could easily work on with a gemmy. The wood splintered at his first hard wrench, and he heard the interior locking bar spring loose.

Inside, he found a small agricultural tractor and an array of well-used farm implements. Even though the barn had an enormous capacity, there was nothing, at first glance, to suggest that McGraw's furniture had ever been stored there. But after a thorough search he discovered the evidence he was seeking. In one of the cement block pigpens he found a stack of flattened packing cases and scraps of protective foam. The cases were identical to the ones he had seen at Le Rêve.

The property, Eddie realized, had been a halfway storage solution, somewhere for McGraw to cache his valuables while he found a more suitable hiding place. Or perhaps it had been a defensive move, a means of covering his tracks, blurring the connection to his previous address.

It was getting on for six in the evening. Tomorrow was Sunday – a lost day if he didn't act fast. He returned to his car and drove along the winding road that ran beside the Aveyron, heading towards the nearest big town, St.-Antonin-Noble-Val.

He parked in the market square and set off through the narrow mediaeval streets in search of a real estate agent. *Immobilier* - that was the sign he was looking for. The first one he found was open, and had a number of photographs of country properties on display in the front window. Fortunately, the agent who welcomed him was used to dealing with English-speaking clients.

'I've seen a property I'm interested in buying,' Eddie said. 'I have some pictures.' He took out his digital camera and scrolled through the images he had taken of the farmhouse.

The agent looked at him with incredulity. 'That is not a very attractive property,' he said. 'I have much better in my window. Here - '

'No, no – I like this place,' Eddie said. He took out his map and showed the agent its location. 'You know this area?'

'Of course. I also have a property near there I can show you. Perhaps more suitable for you, too.'

'But do you know the owner of this one? It looks abandoned.'

'No – and I don't think it's for sale,' he said.

He took a well-used ring binder from the shelf behind him. It contained street maps, domestic plans, and handwritten assessments of hundreds of private properties in the commune.

'Do you have this place listed?'

The agent continued turning pages until he found what he was looking for. 'Yes – it belongs to a man called Albert Laussier. I don't know him, but it says here he's a harvest worker. He's employed on other people's farms. You understand? Cutting the crops.'

'Sure,' Eddie said. 'May I?' He hastily copied down the name. There was no telephone number.

'But now I have better things for you to see.' The agent directed Eddie's attention to another, even thicker, ring binder that was lying on his desk. He thought it wise to indulge the man a little.

'How much do you want to pay? What is your limit?'

'If I love it – no limit,' Eddie beamed.

The agent wasn't sure whether he was dealing with a wealthy sucker or a time-wasting idiot.

Later, Eddie took a look around the town. There was nowhere obvious to stay. Besides, he didn't want to be too widely noticed in the area.

In the calm twilight, he headed back to the *département* capital, Montauban, where he found a hotel vacancy down near the railway station. After dinner, he consulted the Tarn-et-Garonne phone directory, where he found a telephone number for Albert Laussier.

He dialled the number and left a cryptic message, in which he requested a meeting to discuss the possibility of buying the man's property.

When Eddie returned to the farm the following morning, he found the owner waiting for him.

Albert Laussier was a stringy, stiff-jointed man in his late sixties. He was dressed like a farmer on an excursion to town: tight chequered sports jacket; baggy woollen trousers; shiny shoes; and a leather cap pulled down low on his brow.

'Bonjour, Monsieur Laussier,' Eddie said. *'Ça va?'* His practice was paying off. He was acquiring a cheeky confidence with the stock phrases of address.

Albert Laussier kept his long jaw clamped shut as he gave Eddie a sullen nod.

Eddie had decided to be as direct as possible. He presented his fake AFP badge and said, *'Je cherche la maison de Michael McGraw. Je suis un ami.'*

Non - Je ne le connais pas,' he said, with a shrug.

Eddie ignored the obvious lie and produced the sketch that Paul Rigal had made of the barn and the pile of boxes. *'Les boîtes de Michael McGraw,'* he said, pointing vigorously at the drawing.

'Non, non,' the old man said, vehemently.

'Okay,' said Eddie. *'Venez avec moi.'*

He beckoned Albert Laussier towards the barn.

'C'est fermé,' he said.

'I know it's *fermé*,' Eddie said. 'And I'd like you to open it up for me.'

The old man hesitated and dug in. He was hostile about being intimidated on his own property. Eddie placed a strong hand on his shoulder and spun him in the right direction. With a hiss of breath, the old man shook him off and strode away towards his house. Eddie waited for him, keeping an eye on the open door.

When Albert Laussier reappeared he was brandishing a shotgun in his shaking hands. In the instant that he saw the weapon, Eddie side stepped and struck the barrel with the back of his hand. The old man lost his grip and the weapon clattered against the paving tiles. In what seemed like a single practised move, Eddie drew the Beretta from his pocket, slipped the safety, and jammed its snub nose into Albert Laussier's neck. The old man gasped and shrank back against the doorframe. With his free hand, Eddie grabbed his collar and shoved him back into the dark interior of the house.

'Keys to the barn door? Where are they? Keys?'

Eddie took hold of his jaw and forced him to watch a key-miming gesture. The old man understood well enough. He groped in a dresser drawer and took out a huge iron key coated with rust.

'C'est pour la grange,' he whined, already in a state of shock.

Eddie trundled the old man outside, and with the Beretta jammed against the back of his neck, urged him towards the barn.

In spite of the tremor in his bony hands, the old man managed to unlock the doors. Eddie shoved him inside and steered him towards the pig pen, where he forced him to look at the pile of cartons.

'So where did the furniture go, huh? *Les meubles? Où?'*

The old man looked back up at him, uncomprehending. Eddie wondered whether it was his lousy pronunciation, or the wily old bastard's ability to hold out.

Eddie continued to repeat the words, and still the man ignored him. He was beginning to lose patience. He gave the old man several sharp kicks in the crook of each knee, causing him to crumple to the floor. Then he took a pair of NSW Police Department issue handcuffs from the back pocket of his chinos. Their stainless steel jaws were dulled from years of use. He had carried them on this trip for just this purpose. In a sequence he had performed many times before, he took Albert Laussier's arms, and in turn, cuffed them behind his back.

Laussier began to whimper. Eddie kicked him low on the spine and told him to shut up. He left the old man squirming on the dirt floor of the barn while he returned to the Renault. When he came back he was carrying the coil of 10mm climbing rope. He proceeded to truss the old man, and then fasten him to a steel cow-tethering ring attached to the manger.

Eddie returned to the house and spent fifteen minutes scouring it for any possible clues to McGraw's movements. He found no evidence of any connection. He returned to the barn, carrying a dog bowl full of water, a half-loaf of bread, and a bag of oat cereal, which he placed in reach of Albert Laussier's face.

The old man turned his head away sharply. There was a murderous ferocity in his grimace. Perhaps, Eddie thought, he was expecting torture, or at the very least, to be left to starve like a tethered animal. Eddie took hold of the old man's right arm and unlocked the handcuff. He floated the area map in front of him and ordered him to point to McGraw's house. The old man refused to even look. He tensed his body, expecting violence.

Instead of persevering, Eddie slipped the right handcuff back onto the old man's bird-like wrist and stood up. He used his foot to nudge the food and water well out of reach.

'Okay,' he said, bouncing his car keys in his hand. *'Au revoir, mon ami.'* He headed towards the barn door, whistling an old Stevie Wonder tune.

While he was in the process of bolting the barn doors, he heard the old man call out, *'Arrêt!'*

Eddie returned to the pig pen and stood over him.

'Montrez-moi la carte,' he said, in a choked whisper.

Eddie understood well enough. He repeated the process of releasing the right handcuff.

Albert Laussier studied the map. His eyes were clouded with tears. Finally, he raised his shaking hand and pointed to a cluster of farm buildings to the south of St.-Antonin-Noble-Val. It was a *château*. Eddie should have realized. Saved himself the agony.

'*Merci*,' he said. 'Sorry – but you're going to have to stay here a while.' He replaced the right handcuff and returned the food and water to within the old man's reach.

The old man cursed as Eddie walked off. But with no second thoughts, he locked up the barn and drove away. He was heading south-east, back to Montauban. He needed to have a long talk to Leon Meyer before he made the next move.

18

August 16: Paris, rue Roger Verlomme

Chez Janou, a bistro that Mitchell had suggested for their next meeting, was tucked away in a narrow side street, not far from the Place des Vosges. It was popular with locals, but largely unknown to tourists. The menu was traditional Provençal, served in an atmosphere of brisk efficiency. One came there to eat and drink, then move on.

He worried – briefly – that she might find the place ordinary, but then thought she might appreciate something simple and unpretentious after all the chic guidebook dining she told him she had been experiencing. Unfortunately, it was also out of her way: she was staying at the Hôtel-de-Fleurie in St.-Germain. But, when he suggested an alternative that might have been more convenient for her, she protested. Underlying his anxiety was the thought that she might cancel at the last minute, or worse, regret the arrangement and not show up at all. His concerns were unfounded.

She arrived at 7:00 p.m. precisely, wearing another of her elegant, expense account suits: this one was of a loose and extremely flattering cut, tailored from a lightweight silver-grey fabric. She caught Mitchell's eye at the crowded bar and smiled. He squeezed through the gap in the drinkers, and made his way towards her. She offered her cheek like an old friend.

They were shown to a tiny table, wedged between two parties of noisy diners: an intense, theatrical couple, both clad in black leather, who waved their arms wildly when they argued; and a surly pair of Russian girls with big hair, who seemed to say nothing that wasn't a gruff complaint about their bad day in Paris. Mitchell was concerned that Ilena would soon be irritated by the strain of having to raise her voice above the competing conversations. But shouting seemed to animate her, appeared to lift her spirits. He knew he had been worrying too much and began to relax.

She snatched up the menu, as though on a ten-minute lunch break.

'What do you suggest? What's good here?'

He craned around to see the blackboard.

'Well – the *lapin au moutarde* is on special. It comes with beans and roast potato.'

'Great,' she said. 'I'll have that.'

'Yes, sounds good. May I also suggest we get a bottle of Bandol and some Perrier, and I'll try to catch his eye.'

A waiter arrived and took their order. In the awkward silence after he left, they found themselves resorting to small talk. But he could see that she had something more than food on her mind.

'More interviews today?'

'No – just frustrating postponements. But it gave me the chance to get back on the McGraw case. I had an interesting meeting with my contact at the embassy. But better than that, the network has finally given approval for me to stay over here longer and make a documentary special on the McGraw débacle.'

Mitchell couldn't understand the cause for excitement. 'I thought that you were already doing that.'

'No, no – they were just planning for a few short items. Following the story as it developed. This is to tell the whole sorry saga: McGraw's rise to prominence; his spectacular collapse; and finally, his attempt to outrun his creditors. A three-part, ninety-minute special to be called: *The Hunt For The McGraw Millions,* or something equally pretentious.'

'Congratulations, then – it is what you wanted, isn't it?'

'Turning my book into schlock before it's even finished.'

'It'll boost your sales.'

'Kill my interest, you mean.'

'But a wonderful title, though' he said, facetiously.

'Oh, sure. Coming up, we have Ilena Vadas in a *Late Night The World* special, when she crosses three continents in pursuit of controversy and high drama in: *The Hunt For The McGraw Millions.'* This she delivered in the ultra bass, portentous voice of a network television announcer.

Mitchell quickly took up the challenge himself, offering equally moronic alternative titles in a similar voice:

'Mike McGraw: Fugitive... The McGraw Quest... Criminal in Paradise: The Mike McGraw Story.'

'You're very good,' she said. 'Your voice, I mean You actually have the perfect delivery for that crap.'

'Thank you. But getting back to the question of content. A ninety-minute long programme about a man who refuses to talk to anyone, might be lacking a certain - '

'Substance? Well, yes. I'm going to have to rummage through the archives in order to pad it out. There'll be a lot of colourful back-story and meaningless picturesque B-roll. But I'll also be documenting the current attempt to extradite him - as far as anyone will let me. And yes - there'll be a lot of filler. Plenty of speculation, hearsay, and pure fantasy. Mostly performed by me, looking serious and authoritative, standing outside the gates of various McGraw haunts.'

'You're going to film down in Provence, then? Wherever it is he has that place?'

'Probably have to. There I'll be, walking up a dusty road, towards McGraw's villa in the hills.' She slid back into the network announcer's voice. 'Menton. Playground of Renaissance royalty. Watering hole of the wealthy English. With a history written in pleasure, profit and intrigue. And in our time, home to Australia's most notorious fugitive from justice: Michael McGraw.'

'You're too cynical for television.'

'I know. It's a cuddly medium, and I don't belong.'

'I suspect you were born for it.'

It made her laugh. 'Watch it – I might have a proposal for you.'

Their waiter returned with a bottle of Bandol. Mitchell indicated for him to skip the tasting rigmarole and pour. They toasted one another like old friends. Then she took a long sip, and allowed the glass to rest against her lower lip while she remained in thought. He wanted to meet her gaze, but she continued to look away, out at the clamouring crowd. When her attention finally returned, he changed the subject.

'You said before, you saw someone involved with the extradition process. Was that a breakthrough?'

'Yeah. I've been handed to a guy called Roger Knight, in the Attorney General's Department. He seems prepared to talk. About what, I'm not yet sure.'

'But it's all happening right now. So there's obviously a limit to how much he can divulge, right?'

'Yes. I'm up against it, I know. Personally, I'd be a lot happier if I could treat the story as a manhunt, following in the footsteps of the investigation team. But, of course, it's all fairly undramatic stuff. Endless meetings with the French authorities. Boring documentation. International treaties. Legal interpretations. Naturally, the network doesn't think their audience could follow anything as intellectually taxing as that, especially if there's no pay off. It's hard to make television for people who think their viewers are nincompoops.'

That was her problem, he thought. Her disdain for television wasn't just the pose of a jaded practitioner. She really did despise the medium.

'The seven minute attention span, huh?'

'Where'd you get that idea? It's down to three, now. Three! And, hey, aren't you going to ask about my proposal?'

'Sure – tell me about it.'

'Where to begin? You see, now that it's feature length, I'm going to want a segment of the story that deals with McGraw's art collection. The man stole millions, claims to be bankrupt, but still owns a lot of highly valuable art and property over here.'

'Including several Picassos.'

'Exactly. So I want you to tell the story of your encounter with Marlo McGraw. Leaving nothing out. How the woman contacted you to set up an appraisal, told you her name was Alana someone-or-other, played you for all she was worth, then suddenly acted coy about who she really was. And how, just when you've taken the bait – thinking, *wow*, I'm working for McGraw's woman - and are prepared to do anything to help her with her priceless Picasso, she inexplicably disappears. And on top of that, you get kidnapped and assaulted at Nice airport by a gang of French mafiosa. Now you have no idea what's going on - but you're hooked. You've become obsessed with this woman and with this painting. You're going to have to pursue this mystery to the end. There. That's great television. That's a story worth telling.'

She had made his adventure sound preposterous, even without the absurd complication of the 'other' Marlo – the woman he had still never mentioned.

'I'm not sure. It sounds like all set up and no pay off.'

'That's how my show works,' she said with a sly smile, 'If they want closure they've always got the commercials.'

'So how would I be telling this? Am I just a voice-over commentary, or what?'

'Meaning?'

'Do you want me to tell this story in person? On camera?'

'Of course. At some point, I'd like to whisk you off to Provence. Sit you down in the Colombe d'Or - wasn't that where you first met her? - and have you tell your story. And there'll be no dreary old sticking to the facts. Viewers can't take too much reality. You're going to have to zoosh it up with layers of mystery and sexual intrigue.'

'What makes you think I'd be any good?'

At that she hesitated, aware for the first time that she might have presumed too much.

'You're good. I can tell. Besides, we'll script every word you utter. You and me. Or just you, if you prefer. This is commercial television - we don't like *actual* spontaneity, either. Only the illusion.'

'So I'm to be a performer.'

'No - just yourself. I realize that's an art - but I can tell you'll be great. You'll take to it.'

'Don't be so sure.'

'We'll practice along the way. I'll interview you, point a camera at you, until you couldn't care less. And we'll pay you, too. Only a few days' work, but it'll be worthwhile. I have small crew over here. Camera person, sound recordist, and a research assistant who also doubles as a driver. It'll be fun. Please say yes.'

'Give me a chance to think this through.'

At that moment their meals arrived. Already the aroma from the neighbouring tables' *soupe à l'ail* was giving them regrets that they had skipped the entrées - always a mistake in France - and gone straight for the main courses.

Mitchell didn't need to give Ilena's proposal too much hard thought. Contemplation of the excitement of travelling with her, of getting to know her better, far outweighed any sense he had of the possible futility of the endeavour. His commitments at the Musée would just have to be squeezed into the schedule somehow. How could they refuse him permission?

He said 'yes' to her without voicing any reservations. But privately he wasn't sure which made him the more apprehensive: the likelihood that he might disappoint her as a television performer, or the even more troubling possibility that he might disappoint her as a companion. And there were other factors. Maybe an appearance on her show would do something for his confidence as a purveyor of opinions on art; or then again, maybe it would simply expose him as a hopeless poseur and scuttle for all time his prospects in that direction.

But overriding everything was the obvious fact that he was now more than a little bit in love with her. Other considerations hardly mattered.

'It's a pity you don't know how to find Marlo McGraw,' she said after they had been eating in silence for a while.

He almost answered: 'which one?'

'Do you think there's a chance she might try to contact you?'

'Not me – but Luc Pellegrin's gallery, perhaps. Anyway, I'm sure she'd hardly want to go public with all this.'

'Maybe we could persuade her to recreate your first meeting,' she said. But he knew she was fantasizing.

After their meal, Mitchell walked with Ilena, back to her hotel in the sixth. They passed by the Places des Vosges, crossed the rue de Rivoli, and approached the Seine via several quiet back streets. While walking over the Ile Saint Louis they resumed their conversation about Mike McGraw.

'Is your book really in serious trouble?'

'Trouble? I don't know. Overload, maybe. My mental picture of the work I've taken on is of an open cut iron ore mine. I see myself driving one of those giant trucks that look like toys – hauling endless detail out of this massive pit. I seem to have spent all my spare time in the last few years investigating McGraw's public life in Australia - his corporate dealings, his labyrinthine financial scams, everything. Of course, I've had a lot of help - from ex-business partners of McGraw's, from friends in ASIC, from lawyers and finance journalists. But the amount of material I'm trying to process is overwhelming. I probably know as much about the man as anyone – for all the good it's doing me.'

'As much as anyone?'

'Well, anyone outside his immediate circle - whatever that's worth.'

'But why do you need to tell this story? There must be an army of journalists all over it by now.' He could see that the question offended her, as though it had pierced to the heart of her problem.

'I suppose I feel a responsibility to push through and do something worthwhile with it.'

'So what is there to write about that's unique? It seemed the obvious question, in spite of the fact that it suggested her enterprise was futile.

'I live in hope that I'll find the key to his criminality. Why does a man who has created so much, who has more than enough of everything - why does he need to risk it all by devising the ultimate greedy scam? Why does he flirt with self-destruction? What's behind it? If I could answer that, I think I'd have an extraordinary story.'

'And what if it isn't extraordinary? What if it's just banal and grubby, and as predictable as the life of any other greedy entrepreneur?'

'I don't think there's any risk of that.'

'He's *that* different, is he?'

'I think so.'

What is it then? What does he represent to you?'

'You're wanting the same answers as me. So, let me finish my story.'

'Next time I interrupt - slap me, please,' he said, offering the back of his hand.

'My pleasure. Well, I published part of an early chapter - it wasn't the one you must have seen in the *Australian* - this was an exposé of McGraw's unscrupulous methodology in the early days of his rise and rise. I drew on a lot of sources. Went out on many a slender limb. But not before testing every handhold. At the time I was very proud of it, and people seemed to like it - I mean the readers, not McGraw's old mates. They liked it, not because of the unflattering facts I'd uncovered, but because of the recklessly libellous territory I'd strayed into. But still, I have to admit, it was not particularly inspired; probably no more than a painstaking piece of journalism. I knew I'd have to rework it completely if there was going to be a book.'

'So how did you portray McGraw? Charming rogue, or ruthless bastard?'

'Dangerously clever, I think. The most entertaining parts were about his early days as a henchman to various corporate raiders. This was well before he established McGraw Securities, and long before the financial crash of '08. Back then he'd court gullible investors, portraying himself as a little guy taking on the nasty big players. He could always find suckers who'd fall for that one. Having flattered their egos, he'd borrow heavily from them, bind them into his schemes - then, once the takeover was accomplished, he'd turn on them, slough them off and undermine their equity. Do anything to come out of the arrangement holding everything. Monstrous stuff. Such terrible behaviour that unless you were an insider you'd hardly believe it possible. And all done with such secrecy that it was always easy to ensnare the next victim.'

'So how did you unearth all of this?'

'That wasn't the hard part. There were no end of bruised people willing to talk about Mike McGraw. The risky part was in the writing. It was impossible to explain that era without referring to individuals and the facts surrounding their deals. But too many of these players are still active, and still in a position to take action.'

'So how did you manage to get it into print?'

'With great difficulty. The newspaper's legal department were at me day and night. They put me through weeks of scrutiny; had me jumping through one legal hoop after another; most of them landing me with cuts, or compromises. I was made to haggle endlessly over phraseology, forced to hedge every bold statement, and back off on the explicitness of so many references. At times I considered tossing it all in. I no longer believed that anything worthwhile or even close to the truth would survive the process. That kind of second guessing can finish you off. It sure wasn't part of my style. If I can't express my opinions in my own way, I'd rather not go into print at all.'

'Was that really an option?'

'I think you know it wasn't. By that stage you don't even own the article any more - they've spent so much money paying lawyers to crawl all over it, they couldn't afford to let you pull out under any circumstances. They own the crappy thing, and they'll put it to print one way or another. And of course, once the thing's in print, that's when your troubles really begin.'

'I can imagine.'

'It was something I'd never expected. After those pieces appeared in the *Australian* my publishers were served notice that legal action might be taken on my book. No specific objections, just generalized threats.'

'This was from McGraw's lawyers, was it?'

'Yes, as far as I know.'

'But surely if your publishers agreed to a book on McGraw, they knew what they were in for.'

'Of course. Normally a threat like that wouldn't faze them. They'd regard a controversy like that as good publicity. But this must have been on another level entirely; something that posed a threat to their financial security - or their reputation. Whatever it was, they weren't prepared to take the risk.'

'What exactly did they tell you?'

'Nothing really. Nothing I believed. Nobody seemed prepared to discuss it openly. Sure, they were supportive, but only to the extent of saying that they'd take their own legal advice once the manuscript was ready for publication. But at the same time, they were urging me to avoid certain areas of investigation. Giving me all sorts of excuses, claiming that opinions on the legality of certain McGraw financial moves might be more appropriately left to the courts, that kind of thing.'

'They didn't want to shut you up exactly - they just want to back you off into some safer area?'

'Something like that. Now they're claiming what they want - and always have wanted from me - is an inside portrait of McGraw the risk taker, mover, the celebrity, the star fucker. They like the fable of the exemplary Australian with the corrupt heart - yadda, yadda, yadda.'

'I can see you already, signing a mountain of copies in book shops.'

'The last session I had with my editor was more than disconcerting. I was having to negotiate the hard content of the book down at every turn. And always the claim was, the book they expected from me needs to have a balance, tastefully poised somewhere between investigation and sophisticated gossip. Inspiring, huh?'

'What do you want to do with your book now? Do you know?'

'Not sure. Everything's changed now, anyway. If they extradite McGraw – which I have no doubt they will – then I'll have to wait until his trial has been concluded before I can publish. It could all take years.'

'Don't you believe strongly in your own path?'

'I did. And maybe I still do. I suppose the best compromise I can make is to steer it towards honest biography. But when I think of how I've written about him so far, I could weep. There's too much emphasis on the financial and corporate side of his story. The intimate observation of his life itself just isn't there yet. Of course, the explanation is simple - I just don't know enough about the man. Can't get close enough to ever portray his life the way a good biographer might.'

'And so you're still caught between gossip and investigation?'

'Yes. Writing bland reportage. Not through lack of trying for something better. Just a special category of failure: an inability to get close enough to the person I'm writing about. For all my efforts, what I'd written was probably no more than a record of my circling around the problem.'

'So why are you wasting time working for the Seven network? Why aren't you dropping everything and pursuing McGraw?'

'Believe me, I'd like to – if I could afford it. If I thought I'd succeed. A couple of years ago, when McGraw was briefly hanging out in the USA, I spent three months in California, trying to track him down. I must have interviewed at least a hundred of his former friends and associates - and none of them told me anything I didn't already know, one way or another. Nothing fresh or reliable about his life on the run - just the same old mythic bullshit.'

'Did you confront him personally at that stage?'

'No. He was too elusive. He moved in this fluid, moneyed world of people who barely knew him. He attended their parties and their weekenders up in Santa Barbara - even gave a few parties of his own. He made love to their bored wives, and their spunky daughters - at least the one's who were aspiring to be models. He was incorrigible. Like a completely free agent, he turned up wherever the fun was. Everyone appeared to know him - and yet, no two people ever seemed to describe him in quite the same way. *'Had he committed some crime?'* they'd ask me. *'He seemed too, too wonderful to be true,'* they'd say.' Any attempt I made to get to the everyday details of the man's life ended in failure. Most of the people I talked to could spin a story, but very few were convincing on any level; and none of their tales were on a human scale. Every line of inquiry just delivered up another myth. It seemed that McGraw had managed to guard his privacy and control his public image, just as he had done back in Australia.

To even attempt to write about his time in California just put me back in the realm of tabloid speculation and celebrity gossip. After a few months, I gave up in disgust with my efforts.'

'Gave up? You mean, you abandoned the book?'

'That's how I felt at the time. I remember leaving America determined to give up biography and return to straight reporting. I was angry, and I felt as though I had been outwitted. I thought if I couldn't get anywhere trying to uncover the private man, I was going to attack and expose the corporate identity. It drove me back to my ASIC contacts and a mountain of financial reports from the files of daily newspapers. It also made me absolutely certain that my book was a failure. My subject wanted nothing to do with me. My publisher was hoping the book would just disappear. And I was short of inspiration. I had to face it - I was a journalist, nothing more. I'd lost all faith in my ability to produce anything that met my own standards of literature and biography. I was stuck with a clunker - and the knowledge was painful.'

'What do you want to do about the book now?'

'Toss it in.'

'If only you could.'

'All right - I'm exaggerating. But the thing is like an unhealthy obsession. Common sense would tell me to put it aside until there was some significant breakthrough in the ASIC investigation. Wait until McGraw is caught and extradited back to Australia for trial, and then maybe cannibalize the contents to feed a few newspaper articles.'

She was trying to sound tough about her resolution to abandon her ambition, but somehow Mitchell didn't quite believe her. Walking alongside her had made him aware of her vulnerability. In spite of her celebrity, her aura of being in control and at heart a cynic, she had revealed herself to be riven with self-doubt and beset by unanswered questions. She seemed to him almost adolescent in her single-minded pursuit of an idealized, improbable ambition. There was even something a little sad about her struggle with her extravagant writing goals. For all her apparent connections, in this she was truly alone, unsupported, and most evidently in need of confidence.

Twenty minutes later, they arrived at the rue Grégoire de Tours in St.-Germain. All too soon for Mitchell, they were standing outside the entrance to her hotel.

'Anyway, before we can plan to shoot any of this, we're going to need another meeting. I want to take down every detail of your story. I'll probably have to interview you – that's the easiest and quickest way.'

'You'll blow my spontaneity before I even make it to tape,' he joked.

'We need to distil your story down to its essentials.'

'My three minutes of fame.'

'How are you for tomorrow evening? Here – say, at six?'

'Sure. I can do that.'

'Thanks for tonight,' she said, with tender emphasis. 'I enjoyed banging on about myself, as usual.'

She offered her hand - which he shook, lightly - then surprised him by giving him a darting peck on the cheek. He watched, still disoriented from the glancing kiss, as she backed away, smiling, into the amber glow of the foyer.

Moments later, as he headed for the entrance to the Métro Odéon, he was cursing his failure to tell her about the 'other' Marlo. Why had he held back? Did he imagine she would have found his story ridiculous? Was he afraid she would regard the complications too absurd, too distracting to be of any use in her documentary.

He stumbled onto the metro escalator, vowing to confess the whole story on their next meeting – if he could only be sure what that story was.

19

August 17: The Gorge de l'Aveyron

Eddie took the winding trip up river with his speedometer on one-twenty. He was getting the hang of driving like a Frenchman. Taking the blind corners with two wheels hanging out over the line. Pulling in at the very last minute to avoid the oncoming cars. The scenery meant nothing to him.

The place wasn't too difficult to find. It was a large two-storied *château*, clearly visible on a prominent ridge on the opposite side of the river. It was built of pale orange stone, with a high-pitched slate roof and an impressive tower at one end. There was a row of dormer windows in the roof and high windows in the tower. Many of the pale grey shutters were closed, and his first impression was that the place was deserted. But from where he was parked, a high stone wall made it impossible to see whether there were any vehicles in the grounds. Nearby was a large barn, and further away, a *pigeonier* situated on a sunny rise above the river. There were several massive oak trees and a few chestnuts. An orchard of espaliered pear trees ran down to the river flat. On the sunny slope above the house there was a field of ripe corn.

He didn't approach the house directly. Instead, he parked his car off the verge of the D115 in a small clearing used - judging by the dried severed fish heads - by local anglers. Taking an indirect route, he walked back along the road in the direction from which he had come. Several hundred metres along the road was an old stone bridge across the Aveyron. He crossed it and entered the *hameau* of Cazals. Apart from a naked marble Christ on a grey oak cross, there was nobody about. People must have lived there - pink and white petunias overflowed from tubs outside every house. But all of the windows were shuttered. There were no dogs, no cats, and no cars in the street.

A narrow bitumen road rose out of the *hameau* and followed the course of the river. He walked along it in the direction of the *château*. As he got closer he could see the tall iron entrance gates. Two cars parked inside: a dark blue BMW sedan and a silver Mercedes coupé. He realized he could be observed from any of the several open windows and so adopted a less suspicious walk. He began looking around like a nature lover out on a stroll: he considered the limestone crags across the river; paused to watch the swallows circling and diving above the willows; gathered up a fistful of thyme and crushed it under his nose. If they had known his intentions, they might have picked him off right then and there. A silent country road. No witnesses.

He didn't need to speculate on whether he had been noticed for very long. As he neared the iron entrance gates, two German Shepherds came bounding at him. They hurled themselves at the iron bars, snarling and barking as they tried to get at him. Anyone in the house could have seen him easily. He had no choice but to continue his hike, without so much as a glance in the direction of the farmhouse.

He knew from his map that there was a second bridge a

kilometere or so further back in the direction from which he had driven. He did his best to ignore the dogs, and walked on. Ten minutes later he reached that bridge, crossed it, then took the long walk back along the D115 to his parked car. The wasted time was beginning to irritate him, but there was no other way. He was going to have to settle for surveying the house through binoculars.

It didn't look easy. Maybe it wasn't even possible. At least not a clean, walk-in job the way Gornik and Toop had put it to him. In the first place, he had no way of knowing whether the painting was even in the house. He was going to have to lay the carpet without a friendly inspection and quote. And the dogs were a serious impediment. He'd have to bait them or shoot them from a distance. And then what? Hope that McGraw and his pals wouldn't notice? The trouble was, they were probably only out in the yard and up at the gate in daylight hours. At night, when he wanted to do the job, they were most likely kenneled somewhere. Dogs didn't sleep. They'd smell him and wake the household before he could silence them. It was all too complicated. What he needed was time to prowl the house with everyone out to it. Time to locate some paintings that might not even be there. On the other hand, if he tried for a daylight raid and took out the dogs, he would have to use a weapon in the house. Probably even need an accomplice. More than likely somebody was going have to get taken out. But they weren't paying him enough to take risks like that. There were just too many ways it could all go wrong, and the last thing he wanted was to involve someone else.

He paused in the cover of the bushes that lined the roadway to take a better look at the house through his field glasses. The upstairs dormer windows were all curtained. Only on the second level - the living area - could he see into the house. He lit a cigarette and settled in for a long wait. Thirty minutes passed while he kept his binoculars trained on the open windows, waiting to see any sign of life. He ate half the chocolate bar, smoked two more cigarettes, and fought off a column of ants that threatened to climb his inside leg.

Finally, four men came out - one of them, from his recollection of the picture Toop had shown him, was unmistakably McGraw. The other was a man of similar age - most likely the owner, the banker. The banker played with the dogs. They leaped at something concealed in his hand. The other two men were much younger. They appear fit and physically adept - bodyguards, maybe.

After a conversation with McGraw and the banker, one of the younger men got into the BMW and drove away. Perhaps it was to see what had happened to the strange looking man who walked past the gate and spooked the dogs? But why would they have waited so long to investigate? Perhaps it was merely an errand. One man goes, one man stays.

In an irrational way, it reassured him that from his position across the river, a good marksman could have taken any of them out. He hurried back to his car and started the engine. With any luck, he could follow the BMW and learn a little more.

Down by the bridge to Cazals, the BMW turned onto the D115 and took the direction to St.-Antonin-Noble-Val. he followed in his little grey Renault, keeping a sensible distance behind. The BMW skirted the ancient part of St.-Antonin and drove into a *supermarché* parking lot at the modern end of town. He parked across the road, watching the man's movements with one eye while he pretended to consult a road map. The man left the parking lot with no sense of caution or subterfuge. He was whistling as he crossed the road twenty metres in front of Eddie's car, and entered an unpromising cafe and pizzeria. Minutes later, he reemerged carrying a stack of take-away boxes and a carton of beer.

As he watched the BMW drive away, Eddie knew for certain that they weren't paying him enough.

20

August 17: Paris, Saint-Germain

When he dashed into the foyer of the Hôtel de Fleurie, ducking a sudden summer downpour, Ilena was already waiting.

'Bon courage,' she said, not sure whether it was an appropriate greeting to give a man scrambling to stay dry. She offered both cheeks for kissing. 'Your day? Good?'

'Busy in the dusty Picasso archive,' Mitchell said, making an exasperated face.

He saw that she was carrying a small umbrella and a compact digital sound recorder.

'Trust me,' she said, 'this will be completely painless.' To his surprise, she began fastening a tiny lapel mike to his shirt pocket, switched the recorder on, and told him to slip the device into his pocket. 'I want you to forget you're even wearing it.'

'So I can blather as I walk along?'

'Exactly. Let's have an *apéritif* in the Café de Flore.'

'Won't they object to me giving forth on the terrace?'

'You can speak at normal volume – even in the street.'

'Let's go, then.'

They walked, pressed close together in the shelter of the umbrella, arms sometimes brushing, hips bumping. As soon as they hit rue Grégoire de Tours Ilena initiated the interview.

'Okay, ready? The truth is, when you told me your Marlo McGraw story I became excited about my project all over again. Nobody I've spoken to has gotten quite so close to either of the McGraws for ages - not in that way, at least. I mean, I'm assuming that the woman you met in Nice - or wherever it actually happened - was Marlo McGraw. If so, wow - what an extraordinary encounter. I want you to tell it me about it all over again - this time giving it to me in every excruciating detail.'

Mitchell was conscious of passers-by staring with curiosity at this hectoring woman in faux-interview mode.

'I have to confess' he began, with stilted formality, 'there was one excruciating detail I left out.' It was the opportunity he had been preparing for, and his departure from the anticipated script took her by surprise.

'That's all right. You weren't under oath.'

'Oh, but this was something important. Something significant. Hard to swallow - I'm warning you - but completely true and totally bizarre.'

'Really?' she said coolly, refusing to rise to the bait. 'Even better.'

'There were two Marlo McGraws.'

'What?'

'After I met the woman down in Saint-Paul-de-Vence, another woman turned up claiming to be Marlo McGraw. She telephoned me in Paris, a day or so after I returned, and I arranged to meet her at a café down by the Louvre. Naturally. I thought I was going to meet the woman who had stood me up at Nice airport. I just couldn't believe it when this stranger introduced herself as Marlo McGraw.'

'My God. This is better than I thought.'

At the intersection of rue Bonaparte and the boulevard St.-Germain, they crossed at the lights. They were almost oblivious to their surroundings. Spray from passing cars was wetting their legs, but they didn't mind.

'Well – if only it had been better,' Mitchell continued, as they reached the northern pavement. 'I was very disturbed by it all. This new Marlo was very confident and utterly convincing. She produced a passport in her name. She talked intimately about herself and Mike McGraw. She knew all about the Picasso portrait – had real authority on its history. And she had a very persuasive explanation for what the first Marlo might have been up to. Frankly, I'd have preferred it if the first one had been the real Marlo. She was a far more appealing person. Far more glamorous, too. But in the end, I'd have to say I'm still confused. The first one made perfect sense until I met the second. But maybe neither of them is genuine. Who knows?'

Ilena uttered a sigh of disbelief. 'Well – this *is* a story.'

'I'm really sorry for not telling you any of this before. I do apologize. My only excuse is – I didn't know what to make of it all myself.'

'Now you're going to have to start at the beginning and tell me everything you can recall. This is marvellous.'

They arrived at the Café de Flore, shook the water of their umbrella, and found a table just inside the terrace. Over *apéritifs,* he told her everything: no omissions and no embellishments. He soon completely forgot the omni-vigilant presence of the lapel mike and the silent incrimination of the digital recorder in his pocket. Urged on by her enthusiasm, he found himself recalling half-forgotten personal details and revealing moments of the woman's conversation. Still, he thought Ilena would find it all wildly improbable, a liar's concoction.

When he had exhausted his memory of the encounter at Le Fumoir, he concluded by plucking the mike from his pocket and placing it gently on the table. He leaned back in his chair to invite her response, and saw that she was staring at him in mock astonishment.

'You're right, it's all very hard to believe – and hard to fathom. But now I'm more intrigued than ever. I only wish I'd had a camera on you the whole time. You know I'm going to need you to tell the story all over again some time soon.'

'And I suppose you're going to want copyright?' he said, amused. 'Permission for publication, as well?'

'Well, naturally. Or is that straining a new friendship?'

'Not at all. You're welcome to it - all of it. But what exactly did you make of it?'

'Nothing that I can pretend to understand. Presumably, one of those women is the real Marlo McGraw – but which one? The second woman sounded more convincing, except for the fact that the first was doing exactly what I'd expect of McGraw's partner: trying to unload one of his valuable paintings. The possibility that he was using her to unload it fits with the McGraw that I know.'

'There are too many possibilities,' Mitchell said, 'and they're all hard to rule out. What if – as the second Marlo claimed – the painting was stolen from the McGraws? Or what if was a fake, copied somehow from their Picasso?'

'Or maybe McGraw has nothing to do with either of these women. Maybe they've been separated for quite a while. Possibly he doesn't have a clue where Marlo – the *real* one, whoever she is - has gone? And what if selling the Picasso was solely her idea?'

'If those things were true, I'd say that's because he's driven her away, and this is the only worthwhile chip that the desperate woman can cash?'

Ilena covered her face with her hands, then re-emerged and gave Mitchell a look of utter bewilderment. 'I think I should've just stuck with hedge-funds.'

'Well – I don't know what this does to your plan.'

'I guess there's only one way you'll learn anything more, and that's to talk to her again.'

'But which one?'

'Oh, stop it. I mean get back in contact with the one you met in Paris and try to learn even more.'

'She gave me her number, but I've got a hunch she's going to be as impossible to find as the first Marlo.'

'Could you try?'

'Why? To test her story? Expose whether or not she's the real thing?'

'Sure. All of that. Couldn't you offer to do a little of whatever it is she's wanting?'

'What she wants, I definitely can't do. She wants me to help her find the woman from Saint-Paul-de-Vence. But I will call her, if you like – as soon as I work out what I can say. I suspect it won't come to anything.'

'Don't worry, you're talking to a veteran, with a doctorate in futility.'

They spent some time discussing possible reasons Mitchell could have for contacting the woman. Ilena suggested that he should simply request more detail about the *Portrait of Dora Maar*, and see what else the woman was prepared to tell him. Alternatively, he could offer her the results of his own research on the painting. Whatever the approach, the intention was to secure another face-to-face session with her, in the hope that her true identity might be revealed.

Ilena allowed Mitchell to pay for their *apéritifs* but insisted on paying for dinner. He suggested Le Petit St.-Benoît, just around the corner. It was a cheap coach-house style bistro that served solid traditional fare. He didn't want her running up a large bill on his account.

Once they were settled at a table in the bistro, Mitchell asked Ilena about her shooting schedule.

'I want to set off for Provence on the twentieth – starting work down there on the twenty-first. We'll be driving down via the Rhône valley. I've got a crew of two – camera and sound – and a ton of equipment. The idea is to begin our filming at McGraw's villa in Cap-Martin. It'll be locked up, but no matter. I just want to evoke the ambience of his old lifestyle. Also try to get Lavelle, his former lawyer, on film. He probably won't agree – so I'll just have to ambush him at his premises in Menton. After that, I'd like to travel up to Saint-Paul-de-Vence and tell your part of the story. So you can come down with us, if you've got the time to spare – we should have the space for you. Or you can fly down just for the day, if that's all the time you've got.'

'Sounds good to me. I'll see what I can arrange.'

'This timetable may change if, in the meantime, anything breaks on McGraw's extradition I'm in regular contact with the investigation team as ASIC and the Attorney General's Department. I've already interviewed a couple of those people here in Paris, documenting what I could of the process.'

'I guess you have to be there for the bust.'

'I just hope it's not an anti-climax.'

'What? You and an entire army of television cameras trying to get a shot of a man in handcuffs with a bag over his head?'

'No - I'll be the first there.'

'With the help of these friends?'

'My men at the source.'

'I'd like to see it.'

Mitchell knew that setting out with her on this open-ended jaunt was somehow adolescent. It indicated he was prepared to put aside plans and give over his time to a woman he barely knew. It suggested her company was everything at that moment. But although he did his best to conceal it from her, he was thrilled by the possibility of further recklessness. The truth was, he was open to anything she might suggest.

While they ate, Ilena told him even more about her plans for the documentary. It also seemed that she wanted to talk, not so much to learn whatever she could about McGraw in France - and after all, what did Mitchell really know about McGraw? - but to test her belief in her plans. By committing them to a sympathetic but critical ear, by imagining, by fantasizing, she was edging closer to some kind of resolution.

Mitchell also learned about the crisis that travel engendered in her: a suspension between exhilaration and anxiety. She wanted to be set free in the world, but she knew all too well there would be a downside. She had already accomplished so much, but what did it mean to her? All her passion was for the pursuit of something far less glamorous, much tougher, and only rarely rewarding. And it was all driven by something he couldn't even begin to understand. Maybe it even had something to do with her barely explained relationship with her new employers. But even that could hardly account for such an obsession.

He tried to imagine what was at stake for her in this decision to want to tell the story of a man so deeply despised by the Australian public. By overreaching, she could easily alienate everyone and lose her foothold, and her career, in commercial television. Not that she seemed to care about either of these things. But she might discover, at the end of her struggle with the McGraw story, that she was neither an author, nor a documentary filmmaker. And such knowledge, he believed, would be devastating.

21

August 18: Toulouse

Eddie made two phone calls back to Australia, both to old cohorts from his days with the Feds. He wanted the contact numbers for a Frenchman he had once known called Didier Lapage. Eddie had met Didier back in ninety-five, when he was with the *gendarmes*, posted out to Vanuattu. They were working a case together, tracking a yacht load of heroin headed for the Queensland coast. Up there in a coast guard chopper, tailing the smugglers for a thousand kilometres across the Coral Sea.

Crazy Didi. Didi the head fucker. That's how he was known back then. A man capable of anything. He had wanted to fly in low over the yacht and dump a plastic canister of aviation fuel on its deck. Watch it burst open. Soak the sails. Panic the crew. Then fire on it. Burn the yacht to the waterline, and watch the rats abandon ship. But common sense had prevailed. The fuel was for emergency use. There were property rights involved. People might die. Crazy Didi just laughed. You could never tell when he was serious.

Days later, with the yacht grounded on a sand bar, Eddie and Didier had boarded her from a patrol boat. It was a pirated vessel, reported missing in the Gulf of Tonkin, no trace of the Dutch crew. Didier was the only one who could communicate with the bunch of half starved Vietnamese pirates. No one quite knew what he'd said to them - something about hanging them by the nuts with fishing line while they watched the boarding party take turns fucking the youngest kid on the crew - but it spooked them enough to leap overboard and take their chances heading for the palm trees. Didier enjoyed cutting them down as they ran.

Years later they met up again in Thailand. Didier took Eddie down to Ko Pha-Ngan for a weekend of drinking and screwing. Rows of tacky bars along the beachfront, all of them with names like Irish pubs. Everywhere you looked, ugly old white guys with skinny bar girls on their laps. For twenty bucks they'd be yours for the night, do anything - feed you, bath you, wash your socks, let you take them any way you'd like. He remembered the look on Didier's face as he watched Eddie walk off into the tropical night, wrapped tight around a Thai princess in a tight little black lycra cocktail dress.

'You better check that one really good,' he shouted, with a smirk. 'I think you got yourself a boy.'

Didier was right. Eddie recalled, with some embarrassment the half-naked kid, his dick on full jut, chasing him along the breezeblock corridor of their two dollar a night beach hotel, screaming for his money.

They were different days. Eddie had been lost, beyond reach, out of control. Surrendering to some darkness within. Nothing he understood. Nothing he could ever quite forget.

So why was he contacting Didier again? Didier was no real friend. Once they stopped working together they never saw one another again. It was a life Eddie believed he'd left behind for good. But now he'd crossed that line again. He'd left the old man tethered in the barn – perhaps to die – and felt what? Remorse? Then where was it now? He'd taken the money to do this thing, and in doing so, let himself in for absolutely anything. Was he looking for someone to do the dirty work? A moral scapegoat? Or was he looking for a catalyst? Someone to edge him over the line? Tell him it was all fine? With Didier, maybe it would be painless. They'd shared some dark and dangerous times, and if he was going to seek help with this nasty little escapade, it would have to be from a man like Didier.

'Hello Eddie, my man. What you into these days?' Same old Didier. Rasping voice, coming down the line through a cloud of cigarette smoke. Punctuated, as always, by a lot of ugly hawking.

'Freelance,' Eddie said, coolly. 'How about you?'

'Ugh,' he sighed, 'I got myself a restaurant, down here in Toulouse. But the thing is making me broke. Believe me, no fucking money in a tapas bar. Wife's family, they have this idea. Stupid. Killing me. So now, what? I drive trucks to pay for a restaurant I don't want.'

It wasn't like Didier to moan, but once he started the man didn't want to shut up. He told Eddie about his trucking escapades. Driving uninsurable, high risk cargoes overnight from Toulouse to Britain. Screaming up the A61 at two in the morning with a container load of stolen cigarettes. 'At least I'm gonna kill a few Englishmen.' Making the first channel ferry of the morning from La Rochelle. Back home late the next night, feeling like a shot duck. Just in time to set up the tapas bar. This was his life. No sleep, no sex, no good times.

Although it didn't seem such a good idea any more, Eddie laid it all out for him. Told Didier if it didn't interest him personally, maybe he could find him a reliable man to do the job. Eddie came right out with a high figure and cash up front for extra encouragement. That was how much he trusted the man. But Didier made a lot of hedging noises. Complications, no time, responsibilities. Went into a routine about his wife and kid, and things not being like the old days. Driving a heist-magnet semi and running a dead-loss restaurant at the same time was already too much for his nerves.

'What the fuck ever happened to Crazy Didi?' was what Eddie wanted to know. Didier just laughed, and still baulked, even when Eddie bumped the figure to six thousand Euros. No, the best Didier could do for Eddie was to find a good man, a guy who wasn't afraid of going all the way for a sensible fee. Give him a day and he'd have someone lined up. They could meet up in Toulouse and settle the deal.

That evening Eddie took a cheap room in a one star hotel down near the Basilique Saint-Sernin. He ate *magret de canard* washed down with a *pichet* of tasteless red in a tourist restaurant, then took a long walk through the city. The architecture and the ambience meant little to him. Just another old French town, only bigger. Eddie was looking for a supermarket, a corner shop, any place that would sell him cigarettes. He found a small late night mini-mart with crowded aisles that smelled like stale spices. A bearded North African man sold him cigarettes and a bar of dark chocolate, as well as a hand of bananas, and a bottle of cheap Bordeaux. Afterwards, he headed straight back to the hotel, where he drank himself drowsy, and fell asleep in his clothes on top of the bed cover.

The following afternoon at six, Eddie was to meet Didier in a bar down on the Promenade Henri Martin. Eddie arrived early and sat at a table with a view of the Garonne. It wasn't Paris, there was nothing happening down on the river.

Didier's approach took Eddie by surprise. The man was almost unrecognizable. They shook hands and made the obvious noises of greeting, then both men sat back for a while and silently observed the changes that a decade had wrought in the other. Didier was a fat man now, a physical ruin. He looked like a hard drinking truck driver. He also looked like a sedentary restauranteur. Definitely not someone to involve in a business that might involve speed and stealth. The complexion was brick red, and the huge chin - once an indicator of the man's virility and cavalier spirit - was now beleaguered by flesh and patterned with a network of fine dark veins. Watery blue eyes squinted over purple bags. The moustache that had once been clipped and dashing, was now a salt and pepper unkempt bush that all but concealed his mouth. His dirty grey hair, still worn long, looked as though he combed it with his fingers. Crazy Didier had gone missing. Eddie wondered whether he was throwing his money away.

Didier ordered a double Calvados, while Eddie took *un express.*

'Tell me about this man of yours,' Eddie said, trying to conceal his irritation that Didier had shown up without him.

'He's what you looking for. Name is Jacques Craïssac. Has a farm near Caussade, a vealery.'

'Why is a farmer going to want to get involved in this?'

Didier laughed.

'Because Jacques is a crazy fuck like I was one time.' At least his sense of humour hadn't changed. 'Four years he worked for me down in Marseilles. Jacques - believe me, Eddie - he don't say no to nothing.'

'I told you I need a marksman. Can this guy shoot?'

'Yes, yes - he's trained for this. The guy wins prizes. He has - what do call them? – gold things? Ask him to show you.'

'I don't want to see his fuckin' trophies. I want to see what he can hit.'

'Jacques, he was in the Olympic team - small bore. He was gonna go to Barcelona, but they got him on a drug charge. What you 'spect him to hit?'

A waiter interrupted them to bring their order. Within moments of it touching the table, Didier had taken a shot of his Calvados. Eddie broke open his paper packaged sugar cubes and dropped them into his *express.*

'Dogs,' Eddie said. 'I need him to take care of some dogs. From a distance.'

Didier laughed again. 'Dogs! No problem. Every farmer here happy to shoot a neighbour's dog. I thought you was gonna say kill a man. Even so - no matter - wouldn't worry Jacques.'

'That a fact?'

'So - how much you pay Jacques for this?'

'Let's meet him first. How soon can I do that?'

'Soon as you pay me.'

'All right, Didi. I'll give you two thousand euros today. Then two thousand more if it turns out I like this Jacques character. And you get the rest when the job's done,'

Didier stared past him, his bleary eyes focused on nothing, while he made his calculations. 'Okay - tomorrow morning, early. We take a trip to Caussade.'

22

August 19: the Marais and Montmartre

Mitchell was working in the archives of the Musée Picasso when the telephonist on the information desk called. He had been sifting through a portfolio of photographs of Picasso at the villa *La Californie* in Cannes, trying to make a selection, which he would later propose for inclusion in the exhibition catalogue.

'Monsieur Jameson?'

'Oui.'

'Il y a une madame pour vous.'

'Elle s'appelle?'

'Elle ne dit pas.'

'Okay.'

Ilena, he thought. He was going to have to break the news of his failure to reach the 'other' Marlo, the woman he had met in Paris. There was little to explain. The number he had been given by the woman was *coupé* - disconnected. But he welcomed the interruption. It was already two days since he had spoken to her.

The voice on the telephone, however was not Ilena's.

'Mitchell? Hello – it's Marlo.'

'Who?... Marlo?'

It was the woman he had met at the Colombe d'Or. The woman he had never expected to see, or hear from, again.

'I can't talk now, but I need to see you.'

'Sure,' he said, prepared to agree to anything she proposed.

'I'm in Paris. Can I come to your place? Tonight, if possible. You do have an apartment?'

'Yes, of course you can. I'd love to see you.' Such innocuous words of acceptance after all the frustration she had caused him.

He gave the address and the code for his door, and immediately afterwards, she hung up.

She stood at his door holding a worn Louis Vuitton suitcase.

'Mitchell. Thank God,' she said, breathlessly as she took his hand.

He led her inside and invited her to sit on his ratty sofa.

'When I came to Paris, I prayed you'd still be here.'

'If I'd passed you in the street, I might not have recognize you.'

It was true, she looked very different. Her shoulder length black hair had been reduced to a boyish, spiky cut that revealed her pale, pixie ears and threw the focus to her troubled eyes. Unlike previously, she was not dressed extravagantly, but looked quite anonymous in black jeans and a white crew top. Only her simple, but elegant, silver jewellery was there to remind him of her previous incarnation. Even the model's poise and the low, thrilling voice had been disposed of since their last encounter. She had been playing a part on that day, and was someone else entirely now. When she spoke again, it was in a broken voice, shot with fear.

'I've brought something with me,' she said, bending over her suitcase and unlocking the clasps.

She lifted out a package, whose dimensions he immediately recognized. She seemed to be perspiring. Was it fear or exhaustion?

'So you've finally brought *Dora* to Paris?'

'Yes. That's the reason why I'm here.'

`Last time, your charming boudoir. This time, my little pig sty.' He couldn't help his facetiousness, she had made him feel a ninny down in Saint-Paul-de-Vence, and he wasn't about to fall at her feet a second time. At least not in the first five minutes.

He poured her a glass of Perrier, all that remained of a bottle he had in his tiny refrigerator.

'What happened to make you change your mind about your painting?' he asked, after she had calmed a little.

'I'm so sorry about what happened in Nice,' she said between nervous sips of the water, 'It was an awful thing to do, but I was terrified of letting the Picasso out of my hands. I packed and left that same night.'

'I figured that out,' he said, tersely, 'and I haven't exactly forgotten.'

'But truly, I just didn't know what to say to you. There was so much more going on than I could ever explain.'

'Like what?' Mitchell was already losing patience. It seemed her new act was shaping up to be a repeat of her last performance.

'I know it must have caused you and Luke a lot of unnecessary trouble,' she said, looking up at him, her mouth trembling in apology. 'If you can...I could...'

'Forget it,' he said, trying to temper the harshness in his voice. Still, he was determined to a get a straight story from her. And he wasn't going to help by telling her about his own adventures in Nice. 'Just tell me why you ran.'

'I was being watched, followed by somebody. They knew where I was living. I knew I wasn't safe in that villa. It's not something recent. It's been going on for a long time. Sometimes I've been driving in traffic and suddenly become aware that one car seemed to stick to my tail no matter where I turned. Other times I've be followed in the street, from the moment I walked out of my apartment. I've been aware of the same man turning up several times in the same day. Always keeping his distance, half a block behind. Lurking around. Stalking me. I mean, there'd never be any eye contact. I'd turn around and he'd be doing something innocent - entering a shop, buying a newspaper. But I could tell what was going on. I knew with absolute certainty that he was following me. Not always the same man every day. But wherever I'd go, I'd feel the constant threat of somebody just over my shoulder, somebody that I didn't know, somebody who seemed to know me. It was terrifying. And that's why I ran. I was certain they were coming after me that same night.'

'Who are these people?' He had no doubt they were the same gang who had abducted him in Nice, but still he refrained from telling her anything.

'Scavengers. People who knew about Mike's problems. People who thought they knew about the money he was supposed to have hidden away. People who are after this painting and others.'

'So, they're not people that he owed money to?'

'No,' she said, vehemently, 'they're thieves.'

'Are you sure they're not with the French police? Corrupt undercover cops?'

'Maybe. I don't know who they are. But sooner or later they'll show up, no matter where I go.'

'Even here?'

'I'm getting better at shaking them off,' she said, with empty assurance.

'Relieved to hear it.'

'It's all right - they never approach me. Nothing ever happens. But that's because they're waiting for me to slip up and lead them to what they're really after. They don't seem to realize that I'm never going to lead them to Mike, and they just haven't figured where I've been keeping the Picasso.'

'You weren't exactly hiding it the day you showed it to me. And you wouldn't have to be a genius to guess there might be a Picasso in your suitcase.'

'I had no choice. I had to take a risk.'

'Isn't that what you said in Saint-Paul-de-Vence?'

'In Saint-Paul I thought I was safe. I thought I'd left them behind when I went there. God knows, I'd moved around enough. But that night, after I saw you, I drove back into town. I had nothing to eat in the house. I'd run out of essentials. And while I was there I saw a man, someone I'd seen before in L.A. and in Nice. I caught him looking at my car. Fortunately he didn't notice that I'd seen him. When he moved on I just got back into that car and drove right out of there as fast as I could. I took a one hundred kilometetere detour. I used all the back roads to get home. And believe me, I just threw my things in a suitcase and ran. That's how my life has been these last months. I can't feel safe anywhere.'

'But nobody has approached you directly? Threatened you? Demonstrated beyond all doubt that it's you they're after?'

'That's why I'm here. I've been in here for the last few days. Living in a quiet street that nobody visits. But yesterday, my apartment was ransacked. Everything overturned and torn apart. The kinds of things junkies look for were left lying around for the taking everywhere. In fact, nothing was actually missing.'

'Well, that was a bad mistake on their part, wasn't it?'

'They didn't care. They were after the Picasso. I know.'

'So why didn't they find it?'

'I don't live with it under my bed any more. This is the first time since I've been in Paris when I've dared to have it in my possession.'

'You don't think they might be people working for your husband. I mean you did walk off with his painting.'

She shook her head. 'I told you – it was a gift.'

Mitchell wasn't sure that he believed her. With Marlo he had no idea where the truth began and ended. He made a point of not confusing the issue by mentioning his encounter at Le Fumoir with the 'other' Marlo McGraw. Since he still had no certainty about that woman's agenda, he wasn't going to give this Marlo an advantage, nor feed her anxiety. Throughout the entire explanation, he wasn't sure whether she was exaggerating the situation, exhibiting signs of paranoia, or whether this was just another move in her manipulative game in which she planned to walk away with everything. Where it was heading, he couldn't anticipate, but at least he was being offered another seat at the table.

'Then what would you like me to do?' he asked.

'I want you to take the painting to your friend here in Paris, the Picasso expert, the man you were working for.'

'Luc Pellegrin. So you do want an expert opinion? An authentication so that you can go through with a sale?'

'Yes. But I don't want the entire Musée Picasso involved. Just one man.'

'When do you want me to do this?'

'It has to be now - right away.'

'All right. I'll call Luc and see if I can arrange for us to bring *Dora* to him this evening. And we'll take it from there.'

'I always believed you'd be able to help me. I won't mess you around.'

'Oh, no, I'd be disappointed if you didn't,' he said, lightly. 'Go ahead and surprise me as much as you like.'

Mitchell telephoned Luc Pellegrin at his apartment. When told of the situation, his disbelief soon turned to excitement. He insisted that they come over straight away.

Mitchell and Marlo took a long taxi ride to the rue des Martyrs in Montmartre, with the suitcase resting securely at Marlo's feet. While they drove through the chaotic Paris peak-hour traffic, Mitchell's thoughts returned to Ilena. How could he tell her any of this without breaking Marlo's fragile trust?

After buzzing them into the building, Luc waited for them

on the landing outside his door. When Marlo stepped out of the lift cage, Luc took her hand effusively. He greeted her as though he had known her for years.

'You're even more beautiful than your unforgettable telephone voice,' he purred.

Mitchell was amused by Luc's shameless flattery, but Marlo was on guard. Clutching the handle of her suitcase even more tightly, she followed the welcoming sweep of his hand and entered the apartment.

Before getting down to the business of examining the Picasso, Luc led Marlo to the balcony window of his *salle de séjour* with its uninterrupted view of the western facade of the Sacré Coeur.

'I do this for everyone who comes,' he said, pointing to the *basilique,* which had now turned mauve in the last gasp of twilight.

In spite of her anxieties, she indulged him his tour.

'You see why I love my apartment,' he said. 'On my balcony, I'm always a tourist. Every morning I have my coffee right here and look at that magnificent view. For me, it is perfect. But looking the other way - is not so good.'

He was referring to the fact that that the room was a chaotic last resting place for thousands of newspapers, books, magazines, CD's and art works of all kinds. All available shelf space had long ago overflowed. To make even the smallest journey across the apartment, one had to navigate around stacks of books, odd pieces of spiky modern sculpture, sheaves of rolled up canvases, or risk skidding on CD covers or art magazines. One had the impression that nothing was ever thrown away. Every reference work that might be needed was right there at his fingertips, assuming it could ever be found again. It was a shambles, a monument to intellectual overload, a model of dysfunctional urban living. But clearly he was quite at home in the mess.

'I must get organized, sort things out one day,' he said with a sad, philosophical laugh. Mitchell couldn't help but connect the disarray with his recent loss of Catherine.

Luc shovelled some of the mess from one end of his shaggy sofa to make room for Marlo, while Mitchell was offered a stiff chrome and leather monstrosity. Luc then disappeared into a bedroom and returned with a small wooden easel, which he erected at Marlo's feet, before inviting her to display the painting.

They both watched in near silence during the five minutes it took for Marlo to unpack the layers of cardboard and bubble wrap. The portrait of Dora, at its moment of revelation, once again worked its magic of shock and acute pleasure upon Mitchell, while Luc was speechless with astonishment. It was a work by his revered Picasso that he had never seen before, and yet one that was so absolutely familiar.

Although Luc had been speaking English with them, his first words, muttered several times like an incantation, were: *'un vrai chef-d'oeuvre.'* His hands hovered near the surface of the canvas. Mitchell could see that he wanted to touch it, so acute was his need for contact with the work, but he refrained in deference to Marlo. And then slowly, he began to relax in front of the painting. His intuition began to free up as well as his fund of knowledge.

'Do you know in which year it was painted? I would guess nineteen-thirty-seven. Possibly painted during their time at Mougins. He was still very much in love with her then. See - she has the *'miranda feurte'*. It's what Picasso used to call that look in her eyes. That fierce stare. That mysterious female power. It used to scare him. Dora, the dangerous bird of prey, A little bit crazy.'

Mitchell caught Marlo's eye, and could see that Luc's brand of rhapsodic gush was beginning to irritate her. He feared she was beginning to form the impression that Luc was a mere fan, definitely not *un homme sérieux*.

'I understand you don't have an expertise for this painting' Luc said.

'You've discussed this?' she asked of Mitchell.

'A little.'

'He told me quite a bit about the painting,' Luc said.

For almost an hour, they went on to discuss every stage, real and imagined, of the painting's history, while the portrait stood before them. There was no longer light in the sky. Floodlights lit up the facade of Sacré Coeur, and the *salle de séjour* grew cool and shadowy. Mitchell saw that Marlo was appearing to fall under the spell of Luc's erudition. She almost seemed to forget the purpose of their visit. Or was it an elaborate act, a strategy to secure his sympathy?

Mitchell's tension had begun to rise. Finally, he posed the question that he knew Luc would rather have avoided answering. 'So now, do you think you know enough to provide an expertise?'

'Without any supporting papers? Without any kind of provenance? It would just be the word of a friend? It's always a risk for one's reputation.'

Marlo unfolded her legs and rose up from her deep reclining position on the sofa. 'All right. You can hang onto my painting for a very short time. Go ahead - do any of the tests you might need. Just so long as you look after my *Dora*.'

Mitchell knew how much such a concession was costing her.

'With Picasso it's never a matter of chemicals,' Luc said. 'It's the eye.'

'Well, what is your eye telling you?' Mitchell asked.

'Right now? *Dora* looks good. But we've only just met. Can you leave her with me until the end of the week?'

'When do you mean? ' Marlo asked. 'Saturday?'

'Yes, if that's possible.'

'Not really,' Mitchell said. 'Not if you want my involvement. I'm due to be in Nice on Friday.'

'Then, it will have to be by tomorrow,' he said with a sigh. 'For a mysterious new Picasso - no problem.'

'Do you have a safe room?' Marlo asked.

'Look around you. Who would ever find it in this mess?' They all laughed, but Mitchell could see from the strain in Marlo's eyes that she believed she was risking everything.

23

August 19: Caussade, La Griffe

In the late afternoon, when the valleys had become etched in shadow and the high slopes had taken on a retreating, tawny glow, they drove out into the countryside to the West of Caussade. Didier was far too large for the seat of his old Renault 4L. His pig shooting van, he called it - his wife, Cécile, had taken his good Citroën for the day. Didier drove with his massive body hunched forward, embracing the wheel with his meaty forearms, squinting ahead through the mud-splattered windscreen like a man forever lost. The contorted posture meant that his emergency steering capacities were minimal. Eddie reflected that it probably didn't matter, since it also appeared the man's vision was impaired. Looming potholes and soft road edges seemed to escape his attention, and the poor suspension on the 4L made every bump feel like a kick to the coccyx. Eddie's attempts to warn him of road conditions ahead seemed like nervous back seat driving. He decided to shut up and enjoy the scenery.

The holdings were all small. The modest, grey limestone houses with their grimy tiled roofs all looked as though they belonged to local farmers. None of them appeared cosmetically renovated. Most of them had tired looking farm equipment stored beneath ugly, terra-cotta brick outbuildings.

The lower fields were given over to wheat, corn and recently emerged sunflowers. On the higher slopes, strips of clear plastic - which from a distance looked like cascading water - covered rows of young green melons. Forests of scrub oak covered the peaks of the ridges.

Eddie made the comment that the place looked fertile and amazingly productive, considering they had been working the land for centuries. Even more amazing when you compared it to Australia where it had only taken two hundred years to thoroughly root the landscape.

'What land?' Didier responded with a grunt. 'It's all fertilizer. They ever stop growing these crops, they end up with weeds the size of oak trees.'

'Anyway - it looks good from a speeding car.'

'Wait till you see this place of Jacques. Looks like shit. Ecological disaster zone.'

They came to a crude wooden signboard for Jacques' farm, La Griffe, and turned up a winding dirt road that led to a hidden fold in the hills. They had risen above the level of the mist, able to look out on the valley below as though they were skimming above a cloud.

Didier hadn't exaggerated. The place looked like a 747 had recently crash-landed in the back paddock. The approach was littered with broken down corroding cars and farm vehicles, some of them as old as the nineteen-forties. The house, a squat, single storied building of peasant construction, might have once been charming, but had sunk, through years of cheap patch-ups and unsympathetic additions, into a state of irreparable ugliness. The tiled roof was now half sheeted in rusty corrugated iron.

The old oak windows had been gutted and replaced with bland aluminium frames. Dirty green fibreglass covered the concrete patched traditional stone terrace.

A pack of scrawny hunting hounds, all of them the colour of milk chocolate, set up a mournful baying from their cage at the cold end of the house as Eddie and Didier climbed out of the 4L. At the same time, down at the Southern end of the building, a hundred or more outraged ducks began quacking a warning and beating their wings against the slimy earth of their stinking, overpopulated run. Didier knocked on the kitchen door a few times, and peered through one of the windows, but the place seemed deserted.

Eddie took a good look around. Spread out in every direction from the tragic dump of a house lay the evidence of years of neglect and blighted enterprise. There was the debris from unfinished building projects; yawning foundation excavations with adjoining heaps of yellow clay, limestone boulders, and broken tiles. Split bags of solidified concrete formed an unstable mountain near the driveway. Stacks of raw concrete breezeblocks, still on their pallets, were being slowly concealed by tall weeds and were already developing a skin of lichen. Melons were growing around the wheels of the rusted out remnants of a steam engine. There were dumps of empty oil drums and coloured plastic fertilizer canisters, a barn-sized stack of blue plastic animal feed protected from the weather by a few sheets of corrugated asbestos, an upended galvanized water tank, and hundreds of empty wine bottles stored in rotting crates.

'Nice place, huh?' Didier asked with a shit-eating grin.

'Christ, Didi,' was the best Eddie could summon in response. 'Where the fuck have you brought me?' He might have got back into the 4L if Didier at that moment hadn't slapped him on the arm and pointed at a building further down the hillside.

'I heard something down there,' he said.

They headed down a worn, stony pathway to a long, low concrete building that Didier jokingly called the *'maison de veux'*.

With its grey asbestos roof, its pig-pen sized shuttered windows, and its sinister row of hooded ventilators, it evoked for Eddie some notion of an administration wing of a concentration camp. As they descended, the breeze shifted, and with it came the stench of blood and bone.

A man peered around the far end of the building, disappeared for a moment, then reemerged to greet them with a blank stare. He was wearing a bloodstained leather apron and tall rubber rain boots over his blue jeans and dirty yellow T-shirt. A long knife, slicked with blood, hung slackly in his right hand. Skin the colour of dark honey, black stubble shaped in a goatee, lank black hair tied back in a ponytail - the man didn't look French to Eddie. More like some kind of Eastern European gypsy. It wasn't even apparent that the man recognized Didier. He just stood his ground, knife in hand, no plan to shake anyone's hand, an unreadable expression in his berry black eyes. Until he spoke, Eddie thought the man might even be mentally disturbed. He didn't know what was on Didier's mind, but he was ready to make a hasty retreat to the 4L.

'Bonjour, Jacques,' Didier offered, with all the caution of a man approaching a guard dog on a chain.

'Bonjour, Didier,' the man said slowly, mimicking Didier's tentative tone.

From the cautiousness of their embrace, it struck Eddie that they had not seen one another in a long while, and that possibly some bad shit had poisoned their relationship. Didier immediately began assailing the man with an impassioned monologue, a torrent of indecipherable French, which sounded to Eddie like some kind of apology. His frantic hand gestures were suggestive of a struggle to achieve credibility. Eddie followed the two men as they drifted down the slope, back to the end of the building where Jacques had first appeared. Not for an instant did Eddie take his eye off the man's knife.

The argument, or whatever it was, continued to the complete exclusion of Eddie. Didier was hardly allowing Jacques to get a word in. Sometimes it sounded like a father lecturing a son, at other moments it was like a man pleasing for forgiveness. All the while Jacques maintained a look of complete indifference. Eddie had no idea at all of what he had blundered into, but these didn't seem like the guys he needed to do business with.

As they reached the end of the building, Eddie saw the cause of the man's disturbing appearance. A flayed calf's carcass hung from a primitive iron gibbet. Blood still dripped from the mouth and nostrils and lay in dark pools on the concrete slaughter pad. The calf's milky brown hide had been hung over a low wire fence, and was now encrusted with blowflies. Didier turned to Eddie to offer an explanation.

'He found this one dead in there, this morning. Now he cuts him up for dog meat.'

While Didier and Jacques continued with their voluble negotiations, Eddie wandered through the entrance door and took a look into the vealery. In the gloomy light he could see the heads of hundreds of pale, docile, calves, each one chained into its cramped pen. The stench was overpowering. The calf on the gibbet was actually the lucky one.

By the time Eddie had satisfied his curiosity and walked outside again, Jacques had resumed his butchering of the carcass. Didier approached Eddie with an enthusiastic grin.

'Jacques - he like the deal. He need the money.' Didier lowered his voice and solemnly touched his breast. 'His wife, she got the cancer in here. For five thousand euros, he do whatever thing you want.'

'But can he shoot?' Eddie asked.

'Okay - I ask him. He will show you.'

Didier re-approached Jacques, who now had his back to his two visitors. There was a sudden flash of light as the knife blade caught the sun. In one swift downwards stroke Jacques had opened up the rib cage. A steaming mess of purple entrails flopped out onto the concrete. Didier leapt back as he saw his fawn corduroys receive a splash of blood. Jacques hacked away at the remaining yellow fat while he listened to Didier's request, then took a hard, appraising look at Eddie. After a while he nodded slowly. He spun the knife and embedded it in the carcass flank, wiped his bloody hands on the rump of his jeans, then strode off in the direction of his house.

Didier appeared relieved to see Jacques' co-operation.

'He's a strange fucker - but he show you he can shoot.'

'He's not a man for conversation.'

'What you mean?'

'He's got fuck all to say.'

'That's him. Same in French.'

'Yeah? Well you seemed to have a lot to say. What was the problem?'

'He wants to know who you are. Asks me how I know you. I have to tell him the stories. The old good days.'

'Yeah - the good old days. So, how's he going to know what I want him to do?'

Eddie looked in amusement at Didier, who took a few moments to compose his line of bullshit.

'Okay - he don't speak too much English, but he understands pretty good. You'll see - him and me, we work with American guys, DEA agents. No problems. Whatever you want him to do - you just talk slow, point. Jacques - he will get it.'

Several, minutes later, Jacques returned down the pathway. The bloody apron had been left behind. Now he was cradling a shotgun. Eddie saw that it was a German gun, a Krieghoff over-and-under, five thousand dollars worth. The front pockets of his jeans were crammed with red shells.

Jacques came up alongside them and took his time loading the shotgun. He looked out across the valley, squinting as though lining something up. Then, with the weapon halfway to his shoulder, he executed a slow three-sixty degree turn, his eyes focused on the horizon. Eddie and Didier shifted to keep clear of the line of fire. What in Christ's name was he planning to hit, Eddie wondered.

'Fifty metres away, a thrush had settled on the ridge line of the broken down barn, chortling its evening song clear out across the valley. Jacques raised the patterned stock of the shotgun to his shoulder.

'Une grive musicienne,' Didier whispered to Eddie. Both men holding their breaths.

The thrush was a mere dark speck of black, silhouetted against the failing light on the far hillside. Jacques only gave it the one barrel. There was nothing to see. The bird simply vanished from the ridgeline. The shot echoed back across the hills, died away, and then there was silence. Jacques gave Didier a satisfied smile and muttered something under his breath.

Didier reported the conversation to Eddie. 'He want to know if you need to see the feathers.'

It was raining heavily when Didier drove Eddie back down the A62 to Toulouse. Semi-trailers sprayed sheets of dirty water across their windscreen. The tired wipers scraped away the slush. Eddie's thoughts had turned dark. How far could he trust this dead-eyed cow-killer, Jacques? How far could he trust Didier, for that matter? Then there were the crazy logistics of breaking into McGraw's well-guarded *château* without provoking a lethal shoot-out or resorting to the cold-blooded approach.

But gnawing at him even more than these problems was his anxiety about Albert Laussier. It had been three days since he had left him trussed on that barn floor. How long before he would have been discovered? Or found some way to untie his tether and crawl away? It was a massive distraction to have Albert Laussier on his mind.

He took a late-night walk in the streets of Toulouse. The rain had abated to a mere drizzle, but still it soaked him completely. In a street behind the Place du Capitole he found an open Moroccan *supermarché,* where he bought a supply of packaged instant meals, as well as cereal, bread, milk and apples. If the old man was still alive, he'd have to feed him.

That same night, he drove back to La Serre. At the entrance to the farm, he switched off the engine and sat for several minutes, listening, with the windows rolled down. There was no traffic, hardly any night sounds, only the occasional hooting of an owl from across the valley. But soon he heard what he was hoping for: Albert Laussier's weak cries for help.

Eddie took a torch and the massive old key from the glove compartment, and walked up the slope to the barn. Once inside, he went straight to the pigpen, where he saw the writhing, ugly shape on the ground. The air smelled of shit and vomit. The old man was wild-eyed and muttering frantically. Eddie received a lashing boot in the shin.

Suddenly, the old man appeared to realize that this was no rescuer. Almost instantly, the energy drained from his limbs and his eyes went dead. He lay back stiffly, his teeth chattering involuntarily. He was expecting to be executed.

Eddie knelt beside the old man. The food had been mauled and the dog bowl of water overturned. He untied the rope and unlocked the handcuffs. The old man could barely move his arms without wincing in acute pain. His lips were dry and flecked with peeling skin. Without speaking, Eddie eased the old man onto his feet. His legs bowed beneath him. His knees wouldn't unlock. It took Eddie twenty minutes to get him moving in slow circles around the barn, the pair of them, stumbling like drunkards in the dark. Then he supported him for the slow, stumbling trek up to the house.

Eddie switched on all the lights and led the old man through to the primitive bathroom. While the old man rested on the rim of the tub, Eddie ignited the gas heater and got the shower flowing. In the confined space, the stink of old man's shit and piss stained trousers was nauseating.

'Undress,' Eddie said, miming the action by unbuttoning his own shirt.

When he'd seen enough of the old man's compliance, he withdrew to the door. *'Douchez,'* he commanded. Another useful term he had committed to memory. He wedged a chair in front of the bathroom door, then went in search of fresh clothing.

Later, in the filthy kitchen, he unpacked the food parcel, lit the gas stove, and began preparing a meal. When Albert Laussier was finally coaxed to the table, he couldn't hide his extreme hunger. He mopped up the entire plate of *confit de canard* and boiled potatoes, took two glasses of wine from one of his own bottles of *Fronton,* and ate a huge slice of apple tart, washed down with strong black coffee. The entire process had taken over an hour. It was almost midnight when Eddie trundled the old man back to the barn.

On this occasion, Eddie used some of the old man's supply of rope to tether him to the manger. (Eddie knew he still had need of his own 10mm climbing rope.) But after he had seen the old man's acute discomfort at being once again hog-tied on the floor, Eddie made another trip back to the house, and returned with a narrow mattress, a pillow, and two thin blankets. He didn't want the old man dying on him, unexpectedly.

After Eddie had been through the process of once again handcuffing and securing the old man to the manger, he set out the rest of the food and water within easy reach. It occurred to Eddie that they had been together for almost four hours and spoken no more than a few words. But what was he expecting? Gratitude? Honest resentment? Albert Laussier appeared to recognize the care that was being taken, but seemed to take it as a sign that he was going to be abandoned for an even longer period. He still seethed with hostility. Eddie laughed out loud at the absurdity of the peculiar concern that he felt for the old man. It was as though he had burdened himself with an injured dog. He wasn't surprised that his departure was met with the same stream of muttered abuse.

On the lonely drive back to Toulouse, Eddie tried to think through his next moves. The mercy dash had left him weary and shot his concentration completely. But at least he could put the old man out of mind for a while.

24

August 19: Le Métro

Luc offered to call Marlo a taxi, but she protested, claiming to prefer the *métro*. Mitchell knew it couldn't possibly have been a matter of money. Perhaps she feared it would entail sharing the ride with him. Etiquette would require that she was dropped off first, creating the risk that he would learn too much about the location of her apartment.

After arranging to return on the following Saturday, she bade them both a hasty goodbye.

Mitchell watched her from Luc's balcony as she scurried down the hill in the direction of the Place des Abbesses. She was intensely watchful, hardly daring to cross the street without scrutinizing every person and automobile in her vicinity. Luc joined him in observing her cautious departure.

'Vous l'aimez?' Luc asked, reverting briefly to French, with a knowingly raised eyebrow.

'Peut-être,' was all Mitchell could say for certain. *'Mais je suis curieux.'*

Mitchell waited until Marlo had rounded the corner into the rue Yvonne Le Tac before making a move. He had to be absolutely certain of her direction. And in order to follow her into the *métro* unseen, he needed to allow her a head start.

'I'm off, too,' he said, and placing an arm across Luc's shoulder, he led him to the door. 'I just wanted to see which way she was going.'

'Naturellement,' Luc replied. His insinuating smile was totally amicable.

Mitchell headed straight for the entrance of the Métro Abbesses, and descended the steps beneath the glass art nouveau awning. He bought a single ticket and waited for the lift that would take him down to the platforms. Fortunately, he was joining a small crowd: a party of young English tourists; an aloof Parisian woman with a perfectly groomed St. Bernard on a leash; and several harried looking office workers obviously returning home from a long day's work. The English kids were rattling on in cynical terms about the absurdly large contingent of portrait artists they had encountered up in the Place du Tertre. There was an outbreak of raucous, uncontrolled laughter. The St. Bernard's ears pricked up and it emitted a low warning growl, requiring the woman to tauten the leash. The French workers exchanged sardonic glances. *Idiot tourists.* And then the lift arrived, with a loud, sustained buzz and a flashing red light.

As he stepped inside, Mitchell calculated that Marlo had a three minute lead on him. Most likely, she had already caught a train. There were only two possible directions she could have taken: north towards Porte de la Chapelle, or south towards Mairie d'Issy. From what he knew of Marlo, he guessed she would be staying somewhere in the heart of the city, and so he gambled on the Mairie d'Issy platform.

The moment of emerging from the access tunnel onto the

platform was crucial. If she feared being followed, she would probably be watching each new passenger's arrival, with her escape already planned. As a precaution, he stayed out of sight just inside the tunnel exit and studied the *métro* map on the wall. He wanted to quickly memorize the names of all the stations on the line, at the same time trying to estimate which of them would be her most likely destination. Pigalle. St-Georges. Notre Dame de Lorette. Trinite d'Estienne d'Orves. St-Lazare. Madeleine. Concorde. Assemblée Nationale. Solférino. Rue de Bac. Sèvres Babylone. It was a fairly hopeless task. She could even change lines at the next stop, Pigalle, but he had to hope that she wouldn't. He needed sufficient time to locate her on the train before she disembarked. Her next opportunity to change lines would be St-Lazare - a nightmarish proposition, since it connected with at least three other *métro* lines; and then again at Madeleine and Concorde. The only hopeful clue in the entire enterprise lay in the little he knew of Marlo's taste. It was reasonable to suppose that she would choose to stay somewhere on the Left Bank, most probably in the Seventh. That would mean she would be getting out somewhere between Solférino and Notre-Dame-des-Champs.

And why exactly was he following her? To impress upon her the seriousness of his unlikely commitment to her cause? To see whether the little she had told him already about herself was indeed true? To confront her alone in the hope that when pressed she might divulge a little more of her crazy story? Or simply to satisfy a growing curiosity? The stirring of desire? He had to admit that all of his motives were abstract and unplanned. But he couldn't simply turn away and allow her to vanish once again.

The train arrived in less than a minute. Good. It meant that she couldn't have caught anything earlier. Mitchell had no choice but to board the first carriage. Advancing further along the platform would have entailed the risk of encountering her.

The carriage was moderately crowded - only one or two

single seats remained unoccupied. But he decided it was wiser to stay on his feet. It meant that he could be more easily noticed, but it was also the only possible way he could see further along the compartment.

A trio of musicians - an accordionist, a double bassist, and a guitarist - had set up halfway along the carriage. Although they were only in their twenties, they were dressed like fifties bohemians: all were wearing shabby plaid sports coats and pork pie hats. They launched into a version of an old Jacques Brel song. Mitchell couldn't recall its name, nor a single word of the lyric, but heard this way on a plangent accordion, accompanied by the rattle of the carriage and the indefinable smell of the underground, it instantly summoned up for him a half forgotten Paris. It was a performance for the tourists. The Parisians barely lifted their heads from their newspapers or stirred from their sombre staring ahead.

With as little movement as possible he surveyed the passengers and soon satisfied himself that Marlo wasn't among them.

When the train pulled into Pigalle, he ignored the plastic cup proffered by one of the musicians and joined the push towards the platform.

His plan was to head for the rear of the train and then work his way forward in search for Marlo. In all likelihood she would be facing in the direction of travel. He had barely thirty seconds to reach the end carriage, but he couldn't risk drawing attention to himself by running. The train had already begun to pull away as he drew level with the rear door of the second last carriage. There already seemed to be far too much momentum for him to attempt to leap aboard. For an instant he considered abandoning the pursuit. Forget her. He had blown it. Then, on a reckless impulse, he struck upwards at the chrome door handle. It was a futile gesture. The doors were supposed to lock once the train was in motion. But this one was faulty. Miraculously, the handle moved and the doors sprang apart. The risky leap was tantalizing, but he could barely keep abreast of the narrow opening. There was barely a second in which he could either make the terrifying jump or give up altogether. Without thinking, he accelerated his stride, committed a handhold, and took the leap. There were gasps of condemnation as his body weight connected with a few standing passengers. What kind of fool takes risks to catch a *métro* train? One waits five minutes - there's always another.

He spent some time supporting his weight against a chrome overhead pole, regaining his breath and his composure, before taking a good look around. If Marlo was anywhere nearby she would most certainly have witnessed his disruptive arrival. But knowing there was no point in worrying - all that mattered now was finding her - he pressed on through the carriage.

What exactly had she been wearing? Jeans and a plain white T-shirt. As far as he could recall she had arrived without a jacket or pullover, but he may have overlooked something. Her new spiky haircut, however, was unmistakable - unless she had brought a beret or some other small item of head wear.

There was no one in the carriage even remotely like her, and so he moved on up the train, struggling through the connecting doors as it negotiated a steep upward curve.

It was in the second to last carriage that he found her. She was sitting alone, facing ahead, resting her face against one arm, like a traveller submitting to a long and tedious journey. Mitchell took a window seat five rows behind her. She would need to turn around completely in order to see him. They passed Notre-Dame de Lorette, Trinité, St. Lazare and Madeleine. At each stop she barely moved from her place alongside the window, but from the slightest movements of her head, he could detect that she was carefully checking the movements of every new departing and arriving passenger.

But at Concorde, she stood abruptly. Mitchell barely had time to sink low in his seat, avert his head, and partially conceal his face with his hand. He didn't look up again until the train had come to a complete halt. By then she was at the door, anxiously preparing to alight.

Two other lines connected at Concorde. Was she leaving the *métro* or changing trains? It was essential to stay in close proximity to her from this point on.

He shadowed her in the maze of correspondence tunnels, sticking as close as he dared, without risking discovery. But the further they went, the more difficult this became. There were barely enough commuters to conceal his presence. His technique became one of hanging back until he had seen her take a definite direction, and then plunging on as rapidly as possible to make up the lost ground. The only factor in his favour, the thing that he was absolutely counting upon, was that his was probably the last face she was expecting to encounter.

And then he saw that she was once again heading towards the Porte de Clignacourt - Mairie d'Issy line. She hesitated for a moment at the juncture of the two tunnels, looked back furtively - at that stage Mitchell was fifty metres away, concealed by at least a dozen commuters - and then darted away. It hardly surprised him that she was once again taking the direction, Mairie d'Issy. The fact that she had broken her journey in this elaborate way was a measure of her extreme unease.

For a brief moment he caught himself forgetting his mission and losing himself in admiration. At full stride, she had the most elegant carriage of any woman he had ever seen. Held erect by some strong, invisible cord, was how it seemed. Even under stress, as she certainly was now, she moved with a mesmerizing grace. She was intrepid and amazingly self possessed in a way that stuck him as uniquely American. She might not have been who she claimed to be, but in the role she had created for herself - or for him - she was endlessly intriguing. If it was a mere performance, it held him completely. Maybe like some actresses he had known, it was possible that her true self was disappointingly dull and unformed, and that only through playing a role could she construct for herself a commanding and complex personality. If that were the case with Marlo, he didn't entirely mind. All he wanted was the opportunity to know more about her - whoever she was.

He followed her down onto the platform, anticipating the same difficulties as before. But on this occasion things were much simpler. The tunnel had delivered them to the rear end of the platform, and once again Marlo had walked towards the mid-point. This meant that when the train arrived Mitchell was able to board the carriage behind hers without any subterfuge. Once they were underway, he walked through to her carriage and took a seat some distance behind her.

Almost as he had predicted, she stood up as they approached Sèvres Babylone and walked to the door. When the train came to a stop she appeared to panic. She leapt from the compartment, and took off at a furious walking pace. Mitchell had to scramble and shove rudely past a group of passengers in order not to lose sight of her.

When she emerged from the *métro* she entered the small park opposite the Bon Marché department store. Mitchell hovered at the head of the *métro* steps long enough to see her pause at a bus shelter. She appeared to be carefully surveying the street before continuing on her way. He worried that there were too few commuters to conceal his presence, so he backed down the stairs a little way.

Moments later, he risked re-emerging, and saw, to his horror, that she had vanished. He scanned the surrounding streets. No sign of her. If he stayed half concealed in the *métro* entrance he might lose her altogether. He had to get out on the street and search. His only strategy was to take a rapid circumnavigation of the streets bordering the park. He set off at a brisk jog, dodging and weaving around the occasional pedestrian, all the while keeping his eyes fixed on the streets leading away from the park. To the people in the rue Velpeau and the rue de Babylone he must have looked like a frantic father in search of his lost child.

Then, to his immense relief, he caught a glimpse of her on the far side of the rue de Sèvres. She was heading along one of the side streets in the direction of the rue de Rennes. He made a reckless of crossing of the rue de Sèvres and followed her along the rue Saint Placide, keeping to the opposite side of the street. It was crucial to keep her in sight from this point on. At any moment she might round a corner and disappear unseen into an apartment building. When at last she turned into a laneway leading, he presumed, to a small courtyard, he made the decision to approach.

The forlorn little courtyard was empty, except for an old grey Renault van and an Italian motor scooter. A fat ginger cat kept its distance, watching from behind the iron railing of a stone staircase. Mitchell found Marlo, keys in hand, at the entrance door to a series of apartments. Her back was towards him, and she was preoccupied in her struggle with a complicated old lock. When she turned at the sound of his tread, her features were frozen in shock .

'What are you doing here?' she demanded.

'I needed to see you again...there was no other way.'

'How did you follow me?'

'With great difficulty. You were very careful.'

'I don't like being stalked,' she said coldly. 'I told you I was being watched. But I didn't ask you to protect me.'

'I suppose I could have called out to you in the street. But you might have fled.'

It was a lame explanation and he could see that she didn't believe him. 'What do you really want to talk about?'

'Should we go to a cafe?'

'No. I feel safer here. It's better we go inside.'

'I presume this is your apartment.'

'My borrowed apartment,' she said with defiance. 'You don't trust me at all, do you?'

'Should we go inside?'

Marlo nodded. She knew he was owed an explanation.

He observed her, fascinated, as she returned to her struggle with the lock. Her confusion about the correct sequence of keys added to his sense that she was perhaps even lying about the apartment. But after another minute of key thrusting and door rattling, all to the accompaniment of a reassuring stream of American cursing, the locks surrendered.

25

August 19: The Seventh

She led him up a dimly lit austere staircase to a shabby door on the third storey.

'Is this your apartment?' Mitchell asked, while Marlo faltered with another unfamiliar lock.

'My older sister, Ashley, owns it. She worked for Air France in New York for a long time. Now she's married to a very successful IT executive. She has two kids. Lives out in San Francisco. But she still somehow manages to come to Paris twice a year.'

She pushed open the door and invited him inside.

'It's nothing special, just a bolthole in Paris. At least that's what she calls it.'

There was even less to the apartment than he had expected. It could be seen in its entirety from the pokey foyer: a compact living-dining area with a view of the street below and apartments opposite; a narrow kitchen nook hung with the kinds of expensive copper plated cooking pans owned by serious chefs; and a petite bedroom, oppressively wallpapered in a mauve and blue love-bird motif, suitable only for one. He imagined that the closed door concealed an impossible bathroom. It was furnished throughout like a set for an Audrey Hepburn romance from the late fifties. None of the furniture looked quite fit for normal use. The sofa, the chairs, the bed, all looked chic, but insubstantial.

Marlo had barely occupied the apartment. She claimed she had only been in Paris a day or two, but there was little evidence that she had ever moved in. Unlike her previous bedroom, this one was pristine. The bed was fastidiously made. There was nothing on the floor. No luggage. The kitchen looked as though it had never been used. There were no dishes in the sink. No food. Not even a comforting purr from the tiny refrigerator. The cushions in the living room looked undisturbed. And there were no newspapers or clutter of any kind on the dining table. In the few moments it took for him to take it all in, his confidence in her evaporated once again.

They locked the door behind them and entered the shadowy apartment. The summer day had been left behind in the courtyard. It was almost chilly in those claustrophobic rooms.

'Are you going to be staying here long?' he asked. It was a provocative, almost facetious question.

'That depends.'

'On what Luc makes of your Picasso?'

'Yes - I suppose.'

'And then where will you go?'

'I'd rather not say.'

'I know you'd rather not say, but I think it's unreasonable of you not to trust me. You already know enough about me.'

'Mitchell - I'm married to Mike McGraw, remember? I operate on the assumption that everyone's after something and everyone's secretive. It seems to work for me.'

'Like nothing else?'

'Like nothing I've discovered.'

They were both standing in the austere living room. Marlo had become edgy and defensive. She had her arms folded tightly against her body, as though the cold had already penetrated her. He stood before her, wanting to engage her, but feeling at a loss, and occasionally looking beyond her to the bleak row of curtained windows of the apartments opposite.

When he finally took an impulsive step towards her and enfolded her in his arms, it shook him as much as her.

'Of course I trust you,' she said, almost breathless. 'I just don't know how to get off this path I'm on.'

Somehow, in the rush of emotion, the question of whether she was the actual Marlo McGraw had been brushed aside. In time he might know the answer. Something extraordinary might happen to reveal the truth. But until then, he would take her as he found her.

He drew back a little, just far enough to see her face up close. Her eyes were glistening and seemed larger. The whites were reddened with emotion. He hesitated before her, as though wanting some sign. Something she couldn't quite give. Until she saw that he was frozen. And out of need she pressed her fingers hard against his back. He calmed, and pressed his lips against hers. The warmth of her skin, her hot breath, overwhelmed him.

They clung together through a succession of hungry kisses, moving in a slow dance, unaware of their surroundings. He unsnapped her jeans and slid his hands inside her pants, feeling the smooth curves of her bottom. She wrapped her arms around him, drawing his chest against her breasts. And then found his cock, held it through the layers of clothing. He was stupefied, clotted with desire. Lost in the moment, until suddenly, she collided with one of the copper pans hanging near the kitchen entrance. She abruptly pulled away from him, nursing her head, laughing at the absurdity of the interruption.

He took her in his arms again and supported her weight with his back propped against the kitchen bench. Both of them, breathless from their body heat and dizzy with arousal. She grappled with his belt buckle and unfastened his chinos, then tugged at his shirt-tails until they were free. With comic coordination, he dragged down her jeans and pants until they were bunched above her knees, while she slid his trousers over his arse and let them fall to his shoes. At first her hands were cold against his skin. And then her fingers felt electric as they touched his cock. He wanted to arouse her, too, but she was too impatient for experimental touching. Instead, she guided him inside her.

In that strangely forlorn kitchen they fucked where they stood. He might have prolonged the encounter, but she gave him no opportunity. The sudden abandonment of mistrust and suspicion had made them reckless, heedless of anything beyond the immediate rush of pleasure. He slid down against the bench until he could feel the deepest possible fit of their bodies. With every movement into one another, a small sigh escaped Marlo's lips. Her eyes stayed unfocussed. She was lost inside her own experience.

In the moment of coming, he held her head with both hands and spoke her name aloud. Afterwards he felt remorseful. He knew that she hadn't made it, and she uttered a soft anguished moan at the discovery of his diminishing cock. As he withdrew, he wanted to arouse her in an unspecific, apologetic way, but she gently brushed his hand away.

'Too late,' she said, already recovered from her sharp mood, 'I couldn't keep up.'

'Sorry - wasn't thinking.'

'Not exactly a situation requiring thought, I suppose,' she said with a rueful smile.

Their fucking had filled him with an extraordinary calm, but as the pleasure receded he had become aware of his own peculiar remoteness from the experience. He felt selfish, private, enclosed.

'My God - no condom either,' he said with slow dawning.

'My fault, too,' she said. 'We just went a bit wild.'

'I'm truly sorry. You aren't concerned?'

'Forget it, please. I take the pill, and I'm sure you're safe and sound. And hasn't everything between us has been a bit like this?'

'You mean - we have to trust one another now?'

'Something like that.'

'Then, yes - I trust you, and I trust your story.'

'Liar,' she said, giving him a playful jab in the ribs.

'I don't have an honest Australian face? Is that what you're telling me?'

'But you have a nice cock.'

She kissed him on the mouth. When at length they parted, she pointed in the direction of the bathroom.

'Let's go in there,' she said. We could take a long hot bath together and start this all over again. Slowly.'

Hobbled at the feet and knees by their underwear and trousers, and laughing all the way, they shuffled their way out of the kitchen. 'It's the best room in the house, 'she said, 'with a beautiful bathtub - made for fucking.'

A *frou-frou* monstrosity was how he might have described it. Tiles of a nauseating violet hue, with a border pattern of *fleur-de-lis*. A gilt framed mirror, supported in each corner by smiling gold cupids. Candy pink porcelain basin and bath. Rococo gold taps with spouts like gaping frogs. Baskets of dried herbs. Hand made soaps from Provence. Arrays of expensive oils and body lotions. Mitchell was afraid that running a bath might trash the place. He hung back in the doorway to watch.

Marlo turned the hot tap on fully. A jet of water gushed from the frog's mouth. A few moments and it was steamy. She stepped out of her jeans and draped them across a twee, wicker clothesbasket. Down to her T-shirt alone, she drew Mitchell into the room. He discarded the rest of his clothing and joined her, balanced in an embrace on the slats of the wooden drainage board. Like a bird about to take flight, she made open wings of her T-shirt and fluttered it over her head. Something made her turn away to unclasp and discard her skimpy black push-up bra. Perhaps she was afraid of the moment of comparison, when he would discover that her breasts were not quite so full, not as well postured as the bra had proclaimed. She need not have worried. When she turned back, he couldn't disguise the rapture of this intimacy. He saw that her breasts were the same even tan as her throat. She had spent the summer sunbathing. That was her life. He kissed her nipples in turn, closed his lips over them until he felt them harden. Her hands were around his neck, clinging. There was the danger that they might fall from their raft and end up barefoot on the cold floor tiles. He held her to him and felt his quiescent cock brush against the soft curls of her pubic hair. It would need to be a long bath if he wasn't to disappoint her again.

The bathroom rapidly steamed up. Even the pretentious mirror - in which he could see a ghostly sliver of her back. her skin, beautiful as an Ingres nude - had been transformed. It too was playing its part in making the room miraculous. While she tested the water, he ran his hands from the curves of her bottom, up her spine, all the way to her goose-dimpled shoulders, then pressed his body against hers.

'No, no,' she said. 'First we must set sail.' It made him laugh. Both their minds were swimming in childhood bathroom fantasies.

The water was far hotter than she had planned, but they both ventured in, cautiously willing their bodies below the surface, grimacing and laughing at the tentativeness of their moves.

Fascinated, he watched her golden brown pubic hair, as it turned suddenly ebony, then drifted like fine seaweed beneath the distorting surface of the choppy bath water.

Marlo groaned with the pleasure of it all.

'Turn around,' he said. 'I want to wash your back.'

She did as she was ordered. In the clumsy process, the warm red moons of her bottom were suddenly in his vision. He leaned forward, and kissed her steamy, puckered skin. When she settled back into the water, he eased his thighs around hers. He wanted to keep her warm, to protect her, to stay with her as long as she needed him. It was almost enough to feel his cock resting against her spine. She must have known it was too soon for him to be making love again, but everything told him she craved the simple intimacy as much as he did.

He took the pristine cube of lavender soap from its ledge, soaked it, then slowly and tenderly began to lather her shoulders.

'Was this your plan all along?' she asked, almost purring. 'Was this why you were stalking me?'

'No - I don't think so. I may have fantasized about it, but only for a moment.'

'That sounds like an admission.'

'All right. Perhaps it was an unconscious plan.'

'A plan, huh? And when do you think this plan took shape? When you met me at the Colombe d'Or? When I showed you my bedroom in Vence?'

'I think you can imagine when.'

'The bedroom?'

'That may well have planted the seed.'

'What did it, exactly?'

'Just the unmade bed, I think. It seemed to tell the whole story. I could imagine you in it. Then after a while, I could imagine me in it. I think that was it. Until I saw you again, today.'

'On your doorstep, like a lost dog?'

'No - later, when you were running away from me. Like a woman in fear of her life.'

He continued soaping her back, from the water level to the nape of her long neck. And then he scooped water in his hand and rinsed the suds away. Daylight from the tiny bathroom window turned her glistening skin phosphorescent. She half turned towards him to receive his kiss. As though by invitation, he slid his hands beneath her armpits and sought the soft slopes of her breasts. Soon her breaths changed to quick sighs of contentment.

Before surrendering completely, she reached out and chose a body oil from among the dozen or do products arrayed along the bath ledge. After filling the valley of her palm, she submerged her hand in search of his dormant cock.

'So - it isn't possible to stay hard underwater?'

'Technically, yes. But only if the water is hotter than thirty degrees.'

'How can we be sure we'll stay hot enough?'

'We can't. It's a huge risk.'

'Should we go ashore? Find some warm beach to lie on?'

'You have an appropriate setting in mind?'

'There is the little bed.'

'The Goldilocks suite?'

'Mm.'

'You're sure we wouldn't break it?'

'We're not anticipating any frantic moves, are we?'

'Course not. So - should we take along some of these essential oils?'

'I'll dry you off.'

'No, please - allow me first.'

They hauled themselves reluctantly from the bath. Standing face to face, they towelled one another in turn. A mutual tenderness, a patient care in seeking out and drying every fold of skin, became their substitute for foreplay. When finally she led him into the bedroom, he was hard for her again.

They lay together for a long time, touching and kissing, luxuriating in the radiant warmth of their perfumed bodies. When finally they progressed to fucking there was no frantic rush, no isolating otherness. With open eyes they drank in one another's pleasure. Afterwards, they slept enfolded. Marlo was the first to stir.

'We'd better make a move.'

'Why? I thought you'd only feel safe right here.'

'I don't know. Aren't you hungry?'

'A little.'

'Well then, let's dress and go out. I know a good place nearby.'

It was late when they left the apartment. Hurrying through the streets of Saint-Germain in the direction of the Jardin du Luxembourg, they hardly cared whether or not they were under observation. Their newly entered intimacy gave them the illusion of protection. But Marlo had taken the precaution of disguising herself with lightly-tinted sunglasses and a shapeless felt hat that completely concealed her hair.

The restaurant she took him to was a cheap, popular eatery specializing in the cuisine of old Burgundy. The patron wasn't sure whether his kitchen was still serving. He directed them to the smoky bar while he found out. It wasn't exactly what either of them had planned. There was something irritating about propping up a bar when one was ravenous, particularly after making love with a virtual stranger for the first time. The plangent harmonies of Simon and Garfunkel, issuing from a pair of tinny speakers above the bar, weren't helping. The barman suggested martinis. Marlo liked hers very dry. But when they landed, Mitchell found them to be more George Lazenby than Sean Connery.

Mitchell took a good look around. The decor was amusingly rustic, a tacky attempt to evoke rural France circa 1850. The dining room furniture was all dark, rickety, worm-eaten oak. The rubble-stone walls were crowded with primitive farm implements: hand-forged rake heads; menacingly curved hay forks; oddly elongated spades. All of them rust-eaten and coated in a gravy-coloured glaze. Suspended from the ceiling beams were various hanging baskets, cast iron scales, a wooden bullock's yoke, and a massive blacksmith's bellows.

'Another tragic little museum of rural poverty,' Mitchell commented in the patron's presence, tactlessly assuming a lack of English.

'Yes, yes - but we're here for the food, aren't we?' Marlo said.

'So long as it's not as authentic as that stuff threatening to fall on us.'

They sat with their Martinis for ten minutes, waiting for the patron to stir up his chefs. Marlo talked about the places she loved to visit in Paris: several bars she adored; a favourite club that was never boring; and three or four museums and walks she never tired of revisiting. But the effect of the conversation on Mitchell was to place her at an even greater distance. He soon fell into an introspective silence. Their intimacy had come about as a consequence of the strain of dishonesty on their relationship. It was more a breaking down of a barrier than a genuine coming together. He wondered how long it would be before their old contract would be invoked. She must have seen that he was already mourning the loss of their afternoon together, must have also realized that it was over and unrepeatable and that it was time to resume their true business together.

Unlike Mitchell, Marlo wasn't sentimental. She opened her bag and took out a worn leather bound Filofax. From between its bulging pages she extracted a torn column of newsprint.

'Here - have you seen this?' she asked, handing it to him.

Mitchell read it hastily. It was a story from the *Australian,* dated two days earlier, written under the byline of Ilena Vadas. In essence it was no more than a piece of self-promotion. She had written in sketchy terms about her planned documentary on McGraw, promising revelations about his *'secret horde of art'* as well as interviews with *'the hunters'*. Mitchell couldn't believe that Ilena had written this overheated prose herself. He also saw that his own name was included under the absurd sobriquet *'Australian art expert'*. He was described as a man *'close to the chase'*. There was even a vague, disingenuous reference to *'a major twentieth century masterpiece - believed to be a Picasso - which may prove to have been missing since WWII.'* If the piece hadn't been under Ilena's name, it would have made him laugh. But whether Ilena had written it herself was not the issue. She was clearly implicated. Most likely she had initiated it. The conclusion hit him like a betrayal.

'My God. How did you come to stumble on this?'

'A habit I picked up from Mike. Wherever he was in the world, he consulted all the important Australian dailies online. You can understand why, I'm sure. Me – I'm constantly searching on Google for news of any new Picasso sales.'

'Why did you want me to see this? You think I've been untrustworthy? Disclosing your business to the press?'

Marlo shrugged, gave him one of her feline smiles from the other side of her Martini.

'No, I thought it might help your to see why I'm scared of being followed.'

'How?'

'Have you heard of a man called Leon Meyer?'

'Vaguely. Partner of you husband's, isn't he?'

'Was. He's an American. A guy in his mid-fifties. He ran the New York branch of McGraw Securities. This was all before my time, you understand. I've only met him once. Well, when the panic hit and a horde of investors called for their money that was no longer there, Leon went to ground, same as Mike. Now they're both wanted men. But I suspect Leon has done a deal with the U.S. authorities.

'Betrayed your husband, you mean?'

'I think so.'

'Is he in France, too? Looking to get his hands on your husband's assets?'

'Possibly. I don't know what he's up to.'

'Maybe the French woods aren't going to be big enough to hide two outlaws.'

'We'll see.'

'So does Leon have some claim on Mike's art collection?'

'I'm sure he's bitter enough to think he deserves half.'

'What about your Picasso?'

'That, too.'

'He knows you've got it?'

'Of course. Leon knew all about Mike's art collection. He should have - he helped Mike to put it all together.'

'Do you mean he had some knowledge about art?'

'He'd certainly been around it. Back in the mid-eighties, Leon had been an attorney to a lot of New York artists. Not the biggest reputations. Not Julian Schnabel, or anyone too famous, but he did have some real names on his client list. Significant figures.'

'So he'd probably know exactly what do with your Picasso - if he ever got his hands on it.'

'Sure, he'd certainly know how to unload it for a big figure and no fuss.'

'Do you think he was the one who helped Mike to buy it in the first place? Was he that involved?'

'Most probably. But then, I couldn't be sure.'

'Then, in that case, he might already have his hands on the authenticating documents that you still seem to be missing.'

At the reference to the authenticating documents Marlo's face suddenly flushed, as though it was something she had been hoping would never come up again.

'Yes –I suppose that's possible, too.'

'Was he acting alone? I mean, presumably he was a part of some kind of organization.' Mitchell was thinking of the thugs who had abducted him in Nice.

'Mike never talked to me about Leon's operation.'

'You don't think maybe Leon Meyer is the man behind whoever is stalking you?'

'Obviously, he could be. But I don't have any idea.'

Mitchell sat for a while staring into his Martini. The barman changed the CD: now it was the piercing uplift of Céline Dion, played low, but till soaring above the clamour of conversation in the restaurant.

When, at last, they were shown to a table they were seated alongside an obviously drunk pair, who had long ago finished their meal and were now lost in a fug of cognac and cigarettes (the smoking ban apparently not being enforced after midnight).

Mitchell and Marlo lapsed into a gloomy silence. In spite of their flirtation with intimacy, they had not been honest with one another. It was as though each revelation, each admission, had been offered in expediency, to explain away a lie. Hers, a misrepresentation of the truly enshrouded and compromised dealings surrounding the Picasso. His, a concealment of the profound doubts he felt about the woman sitting opposite, in the light of his dealings with the 'other' Marlo and Ilena Vadas.

The menu was as uncompromisingly authentic as the décor. They went for the obvious, *boeuf bourguignon,* and accompanied it all with a bottle of '98 Volnay.

'My plan hasn't changed,' he said. 'I have to be in Provence on Friday.'

'Is this work you're doing for the Musée?'

'In a way – yeah,' he lied.

But she didn't take it up – as though her thoughts, too, were now elsewhere.

He couldn't contemplate the futility of trying to sustain, or even fathom, whatever had happened between them. He needed a little time and distance. Then, if it were to happen all over again - wonderful - but he wasn't about to push his luck. He briefly considered telling her a little of his true reason for traveling south, but had no idea of where to begin. There had already been too many omissions. It would now all seem like gross disloyalty and double dealing – which, to an extent, it was. The irony of having the documentary's true subject, sitting opposite, was too crazy to contemplate. Marlo had possession of the painting, and she knew McGraw better that anyone, yet he couldn't possibly bear to expose her.

It was almost one in the morning when he walked her back to her apartment. The streets they entered were eerily empty.

They kissed in the shadowy courtyard, clinging to one another like lovers anticipating a long separation. There was a moment when Mitchell might have gone upstairs with her again. Both of them, perhaps wanting it with equal urgency, but neither having the conviction to press for an outcome.

'You have to telephone me on Saturday morning from Provence,' she said. 'We have to talk about my painting. Luc said he'd have something to tell us by tomorrow.'

'Of course I will.'

'I'll be here in the evening after eight.'

'And after that?' It was the wrong question. He knew it was more than she would be prepared to disclose.

'Perhaps Luc and I will be in business - trying to find a buyer here or in London.'

'That would be something,' he said, wondering what his empty encouragement meant to her.

It was the kind of weak ending he had dreaded. Letting her slip away again with no commitment. Mitchell watched her mount the stone steps to her apartment, only a silhouette now. And then he saw her suddenly step backwards in alarm. She called out to him, urgently. He sprinted up the stairs, rushing to her aid.

'What is it?'

'Someone's broken in.'

He edged to one side and cautiously pushed open the door. She stood at his shoulder and pointed out the switch.

When the lights sprang on they revealed an apartment in complete disarray. Cupboards had been flung open and their contents strewn across the floor; sheets and blankets had been torn from the bed; Marlo's luggage had been ransacked and scattered.

Mitchell listened for almost a minute, then entered the apartment. He checked all possible hiding places to ensure that no one was waiting in ambush.

Marlo was still trembling. For a while, she sought comfort on his shoulder.

'Thank God the picture wasn't here,' he said.

A haunted look came over her. 'I have to leave – right now,' she said, in a fragile voice. With robotic determination, she went into action, gathering up her clothes and personal items, and heaping them onto the mattress alongside her suitcase. 'Please – can you telephone a taxi,' she said, as though speaking to a stranger. 'You have a card in your wallet, don't you?'

He did as she instructed, while Marlo hastily sorted and packed her belongings.

'Where shall I say you want to go?'

She gave him the name of an international hotel at Charles de Gaulle.

'And after that?'

She looked at him blankly. 'Until I collect my painting, I have no plan. Surely you can understand.'

Mitchell put in the call to the taxi company.

'What's the address here?' he asked her.

She hesitated at its unfamiliarity, and needed to consult the Filofax in her handbag.

Mitchell gave the operator the details, and was told that the taxi would arrive within thirty minutes.

'Will you wait for me until it arrives?'

'Of course.'

Later, when she had closed her suitcase, she surveyed the chaos of the overturned apartment. He saw that she had attained an icy detachment. Her mind was already moving ahead of events. Once again she was lost to him.

26

August 20 - 21: The Gorge de l'Aveyron

The three men met again at Jacques' vealery. Didier proposed they all have lunch at the Café du Commerce in a small village outside Caussade. A chance for Eddie observe the man a little, ease the tension, was how Didier put. By twelve-thirty they were sitting around an outdoor table with a *pichet* of red wine and plates of *bifteck et pommes frites*, settling the deal.

Didier told stories about Jacques' exploits in Marseille. He was talking them up, embellishing as if his life depended on it - that's how it seemed to Eddie. But if even half of them were true, Jacques just might be the perfect man for the job.

Didier claimed Jacques had worked undercover on the docks, posing as a cashed up local criminal, all the while keeping track of the trade in hash and heroin. The man was so convincing he had been mistakenly arrested three times by their American

DEA partners. The narcotics department in Marseille had given him a budget of ten million francs to negotiate deals with major importers. Jacques - calling himself Serge in those days - had been flown to palaces and resorts all over North Africa, to fraternize with crooked sheiks and the princes of the Arab underworld. There was nothing they wouldn't do for the man - women, imported cars, anything at all, so long as the Koran didn't rule it out. For two years he had played their man in Marseille and gotten away with it. But then, for reasons neither Didier nor Jacques cared to explain, the police department had lost faith in his integrity. They claimed too much of the money had gone missing. But then - like Didier said - what was the money for if not to spend on illegal drugs? Rivalry - that's all it was. Greed and rivalry. Someone always shows up, gets a sniff, and wants a cut. Finally, it all went south. There was a departmental inquiry, and soon after Jacques was dishonorably relieved of his duties. Now he was out in the wilderness, getting his agricultural subsidy, same as all the other peasants, living like a hermit on a broken down farm, trying to scratch some kind of living out of vealers. Was he bitter? Maybe. Like any man who had once been sitting on top of the heap, it hurt to look back up. *'Passer éponger,'* was the expression Didier used. Forget the past. Eddie had remembered that one, he liked the sound of it, tried it out loud himself.

Didier leaned over and draped his fat arm across Jacques' shoulder. He told Eddie he was looking at the most philosophical man he'd ever meet. See - he was telling Eddie. That's what the long silences were about.

With Didier translating - saying Christ knows what - Eddie described his plan to snatch McGraw's paintings. He made it all sound as simple as he could; made Jacques' part in the scheme sound like a breeze. A little shooting from a safe distance. Pack up your weapon and go home. Forget you ever saw a thing. Couldn't be easier. Jacques maintained an air of insouciance and nodded his assent to everything he was asked, but Eddie had no idea how much was going in. Five thousand euros, a neat little stack of notes, was probably all Jacques was seeing.

The following day, Eddie took Jacques for a drive out along the route to Saint-Antonin-Noble-Val. He wanted to take another look at McGraw's hideout and see if the plan made sense to Jacques. Didier declined to come along, muttered something about wanting no connection with the scene of some crime. That was probably smart on his part, but Eddie hoped it didn't signal some kind of rip off, like having a taste of the money and delivering nothing.

The drive was uneventful. Jacques sat alongside him, eyes to himself, gnawing his way through a nasty looking goats cheese and sausage sandwich. By that stage of their relationship Eddie and Jacques had made progress in their primitive means of communication. A close reading of the man's facial reactions convinced Eddie that Jacques understood more than a few words of basic English. Compared to Eddie, when it came to foreign language skills, Jacques was a silent master. This didn't discourage Eddie from employing the few essential French words he knew or utilizing a clumsy language of hand signals to register his most basic intentions. Jacques, however, never seemed to concede that Eddie understood none of his impenetrable Occitan accented French. He relied on the blunt repetition of simple French utterances, backing them up when necessary with emphatic bursts of mime. The bottom line for Eddie was reassuring enough: when it really mattered, the man understood plain English. In the meantime, the trick was to indulge Jacques' pretence of ignorance.

When they the reached the bend in the D115 with the view of the house across the river, Eddie parked the car as he did previously. It was enough to survey the place through binoculars. He took a long and thorough look across the landscape and then offered the binoculars to Jacques. Eddie saw that Jacques' gaze was fixed on the wheat field that bordered the farmhouse.

'Le blé - derrière le mur,' he said, then repeated in a tone that

suggested he was hatching a plan. An animated expression - the first Eddie had ever seen - developed around the man's eyes.

'Un feu dans le blé!' he said with some excitement, then said it several times more, hoping to make Eddie understand. When language failed he produced a cigarette lighter from his jeans pocket, mimed rolling the striker a few times, then smacked it alight and waved a tall gas flame in front of Eddie. But the concept of setting fire to the wheat field wasn't getting through.

'Burn 'em out of the house? Are you fucking crazy?' Eddie said. 'We-no-burn-the-*maison!* No way.'

'Non, non! - le blé!' Jacques shouted, thinking he might be on the verge of a breakthrough. *'Quand ils sortiront de la maison... boum - boum - boum!'*

It was the malevolence in the man's voice that bothered Eddie. He was getting the idea that Jacques was hoping to take out more than just the dogs.

Finally, out of desperation, Jacques snatched the notebook that was protruding from Eddie's jacket pocket and demanded the use of his biro. Spreading the pages open against the roof of the Renault, he quickly sketched a map of the house and the wheat field. It was like a child's drawing. A two-dimensional, kindergarten kid's house. Lollypop trees. A jagged series of leaf-shapes representing the fire front. Then he added several running stick figures, with arrows indicating the direction of their travel. Eddie got it immediately. Burn the field and pop the lot of them when they come out to see what's up. No fucking way.

Eddie took the notebook and struck a line through Jacques plan of action.

'We're not shooting anyone - understand? No *boum-boum-boum* at the men in the house,' he said, jabbing at the stick figures. 'See here -' Eddie made some hasty additions to the man's map - the front yard, the tall iron gates, and two simple representations of savage dogs, all ears and fangs. Next he drew a figure on a bicycle.

'C'est moi,' he said, poking himself in the chest, pleased to see that Jacques was following.

A dotted line was added to represent Eddie passing the front gate. (What Eddie had in mind was dressing in the full cyclist's kit and cruising past, Making enough of a racket near the gate to stir up the dogs. If anyone from the house saw him, he'd just look like a cross-country cyclist out on a training run. He figured that a bicycle would make it easy to get in and out of the area quickly and silently, as well as make it easy to conceal and carry the necessary hardware for the job.)

'Vous,' he said, pointing to Jacques. *'Vous - boum, boom, boom, les chiens.* Except you're going to be using a silencer, nice and quiet - *boum, boum, boum.'*

The rest of the plan was far too complicated to convey in a diagram. Didier was going to have to earn his money and have another session with the man. There was no way Eddie was going to stand there by the roadside, trying to explain what would happen next. How he was going to dump the bicycle behind a small stand of nearby trees as soon as he heard the dogs fall silent. How he would scale the wall on the northern, blind side of the house, while Jacques provided a little distracting rifle fire from across the river. All that detail would have to be sorted out later.

Jacques was getting bored and restless with all the standing around in the sun, looking at nothing. He had run out of sausage sandwiches and Gitanes. Eddie could sense that the man was about to turn belligerent. He gestured to Jacques to get back into the car and pointed further up the road. Before heading back to Toulouse via Caussade, Eddie wanted to cross the river and head up the hills a short distance. From there he would be able to take a look at the house from a different perspective. Maybe see over the wall, see into the grounds a little better. Jacques shrugged. For five thousand euros he was prepared to stay a while longer.

The first thing Eddie saw when he stepped out of the car again and trained the binoculars on the house was a white Citroën sedan. It was visible from the headlights up, parked in the previously concealed side driveway. A few minutes later, he saw three people come out of the house: McGraw, the man he had followed into Saint-Antonin the day before, and a young woman. The young woman was in her early thirties at most, trim, good looking, and dressed in a contemporary big city way. Sexy black stuff, head to toe, was how Eddie would have described it. She seemed to be in conversation with McGraw, but neither party looked too happy. A girlfriend, maybe. Toop and Gornik hadn't told him anything about that. Their research was shit.

On the drive back to Caussade he reflected on the situation. There were things about the job that bothered him far too much, and they were starting to stack up: he had no clear idea of what he was looking for or where he was going to find it; he had back up he couldn't talk to, let alone trust; and now it looked like McGraw was on summer holiday, guests coming and going, not a situation you could count on at all. Eddie had half a mind to call up Toop and Gornik and tell them to stick it.

27

August 21: Paris to Menton

Several times on the Thursday afternoon, Mitchell had tried to telephone Ilena. He wanted to learn the final arrangement for the following day's trip down to Menton, but more urgently, he simply needed to hear her voice again.

He had already squared things away with the Musée Picasso. Since they weren't footing the bill for the excursion, they had no objections to him taking a couple of days off. They were in fact pleased that he would be able to make the previously aborted side trip to the museum in Antibes. (There was now the need for a considerable amount of liaison between the two museums, to coordinate arrangements for the forthcoming exhibition. Mitchell was to deliver a bulging file of correspondence.)

When he did finally get put through to Ilena's hotel room, she sounded breathless and preoccupied. She told him she was perched on her impossible little hotel chair, trying to hammer out some semblance of a script. He felt as though he was interrupting something important. Her own priorities were clearly all consuming.

'Today was insane,' she said, with exaggerated weariness, 'Don't ever try taping an interview outside the Australian Embassy. It's right near the Tour Eiffel on the Rue Jean Rey. Tourist traffic roaring past all the while. Me and the guy from the Attorney General's Department, out there on the footpath, bellowing into the microphone. Like front line reporting. Terrible farce. I can't wait till we head south.'

'Have you got time for quick drink?' he asked, without expectation.

'Drink? In my frame of mind? That would spell catastrophe,' she said, with a wicked laugh. 'Honestly, I can't possibly, Mitchell. This evening I have to have an aperitif with some press guy from Sarkozy's office. Waste of time, of course. And then there's the obligatory Paris dinner and drinks with the crew. Apparently they're hoping for the full ghastly La Coupole experience. What could I do? And right now I'm trying to write this scenario. I know how Hemingway felt. Sitting with a coffee and a notebook, trying to write the one true thing. A very *empty* notebook, so far, as you can imagine. And oh, yes - you're contract is en route. E-mailed direct to you from Australia. I stirred them up down there. If I sound a little scatty, that's what this kind of schedule always does to me. Oh - and I've been making notes, preparing the questions I'll be asking you. Just to keep you on your toes. You'll have plenty of time to prepare your scintillating answers while we're driving down.'

'What time are we leaving in the morning?' he asked.

'At six, from my hotel. Is that all right for you?'

'Of course. I'll get an early night, then.'

'We've hired a comfortable vehicle – one of those ghastly family bubbles – a Citroën, I think it is – the French answer to an SUV.'

'Who's driving?'

'I think the plan is to each have a turn. We want to get to Menton by five, then go straight to McGraw's place at Cap-Martin and film your interview.'

'That's pushing it a bit, isn't it?' he teased. 'I won't be at my freshest.'

'But we'll have beautiful late-summer evening light. Very flattering. You'll look gorgeous in it.'

'Okay, then. Enjoy your blowout at La Coupole. I'll pack my bag and get an early night.'

'I like your attitude.'

'Till six.'

Todd Sigalas, Ilena's cinematographer, was at the wheel of the Citroën when they left Paris. Ilena had nominated him – being the most intrepid of drivers – for negotiating the complicated grid of city streets.

Todd didn't have a lot to say, about travel or anything else. He was several years older than Ilena, but far less worldly, and in fact, somewhat doleful. It soon became evident that he was content to sit in silence at the wheel for ages, his steady eye taking in everything on the road ahead. He dressed like a kid, Ilena had commented, hardly ever seen in anything other than sloppy t-shirts, long, baggy, multi-pocketed shorts, and promotional caps. Europe didn't do much for him; he lacked the education that might have opened it up for him, but – judging from the sighs of pleasure he uttered as each fresh Provençal vista loomed into view - at least he responded fully and openly to the beauties of the French countryside. Ilena boasted that his camerawork was extraordinary. She thought he was far too good to languish forever in the anonymity of television current affairs reportage, but was determined to hang on to his services as long as possible.

Ilena and Mitchell, both barely awake, were slouched in the rear, gazing out their windows in mute farewell to Paris There had been a storm in the night, and the streets and buildings had taken on a pearly, monochromatic sheen, a forlorn beauty that demanded attention.

By the time the sun had fully risen, they were hammering down the A6 through the Burgundy countryside. They made good time, rarely dropping below 120ks per hour, stopping only for coffee, petrol, and toilet breaks.

Ilena took the wheel at Beaune. She was a far more brazen driver than Todd. She would swing into the fast lane to overtake anything slow without a moment's hesitation and exceeded the speed limit as a matter of principle. Mitchell's job – he was now sitting alongside her up front, while Todd and Brooke, the sound recordist, dozed behind them - was to keep her fed and provide stimulation. He peeled baby *clementines* one after the other and pressed the juicy quarters to her lips. He snapped off squares of hazelnut studded dark chocolate and juggled her take-away paper coffee cups on his lap. Ministering to her was sheer pleasure, and he loved sitting alongside her in a cabin smelling of new leather, hire car detergent and her dying perfume

After an indifferent early lunch at a *routier* near Mâcon, Mitchell volunteered a turn at the wheel. He was no risk-taker, and he found himself apologizing frequently for his slower average speed and refusal to overtake every truck that loomed into view. He felt a heavy weight of responsibility for his dreaming charges.

It wasn't until they reached Orange, and the wheel had been surrendered to Brooke Hartley, that Mitchell could once again relax. She drove with calm assurance – the only true adult at the wheel.

Ilena had already told him a little about Brooke, who was in her late twenties, gay and unattached, and claimed to have no special affinity for the Mediterranean world. Growing up in the western suburbs of Sydney had crushed any possible romantic illusions in that direction. Third world Asia was more her thing. And as for eating in foreign places, Brooke claimed that French *routiers* were no more or less interesting than Michelin-starred

Parisian restaurants. She wore an outfit of cut-down combat fatigues, an El Salvador army cap, and SAS issue tropical boots. This shouldn't have bothered Ilena, but down in rural France, she wasn't confident about the message being unwittingly transmitted

Mitchell was pleased to be once again sharing the rear seats with Ilena. He had become bored with rehearsing his interview answers in his head, and was happy to respond to Ilena's questions about Mike McGraw's art collection. On an earlier occasion, he had already told her a little of the *Portrait of Dora Maar's* history during World War Two. But now he had fresh information. On the previous evening, Paulette Berg had e-mailed him with her latest news.

'Do you recall me talking about a man called David Kaufman?'

'Vaguely – wasn't he the gallery owner who bought all of Picasso's work?'

'No – you're thinking of Paul Rosenberg. Anyway, Paulette Berg has confirmed what she already suspected: that the original purchaser of the work was David Kaufman, a Jewish banker and serious contemporary art collector. He bought it, of course, from Paul Rosenberg's gallery. This was some time in 1938.'

'And what happened to David Kaufman?'

'It's a long and complicated story, but - '

'Briefly, then.'

'Well, Kaufman had a huge collection - over three hundred impressionist and post-impressionist canvases - which he housed in his *château* near Paris. But during the Phony War, he became nervous and had everything shipped to his uncle's *château* down in Bergerac, on the Dordogne. Unfortunately, the Germans had heard of his collection and were very keen to locate it.'

'In spite of the fact that they hated modern art?'

'They knew its value in trade.'

'But soon everyone was after this collection: the Vichy Government's General Commissariat on Jewish Affairs; the predatory German dealer Haberstock, who was active in Paris at the time; and Herman Goering himself. Bribes were being offered. Kaufman's family was being questioned. Friends were being threatened. It was only a matter of time before someone betrayed its wherabouts. Finally the head man from the Commissariat managed to track down the small firm of removalists who had secretly transported the collection. One of the drivers led them straight to the *château*.'

'And the *Portrait of Dora Maar* was amongst these paintings?'

'It seems so, according to Paulette Berg.'

'So the Vichy French got hold of it?'

'No. Goering soon discovered the location of the *château*, and arranged for the Gestapo to hijack the entire collection from under the noses of the Vichy guards. Just to cover his tracks, he employed a gang of Bony-Lafont 'French Gestapo' members to make the raid. They spoke French and claimed they were working for another branch of the Vichy Government. Meaning that the collection would have probably ended up in the Jeu de Paume, where it would have been traded for the kind of Germanic art that Goering was really after.'

'And David Kaufman?'

'The following year he was arrested during the roundup of French Jews and taken to Drancy. Later they railed him to an extermination camp in Eastern Europe. She said there were relatives who could verify this.'

'And he died there?'

'Yes.'

'I'm sorry. What about the painting? Where would that have ended up?'

'Traded to some corrupt dealer in Switzerland most likely. Probably bought by some criminal who didn't care that the work was obviously confiscated Jewish property. At least, Paulette Berg thinks it's been out of circulation since the war. Bought and sold by criminals. Lost to public view for fifty years.'

'The Lost Picasso,' she said. 'I think I'd like to use that title for your segment. What do you think?'

'But it wasn't exactly lost, was it.'

On the run down to Marseille, Todd was back at the wheel. He opened the sunroof and they all felt the first hot breath of the Mediterranean. Ilena, revived by the rush of aromatic air, cheered at her first glimpse of the sea.

'Fucking awesome,' Todd concurred.

For a long while they remained silent, taking in the dramatic landscape of the south. The mountains of jagged grey limestone. Slopes covered in vines, olive groves, and outcrops of stringy Aleppo pine. The geometry of clustered village houses. Waves of roman tiles, basking in the sun. And in their ears all the way, the wind-driven thrumming of a million cicadas.

The only dampener on their spirits was the discovery, after Fréjus, that they had joined a peak hour traffic crawl along the Côte d'Azur. There seemed to be a *paeage* station every couple of kilometers.

It was after five when they arrived in Menton. They left the *autoroute* and saw, far below, at the foot of the vertiginous hillside, a perfect expanse of azure sea dotted with pleasure yachts, a palm lined seafront promenade, and descending levels of pastel hued apartment blocks. Another nightmarish Mediterranean playground for wealthy retirees, was Mitchell's first reaction. But then, with relief, he soon caught glimpses of the terra-cotta tiled roofs of the old town on the peninsula, with its dense pattern of ancient streets, ascending geometry of ochre-coloured stucco walls, and at the summit of it all, the magnificent Italianate bell tower of the Cathedral St.-Michel.

Ilena had chosen to book them into a hotel in the newer section of town, simply because of its proximity to the main shopping streets as well as numerous cafés and restaurants. She claimed she didn't crave insular five star luxury. On a brief visit she only ever wanted stimulation and local colour.

The party checked in, unburdened themselves of their

luggage, and met again soon after in the foyer for the excursion to Cap-Martin.

They set off in the Citroën, through the quiet streets of the town, traveling south along the Promenade du Soleil. The late afternoon sun was turning the rows of apartment buildings into cliffs of dazzling white light.

Michael McGraw's villa, Le Rêve, was only a three-kilometer drive. Todd took the wheel, while Mitchell navigated.

He had no difficulty in locating the mandatory car park at Cap-Martin, the closest place they could bring their car to the exclusive reaches of the peninsula. Todd and Brooke complained about having to lug their camera and sound gear the remaining two hundred metres. But their first sighting of Le Rêve made them whoop for joy. The extravagant Italianate villa took on an inviting, roseate glow in the late sunlight. They peered through the iron gates at the shuttered windows and the derelict gardens, and they walked its perimeter, as far as the sea wall would allow. Not for a moment did Ilena imagine that McGraw might be still in residence.

Todd set up several different shots of the villa from the narrow apron of roadway in front of the driveway. He also walked to the top of the knoll to obtain a deeper perspective. Later, Ilena stood in front of the barred gates and recorded some of her prepared McGraw narration. The experience left her feeling forlorn. Her subject had departed long ago, and her efforts had the hollowness of mere television rhetoric. It took her many attempts to perform her own words with any spark of investigative conviction.

When she crouched on the rocky ground, shaded by the eastern wall, to play back the disappointing rushes she felt the disgust of failure rise up in her. Perhaps if they had been able to film within the grounds, or even entered the villa itself, the segment might have had some resonance. As things stood it seemed a long way to travel for so little impact. She said she could have done the piece back in the Sydney studio against a projected blow up of the villa. At least she was complimentary about Todd's compositions, believing that they successfully highlighted the crazy opulence of the man's lifestyle. Todd suggested that, if they were prepared to hang around until dusk, the rapidly failing violet light might transform the view of the villa into something more suggestive of loss and abandonment. Ilena rejected the idea; she had no intention of romanticizing McGraw's disappearance. Nevertheless she was grateful for the idea. That was always Todd's special contribution. Suggest a shot to Todd and he would almost always stroll off to find a better angle. Ask for a big close up and he would question why you didn't want to put on a wide angle and see the whole room transformed by an unusual perspective.

They were on the point of packing up the gear when Todd realized that if he were to descent the steep, rocky slope on the seaward side of the wall, there was the possibility of a dynamic, strongly back-lit angle on the villa that would give it the appearance of a fortress. Given their limited creative options, Ilena couldn't think of any reason to deny him the shot.

Todd was twenty metres down the difficult slope when Mitchell heard an approaching car. Moments later, a black Mercedes with tinted windows loomed into view and slid to a halt. Out of the eddy of dust stepped two men who looked like bodyguards. The younger of the two wore reflective sunglasses and a tight black body shirt over his tanned, muscular torso. He advanced on Mitchell, Ilena and Brooke, greeting them with an arrogant smile, without bothering to raise his sunglasses.

'What business you got here?' he demanded bluntly. He shot a look down at Todd, who was steadying himself against a rock ledge while he strained to hear what was being said.

'We're taking a look at this extremely attractive villa,' Ilena said, with as much innocent cheek as she dared summon. 'You don't happen to know who owns it, do you?'

He ignored her and pointed in Todd's direction. 'You trespass,' he said.

Over at the Mercedes, the second man, who wore a canary yellow sports jacket and tight black leather trousers, was leaning on the door, muttering in belligerent patois into a mobile. When he glared in their direction, Mitchell tried to memorize his appearance: thick Zapata moustache; lank black hair that fell to his shoulders; a crooked aquiline nose; and most alarmingly - what seemed to be a thick white scar that almost encircled his throat. Neither of the men resembled the ones who had waylaid him in Nice.

Without warning the first man stepped forward and lunged at the carry strap of Brooke's digital recorder. Brooke cringed backwards and the man sniggered. 'You lie, too. What this for?'

Mitchell wanted to defend her, but felt helpless in the situation.

'We're making a holiday video,' Ilena protested, 'Anything wrong with that?'

The man pointed at the dials of Brooke's recorder. 'Switch it off, or I take.'

'Okay - sorry,' Brooke said sheepishly, fumbling for the 'off' toggle.

Mitchell felt the need to intervene rise in him like nausea. 'What's the problem?' he said flatly. 'This is a public thoroughfare, isn't it? In fact, I thought cars were prohibited along here.' He was trembling as he spoke and knew that they could see his fear. He had no idea who these men were, but he certainly wasn't going to toss them McGraw's name. 'So, who says we can't be here?'

'Me,' the first man said. 'Get back in your car and go.'

He grasped Ilena by the upper arm, and ignoring Mitchell, steered her back towards the door of the hire car.

By that time the second man had completed his mobile conversation. He stepped around the front of the Mercedes to join his friend. As he approached Mitchell, he spat in the dust and brushed aside a flap of his sports coat to reveal the butt of a silver revolver.

Mitchell saw that it wasn't worth the risk of antagonizing these people any further. He caught Ilena's eye and shook his head urgently, signalling that they should leave. She got the message and yelled for Todd to come back up the slope. The panic in her voice told Todd that things were serious and warned him not to try anything smart.

In less than a few minutes they had been herded back to the car park, where they nervously climbed back into the Citroên. The two men hovered with the belligerent empowerment of nightclub bouncers. They remained on the roadway, watching, as Todd nervously backed up, turned the hire car around, and drove away swiftly.

'McGraw's friends, do you reckon?' Todd said, with a catch in his voice.

'God knows,' Ilena said. 'But did you manage to video any of that?'

'I buttoned on for a minute or so - until I saw the gun.'

'Interesting,' Mitchell said. 'If we only knew what it all meant.'

Under a waning sun, and in markedly deflated spirits, they drove back towards Menton.

'Did you get everything you were after?' Mitchell asked Ilena.

'Enough. There's a limit to how many shots of abandoned houses I can hope to use.'

'So, what's up next?' Mitchell asked. 'Me, I presume?'

'Not so pushy,' Ilena said. 'While we're in Menton I want to seek out anyone of consequence who knew McGraw from those earlier days. People who are prepared to talk about him. The most significant one, obviously, being his former lawyer, Pierre Lavalle – if I can manage to corner him. I'll visit him first thing in the morning.'

'Might be a good time for me to slip up to Antibes on the train and deliver my package to the Picasso museum.'

'And meet back here at six for cocktails on thee promenade.'

'Perfect.'

28

August 22 - 23: Menton to the Gorge d'Aveyron

After a shared breakfast with the rest of the party in the hotel's *salle de peitit déjuner*, Mitchell set off to walk to the railway station. He had no idea how long the Antibes trip might take, but urged Ilena to call him on his mobile if there were any developments. He was secretly pleased not to have to be performing to the camera on that day, preferring instead to be getting on with his legitimate Musée Picasso obligations.

Ilena suggested that Todd and Brooke take the morning off to look around the town, while she visited Pierre Lavalle on her own. Taking the crew on an initial meeting was tactically unwise. It carried the presumption of co-operation in securing an interview. Alone, she believed she could be as pushy and as devious as the situation demanded.

The address she had been given was nearby, in a narrow street on the north side of the old town. Maître Pierre Lavalle's office was on the ground floor of a pale ochre corner building that had been recently restored to its full sixteenth-century splendour. Tall Canary Island palms in the square opposite cast lazy, jagged shadows on the stucco wall. Through the partially open olive green shutters, Ilena could see no sign of movement in the gloomy wood-paneled interior.

After entering the alcove, she knocked for fully a minute on the pebbled glass door, and was on the point of leaving when she heard footsteps approaching from within. The door was cautiously unlocked and a tiny, dark complexioned woman with a severe Frida Khalo hairstyle glared up at her with undisguised irritation.

'Bonjour, madame,' she said sharply, like a warning.

Ilena stood her ground. 'I'm hoping to see Maître Lavalle,' she said.

'English, yes?' the woman said, with a note of contempt. 'I speak to you a little, but I can no help. He no here. No this time. No tomorrow. No more.'

'Can you tell me where he is?' Ilena asked patiently, already falling into step with the woman's staccato syntax.

'No. You must go now. This is the after hour.'

'I've travelled here from Paris to see him. In fact I've travelled all the way from Australia.'

'Australia? Is worse for you. He no talk to Australia.'

'But I'm a friend of Mike McGraw's. He told me that I could talk with with him through Maître Lavalle. So I'm going to leave you the telephone number of my hotel here in Menton. Please give this to him.' Ilena had no idea how much or how little the woman understood, but she was prepared to be patient.

It was at that moment that Ilena heard the sound of another presence behind the office partitioning. It was like the exhalation of a long held breath, and then the shuffling of a body on a leather chair. Ilena held her own breath, knowing that the woman was fully aware of what she must have heard. Ilena knew that it could only have been Lavalle, but the woman's lie had paralyzed her initiative. With a shaking hand, she scribbled her number onto a network business card and handed it to the woman, who studied it with no relenting of her attitude. 'If you do see Maître Lavelle, would you please ask him to telephone me?'

'Oui, oui,' she said, indifferently. 'But I no think I see him.'

'Yes, I understand,' Ilena said. 'but please do your best.'

'Au revoir, madame,' the woman said, offering Ilena a tight, insincere smile, while closing the door in her face.

Instantly Ilena regretted not bringing the crew along. It might have given her the courage to challenge the woman's defensive lies. They might have had the nerve to storm straight into the office and confront Lavelle directly. At least the encounter would have been entertaining. Now she was left in the agonizingly passive position of having to hope that Lavalle would decide that it was in his interest to contact her.

She returned to the hotel and took the opportunity to review her position. She left the door ajar in the hope that the telephone might ring. Two hours passed while she ordered room service coffee and rehearsed what she might say to the man. The irrational thought that everything might now depend upon his co-operation began to prey upon her. At midday, when she knew that all the offices would be closing, she abandoned any hope of a phone call and tried to calm herself.

She telephoned Brooke and Todd and told them she was expecting calls and would need to eat in her room. In reality she had no desire to share the truth of the situation with them. She ordered room service sandwiches and soda water and sat on her shaded balcony to contemplate her dilemma.

The McGraw project was looking shakier by the moment. The day should have been devoted to tracking down anyone who had enjoyed any kind of meaningful contact with him. She had been counting on Lavalle to provide some openings. Now it was clear he had no intention of meeting her. The idea that the Provençal junket would amount to no more than a piece of badly performed to-camera waffle outside the barred entrance to an empty villa was already humiliation enough.

She considered calling Mitchell on his mobile, but then decided not to burden him with her doubts and failures.

Being in no mood to face the hot streets without a plan of action, in the early afternoon, she took a nap. She was woken by a persistent telephone.

'Hello,' she croaked, making an effort to sound wide-awake. The voice on the line was unfamiliar. It belonged to an older man who spoke French-accented English with intelligent authority.

'I'm speaking to Miss Vadas - yes? I understand you wish to meet an old friend, Mister Michael McGraw.'

'Whom am I talking to?' she asked, immediately on edge.

'Maître Pierre Lavalle. You came looking for me. I am ringing to tell you that Mister McGraw would like to meet you this evening.'

'Tonight? Where is he?'

'You must listen carefully To do this thing you have to prepare immediately for a short plane trip and an overnight stay. Bring very little. Tell nobody about any of this. In thirty minutes, a car will come for you at the hotel. You will be driven to Nice - this has been arranged already. From there, you are booked on a flight to Toulouse. Someone will be at Blagnac terminal to meet you and take you to Mister McGraw.'

'So he's living in Toulouse?'

'Nearby. Exactly where need not concern you.'

'Just a moment - who suggested this crazy timetable? Why not-'

Lavalle cut her off. 'Because this is the only possible arrangement, Miss Vadas. I think this is not a suitable time to talk. The car will arrive at ten exactly. Please be ready. Goodbye.'

Lavalle paused on the line just long enough to take her stunned silence as assent, and then hung up.

Ilena struggled to rise from the bed. The air in the room was stuffy and she felt sluggish and disoriented. Lavalle - if that was who the caller had been - could hardly have been serious. The arrangement sounded like a melodramatic joke, as impractical as it was improbable. Why should she trust this man? Was the purpose of the offer to induce a panic and lead her into some reckless commitment? She feared that it must be some plan to isolate and intimidate her - and then what? And yet she was already rising from the bed, crossing to the bathroom, and sealing herself into the shower cubicle.

For many seconds, her hands remained poised on the taps, while the decision took shape inside her. It came with an impulsive wrenching of both taps to release a stinging jet of water. She was being driven robotically by the lure of this sinister arrangement.

She cradled her breasts in her crossed arms and allowed the scalding water to drum against her face and throat. The idea that she might actually see Mike McGraw before the day began to take over her imagination. It was becoming clear that she would surrender completely to the terms of Lavalle's deal.

Five minutes later she was powdering her bare skin in front of the long mirror in her bedroom. By the shadowy light of the half drawn blind, she studied her naked limbs. In this unfamiliar room she felt raw, insubstantial. It was as though her body belonged to others. The idea chilled her. In ten minutes she would be gone, and the space with its tastefully anonymous furniture would be void.

She rummaged amidst the pile of clothing that she had upended on the carpet and found her only remaining fresh underwear. Her usual habit of laundering each day's worn items in the basin had been abandoned on this trip. She dressed comfortably in loose jeans, t-shirt and light-weight cotton jacket, and then spent several minutes tossing a few essentials into her small carry bag: money, passport, mobile, toiletry bag, address book, mini-tape recorder and notebook. The remaining minutes before descending to the lobby she used to compose a brief note of explanation to Brooke and Todd, which she would leave with the concierge. In it she described the telephone call and the hasty arrangement she had with Maître Lavalle - trying to put aside his warning that there may be consequences for ignoring the instruction to talk to nobody.

It hardly surprised her that the man waiting for her in the lobby was the one who had, on the previous day, ordered her away from the gates of McGraw's villa. This time he gave her a sly, over-confident smile as he extended his hand in introduction.

'Miss Vadas. *Je m'appelle* Philippe. For yesterday, please forgive me. You come with me this way.' He motioned towards the front of the hotel.

It was like a rehearsed speech, delivered in a manner that left no room for second thoughts. With a gentle pressure on her elbow - so unlike the rough seizure at the villa gates - he guided her out through the automatic doors. The same black Mercedes was parked directly opposite. Sunlight splintered off the chrome work. Beyond the tinted windows, it was impossible to tell whether the other more frightening thug, the one with the moustache and the scar, was sitting in wait.

As she crossed the road she was assailed by an attack of pure panic. In the space of a several chaotic moments she considered her chances of making a run back towards the safety of the hotel. But Philippe was already at the passenger door, swinging it open for her, while he held her by the arm. A frantic scan of the dark interior couldn't persuade her that they were alone. Philippe registered her fear.

'You worry?' he said, with another smile. He obligingly opened the rear door as well and encouraged her to take a good look for herself.

'You see - no surprise behind,' he said

With a racing heart, Ilena settled into the luxurious passenger seat. The sharp clack of the seat belt marked the moment of her total submission.

For the next fifteen minutes they drove in silence, westwards out of Menton in the direction of the airport at Nice. She was expecting some kind of further explanation, but none was offered.

On the airport concourse, he pulled over, out of the traffic flow, and once again opened the door for her. It surprised her when she realized that he had no intention of accompanying her into the terminal. Instead, he handed her a piece of folded paper.

'Your e-ticket details. *Bon voyage.*' he said, almost reaching for her hand.

'Thank you...Philippe,' she said, not knowing what to make of his mechanical courtesy.

'I will be here tomorrow at one o'clock, to return you to your hotel.'

He smiled warmly, as though by now they had become intimate, and held her final look a beat too long.

She tried a smile, too, and said, 'I'm sure you will.'

The small turbo-prop aircraft that would make the short hop to Nice was already boarding when she arrived. Ilena collected her e-ticket and joined a queue of sunburned English and German tourists who were shuffling through the departure gate.

She had been given an aisle seat next to an intoxicated, grey-bearded, elfin Englishman who hummed to himself throughout the take-off. In order to get a last look at the coastline back towards St.-Jean-Cap-Ferrat it was necessary for her to lean somewhat into his space. He gave her an opportunistic smile, as though she had made some kind of advance. Fortunately, he was too drunk to pursue a conversation, but soon he began to nudge her and point at the receding landscape outside the window, seeking her agreement about nothing he could manage to articulate. In order to escape she reached for her notebook and tried to jot down as much as she could recall of the conversation with Maître Lavalle.

As the plane strained upwards, ploughing through dark rainclouds, bucking and dipping sharply to a degree that normally would have caused her panic and nausea, Ilena noticed that she wasn't at all anxious. The inexorable nature of her mission seemed to guarantee her safe deliverance. She refused the in-flight coffee and cheese roll and instead tried to focus on the questions that she might put to Mike McGraw.

Twenty minutes later, the plane was descending towards Toulouse.

Once inside the terminal she followed the instructions she had been given and waited by the entrance to the bistro. After several minutes a man approached her, making eye contact with the certainty of absolute recognition. This one also looked like a bodyguard. He was compact, muscular and suntanned, but considerably less attractive than Philippe in his corporate peaked cap and hideous synthetic black sports trainers. He was also completely lacking in charm, greeting her by muttering her name, but not finding it necessary to introduce himself. After listening to a few of his terse directives, Ilena was astonished to realize that he was Australian. She could only conclude that McGraw must have felt safer in the company of his own countrymen.

They walked out of the terminal together side by side. Strangers might have taken them for a tense, travel-estranged couple. Out of curiosity, she decided to initiate a conversation, but the man's sole concern seemed to be get her into his gold BMW as quickly as possible. But before driving out of the short term car park he confronted her with a strip of black cloth in his hand.

'Gonna need you to put on a blindfold, love,' he told her.

Put so politely, the suggestion made her laugh. 'What? And sit up here in front like a hostage?'

'Nah, I'm gonna need you to lie down on the back seat.'

'That's a bit extreme, isn't it?'

'Otherwise, we're not going anywhere.'

'All right...if that's the deal,' she said, before unfastening her seat belt and slipping out of the passenger's seat. He watched warily as she stepped onto the asphalt, opened the right side rear door, and settled herself in the back. When she put her hand out for the blindfold, requesting to be allowed to tie it herself, he refused. It was settled by her consenting to stretch out full length while he secured it with a firm knot.

By Ilena's estimate, they travelled for over an hour. From the frequency of heavy truck engines in nearby traffic lanes, she knew they were on an *autoroute.* After about thirty minutes they stopped at a *paeage* station, and then turned onto a road with sparser traffic. FIfteen minutes later they slowed and took a poorly surfaced minor road, which seemed to wind upwards into a hilly forest. She could smell the pine trees and the dust on the verge of the road, and feel from the absence of flickering sunlight on her skin that they were on the northern side of the ranges. A short while later she knew they were descending into a valley. She could smell freshly cut hay, and hear the barking of a distant farm dog.

The car slowed and finally came to a halt. While the engine idled, Ilena strained to listen to the Australian as he made a call on his mobile. His French was atrocious, but she could tell he was requesting that someone open a gate for him. She heard the groaning of metal on metal as large iron gates swung open. Then the car rolled forward, and she could tell from the crunching and popping of the tyres that they were riding on gravel. When they came to a stop again, he told her to sit upright so that he could help her to get out. Then, after a short, stumbling walk on the gravel driveway, she was led up a flight of stone steps and into a cool interior that smelled of furniture wax and mildewed carpet.

She sensed the presence of a second man, who arrived in the room at the same time and came and stood directly in front of her. Gentle hands untied her blindfold, which was finally discarded on the floor. For a moment she was almost sightless; two hours of total light deprivation caused her to squint.

The man - who was still no more than a silhouette - stepped forward and embraced her. Three times he pressed his unshaven cheek against hers.

'Mike...' she said, her voice failing to rise above a whisper. The relief she felt was overwhelming.

'Ilena, I want you to come with me. We need to talk alone.' He waved away the man who had brought her from Toulouse, and led her into a long, dimly illuminated, stone room with oak ceiling beams and overbearing dark antiques.

'I assume this isn't your place,' she said weakly. She had little sense of how they might begin a conversation.

'No. It belongs to an old mate, a banker in Toulouse. It might surprise you, but I still have a few good friends.'

He led her to a sofa upholstered in unyielding polished leather, then settled himself opposite in a worn, comfortable looking club chair.

'They'll bring us food, if you'd like. Tea, coffee, water - whatever you'd prefer.'

Ilena declined. She had no immediate interest in eating. The strained circumstances of their reunion were far too unsettling. 'Somehow I didn't allow myself to imagine ever seeing you again,' she said, a little too breathlessly.

He sat deep in the chair with his long legs wide apart and his suntanned, boney fingers interlaced on his lap. It troubled her to observe that he appeared careworn, haunted even. But with his calm, indulgent smile, she found him as solid and as elusively attractive as ever.

'We could never have just let it all go as simply that,' he said.

'I thought that was exactly what had happened.' She hadn't meant to sound such a note of recrimination, and fortunately he didn't react.

'I never believed it was over.'

'But we both knew it was impossible.'

'Oh, no - I never thought that,' he said, obviously remembering the course of their affair in a completely different way from her. 'At a certain point my life just became ridiculous. That was all it was.'

Ilena didn't trust his insistence on the survival of their intimacy. She recalled their affair as a period of reckless instability on her part, and of calculating seduction on his. It had amounted to no more than a month of furtive comings and goings from international hotels in three states, while Mike eluded the press, investigators from the securities institute, and his estranged wife's lawyers. It had been a heady and wildly romantic time, but it had proved unsustainable and psychologically costly. When he had telephoned to put an end to the affair, she had been shattered. Seemingly, it had all cost him very little, but it had taken Ilena a year to put him - as a lover at least - entirely out of mind. Consequently, it was impossible for her to believe that their meeting on this present occasion was of any emotional significance to him. Besides, he knew precisely what she had been researching and writing. How could he not see her work as betrayal of the worst kind? She was relieved when he changed the subject to his current predicament.

'This is what they call the end game,' he said. 'They've stripped me of all my pieces. Now they're trying to corner me, and there aren't many moves left.'

'What are your options?'

'I can co-operate with the case against myself, or I can run, and try to conceal what little of my assets I can salvage.'

For the next forty-five minutes they talked informally about his problems with ASIC and the Australia Attorney General's Department. She asked all the obvious questions, cursing the fact that she hadn't had the time to properly prepare herself. He answered them with the bland abstraction that she had been dreading. Nothing was admitted. He knew how to parry demanding inquiries He was impervious to irony, sarcasm and even shame. The session was torture for them both. They might just as well have been in a television studio, such was the failure of candour and true intimacy.

She told him that she would like to have the opportunity to interview him on camera, but he avoided making any absolute commitment. He would need to see the questions well in advance. He had been advised to avoid all comment on certain aspects of his business. Putting anything on record, he needlessly explained, entailed too much potential risk. The lack of trust he displayed hurt and annoyed her, but he held all the cards.

Afterwards, with the weariness of an older man, he levered himself up from the chair and stood in front of her. With a smile that she had never once succeeded in resisting, he offered her his hand. He drew her up and led her to the bank of windows overlooking the river valley. The view was spectacular, a picture of rural tranquility: a winding river beneath gentle, forested hills, craggy limestone outcrops, distant farmhouses, and slopes of sunflowers and ripe wheat. If this was running from the law, it seemed to have its compensations.

'I suppose you have little idea of where we are,' he said.

'An hour out of Toulouse - that's all I know,' she said.

'La France Profonde, they call it here.'

'I love the sound - so safe, so protected.'

He pointed to a distant place where the river disappeared behind a dense stand of trees. 'Right now, I would love to be down there by the river. Walking with you, swimming, lying beneath the willows.'

'When have we ever done that?' she said tersely.

'No - and we can't now, either. For all I know they may already have discovered that I'm here. I feel like Louis the sixteenth. I've got the palace in paradise, but I'm on borrowed time.'

She looked into his eyes - a piercing opaline blue by the strong window light - and saw in them a vulnerability against which she had no defence. He brushed her jaw with the tips of his fingers and guided her face towards his. They kissed where they stood, in a state of silent arousal.

Later, in an upstairs bedroom, they made love, and lay for an hour in one another's arms. Above her, Ilena saw the shadows cast by the limewashed white ceiling beams lengthen and then turn a deep impenetrable grey. She fell asleep, and when she awoke, found herself alone in the cold expanse of the antique bed. Mike McGraw had gone.

The sex had left her feeling cruelly exposed. She felt a confusion of lust and despair, a churning disgust at her weakness. Reeling with panic, she stumbled from the bed into the en suite bathroom and showered away every trace of him. It frightened her, the way she had so easily surrendered all control.

After dressing - all the while struggling to realign her turbulent thoughts - she ventured downstairs where she was met by a man she immediately assumed was Maître Lavalle. The man appeared to be in his mid-forties and had the physique and complexion of a sedentary bon vivant: heavy-jowelled, florid face, sagging stomach, and pear-shaped bottom. His wavy silver hair was worn at collar length and he sported a dyed black goatee. Any hint of his state of mind was concealed behind opaque, yellow-tinted glasses. She had no idea how he had managed to turn up in Toulouse. Had he been there all along, or had he been on the same flight from Nice?

'Mister McGraw has had to leave urgently,' he said. 'I warned you the meeting would be brief. Your plane back to Nice is due in an hour. We can talk on the way.'

He produced a blindfold from his pocket - the same strip of black cloth she had worn earlier - and politely suggested she submit to the process. So eager was she to leave, that when she felt his chubby fingers fumbling with the knot, she assisted by reaching behind her head and tugging the ends of the blindfold even tighter. No coercion was required to guide her outside and settle her on to the back seat of a car. Minutes later, they were turning out of the gravel driveway and accelerating rapidly.

Lavalle - for by then he had introduced himself - informed her that it was essential that Mister McGraw be shown a transcript of anything she was preparing to publish of their interview.

Ilena protested that the conversation had been confidential, of an essentially private nature, and not likely to result in anything publishable - a defence at which Lavalle snorted derisively. It was at that point that he showed his full hand. 'You realize, of course,

Miss Vadas, that this is not a matter for debate. We remain in control of any statements made by Mister McGraw.'

'I don't recall any such agreement,' Ilena said, perversely emboldened by her total physical vulnerability.

'Perhaps you do not realize, but you were secretly taped – picture and sound - in the presence of Mister McGraw. We have a record of your intimate dealings with him. This is now, potentially, no secret.'

She felt a sudden knot of fear in her stomach and a fury at her own gullibility. Of course he would have taped her – while talking about business, and while making love as well. As monstrous as it seemed, it had always been his way, this need for absolute control.

'Naturally, we hope you give us no reason to ever make this tape public. You can easily imagine the consequences. Who could ever take your opinions of Mister McGraw seriously? Besides, I cannot imagine that you would want to appear corrupt, unethical, and in breech of Australian law.'

Lying on the back seat, with the constant vibration of the tyres being transmitted directly into her ear, Lavalle's disembodied words chilled her like a prison sentence. Unable to see the man, she had no way of judging whether he was completely serious or merely bluffing.

'There is also the matter of the book you are writing,' he said. 'Mister McGraw knows about it. He doesn't like the idea. It's of great concern to him. I'm sure you know, it can be very difficult to publish that kind of thing without the co-operation of the subject. All manner of legal difficulties can arise.'

She said nothing. Lavalle's line of intimidation was all heading in the one direction and she had no defence at all.

'It might also be discovered that you have accepted money from the McGraw organization in exchange for your so-called inside story. Bank statements in your name might easily appear with significant deposits attributed to Mister McGraw. These could be very beneficial to you - or very damaging. The choice is yours.'

'What exactly does Mike McGraw expect me to do?' she asked. She knew the question was weak, redundant even, but she could no longer bear Lavalle's menacing vagueness.

'Very little. Nothing, in fact,' he said with false lightness. 'The less you do, the better.'

'I see,' she said, understanding perfectly. There would never be any reassuringly explicit directive to lay off altogether, but instead a threat of consequences for unfavourable reporting. For the rest of the journey to Toulouse, she remained silent.

At Blagnac terminal, when she stepped out of the car with the blindfold removed, helpless tears blurred her vision. The trip had left her feeling nauseous, and she had to struggle to find her balance. Maître Lavalle needed to support her as they tottered across the asphalt of the long-term car park. He said his farewell to her at the doorway to the terminal, squeezing her hands between his hot, pudgy palms. The gesture sickened her, she felt violated, but had no strength, no voice with which to protest.

Once inside the building, she fought to regain her composure by whispering a mantra of reassurance, a fragment of prayer - the same words that had once helped her surmount her fear of flying. At a souvenir shop, she purchased an expensive bottle of aged Armanac, then, sneaked away to a remote corner of the terminal to drink herself numb before boarding the aircraft. On the flight to Nice she twice had to hurriedly vacate her seat to visit the lavatory, where she vomited painfully and inaccurately into the tiny stainless steel hand basin.

Through the crisis of nausea, she struggled to formulate a plan. Upon her return to Menton, she would make immediate arrangements to return to Paris. There was no other sensible option but to place herself in the hands of Roger Knight and the Attorney General's Department. She would share with them all that she had learned, take their advice, and act accordingly.

29

August 22 – 23: Menton and La Cave

It was raining lightly when Mitchell reached Antibes. After a ten-minute wait on the deserted station concourse, a taxi showed up. His driver was a surly, careworn, middle-aged Arab, a man whose every sigh delivered the clear impression that he had no time for tourists taking short jaunts.

As his taxi accelerated along quiet side streets and shot up empty alleyways, Mitchell was, for a short while, able to maintain his bearings, but very soon he couldn't even tell in which direction they were headed. He knew that the Picasso Museum was on the coast, but so far he hadn't even caught a glimpse of the sea. The best he could say about his driver's expertise was that he drove with nerveless authority.

Ten minutes into the trip, while navigating a narrow two-way street that was almost impossibly blocked by parked cars, a large black sedan pulled out from an alleyway and came to a sudden stop only metres in front of them. Mitchell's driver hit his horn, creating a loud wail of panic. He braked fiercely, and immediately began to curse in Arabic.

Two men, both wearing jeans and black T-shirts leaped out and approached the taxi. One man pressed his face to the driver's window and engaged the excitable Arab with a torrent of apologetic explanation. The car had engine problems. It kept cutting out. The taxi would have to back up. With his amused expression and drooping black moustache, he had the countenance of a comic Italian waiter. Within moments Mitchell discovered that it was a ruse. The second man had circled the taxi and approached Mitchell's door unseen. He dropped down alongside Mitchell and pressed a small pistol into his side.

'Out of the car, Mister Jameson,' the man said, in Italian accented English. Mitchell was too astonished to comprehend, let alone obey. With his free hand the man took hold of Mitchell's jacket and wrenched him out onto the footpath.

'This car is for you.' he said, as he steered Mitchell towards a large grey Citroën, which had apparently been following close behind. A rear door was opened for him, and he was thrust into the dark, curtained interior. His captor shoved himself in alongside and again Mitchell felt the barrel of his pistol hard against his ribs. He saw the man properly for the first time. He was a tall, bear like Italian with an ugly bush of black beard that all but concealed his wet red mouth. He also saw through the wiper-slashed windscreen that the comic waiter was retrieving Mitchell's document bag and flinging money at the driver. They were leaving no traces.

'Get out of here,' the man said in Italian.

The Citroën was put into reverse, and the engine whined as the car fishtailed back along the narrow street. None of it made sense to Mitchell. He recalled demanding some explanation, shouting at them at the top of his voice, and having a gloved hand jammed across his mouth.

Two powerful arms pinned him against the seat. He felt the

sharp prick of a needle in his thigh, and then the spreading ache of an injection. Beyond that, he could recall only fragments. Looming splinters of light on an *autoroute*, piercing the fog of some sedative in his system. Rain lashing the windows. The throbbing rhythm of slashing wipers. The whine and shuddering explosion of passing trucks. Loud Italian voices laughing, arguing. The air, thick with cigarette smoke.

Mitchell was bundled back into consciousness by the rough attempts of two men to bind him into a hard chair. Rope burned his wrists, forcing his shoulders back. His ankles were already trussed to the chair legs. Their sharp edges cut into his calves.

Faces loomed over him. The huge bearded Italian, his assailant, and another, also Italian; this one, balding, short, almost obese, his moon face contorted in fury.

'Stretto, stretto,' he urged the bearded man; and Mitchell felt a sharp pain as the rope was yanked even tighter, sending a spasm of pain through his entire torso. He cried out, smothering the agony in the loudest possible roar. The small man dashed forward and delivered a stinging, but ineffectual slap to Mitchell's cheek. He was too groggy to resist any kind of assault, and allowed his head to flop back, as though having passed out. It seemed the only safe condition. He felt a few rousing pats on the cheek, and then a rough thumb pushing against his eyelid.

'E svenuto?' the big man enquired.

'No. He's just faking it,' the other said. 'Look.' And he gave Mitchell a few more sharp slaps on the cheek. 'Don't waste your time!' he snapped. 'Understand? You hear me? Course you can hear me, you fuck!'

Mitchell rolled his eyes back and stared up the man. For the first time he was able to register his surroundings. The dim lighting and the stone, barrel vaulted ceiling made him think he was in some kind of cell or dungeon. But he saw now that they were in a *cave,* a wine cellar. At one end were two immense oak vats and barrels stacked to the ceiling, and all about them, on benches and shelves, were various stainless steel and glass instruments of the trade. But whether they were still in France, or already across the Italian border, he had no idea.

The little man drew closer, and gave Mitchell a malevolent smile that revealed his full mouth of perfectly capped teeth. By way of introducing himself, he slapped at his chest with one pudgy, simian, jewellery-laden hand.

'Franco Orsini,' he said in his squeaky voice. 'Call me Frank.'

'I don't understand...I don't know what any of this is about.'

'You! You are the cause of all my fuckin' problems. You've cost my boss twelve million dollars, Mister Mitchell Jameson. That's what the fuck this is all about.'

As he cursed, he swaggered back and forth in front of Mitchell, rolling his shoulders like a chimp. He could recall thinking that the man seemed to be dressed for a Californian cocktail party. He was wearing baggy black trousers, several sizes too large, held up by a fat gold Gucci belt; and a decadent, Versace-style, silk shirt patterned with purple hibiscus flowers, floating on a strident abstract motif of bright yellow bananas. He reeked of some kind of tropical scented men's cologne. In other circumstances Mitchell might have laughed, but Mister Orsini was in an unmistakably lethal state of mind.

'I'm sorry, I just have no idea what you're talking about,' Mitchell pleaded.

'Let me make it real simple. My boss bought a painting for his house in L.A. A very nice Picasso. A picture of that crazy woman he was with, Dora...Dora-who-the-fuck? What's her other name?'

'Dora Marr.'

'Yeah. You know the painting. Of course you fuckin' know. You're the prick who's been helping the bitch who's got our fuckin' painting.'

Me? Sorry - none of this is making any sense to me.'

The truth was, it was beginning to make *some* sense to Mitchell, but not enough to warrant an admission of anything.

'Listen to me, you fuck. I'm gonna show you a picture. And you're gonna tell me that's you, walking around in Paris with the McGraw broad. And then you're gonna eat the fuckin' thing. That clear, you putz?'

He walked over to his silent, bearded partner and muttered something ugly in Italian. His truculent mood terrified Mitchell, but it also gave him a moment to catch up with the direction in which things were heading. He thought a rational approach was his only option.

Although the beard was new, Mitchell at last recognized the silent partner. He was certain it was Toadmouth, one of the men who had abducted him in Nice. It had taken this long for them to catch up with him again. Maybe, he hoped, they were just a bunch of incompetent amateurs.

Orsini returned with a small digital picture: a blurry, telephoto shot of two distant people walking in a nondescript Paris landscape. They could have been anybody.

Mitchell shrugged. 'Who are these people?' he asked.

'Get the fuck outa here,' Orsini snapped. He rolled the picture into a ball and stuffed in into Mitchell's mouth.

Mitchell spat out the wad of paper. 'Tell me about this deal, Frank,' Mitchell said. 'Whom did your boss buy this painting from?'

'Frank? What's with this fuckin' *Frank?* Who's asking the questions here?'

It was like dealing with a crazy, petulant child. Mitchell could feel the man's frustration and paranoia edging him closer to the point of violence.

'All right. History. My employer bought it from a New York gentleman called Meyer. Leon Meyer. You gonna tell me now you don't know who the fuck is Leon Meyer?'

Mitchell shook his head. Orsini did a double-take, unsure of whether it was a denial or an admission that Mitchell had never heard of Meyer.

'Comes with a recommendation in writing,' Orsini continued. 'It said: *"I, whatever-my-fuckin-name-is, expert on fuckin' Picasso... blah, blah, blah...have examined the aforesaid portrait of Dora-who-the-fuck, and attest that it is from the hand of Pablo Picasso."* Words to that effect.' He had the habit of punctuating every significant word with a sharp jab of an erect little index finger. 'So - Leon Meyer offers my boss this painting for twelve million. I do some research for him, and see the market value for these Picasso things is up around twenty, twenty-five million. So, call me stupid, but I know this is a good deal. Half price for a fuckin' masterpiece. Who's gonna turn that down?'

His voice had risen to a manic pitch. Flecks of white foam were boiling at the edges of his quacking lips. His tiny hands were fluttering with suppressed rage. Mitchell thought the man was going to lash out and strike him at any moment.

'I think I understand what you're telling me, but none of it involved me in any way at all.'

'That may be true - almost. But I looked into you. Had you checked out in Paris. And I know this - you've got the bona fides. You may be no fuckin' genius, but then you tell me why you're working at the Musée fuckin' Picasso? Huh? You have the qualifications, right? So, you gotta be another fuckin' expert.'

Mitchell didn't deny or confirm anything.

'So, naturally my boss buys this thing from Meyer, thinking it's the real thing. Turns out, it's a fuckin' fake. Took him months to find out that he's paid twelve million for a piece of crap.'

His forehead had broken out in big glistening beads of sweat, which he mopped away with an already damp, scarlet and gold Versace handkerchief.

'You still haven't told me who this Leon Meyer is,' Mitchell said. Playing dumb seemed the only safe approach.

'Listen to me, Jameson. Fact - you know McGraw's wife, that Marlo slut. We've seen you with her, followed you round in Paris, the two of you doing who-knows-what-else. So - second fact - you know where this painting came from. Michael fuckin'

McGraw. Meyer worked for that prick for years. He handled all his cocksucking financial deals. So, don't try to tell me you don't know who Leon Meyer is.'

This time the little finger was jabbing Mitchell hard on the bone between his eyes.

'Well, I'm sorry, but the truth is I don't know any Leon Meyer.'

Mitchell was trying to stay calm, and to calm Franco down as well, but it wasn't taking.

'Meyer! Meyer is headed for the fuckin' cheese grater. Same as you, you don't fuckin' tell me something useful. See, why is it I think you might be right there on the inside of all this?' He screwed up his eyes and leaned in closer. 'The one simple question I've got for you, is where the fuck is our Picasso? The genuine one? The one my employer paid twelve million for?'

'I can't help you there, either.'

'I've been having a little difficulty finding Leon Meyer. He's the logical first place to look, right. But he's really got something to fuckin' worry about, so he's disappeared. Or maybe this McGraw woman, maybe she's got it hid somewhere. I mean, why else does she want to see you, Mister fuckin' Picasso expert? Unless she's got a picture for you to look at? Understand how I'm seeing all this?'

'Of course.' Mitchell was desperately afraid that the man's ranting inquisitional technique would shake loose some vital clue as to the wherabouts of the Picasso, and so he closed down the debate as far as possible. Mitchell was trying to sound totally reasonable as well as completely ignorant, but it wasn't working. It only seemed to draw Orsini in closer.

'Good. Step in the right fuckin' direction, at last. That's why I thought you might be the very man to help me with all of this.'

'I meant, I understood your approach to the problem. I didn't mean that I knew the answer.'

'You're an arrogant fuck, Jameson. You think I hauled you out here to have this fuckin' ping-pong talk, then, send you on your way? No. You're here because I-want-to-know-what-happened-to-my-Picasso.'

'If I could help you on that, believe me, I would.'

'What is that? Australian talk? *If-I-could-help-you-on-that-believe-me-I-would?* Give me what you know, arsehole. Or I'll cut off a fuckin' finger, I swear.'

He suddenly produced a small bone handled stiletto and sprang it open with an ominous dry click of well-oiled quality steel. His face developed a terrifying crimson flush.

'Gimme that fuckin' thing,' he squealed, ducking down and making a grab for Mitchell's trussed hand. Fortunately, Toadmouth was quick in reaction. He hauled Orsini to his feet and instantly began a ritualised soothing, patting him down gently until his elevated colour subsided.

'Franco, Franco, Franco,' the man whispered, in his gruff basso.

'I'm on a tight timetable,' Orsini said, with even greater urgency. 'I've got a plane to catch back to L.A. in the morning. I have business to take care of out there. You don't know who I work for, what he does?'

'I can guess. He's in movies?'

'Wilder, you supercilious prick - he *finances* pictures. He backs things people want to see. And he makes enough money to buy your arse. That's why he don't appreciate being fucked over when he buys a work of art. He's in the business of making the fuckin' stuff himself. And that's why you're not sitting here, at this moment, with your feet in wet concrete. I represent a top of the line businessman, I'm not a fuckin' thug.'

'I'm sorry, I misunderstood you. I thought -'

'You thought nothing. He's proud of his pictures. No, not your taste maybe. I can see you'd like that fuckin' European shit. Hard seats and fuckin' subtitles that don't relate. My boss, he finances action pictures. Last year he did a Stallone and a Steven Segal. Not their best works – a little late in their career trajectories, maybe - but he went into profit. Both pictures. That's what matters. And now his profit's on the line cause of you and that Meyer fuck.'

'Can I ask, why he wanted to buy the painting?'

'Listen to me, you dopey fuck, it's a normal thing in L.A. He buys a little art, from time to time. So, he's got a few nice things in his Brentwood house. Got a nice Dave Hockney – even met the man - picture of sprinklers on the lawn of a house just like his own. Sits up there in the conversation pit. Perfect. Also got a nice Francis Bacon - two fat guys, buck naked, squirming in this kinda lounge chair, whatever - but it's worth a fuckin' pile, I'll tell you.'

'So he's a serious a collector?'

'No - more of a hunter-gatherer, maybe. People owe him, so they pay with a piece of art. Eliminates the tax problem, understand.'

He seemed to have explained everything Mitchell needed to know. The scope of his boss's grasping ego. The ugly side of the fantasy of owning art one barely understood.

'I'm sorry your boss got taken on the Picasso.'

'Just shut the fuck up on that. Now - situation. I've gotta make some long calls. You can make yourself comfortable and sit here for a few hours trying to get your fuckin' story straightened out. Then, I'm coming back, and you'd better have some nice fuckin' answers about our missing Picasso.'

A short time later, the combination of fear, exhaustion and sedatives began to kick in. Mitchell spent the next hours passed out in the chair. He was roused by a few stinging slaps on the cheek.

'Oakey-doakey, let's get started.'

It was Orsini. He explained that he was in a restored mood now, after a nap, a shower, and a change of outfit. He was wearing a bright red head-to-toe acrylic tracksuit. Michael Schumaker without the sponsorship patches. The hair surrounding his bald patch was hanging in wet baby ringlets. He smelled of talcum powder and an even more liberal application of the tropical aftershave.

'You took a little nap, too - huh?' he demanded of Mitchell. 'Rested your brain a while? Got your dopey fuckin' story straight?' He leaned in close to Mitchell's face. 'Cause now is the time I-want-to-know.'

Orsini signalled to Toadmouth, who had been watching over Mitchell in his absence. The man gave an obsequious nod and left the cellar, to return a short time later with another man whom Mitchell had not seen before. This one was also Italian. He was a stumpy, compact man in his early forties, with a bodybuilder's physique and a moon faced pugnacity. He was dressed as though having come from a gym, in a taut grey low-cut singlet and a pair of synthetic black tracksuit pants. His glistening skin stank of perspiration and the musky odour of genitalia.

The two men approached Mitchell's chair from behind, took a firm coordinated grip on the backrest, then sharply tilted the chair onto a forty-five degree angle. Mitchell gasped in anticipation of pain. It felt as though he was about to be slammed against the floor.

Orsini smacked his hands together. 'Bath time,' he said, in a cartoon voice.

Mitchell was dragged backwards across the cellar, the chair legs screeching against the tiled floor. Every mortar joint transmitting a painful jolt to his spine. He was carried up a curving flight of stone stairs, along a dim passageway, and into a brightly lit, spacious bathroom. The floor was wet. The air was damp. The window was frosted with steam. Orsini had taken his shower here, was Mitchell's perversely irrelevant observation. As a guest, one might have found it luxurious, or at least admired the elegant free standing porcelain bathtub and washbasin, and the Art Nouveau plumbing. The bathtub, he could see, was almost brimming with water. And, oddly for summer, a gas-burning radiator had unnaturally elevated the temperature of the room.

The two men brought the chair to rest, upright in front of

a tall dark wood *armoire* with a door length mirror. Mitchell lifted his head and saw his reflection in the steam-frosted glass; a picture of abjection and absurdity, the colour entirely drained from his face.

Orsini waddled into the room and made a play of testing the bath water. 'Oakey-doakey. Your turn, smart guy.'

The bodybuilder crouched at Mitchell's feet, then rose, grasping the legs of the chair like a wheelbarrow. The man's face turned crimson, the tendons in his neck tightened. The bearded man took the weight of the backrest. In one shuffling, strained movement, they lugged Mitchell across to the bath, hoisted him up over the lip, and dropped him cleanly into the water.

Panic surged through him as the chair legs slithered against the sloping edges of the bath and a wash of disturbed water sloshed across his nostrils. He wrenched his head upwards, spluttering and gasping for air.

Orsini rested his weight on the edge of the bath and gazed down at him with an expression of simulated concern.

'Maybe it's a little too hot for you? Is that it, huh? You a man likes a party? Cause I got the ice, See - '

Orsini lifted up a sack of party ice, which he began to slice open with his stiletto. He stood to pour the pellets into the bath, ensuring that the bulk of the load was heaped upon Mitchell's stomach.

'I assume you're a Champagne man, Mister Jameson. What I got for us is two very nice bottles of nineteen-ninety Bollinger. Excellent year, according to the *Guide Hachette*. What the fuck do they know, huh? All that matters is - this's the favourite drink of James Bond. Thought that'd appeal to you. Here - two bottles, case we get greedy. That suit you?'

Orsini stuffed the two Champagne bottles into the ice at Mitchell's feet, then, tested the water temperature with his finger tips.

'Tell you something - if that's feeling a little too warm, if you're not entirely comfortable, I got another bag.'

At first the sudden cold had merely alarmed him. Like pins and needles. An urge to move his limbs, to shake it off and leap free. And then it hit. A burning ache that seared his skin and penetrated to his bones. A cruel pain in his gut and a needle behind the eyes. His teeth, his whole jaw, shuddering uncontrollably. The terrifying approach of an overwhelming numbness. He thrashed against the ropes with all his fading strength, but only succeeded in swamping his nostrils. The bite of cold water in his throat and wind passage. Three faces, amused, curious, hovering over him. Detached anaesthetists. No help. Receding. Gone.

Suddenly, hands were reaching into the water. The chair was lifted, streaming water. Ice pebbles bounced off the tiles like hail. The ceiling beams, the high bright window, swirled overhead. He was aware of landing upright in front of the radiator. Splashed water spat against the glowing red heat grille. The toxic bite of burning gas in his throat. A tiny area of warmth, spreading slowly down the front of his body. Still he shivered all over.

And then there was Orsini's puffy hand, dabbing at his face with a towel. Offering him a glass of Champagne. The glass pressed against his lips. Bubbles bursting under his nose. A forced sip that gagged in the throat and was sprayed against the radiator.

You're the first stupid fuck I ever met who knocked back a glass of Bollinger. So - I'm sorry to interrupt the cocktail hour, but I got the same two questions for you. Where's my painting? And where do I find the McGraw woman?'

'I don't know...I can't help you,' was all Mitchell could summon. He kept on repeating the words between mouthfuls of Champagne and tender cheek manipulations from Orsini's pudgy fingers.

'We oughta check that bath water. Whaddya say? Hey - stick that other bag of ice in for my man.'

Mitchell was barely aware of what was happening in the room, his body ached to the exclusion of all other sensation. There was the sound of a second bag being sliced open. A brittle cascading and threshing of the bath water as the ice hit.

'Cocktail hour's up, my friend. Back in you go.'

'Oh, no, no, no. Oh, Christ, no! Please, no!'

'What's that? Oh - you want to know the rules here? Simple. The longer you talk to me, the longer you get to sit here by the fire, glass of Bollinger in your hand. How's that sound?'

Orsini turned to his two accomplices. 'Do it!'

With an appetite for the game they swooped on Mitchell's chair and dumped it once again into the bathtub. For a terrifying few moments the water sluiced over his head. And then he could breathe. But by then the icy water had already assailed him. His mind could barely struggle against the pain of the intense cold. A silent bellow exploded and died in his throat. He was underwater again, clamping his eyes, his mouth, against the terrible cold. The light, fading to blackness.

A painful glare from above, was burning his eyelids. All his teeth were aching. Mitchell gradually realized that he must have passed out. Now, he was slowly becoming aware of the clammy heat from the radiator, feeling a raging fire in the nerve endings of his skin. Numbness had overcome his entire body. He tried to strain against the ropes, to move his leg, to twist his torso. Nothing. He had lost control of all his limbs. They had cut some of the rope away. His hands lay limp against his thighs. His flesh was a dangerous, sickly blue. His fingers were clenched rigid, like the useless claws of some dead animal.

Then Orsini was crouching down alongside him, whispering near his ear.

'You like another Champagne? Or maybe you'd prefer a warm towel and a nice massage? Get the old circulation going again. We up for some more conversation? How's the mouth? Just give me a simple 'yes' or 'no '. You're not looking good at all, Mister Jameson.'

Mitchell was incapable of any reaction. His blood felt frozen in his veins.

'Now. Situation. We've been wasting a lot of time over this. I know you know this McGraw broad. My man saw you with her yesterday, taking a nice little walk together in Paris. Looked to him like you might be gettin' some, too. Hey - hey! Don't pass out on me. I need your full attention. Seems my man - he's got a better memory than you. But - sad thing is, we don't know where the broad is no more. See - last night we had someone take a look in her apartment.'

Mitchell stared at him, unable to conceal the impact of the revelation. Not quite able to believe what he was hearing.

'What's the funny look? Big surprise to you, huh? You gotta remember this apartment. Don't say you don't. We know you been there. My man, he followed you. But next day, we go to take a look ourselves - nothing'. Nobody home. Cute furniture. Nice and tidy all through. No trace of this McGraw broad. No fuckin' Picasso - that we don't expect. It's like she's cleaned up every last crumb. Disappeared again. Which means, Mister Double-O-Seven, that you gotta know where it went. We know she had it with her. We saw her. Too bad it was out in a public place, we might have collected. But she got away in a crowd. Fuckin' Métro. Like a fuckin' mole hole down there. So - where is it, huh?'

'I'm not the one...'

'Oh, Jesus - and we're gettin' low on ice. Only one more bag, and all the shops closed. Oakey-doakey. Rinse him one more time.'

'No, no - Jesus, not again. What do you want to know? I'll tell you.'

'Oh - this is better. This is good. This could have saved you a lot of fuckin' misery, you stupid putz. As it is, you gonna be walkin' round like a stick man for the next week. Ice is a fuckin' terrible thing - I think you know.'

Mitchell had no idea what he might say. He couldn't possibly surrender Luc's name. That would be the most abhorrent betrayal.

He couldn't be responsible for what this demented clown might do next. He would hang on. Tell them as little as possible. Or lie. Mislead them, if he could.

'There's a man...a man in Montmartre.' It hurt terribly to even speak. It was the truth, but he had to offer something of the truth, it needed to sound plausible.

'What? Huh? I don't know where that is.'

'Paris...'

'Paris? I know it's Paris, you cluck. But I dunno Paris from Brigitte Bardot's left tit. Where is this place at?' He turned to his accomplices, who by this stage were warming to Franco's act. 'Any you guys know?'

'Up the hill. In the North. Big white Duomo,' Toadmouth said, slowly, cautiously, making sure he imparted no loose information.

'Ah...that joint. I know it. So - you got a name for me?'

'Pierre...'

'Oh, Pierre?' Orsini's face lit up with mock delight, then, just as suddenly clouded with malice. 'This is good. Lot of fuckin' Pierres in that city, my friend. Pierre who?'

'Pierre Caumont,' he said. Where did that name come from? Why would he think they'd buy it? All the while the name Luc Pellegrin hovered on his tongue. It would be so easy to say the words and end the torture.

'How do you spell this - what is it? Cormon?'

Mitchell struggled with the spelling of the name, his mind sliding, barely grasping the reality of the situation, while Orsini took it down using a silver biro, printing the big letters on the inside of his wrist. He finished with a grunt of satisfaction, then twisted his arm and displayed the name to Toadmouth.

'Hey - go look this up on the net. If this fuck is lying he takes another bath.'

Orsini turned back to Mitchell. 'And this is who's got our Picasso, right?'

'He could have it...yes.'

'Why's he got it, huh?'

'He's a Picasso expert. He's taking a look at it for her.'

'On account of you directed her there. Am I right?'

Mitchell said nothing.

'Takin' a fuckin' look, huh?' Orsini got to his feet. He glared at Mitchell as though he would have liked to give him a swipe across the mouth. 'I'm the one who should be lookin' at it!' he shouted. 'A good twelve million dollar look. So what's the plan you two cooked up? She gonna try to sell my boss's painting? That it?'

'I don't know what her plan was. We never talked about it.'

Toadmouth returned to tell Orsini that there were three Pierre Caumonts listed - 'None of them in Montmartre.'

'You made a mistake, huh, Double-O-Seven? You remember the name wrong?'

Mitchell closed his eyes. He knew what would happen next.

'Oakey-doakey. Back into the tub we go.'

He felt his body hurled through space. Once again, the brutal shock of the icy water. A numbness that spread upwards from the base of his spine. A shower of ice pellets, tumbling slowly towards him. A sky full of white flower petals. Burying him beneath a blinding white blanket. Then the roar of water in his ears, receding to silence.

He woke beneath a strange ceiling. Stretched out naked on a hard bed. Heavy grey blankets, tucked up to his chin. The glow from the windows very weak. Late afternoon light. The shadows of leaves thrown against a white wall. The song of a thrush. And now Orsini, sitting at his side near the bed.

'You've been a real helpful guy, Mister Jameson.'

'What?'

'This new name you gave us - it checked out good.'

'Who?'

'Luc Pellegrin.'

The sound of Luc's name filled him with dread. How could Orsini possibly know?

'Ah - don't tell me you don't remember. You were screaming it out, over and over. Like you couldn't wait to tell me. That's the funny thing about ice. Everything else freezes up, but it gets the tongue going every time.'

So he had told him. He believed he had passed out. Everything convinced him of that. But he hadn't. Something had happened beyond his awareness, and he had done the very thing he had struggled against.

30

August 23: Paris

Another room. Smaller. Faded wallpaper. An intricate pattern of red and orange rose petals. A slash of morning sunlight on the white door. A framed notice of tariffs. A hotel room. Traffic sounds and animated voices drifting up from the street.

He tried to stand up, but he had no strength at all. The pain in his joints was acute. He felt feverish, weak, and nauseous. He was dressed only in underwear - his own, as far as he could recall. His skin was an ugly fish belly white.

There was a chair in one corner of the room. A small pile of neatly folded clothes lay upon the seat. They seemed to be his, but he couldn't be sure.

By holding on to the headboard of the bed he managed to haul himself upright, The window was no more than half a dozen steps away, but still he needed the wall for support. After slowly circumnavigating the room, in the process knocking the telephone from its cradle, he finally ended up at the window. He held onto the heavy curtains like a man in fear of falling to his death. After a few moments, he parted them fully to reveal a view of the river from the north. He was back in Paris.

With great difficulty he attempted to dress. He barely had the strength to force his feet into his shoes. Everything ached. Afterwards, he considered using the telephone, but realized he couldn't recall any of the crucial numbers. Not Marlo's. Not Luc's. Not Ilena's. His small telephone directory had been in his pocket at the time of the abduction, but Orsini had evidently kept it.

Downstairs, he learned where he had been brought: the Hôtel Malliol. He was in the 9th, not very far from the Gare Saint Lazare. The stern young woman on the front desk was at first puzzled by his questions. Realizing how ill he must have appeared, he thought she must have imagined he was suffering from an almighty hangover. For a while she reacted as though he was attempting to lodge some obscure complaint, to which she had no response. But before long she changed her attitude and behaved as if she was dealing with a disturbed man who had lost his memory. She talked to him as one talks to a child, but all the while her eyes kept drifting to the telephone.

'Do you have a record of my booking?' he asked in French.

'Yes, of course,' she said, while locating it in the register. She maintained a veneer of politeness throughout, determined to keep this crazy man placated. Rotating the book so that Mitchell could see the entry for himself, she pointed out that the room was reserved for a Monsieur and Madame Jameson from Nice for the one night only. It should have come as no surprise when he saw that the contact number that they had provided was his own.

'How long have you been on the desk?' he demanded.

'Since seven this morning,' she said. 'Madame, over there - she was here last night.' She was referring to an older, smartly dressed woman with coiffed grey hair, who was in the nearby *salle de petît dejeuner* giving instructions to an African maid who was in the process of clearing away the breakfast detritus.

When Mitchell approached her, she held up a warning hand and told him he was too late. Everything had finished at nine. He attempted to explain his problem and began asking the questions all over again. Still, she seemed preoccupied with the arrangement of her tables. She continued looking over Mitchell's shoulder to point out her preferences to the maid. When she did finally respond, it was to ask insistently whether he was in fact a guest.

'You are Monsieur Jameson?' she kept repeating, having evidently comprehended little of his earlier explanation.

'Yes, I am. But I didn't make this booking. And what I need to know is, who arrived here last night and claimed the key to my room?'

'Your wife - Madame Jameson, of course,' the woman said, with sufficient front to dismiss any notion that she may have been negligent.

'Can you describe this woman for me?'

'But obviously you must know her - no?' she said, with a condescending smile. 'She's your wife, isn't she?'

'No, no - that's the problem, you see. She was somebody pretending to be my wife.'

At this the woman threw her hands up in a pantomime of utter confusion. She took a few steps away from Mitchell to continue with her rearranging of the tables. Mitchell followed her.

'Could you describe the woman to me?' he asked. 'It's very important.'

The manageress hesitated for a moment, unsure about how co-operative she ought to be. 'Oh, she was elegant. Like an Italian movie actress. The make up, the hair, the jewellery - you know - far too much. The expensive designer clothes. Everything too much.'

The excessive description fitted nobody he could conjure. 'And was she alone?'

'Well, you weren't with her. That's obvious.'

'What time did she arrive?'

'Around ten.'

'And what time did she leave?'

'I'm not sure. She went upstairs. Only one small bag. She made some phone calls. I know - we have a record. And then she left, half an hour later. Maybe less.'

'These calls - were they local?'

'One was, yes. The other was a country number, or maybe international - I don't know.'

'And you didn't see anybody else enter the hotel that night? Nobody that you didn't recognize? No Italian gentlemen?'

That made the woman smile. 'No, Monsieur Jameson. I never forget an Italian gentleman. They're rare.'

'The bag the woman carried, could you describe it?'

She closed her eyes and tried hard to visualize it. 'I think maybe it was green. Soft material, you know the type. Perhaps dark green.'

It was his, he was certain of it.

'Monsieur Jameson - I am very sorry if your wife is being... difficult. But if there is anything else I can do to make your stay more pleasant?'

'I think my stay is already over, thanks all the same.' He told the manageress how much he appreciated her concern, then allowed her to resume her fussing with the dining tables.

He had no idea how he might learn any more about why he had been brought to the Hôtel Malliol. And did it really matter? It was obvious enough who was behind it - except for the involvement of the improbable 'Madame Jameson.' Impossible to imagine whom she might have been – unless it had been the 'other Marlo' - or why they would have gone to such lengths to deliver him safely back to Paris. Perhaps, in spite of his brutal methods, this was Orsini's way of saying that he wanted no further trouble.

Mitchell was about to return to his room when the young woman on the desk called out to him.

'Monsieur Jameson - your luggage is here.' She pointed to a dark green bag standing in an alcove near the desk. At a glance, he knew that it was his, and from its bulging sides, realized that it probably still contained the documents intended for the museum in Antibes. The mysterious 'Madame Jameson' had left it without informing the manageress. Maybe the contents would also be intact.

Mitchell took the bag back upstairs. Each step was agony. He needed to pause for thirty seconds on each landing, in order to recover the strength for the climb to the third floor.

Once inside the room, he hauled it onto the bed and unzipped it. Nothing appeared to be missing in spite of the signs of a thorough ransacking.

Still, he was without his telephone directory. Luc's numbers he could easily obtain. As for the missed rendezvous with Ilena in Menton, there was little to be done. All he could do was leave a message for her at their hotel and offer an explanation.

The young woman on the desk found Luc's home number for him in her directory. For some inexplicable reason, Luc's line gave out a long, uninterrupted buzz, a sign that his telephone had been disconnected. Mitchell realized that he would have to revisit Montmartre - or even possibly Luc's gallery - and contact him in person.

Mitchell phoned the hotel in Menton. The woman who took his inquiry was extremely helpful. She explained that Ms. Vadas had already checked out earlier that morning, and had made no return booking. But she added that Ms.Vadas had left a message for him. The woman laughed as she read it out, amused by her own difficulty with the pronunciation of the crucial word:

'Mitchell, my man - where the fuck are you?

Ilena'

He was already weighing up whether he should return straight away to his apartment, thinking he might be able to recuperate there - at least until he could report to the police on the Franco Orsini matter, and sort out what had happened to Marlo, Luc, and the Picasso portrait. He also considered visiting a doctor beforehand, but he could barely summon the energy to bother. Even the thought of having to explain the cause of his condition was daunting. Contacting Luc was a far more pressing concern.

He tried to ignore his frailty and took a taxi straight to Montmartre. He was praying that he would find Luc at home. All the way there, dreading that his betrayal of his friend - or did he merely dream it? - might have had terrible consequences. And finally, seeing what he feared, as the taxi turned into the Rue des Martyrs - the cordon of *agents de police,* the array of police vehicles, and the small crowd of silently curious residents.

Mitchell thrust a ridiculously large note at his driver, and stepped onto the pavement. The surreal logic of the scene confirmed his every fear. He didn't need to look up at the shadowy figures, visible through the windows of the third floor apartment, to know that they were there for Luc. No one had to tell him that the people clad in white and blue overalls entering and leaving the building were there to investigate a death that he had set in motion. An unmarked white mortuary van was parked opposite the apartment block. He was struck by a fearful vision of Luc, already lying on a gurney.

He staggered like a sleepwalker towards the ribbon of flapping yellow plastic and the young *agent de police* who was keeping the public at bay.

'Can you tell me what happened here?' he asked. The request was impertinent. As if every member of the crowd hadn't wanted the answer to that same question.

'Non,' the *agent de police* said curtly. It was an answer he must have already given a hundred times that morning. From somewhere in the crowd Mitchell heard the words he dreaded: *'C'est un meurtre.'*

'I'm sorry, but I'm very concerned,' Mitchell insisted. 'I'm a friend of Luc Pellegrin's, the man who lives in that apartment.' He pointed towards the third floor. 'I've come here today to see him about something urgent. I really must speak to the senior detective.'

The *agent de police* took a long, searching look at Mitchell and considered his options. 'In that case, please come with me,' he said.

Keeping a weather eye on a few impatient, disgruntled members of the crowd, he lifted the plastic tape and summoned Mitchell into the crime scene. They walked past the mortuary van, where two callow looking young attendants were opening the doors of their refrigerated compartment. With their crew cuts, crisp white shirts, and conservative dark suits, and their facial expressions suggestive of holy office, they looked like zealous urban missionaries awaiting the call.

Mitchell was led over to an unmarked royal blue Peugeot station wagon, where a senior detective was leaning on the driver's door, engaged in a volatile radio conversation. Something hadn't been done, and someone was to blame, and the detective wasn't taking any more shit. Mitchell was made to stand directly in the man's line of vision, while the *agent de police* sought his senior officer's attention. The detective cast a distracted glance at Mitchell - another unwanted intrusion - as he wrapped up his conversation with an explosive, *'Connard!'* When he finally had the man's attention, the *agent de police* explained that Mitchell was an acquaintance of the victim with some potentially important information.

The detective had the tired, sardonic demeanour of an aging *boulevardier,* a far less attractive, but recognizable, Belmondo type. He wore his coiff of salt and pepper hair an inch or two on the shaggy side, so that a heavy lock flopped across his brow. His impenetrable wrap around sunglasses were scored with scratches and held together with cellotape. A Gitane hung in the corner of his lazy mouth.

'Inspector Védrine,' he said after ashing his cigarette with a sharp flick of the jaw. 'Who are you?' The question was in English, but the thickness of his accent suggested that his repertoire of phrases wasn't great.

'Mitchell Jameson. Friend of Luc Pellegrin.'

'Montrez-moi votre passeport.'

By chance Mitchell had it in his possession. After the business with Orsini, he was carrying his valuables with him everywhere. He produced it for him for the Inspector, who took his time flicking through the indecipherable trail of immigration stamps. Mitchell seized the opportunity to elaborate on his business relationship with Luc.

'So - you've come here to collect a painting of yours?' he asked, speaking this time in French.

Mitchell felt obliged to formulate his answers in French. *'No - the painting belongs to a woman I'm representing. I've come here to discuss the painting with Monsieur Pellegrin.'*

'Je suis désolé,' he said. *'Il est morte.'*

He was assailed by the simple, devastating fact that he had struggled so hard to deny. But how could he begin to tell this man all that he knew? How could he explain the absurd horror of his last twenty-four hours?

'What else do you can you tell me?' the Inspector asked. The man could obviously read Mitchell's guilt and confusion.

'I can tell you whatever might be helpful about my business with Monsieur Pellegrin.' Perhaps, after the Orsini ordeal, a full confession would be the easiest thing in the world.

The Inspector motioned the young *agent de police* to conduct Mitchell to the mobile operations van, a large white windowless vehicle, parked further up the street. Once inside, Mitchell was offered a moulded-plastic seat in the interrogation cubicle. Comforted only by a paper cup of bitter black coffee, he faced a discreetly concealed camera and sound recording device.

Inspector Védrine, who sat at right angles to Mitchell - so that the camera could photograph them both simultaneously

- introduced himself to camera and stated the time and place of the interview. Once underway, the questioning took place at head-spinning speed. The Inspector seemed anxious to get back to his investigation.

Mitchell was asked to explain his business relationship with the deceased as well as the reasons for his recent visits to the apartment. The occasion of the Marlo McGraw visit to Luc's apartment was the only aspect of the story in which he was encouraged to offer detail. He volunteered a more complete history of his involvement with Marlo McGraw and her Picasso, but the Inspector cut him short. The Orsini abduction elicited no apparent interest at all - or perhaps the Inspector was just being cagey. Mitchell thought he must have sounded like a crank while trying to convey the tone of the *buffo* violence featuring the Hollywood Italian and the bathtub full of party ice. The fact that he could offer no convincing account of how he had escaped from these madmen, nor any sensible explanation of how he had woken up in a Paris hotel, must have made his tale sound even more suspect.

At the conclusion of this perfunctory interview, Inspector Védrine switched off the recording device and slid a document in front of Mitchell. It was a statement of personal details and an affidavit. A biro was placed in his hand and he was asked to sign.

'The painting - this Picasso,' the Inspector said, gravely. *'I don't think it's in the apartment.'*

'I'm not at all surprised,' Mitchell said.

'I want you to come upstairs with me. I have some more questions for you. There are things you might be able to help us with.'

At last Mitchell realized the man's purpose. Get the suspect to commit the story of his last visit to tape. Let him lie as much as he liked. Then trap him upstairs with the evidence.

'I don't know if I...' Mitchell began, wondering whether he had the stomach to see Luc's body, which he knew must be up there waiting for him.

'I'm sure, after your experiences of the last twenty-four hours, you won't be upset by the sight of a little blood.'

Inspector Védrine escorted Mitchell up to the third floor. The entrance to Luc's apartment was guarded by two uniformed *agents de police.* The senior man nodded in deference to the Inspector and opened the door. As he stepped into the hallway Mitchell was astonished by the extent of the devastation. Whoever had come in the night to attack Luc had made no secret of the fact that they were searching for something. Books and CDs and paintings had been flung across the floor. Shelves had been overturned and cupboards ransacked. Out in the living area, a forensic team was at work, dusting for prints and bagging evidence. In the centre of the room, half hidden by the lounge setting, a more sinister scene was taking place. A man and woman, both in white overalls - police medical examiners, he assumed - were down on their haunches, taking a close look at what Mitchell assumed must be Luc's body.

'Your friend is lying dead on the floor over there,' the Inspector said. *'You needn't look if it upsets you.'*

'I'd prefer to see what happened for myself,' Mitchell said. *'Do you mind?'*

'Je vous en prie,' the Inspector replied, with a shrug.

Mitchell stepped around the sofa. The medical examiners ignored him; they were engaged in the indelicate task of ascertaining the corpse's temperature. What Mitchell saw left him unsteady on his feet. The attitude of Luc' s body suggested nothing more odd than an evening spent sitting on the rug, back resting against the sofa, watching television. But his mouth was agape in a grimace of bloodied teeth. His eyes were open wide but without pupils. The exposed whites, hideously enlarged, looked like peeled boiled eggs. The front of his shirt was soaked in dark arterial blood. There was a deep slash in his throat just below the jaw. A coil of what Mitchell supposed was picture hanging wire was wrapped around his neck.

'What do they think happened here?' Mitchell asked, almost seeking reassurance from the Inspector.

'Well - we think he opened the door to someone, probably someone he knew. We know this because there's no sign of struggle in the doorway. Then he showed them into his apartment and - '

'How do you know there was only one person?' Mitchell interrupted.

The Inspector smiled, amused by Mitchell's predictable reaction. *'Because so far they've only found evidence of one other person. But who knows for sure, eh?'*

'At what stage was he killed? Before all this happened?' Mitchell pointed to the debris scattered across the room.

'Yes. Almost certainly. They probably made some demand. Threatened him. Maybe he refused - we don't know anything for sure. The only thing we can assume is that he didn't put up much of a fight.'

'They were professionals.'

The Inspector didn't challenge the assumption. *'But we do know how they did it,'* he continued. *'One hard knife thrust, straight into the chest below the heart. And then - just to make sure he was dead - they used a length of thin wire to garrotte him. Preferable to making a big mess with a knife. No opportunity for screaming, either.'*

'Italian style killing. And it sounds like a job for two.'

'Monsieur Jameson, we can see how it was done, but as to who - let's not assume anything,' the Inspector said without emotion, before continuing his account of the night's events.

'And then, it seems the killer made a frantic search for something. Maybe found what he came looking for - we don't know.'

'I think we do know - it was the Picasso...and I know exactly who's got it.'

This display of angry conviction seemed to amuse Inspector Védrine, who shook his head sagely. *'But we never really know until we absolutely know, Monsieur Jameson. Please - take a look at this.'* He led Mitchell over to the dining table, where a number of items, each sealed in labelled plastic bags, were placed in an orderly line. The Inspector carefully picked up one of the bags and held it in front of Mitchell. It contained a small blue cloth bound notebook whose covers were smeared with blood. *'We found this little address book beside Monsieur Pellegrin's body. I'm sure you recognize it.'*

The sight of his missing telephone directory in a police evidence bag failed to have the predicted impact on Mitchell. It merely confirmed his conviction that Orsini and his thugs had killed Luc. *'Yes, yes, it's my telephone directory,'* he answered with impatience. *'It was the one item that I knew for certain had gone missing after Orsini had finished with me.'*

The Inspector met Mitchell's eyes for an uncomfortably long time. *'I'm sure I can imagine how you could explain this,'* he said. *'But why would anyone believe it?'*

'Yes - of course I realize it's a clumsy way for anyone to try to implicate me. Like something the author Agatha Christie might have used. Steal something significantly personal and stick it in the victim's hand.'

'Pardon?'

'Old fashioned, but still popular English crime writer. Think Simenon.'

'An old trick, yes,' the Inspector agreed. *'But Simenon wouldn't ever use it.'*

'It's just Orsini's idea of a black joke. A bit of payback.'

'No matter,' the Inspector said, hardly interested in Mitchell's convoluted explanation. *'I'm going to need your fingerprints. A procedural necessity, you realize. I'd look stupid if I didn't do my job.'* He summoned one of the forensic officers and asked him to take a full set of Mitchell's prints. While this was being done, with a familiar French thoroughness - each digit, left and right, pressed against an ink pad and guided to its correct place on a form bearing a printed outline of two spread palms - Mitchell and the Inspector continued their conversation.

'This is not as serious as it appears,' he said consolingly. *'We're certain you didn't do it.'*

'But you don't know this for sure?' Mitchell said, risking a joke.

'At least we know how to find you - just in case.'

'I'm immensely relieved. I thought you were going to really put me through it.'

'No. There's more to the story. The Montmartre police received a telephone call from Monsieur Pellegrin at ten o'clock last night. He was very emotional, extremely distressed. He was reporting that he had been harassed by a strange woman who had arrived without notice on his doorstep. She had demanded that he hand over a painting that she claimed belonged to her. He suspected she was a thief.'

"The Picasso?'

'Yes. I'm sure it's the same painting she was after. He gave them a description of it.

'Was this Marlo McGraw?'

'No, it wasn't the woman that you brought to his apartment, the one who owned the painting. This was someone he had never seen before. At least that's what he told the police. She was very well dressed, in her early thirties perhaps, attractive - at least that's how he described her. He said he did everything possible to convince her that he didn't have her painting. She persisted with her crazy claim, but after becoming almost violent with him, suddenly gave up, for no apparent reason, and left without any fuss. At that point he telephoned the police.'

'So, did anyone from the Montmartre police come to investigate?

'No. They would have thought it a minor mater."

'But then, several hours later, in the early hours of the morning, the Montmartre police got another phone call. This was from someone in one of the neighbouring apartments. They had been woken by strange noises. A terrifying cry. The sound of things being thrown around very violently. This time the police came to investigate. And

this is what they found. So you see, it's all much more complicated than you were aware.'

It all confirmed Mitchell's certainty that the murder was the work of Orsini and his assistants - that was never really in doubt. But his mind had leapt ahead to the more startling conclusion that the woman who had arrived on Luc's doorstep demanding her painting was probably the woman he had met in the guise of Marlo McGraw at Le Fumoir. It made perfect sense. Whoever she represented, she had been in determined pursuit of the Picasso for some time; now, with the real Marlo showing up in Paris with the painting under her arm, it was hardly surprising that the trail had been picked up again.

'Do you have any idea who this woman might be?' the Inspector asked, as though having read his mind.

'No, no - none of it makes any sense to me.' Mitchell didn't believe that there was any point in trying to talk to Védrine about the woman. After all, what did he really know about her? Nor did he think it appropriate to say anything about the meeting with her at Le Fumoir. How could it be explained? It barely even made sense to him

'What about this woman who owned the painting, this Marlo McGraw? Do you know where we can find her? She isn't at her apartment - we checked.'

'No - I have no idea.' It bothered Mitchell that he hadn't properly considered the danger that Marlo might be in. It was a pointed reminder of just how confused he had been since their afternoon of lovemaking. In truth he neither had any idea of what she wanted from him, nor of what he wanted from her. And he certainly had no way of reconciling the conflicting emotional claims of Marlo and Ilena. In Marlo's case, he had become so used to her looking after her own interests; until now her safety had never seemed an issue. There were so many questions he couldn't answer. Did Marlo collect her painting some time before Luc was killed? And had Orsini and his thugs found a way to get to her as well?

He wanted to get out of the apartment before the horror of the situation engulfed him completely, but there were things he needed to know. He looked across at the computer on Luc's desk. It was one of the few things that hadn't been overturned.

'Luc was in the process of writing an appraisal of the Picasso,' he said. *'Perhaps it's still on his computer. Could I possibly...?'*

Inspector Védrine walked over to the desk, took a moment to consider the irregularity of what Mitchell was proposing, and then acquiesced.

'Go ahead, open it. You're familiar with a Mac? I'm not at all.'

Mitchell took a seat in front of the outmoded old desktop. He was about to boot it up, when he hesitated, his hands poised above the keyboard. He looked up at the Inspector who instantly understood his concern.

'Fingerprints? Do you really imagine I'm wanting to frame you?' he said with amusement.

'Nevertheless, considering what you're holding over me, it would suit me better if I left no trace.'

Disposable latex gloves were provided by one of the forensic officers, and Mitchell opened up the computer.

At least Luc was organized in his work habits. Mitchell easily located the file containing his most recent writing. The document was dated the day before and was called: *Portrait de Dora Maar*. It took the form of a letter to Marlo McGraw, outlining his findings (scientific) and his opinions (informed but highly subjective). It appeared to be unfinished.

'*Do you mind if I print it out?'* Mitchell said to the Inspector.

The Inspector leaned closer to the screen to see for himself, then, nodded his assent. Mitchell was too unsettled to attempt to read the document closely. Besides, he was sure it would hold few surprises - his eye had already alighted on the phrase: *'beyond question, an authentic Picasso'.*

The printer was given the command to produce two copies - Védrine was equally curious. Mitchell folded his copy and stowed it in the lining pocket of his jacket. He thanked the Inspector for his consideration and requested permission to leave. The Inspector made no objection. The apartment had grown chilly. The air had begun to take on the pervasive, chemical smell of death.

31

August 23 - 24: Paris

Ilena returned to Paris beset with anxieties. She had left her crew in Menton. They were, she had no doubt, perplexed by her behaviour, and wondering what they were supposed to do in her absence; their only compensations, a bar in the most expensive hotel in town, a casino, and a nearby pebbly beach.

There was no easily imagined response to McGraw's coercive offer. To comply was to invite disaster - if not immediately, then clearly at some point in the future, when his attempts to evade the law finally collapsed. She couldn't share the problem with her employees back in Australia - not her network producer, and certainly not her editor at the *Australian.* They could hardly condone a corruption of her journalistic standards; they would have no interest whatsoever in any of McGraw's attempts to gild the truth; and they certainly wouldn't want to be footing the bill for a worthless piece of self promotion. If she withheld the facts about the precise nature of the attempted blackmail, the network would most probably encourage her to interview him - but then the moral responsibility for all the misrepresentations would be hers alone. It was, she suspected, the kind of interview that could only be contemplated by a gullible go-getter, or a corrupt crony of McGraw's.

Her plan - her only option, really - was to share the horrible dilemma with Roger Knight, her contact at the embassy, working for the Attorney General's Department. He could be trusted to keep a confidence, and might even be able to counsel her on a way of conducting the interview that might minimize the humbug. At the very least, she would have shared her story and provided herself with a witness, should things go badly.

The staff of the Hôtel-de-Fleurie seemed untroubled by her unexpected early return. A room was made ready with no hint of the usual irritation and fuss, in spite of the late hour. She had been too churned up to even think of making another reservation. When she arrived at Orly, theirs was the only destination that came to mind.

There was a sheaf of messages waiting for her at the desk. An ironically terse complaint from her stranded crew, who were craving direction; a request for an update on shooting progress from her Australian producer; and a request for further story material from her editor at the *Australian*.

Apart from giving her crew some suggestions of material they might usefully film, she chose to defer answering the other messages. Instead, she rang the embassy and made an appointment to see Roger Knight for early the following day. He was cheery and co-operative, and she gave him no hint of the extent of her concerns.

She was about to leave the hotel, in search of a restaurant where she might obtain an early evening meal, when she received the unexpected call from Mitchell. He told her that he was calling from his apartment. She immediately registered his distress. He sounded ill and disoriented. His words, barely audible, were spoken with difficulty, in a broken whisper. His did his best to tell her what had happened to him in Menton, but in detail so sketchy and fragmented that she had difficulty comprehending his ordeal. He was in a hurry to get past the story of his kidnapping and torture to the real matter that was disturbing him: the murder of his friend, Luc. She listened, in horrified disbelief, to Mitchell's account of his visit to the crime scene at Luc's place.

As soon as she comprehended the full seriousness of the events, she volunteered to come straight away to his apartment. The note of relief in his voice touched her unexpectedly. When she rang off, she dialed reception for a taxi and prepared to depart.

Earlier that evening, when Mitchell had returned home from Luc's apartment, he had completely forgotten his own depleted condition. He telephoned his superior at the Musée on her home number. She, too, was numb with shock and incomprehension. He also tried to contact Luc's assistant at the Gallery Pellegrin, but reached only an apologetic recorded message. He had no idea of whom else he might call.

By chance he picked up a notebook he had been using while working at the Musée, and found that he had scrawled Ilena's mobile number inside the front cover. He called her immediately.

Ilena arrived half an hour after they had spoken. He was by then showing obvious signs of having experienced shock and trauma. Fortunately, she had brought her small medical kit, which included, most usefully, a supply of powerful sedatives. She insisted that he take to bed, while she made him a supper of onion soup and toast. Then, over the course of the next hour, in voices hardly louder than a whisper, they traded stories of their previous twenty-four.

Beginning with the appearance of Marlo McGraw carrying

a portrait of Dora Maar under her arm, and ending with the painting's subsequent theft and Luc's murder in his own apartment, Mitchell held back nothing of what he knew. He wasn't sure of how much she cared about the precise state of his personal distress, but he knew she would want to hear the entire story of his kidnapping in as much detail as he could recall. Although it came out somewhat incoherently, in a jumbled torrent of half-completed thoughts, she encouraged him to persevere, until she felt she understood perfectly what he had been put through. He told her about his abduction en route to the airport, his blindfolded transportation to some unknown destination in the country, and his insane, iced water torture at the hands of the casually sadistic Frank Orsini.

'My God - this is such incredible stuff.'

'Yeah - you and the crew should have tagged along. Captured me naked and screaming in a bathtub full of party ice.'

'This Orsini guy – wonderful, grotesque character. You sure you haven't made him up?' She had been like that throughout the entire telling, keeping a jaundiced eye on Mitchell, expecting at any moment to be told that he had been just kidding, that it was all a fabrication.

'No, he's real enough. And he's still out there with his body builder and his bearded assassin - looking for his boss's Picasso, and I would guess, ready to kill someone for it.'

'Aren't you concerned for your safety? You're making me concerned for mine. Feel that,' she said, taking his hand and guiding it to the back of her neck. 'Goose bumps. Hair standing on end, too.'

'I don't quite know - Orsini let me go when it would have been so simple to kill me and dump the body.'

'Why do you think he let you go?'

'He got what he wanted from me – Luc's name - and I'm sure he's convinced I'm insignificant. And the way thugs like Orsini seem to operate, they're so far outside the system, they imagine nothing can touch them. Orsini doesn't live in France. Nobody knows who he is. What could I tell the police? That stuff they did to me, it sounds like something from a Batman comic. But it worked. I gave them Luc, and they got to him.'

'I just can't get around the fact that this smart Hollywood guy puts down twelve million for a Picasso, and only later wakes up that it's a fake.'

'Well, I suppose he was expertly conned. In the first place it was probably a brilliantly executed copy. And he must have been shown papers of authentication - faked, of course. But once the blinkers came off, fierce Italian pride kicked in. The man didn't like finding out that he'd bought a fake. He must have been determined to get his hands on the authentic merchandise.'

'But how did he find out he'd bought a fake?'

'Orsini didn't explain. Maybe someone with some knowledge took a look at it - probably when he came to resell it. Who knows?'

'Why didn't he go after this Leon Meyer, the crook who sold it to him?'

'I was easier to find. Besides, I'd had this contact with Marlo, and by then he must have figured out the scam and assumed that the McGraws still had the original.'

'So he's still after her I'd imagine.'

'Yes, but I think Marlo is smart enough to stay out of sight. Do you know anything about Leon Meyer?'

'A little. Not as much as I'd like to know. He and McGraw were partners for years, but that's no secret. You knew that, didn't you?'

'Yeah - Marlo filled me in.'

'I didn't realize he was dealing in fake art, but it doesn't really surprise me. He's a very clever, devious bastard, who knows how to cover his tracks. ASIC and the Attorney General's Department will make their move on McGraw sooner or later, but I doubt if anyone's ever going to nail Leon Meyer.'

'Where does all this leave your documentary?'

Ilena laughed. 'Nowhere. That's always the trouble with these stories. They're like icebergs. The more you think you know, the greater your ignorance grows. Same old problem. How can I film any of this?'

'You could have me standing next to a Picasso - any old Picasso - talking for an hour. Would that do it?'

Ilena went suddenly silent. Her mind was elsewhere, on her stalled documentary, he assumed. Perhaps she was calculating how this submerged part of the iceberg might be incorporated into her story.

'Listen,' he said, 'I'd rather not be in the programme at all - that is, if you're still considering...'

'That's okay. I'd lay low, too, if I were you.'

'None of what's happened makes much sense to me, and all of it makes me feel dreadful. I caved in when they tortured me. I wanted to be tough enough to lie to them, but I wasn't. I gave them Luc's name, and that's why he' dead. I can't get that out of my mind. There'll be an autopsy. I may be called. That's my first responsibility.'

'I understand,' she said.

'And frankly, I don't care any more what happens to McGraw and the rest of that crowd. I know you do – but that's your job. If they catch up with him, fine. But leave me out of it. Luc Pellegrin is dead, and he shouldn't be. Orsini and his mob are still around – they're seemingly able to get to anyone. Marlo is fascinating, but crazy. And Leon Meyer means nothing to me.'

'And Dora Maar has been dead for years.'

It made him smile. 'But not for as long as Picasso,' he replied.

'Are you still interested in what happened to the portrait?' she asked.

'I don't know whether it's worth bothering about, either. It's been out of circulation for sixty years. Is anyone really going to care who's got it now?'

He heard himself saying these things, but was he really no

longer interested, or was his mood a consequence of his temporary state of mental disorder? He couldn't be sure.

'Who was the woman who turned up at Luc's apartment?' Ilena asked. 'Did the police have any idea?'

'None whatsoever. But from the description that Luc gave them when he rang to complain, she sounded a lot like the woman I told you about - remember, that odd encounter I had at Le Fumoir with a woman who claimed she was the real Marlo McGraw?'

'Do you think she was trying to get her hands on the painting?'

'Most probably.'

'But the police think that some other, more ruthless bunch, who showed up later, were the real thieves – right?'

'That's their theory, but I'm not sure that they're right.'

''What's yours then?'

'I think the real Marlo collected her painting well before either of them showed up. I think that this woman – the fake Marlo – was working with Orsini. I think she was sent to Luc to persuade him that she was the real owner of the painting. She wouldn't have known that he no longer had the Picasso in his possession. Luc obviously wouldn't have believed her story. He would have resisted her argument. The woman would have probably turned up the pressure, even threatened him. Luc wouldn't have stood for it. He'd have thrown her out. Then, once he'd got rid of her - as we know - he telephoned the police to report the incident. Soon afterwards, Orsini's thugs arrived. They ransacked the apartment, then having found nothing, used other methods of coercion. Finally, they brutally murdered him.'

'So you believe that Marlo got away safely with her Picasso?'

'I hope she did. It's the only comfort I can take from any of this.'

Ilena seemed amused. 'Even though she's also probably a scammer and a crook?'

'Even so. Tell me what happened to you, that same morning in Menton.'

'I got up early to try and catch McGraw's lawyer, Pierre Lavelle at his office. I failed of course. I think the woman who worked for him sensed that a potentially dangerous Australian woman had come looking for him, and lied to me. She told me that Lavelle wasn't around. All the while, I think the man was hiding in his office. Not having any other plan, I went back to the hotel, thinking the day was wasted. I'd already told the crew to go out and photograph odd images that might be useful. There was nothing to do but wait for them to return. I think I was taking a nap, when I got this strange call. It was from Lavalle, offering a meeting with *"an old friend"*. Almost straight away I was picked up and taken to Nice airport and flown to Toulouse. As soon as they got me into the car they blindfolded me, then drove God-knows-where for about an hour. All so dramatic. No crew of course - they'd been left behind. That was the deal. And there I was at last: face to face with Mike McGraw. I hadn't seen him since my days as a junior reporter. He was very charming, at first. We talked at length. He was quite candid about his situation. I even thought he was going to propose a serious interview - his terms, naturally - and tell me everything I wanted to know. But instead, Lavalle revealed that our conversation had been taped, with a view to compromising me if I tried to make any unauthorized use of what had been discussed.'

'So what was the point? Why did he want to meet you?'

'I do think he wants to tell his side of the story – but with absolute control of the interview.'

'Did he suggest you come back with your crew?'

'He left it open. But obviously it would be entirely on his terms. Hardly honest journalism. He'd approve every question, closely vet the interview, and decide how and where it could be broadcast.'

'Then are you interested?'

'Unfortunately – I am.'

'Supposing you do this interview. What's to stop you editing it later – adding whatever commentary you choose?'

She did her best to explain how McGraw might carry out his threat. 'For instance, he has stooges back home who could write about my collusion with his attempts to evade the reach of the Australian authorities. Incriminating pictures would probably appear - he had some taken when we were meeting. They'd make us look like cronies. And there are other, more cunning, things he could do to make me appear corrupt. He could secretly open a bank account in Sydney in my name. An old trick, but effective. Money would be wired into it if I didn't play the game. Ugly, devious stuff.'

'But you're doing this interview at the behest of a major television network. How does he think he can intimidate your employers? If you exposed the ploy, surely he'd have to back off.'

'So I'm being paranoid?'

'Maybe.'

But now that it was all out in the open, Mitchell could see just how tortured she was by her situation. It was the undefined nature of the threat that was so hard to shrug off. Still he wondered why she hadn't sought help

'Your only choice is to go to the Attorney General's Department and tell them what's happening,' he said. 'At least it will be on record. Maybe they can take responsibility for the situation.'

'Yes, yes - I know you're right.' she said soberly. 'I plan to talk it over with Roger Knight, my contact at the embassy.'

'Just to change the subject – did you ask him about the Picasso portrait?'

'Sure. I brought it up. It was all off the record, so I took a chance and put it straight to him. Told him some of what you'd told me. '

'My God - he's going to be after my arse as well.'

'No, no - I didn't mention you. I just said it was known that he had this painting.'

'And what was his reaction?'

'Oh, he muttered some impossible explanation. A weak denial. But I pushed him about it. And he finally told me the whole story. Amazingly, it was very similar to yours. He said that since they had separated Marlo now owned the painting. He said that she had been trying to sell it, but that she was also very afraid - being McGraw's wife - of having the painting taken from her by ASIC, on behalf of the Australian creditors; and by this creep Leon Meyer.

'So if I'm right, and the Picasso is back in Marlo's hands again, does that mean..?'

'That its back in Mike McGraw's possession?'

'If it ever left.'

'That's the other thing I haven't told you. As I was leaving McGraw's place - escorted away would be a more accurate description - I saw something in the grounds that struck me as overwhelmingly significant, but I wasn't sure why. It was a car - a silver Mercedes coupé, parked almost out of sight at the end of a long driveway. I took down the licence plate, and found out later that the last two digits indicate that it was registered in the Alpes Maritimes *département*.'

Mitchell stared at her. He couldn't quite believe what he was hearing. 'Go on,' he urged.

'Well, it made me think of you - your story of the visit to Saint-Paul-de-Vence - but I wasn't absolutely sure I was remembering things correctly.'

'You were,' Mitchell said. 'Marlo was driving a silver Mercedes coupé when I met her down there. And she told me that she had hired it in Nice, which is in the Alpes Maritimes.'

'Interesting, but it doesn't conclusively prove that it's hers,' she said. 'It's a common enough luxury car. There'd be thousands like that in the south of France.'

'But if you consider that she was claiming to no longer have any contact with Mike McGraw - and then a car exactly like hers, registered in the same place, turns up in his driveway - it'd be reasonable to conclude that - '

'That Marlo was in the neighbourhood.'

'Exactly. So maybe the marriage split was just a convenient story, a survival strategy to help legitimize her possession of the portrait. Make it easier for her to represent the painting on her own. Right now they probably have both the painting and the authenticating documents.'

'What are the implications of that?'

'Well, if things had gone to plan, and Marlo had lined up a buyer, she and McGraw could have sold it on the sly. But who knows what the situation is now. They're probably terrified of losing everything.'

'But somehow I don't feel too sorry for them.'

'If we're right, I guess this is a big breakthrough. Brilliant work - thanks to your perceptiveness'

'Not really. It was just one of the silly details we were considering recreating in the documentary. Cheesy, I realize. Exotic woman steps out of a silver Mercedes coupé outside the Colombe d'Or. The sort of nonsense we film when the budget exceeds common sense.'

'Do you think you'll really be able to go through with it?' Mitchell asked. 'Go back down to Toulouse and face this man again?'

'I'll make a decision as soon as I've talked to my contact. I absolutely must sort out the legal implications. I want it well and truly on record that the man is trying to fuck me over before I make another move. That's assuming he agrees to be interviewed – on any terms. And who knows, there might be a favour I can perform for the Attorney General's Department and ASIC gang. There might be things that I can find out by going back into the den.'

'Spying can be dangerous. Besides, he'd be too smart to give anything away.'

'Sure. But it could be very exciting, too. Is that what you're thinking? Would you want to come, too? Or are you going to need more time to recover? I know you're over it all and have your safety to think of. But could you be tempted?'

Although he found it difficult to admit, he did feel – in spite of his present state - drawn again to the intrigue of the missing Picasso.

'You're offering me a job on the crew now?'

'If you like. If you're up to it. You can pose as my producer.'

'The poseur producer? Sounds like my role. Thanks, but I'm not so sure I'd want to run into Marlo again. It could blow everything for you.'

'Surely if she heard that a television crew was about to descend on the house, she'd take off for the day.'

'I wouldn't want to predict anything Marlo might do.'

'I could ask to see the Picasso,' Ilena said, 'see what kind of reaction that got.'

'Count me out of that exercise. The truth is, at this point, I'd much rather see Orsini's fake version than take one more look at the original.'

'Let's hope that opportunity doesn't arise.'

Ilena picked up her mobile and began checking for text messages.

'Anyway, I should leave you alone. Let you get some more rest. I have an appointment at the embassy in the morning, to get some advice on what I'm heading into, and then I'm planning to fly down to Toulouse in the afternoon to meet up with my crew. How about I call you at midday to see how you're feeling and discuss whether or not you're up for it?'

'Hey? You already know the answer. What else would I want to be doing?'

She leaned over the bed and kissed his cheek. 'You sure there's nothing else you need?'

'Jus a lot more rest, I think.'

She gathered her things and quietly left his apartment.

Mitchell was left in a troubled state. What was he doing offering himself up to some new reckless enterprise? What was he was rushing headlong towards? What was driving him?

He cast his mind back to the first time he had seen the *Portrait of Dora Maar;* back to that day spent with Marlo in Saint-Paul-de-Vence; and then even earlier, back to when he had first heard that she was in possession of one of Picasso's works that had been lost since the Second World War. The painting had excited him enormously. That feeling had never diminished. He had wanted to participate in the rescue – was that what it was? - of what might conceivably be a twentieth century masterpiece. Even though he had come to the adventure by chance, he had found the intrigue surrounding the painting vastly more satisfying than anything he had been involved with at the Musée. But now, the murder of Luc had cemented his resolve to have something of consequence come from the escapade.

Marlo had spun a web of uncertainty around her motives. It was clearly psychologically dangerous to stray too close to her, let alone pursue any kind of personal involvement. Frank Orsini was an even more deadly specimin, but with him the threat was palpable, the web was in full view. What could he say about this adventure of Ilena's? There was obviously more to her relationship with McGraw than she was revealing. But what good would it do him to hitch himself to her undisclosed quest? In spite of his intense curiosity about the Picasso and the undeniable stimulation of her company, was the risk worth taking? Still, he would have given a lot to know the true history of the portrait - but was McGraw ever going to reveal it? And did McGraw even know the first thing about the work until it had passed into his hands? Was the mystery of its past ownership to remain forever unsolved, a part of the forgotten history of the Paris of World War Two?

32

August 24: Paris to Val d'Aveyron

Ilena had booked them on a mid-afternoon flight to Toulouse. She had counted on Mitchell coming along. He found the whole experience somewhat disorienting; but, still feeling vaguely ill, found it at least comforting to place his immediate plans and welfare in the hands of someone else. On the flight down, he did his best to go along with what he believed was her agenda.

'What did they tell you at the Australian Embassy?' he asked.

'They simply said: 'go for it'. Give us an unedited copy of your interview tapes and allow us to debrief you when you return to Paris. Other than that, they told me not to worry about the legal consequences. They'd take care of it all.'

'What about your reputation back home?'

'They said, go ahead, double cross McGraw. Do the interview

his way, but reveal within the programme precisely what kind of coercion went on, and point out what a crock it all is. We'll take care of the consequences.'

'They must think highly of you.'

'*He* - not they. I've only got one good friend in that place, remember: Roger Knight. That's who I'm relying on.'

'So there's a risk.'

'Always.'

Earlier, that same afternoon, Mitchell had found himself in brief conversation with Michael McGraw himself. One of the last frantic things Ilena did at the airport, before heading off, was to call McGraw to confirm their arrival time. She had wasted no time in introducing Mitchell (whom she had called Miles) and had handed the phone across to him so that he could negotiate the interview schedule. McGraw had affected a detached casualness, purring into the phone as though there had been no coercion on his part. He had treated Mitchell like a minion, with no attempt to establish a relationship, and nothing that could be construed as friendliness. It was purely a business arrangement, no more complicated to organize than a visit by a plumber. Nothing about the prospect of being interviewed on his own terms seemed to interest McGraw, and nothing appeared to daunt him either.

'He bought it?' Ilena asked, as Mitchell put the phone down.

'I really don't know. But what a voice.'

'I know it well,' she said. 'Aged for ten years in oak.'

'The kind of voice John Huston might have had if he was Australian.

'Or something invented by Peter Sellers. A creamy blend of hokum and charm.'

'The killer touch lurking behind the grand manner.'

'Good, good - you're warming to the McGraw legend already.'

'Can't wait,' he said. 'Let's go.'

Later, in mid-flight, Mitchell was still asking questions about

McGraw and rehearsing his new role as documentary producer. He knew it was a jumped up term, that in fact he was merely a production manager, a man with no creative say, but a worrying amount of organizational responsibility. Maybe he was going to have to talk schedules and budget and production arrangements with the casual fluency of a professional. None of it was going to come easily to a man troubled by the complexities of booking an airline ticket. He imagined there were going to be times when he would have to step in and negotiate with McGraw, all the while pretending to have no particular creative interest in the content of the interview. Overplaying, that was the danger. For the most part he would try to keep his mouth shut and allow Ilena to run the shoot.

In the final stages of the flight, Mitchell gave some thought to the questions that he hoped Ilena might ask McGraw. He sat with his seat at maximum recline, notebook and pen in hand, trying to formulate a sequence that would allow her to lure McGraw into the murky area of the painting's history as criminal currency. Every so often he would try out a question on Ilena, who would give him the expected, cynical, non-response she imagined McGraw would offer.

'So - *Criminal in Paradise: The Mike McGraw Story*,' he announced with a cackle of derision. 'Slate forty-seven, take one: Quite a number of modernist works painted in Paris in the thirties fell into the hands of the Nazis when they confiscated the collections of prominent Jewish dealers and collectors. Do you think the *Portrait of Dora Maar* might have been among them?'

'No, no. Waste of time,' she protested. 'Too on-the-nose. All I'd get in response to that mouthful would be a blunt *no*.'

'Sorry - I'll rephrase it.'

'Don't bother. Even if he knew the answer to that, he'd pay dumb. Probably serve up some platitude about the tragic fate of the French Jews.'

'Well, hey - if you want to write them yourself?'

'Listen, Mitchell. You're offended. Don't be. We've known

one another all of one week. We've got ourselves wasted together. We can say anything to one another. It's just that I'd normally be asking him questions that go beyond mere information to elicit some kind of personal emotional response.'

'What sort of questions would they be?'

'Questions that aren't so obviously designed to entrap him. People like McGraw, - whatever the issue - know exactly what they're prepared to tell you. You can't ever trick them into saying more. The best you can hope for, in the way of truth, is that you'll get an off the record comment offered in a spirit of reasonableness. The moment they sense it's a game, you're going to be the loser.'

'Give me an example.'

'Something like: what do you like about the painting? Or: what was it about *Dora Maar* that made you want to own it?'

'I see. A kind of sucking up. Just like those current affairs reporters you want to throttle because they forever hold back from putting the tough question.'

'No need for you to get personal *and* emotional. But at least my question is open ended. McGraw can relax and say what he feels like because - unlike in the case of your question - he isn't being herded towards an obviously preconceived answer.'

'No need to bang on,' Mitchell said with dumb irony, ' I'm only the producer. Or is it production manager?'

At a little after 4:00 p.m. they landed at Blagnac, Toulouse. Once inside the terminal, they set off in search of Ilena's crew, who had, that same day, driven up from Menton. They discovered Brooke and Todd sitting over plates of *biftek et pommes frittes* in the airport cafeteria. Both had the sheepish look of a couple of teenagers caught necking - but as Ilena later told Mitchell, there was definitely nothing going on between that pair.

Over a round of coffees they had a brief conference on strategy. As she expected, their reactions to Mitchell's role as "producer" elicited very different reactions. Todd found the idea amusing, a lark, but Brooke was immediately suspicious and visibly anxious.

Why the need for this deception? What happens if McGraw finds out? How can this be ethical? She wasn't exactly looking for a fight, but she had very serious objections. As soon as tensions had settled, they headed for the parking lot and loaded up the aluminium equipment cases.

It was after 5:00 p.m. when they headed up the A62 towards the Val d'Aveyron. In spite of the hour, the day now seemed far hotter. A milky haze hung in the air. It seemed at last that they had arrived in the Mediterranean. They passed orchards of peach and cherry, fields of young sunflowers, and rows of espaliered pears beneath tents of bird proof netting. None of the farms or villages seemed prosperous. No châteaux loomed above the trees. It was truly *la France profonde.*

Ilena navigated by comparing a crude map, drawn for her by Roger Knight, and the Michelin map of the Val d'Aveyron. It was almost five when they crossed the river and approached the gates of McGraw's retreat. The sun, which would soon set behind the hills to the west of the river gorge, beat against the stone wall of the tower, turning it the colour of the ripe wheat in the nearby field. Except for a distant thrush, nothing stirred in the small hamlet of farm buildings.

Todd parked the Citroën in front of the iron gates in the expectation of being invited to drive inside. Instead they were met by a man who looked like a bodyguard accompanied by a nervous Alsatian on a short chain leash. Although he was probably no older than thirty, the man had the thuggish physique and battered features of a retired Rugby League player. He was clad entirely in black: expensive synthetic windbreaker with brushed chrome zipper; summer weight jodhpurs of distinctly fascist overtone; and sturdy, tightly laced calf length combat boots. When he introduced himself as Gary, in a voice from Wollongong, the entire party broke into relieved laughter. He was ex-Australian Army, ex-N.S.W. Police Force; and ex-Kingsford Smith Airport Security; and now he was Mike McGraw's personal minder. The

Alsatian, which continued to sniff at each of them with tender curiosity, was called Jodie.

They were told that their vehicle would have to stay parked outside the grounds. This was policy, the only way one could be sure of who and what entered the property. If there was any heavy gear to be lugged, Gary would be happy to assist. Mitchell would have liked a few minutes to wander freely around the grounds. He was desperately curious about the possible presence of the silver Mercedes coupé. But the opportunity wasn't offered. They were clearly going to be under guard and on notice at all times.

Gary, who had the waddling gait of a Sumo wrestler, escorted them up the gravel driveway and invited them to enter the house via a wide stone staircase that led up to a cool, tiled *bolet.* They were led into a large, dimly lit living area. Even the heat of a long summer day had made no impression on the thick stone walls. The room was cooler than a wine cellar. Massive oak beams varnished the colour of dried ox blood loomed overhead. Too many of the shutters on the small west-facing windows were closed to comfortably illuminate the space. Surprisingly, the place was furnished like a trendy boutique in the Marais. All of the pieces appeared to be original or clever knock-offs of late twentieth-century classics.

There seemed to be no particular place for them to sensibly gravitate, and Gary wasn't offering any hints. Nothing to look at on the walls, too few places to comfortably sit; and little to be seen from any of the open windows. They might as well have been sent to a holding cell. When Gary finally spoke to them as a group, it was with a clumsy and excessive politeness that translated unmistakably as a veiled threat.

'I'm going to be escorting Miss Vadas to a meeting with Mister McGraw,' he began, fixing them in turn with his slightly crossed, berry-eyed stare. 'And it would be appropriate and much appreciated if your good selves would stay together right here. Should you be requiring refreshments, or toilet facilities, Berthold - who'll show up any minute - will be only too happy to oblige.'

Before she was abruptly led away, Ilena made pointed eye contact with Mitchell, but said nothing. She was clearly edgy and short of breath. It was the moment when even the most carefully woven plans can seem suddenly threadbare.

Ilena was away with McGraw for over twenty minutes, during which time there was no sign of an obliging Berthold. Brooke and Todd were losing patience. They hadn't expected to be included in the discussion, but neither did they appreciate being treated like servants. Finally, at the far end of the long room, an oak door creaked open, and a man who was unmistakably Michael McGraw appeared out of the gloom.

Mitchell took him in. McGraw was dressed in the Tommy Bahama, American adventurer manner: a pale olive green linen shirt, just wrinkled enough to appear convincingly casual; immaculately tailored brushed cotton bone slacks over dark tan loafers; and discrete rimless reading glasses. His hair was a little greyer than it had appeared in the most recent photographs, and he had abandoned the Kennedy coif for a virile buzz cut and a salt and pepper three-day growth. Mitchell looked for the signs of strain in the strong, suntanned face, but detected nothing. The man was all mask, as measured as a seasoned television celebrity. He still wore the confidence of his former power, or at least had mastered the art of concealing all doubt.

Everyone stood, all of them feeling the tingle of awe that the man inspired. McGraw strolled the length of the room with his right hand in his pocket, giving no hint at all that they were welcome in his house. Finally, he smiled, but only enough to dispel their anxieties.

'Hi, I'm Mike McGraw,' was all he said. He shook their hands and heard their names as though there was little time to spare, and led them through the house and out onto a sunny terrace.

Ilena had already made herself comfortable, sitting on a wrought iron chair in a patch of dappled light created by an overhead grape trellis. The terrace had a view down into a walled garden, where rosemary, lavender, spiky aloes, and climbing roses grew in profusion.

'Sorry for the inconvenience of the delay,' McGraw said. 'There were just a few ground rules we needed to establish. Are you interested in an afternoon snack and a glass of wine? One of my favourite Pomerols has just been released. Worth a taste. A man can be on the run and still live well, I find. In fact I insist you try it. Something to tell your grandchildren,' he added with a knowing smile. Moments later a short, nuggety young woman of Spanish appearance entered with a tray bearing a tear-shaped decanter of red wine and an empty Pomerol bottle. Another minder, introduced as Berthold, an athletic looking unreadable German, followed with a tray of *hors d'ouvres*.

'Is this a suitable spot to set up your equipment?' McGraw asked. 'Nice to watch the sun drop away over the wall. No wind, and it stays warm till nightfall.'

McGraw poured them each a short glass of the Pomerol, then proposed a toast, all the while looking squarely at Ilena. 'To straight talk,' he said, with a smile.

'Or at least, to a good story,' Ilena responded.

In the conversation that followed, Mitchell observed an effortless communication between Ilena and McGraw. He knew that they had met on a number of previous occasions, but her account of their last meeting had led him to believe that it had ended in acrimony. Perhaps it was merely a result of his own preoccupation, this odd impression that McGraw was aroused by Ilena's presence and that the emotion was possibly mutual. It was visible in the subtle tugs of attention between them. Even Ilena's simplest utterances induced an involuntary flicker of readiness on his part. There was the sense that the rest of the party might not have even been present. It was inexplicable, and made even more disconcerting by the fact that there would be no easy time to challenge her on the matter.

The equipment was lugged in from their vehicle with the aid of Gary and the silent Berthold, and an interview setting was created on the terrace. At that stage there were probably no more than two hours of light remaining in the day. Todd wanted to know whether it might be possible to take a wander around the grounds once the interview was completed. He explained that the documentary was going to require some additional angles on the property, as well as some long shots of Ilena and McGraw walking together, deep in conversation. He also wanted access to a window in the tower, from where he could shoot an attractive high angle cutaway of the interview itself. Mitchell noticed that none of these requests appeared to concern McGraw at all. Wandering freely in order to satisfy one's curiosity would be another matter entirely. Mitchell began to wish he had possessed the technical skill to have posed as Ilena's cameraman.

Ilena took a sip of her wine, cleared her throat, then asked, 'Where would you like to start?'

McGraw looked deeply into her eyes and shrugged. Mitchell could notice a visible tension in the man's posture, a rigidity that betrayed his uncertainty. In spite of it being his show, he seemed to be retreating into himself, battening down for the worst.

'Could we begin with a summary of your two billion dollars worth of debt? It's an astronomical figure. Do you accept personal responsibility for all of it?'

'*Two billion dollars*?' he said, with just the slightest lifting of an eyebrow. '*An astronomical figure? Personal responsibility?* That sounds more like three questions.'

'Then - could you explain this figure of two billion dollars?'

McGraw took a slow, apparently unnecessary sip of his water. As far as Mitchell knew, he wasn't a man whose mouth had ever noticeably dried back in the glory days. But then the man had been a long time in hiding. He was out of practice in the once legendary art of selling himself.

'In the first place, the figure is a concoction. And whatever the true number, at the moment it's merely an *alleged* debt.'

'Nevertheless, a significant debt.'

'Well, you call it debt – like I'd run up a bill I couldn't pay. But I call it unsecured investment gone south.'

'The unfortunate consequences of a collapsed market?'

'That's about it.'

'But you lost a colossal amount of other peoples' money.

'Those investors were gamblers. They were chasing huge returns. Some might say crazy, impossible returns. Ten percent, year after year. When you have such greedy expectations, you wear the risk. I was taking an even bigger one.'

'You make it all sound like standard business practice.'

'In a way, it was. Everyone was in on this. That was the financial culture. When I needed credit, huge figures - the banks obliged. They ran after me with their trousers around their ankles.'

'Still, ASIC describes your operation as a well disguised Ponzi scheme.'

'Yes, they've made that accusation. But it's based on no evidence whatsoever. I was like any successful money manager. I was able to inspire trust based on past performance. I was also a clever investor who got caught in a sudden downdraught.'

'You weren't a scammer? Robbing Peter to pay Paul?'

'Never met either gentlemen.'

ASIC have a long list of angry losers who entrusted their money with you. Where did it all go?'

'I assure you, it isn't under my bed.'

'But you owned the hedge fund. So surely you have to take responsibility for the losses.'

'This was no one's sole responsibility. This was a global wipe-out. I didn't pioneer hedge funds, and I didn't invent short selling. And mine was a legitimate and respected business, with a long, sound track record – before the beautiful pie shrank.'

'Sounds more like someone whipped it off the table.'

'Now, now.'

Mitchell wanted to applaud. The man was at last warming to the task of his own defence. For all he knew, Ilena was probably thinking she had struck gold. Far from thinking of it as a piece of slippery self promotion, she was probably imagining it on air and rating already.

'How many of your personal assets have you been forced to sell? Or - to put it another way - how much investment property do you still own?'

'Nothing. It's all gone to serve the debt. Even what you see around here belongs to a generous friend. '

'I have here a list provided by the ASIC of the assets and holdings already sold, and also an itemization of the assets they claim you still own.'

'Well - it's their list. They can claim what they choose to. But I'm right here. I'm a fugitive in France awaiting extradition. How could anyone seriously imagine that I had a controlling interest in anything at all back in Australia? Between the banks and the panicky investors, I've been picked clean.'

'For some years now, you have collected art internationally. I have here a copy of an invitation, dated the fifteenth of May, nineteen-ninety eight. It's an invitation to an open house exhibition at a house in Bel Air, California. According to this, you collection includes...'

'Gone. Some have been stolen and some have been sold. Sold to pay debts.'

'Everything? Right now, you have no art works in you possession?'

'Correct. Although my wife does own a reasonably valuable painting.'

'Sure. You told me that she owned a Picasso portrait.'

'Which she's in the process of selling.'

'Does ASIC know about this?'

McGraw shrugged. 'I do know that a former partner of mine, Leon Meyer, is now working in collaboration with ASIC and The Australian Attorney General's Department.' He leaned in closer to the camera. It was a prepared speech and he was going to give it the emphasis it deserved. 'He is aiding them in their attempts to provide evidence to speed up my extradition from this country. This is the man who personally helped himself to what remained of my art collection. It was all removed from my home in Menton. The place was cleaned out almost immediately after my forced departure. And this is the man that the Australian Government is relying upon to give evidence against me. A Judas and a thief all in one.'

'Are you able to explain the current state of the extradition proceedings?'

'Oh, yes. Things are progressing very nicely,' he said with a wounded glare directly to camera.

Mitchell stood up from his seat at the edge of the terrace and approached Gary who was leaning against the stone wall, guarding the French doors. He asked where he might find a toilet, and Gary directed him to a ground floor bathroom at the rear of the house. It was probably going to be the only opportunity he would have to take a look around. For five minutes he would be free to wander. He followed the directions until he arrived at a large square unfurnished room that featured a broad winding staircase. He knew at once that it was the base of the tower. Instead of continuing on through to the bathroom, he took the staircase right to the top. If anyone found him poking around upstairs he would claim to be confused about Gary's directions. Given the man's broadly accented English, anyone would believe him.

As he reached the landing of the upper floor, he realized he had arrived in someone's bedroom. Male clothing hung on an open rack. The bed was unmade and a German motorcycle magazine lay on the bedside table. A zip lock suitcase yawned open on the floor. Items of erotically pushy male underwear - presumably dirty - were scattered on top of some items packed in plastic shopping bags. The room had an overpowering smell of boot polish and body odour.

There were three windows in the tower, all affording a view of a different area of the grounds. Mitchell took a quick look from each of them. He found what he was hoping to see: the tail of a silver Mercedes coupé protruding from the open hanger of the large *grange*. The only question was: was it really Marlo's? Maybe it belonged to Gary or Berthold, and their entire theory meant nothing. At least it would be worth pushing McGraw to discover what he was prepared to reveal.

Once Mitchell had returned to the terrace, he was relieved to see that Gary suspected nothing about his small detour. Ilena had broken off the interview, while McGraw refilled his wine glass, and Todd and Brooke checked their equipment.'

'That it for today, then?' Mitchell asked.

Ilena nodded. There would be no point in trying to resume the interview. The agreement had been to record some initial responses, then to allow McGraw to review the results overnight. Todd and Brooke made safe with their gear and took a stroll down into the garden, Todd to smoke an overdue cigarette, and Brooke to smell the unfamiliar roses. Mitchell, meanwhile, remained seated on the terrace, feigning attention to his diary.

'Why do you want to talk about the Picasso?' McGraw asked with a distinct undertone of threat. There was a disturbing tension in his face.

Ilena's reply required some courage. 'It's obviously extremely valuable. And given your situation, it's interesting that you've been trying to sell it. '

'As you already know,' he began, with a visible effort to hold his temper in check, 'my wife has sole ownership of it. But since we no longer live together - something you also know - you'll have to put any questions about it to her.'

'Yes, you did tell me all that,' Ilena said, patiently, 'but I'm not entirely convinced. I think that you still have possession of the painting. And I don't believe that you and Marlo are separated. I believe it's just a strategy to keep the painting away from your creditors.'

'Really? What other theories do you have?' He looked like a man who had just abandoned a poker bluff, but a man still hoping to find a safe measure of control in a losing position.

'I've also been told that when Leon Meyer turned against you, he tried to get his hands on your Picasso as well at the authentication papers. He failed to get either, so he forged the papers and commissioned a fake portrait. Now I've learned that the fake was sold to a wealthy Hollywood dupe, who's front man, Frank Orsini, is a nasty piece of work with strong Mafia connections. Naturally, this Hollywood gentleman is very unhappy about being sold a lemon - he wants the real thing. And so does Leon Meyer - maybe just so that he can get Orsini and his thugs off his back. All of which makes your situation very uncomfortable. ASIC, Orsini, Meyer - all of them after your Picasso. What better way to avoid the problem than pretend that you no longer own it? But you're the one who's hiding the pea under the walnut shell - there's no other explanation that makes any sense.'

McGraw laughed out loud. It was an unsettling, mocking laugh. Chilling in its lacerating sarcasm. At that moment, neither Mitchell nor Ilena had any idea of what they had unleashed.

'I think this deserves another bottle of Pomerol, don't you?' He made a signal to Gary, who had all the while been affecting a servant's invisibility. Gary welcomed the errand and slid away.

'Excuse me a moment,' McGraw said, slipping a miniature mobile phone from his trouser pocket. With no sign of panic or pressure he unfolded the phone and dialed a number. 'Yes, it's me,' he said in a warm, jocular voice. 'We need you to clear something up. Could you come over right away? We're on the west terrace.' He folded the phone away with a sign of resolution and relief, and turned to face Ilena.

'All right. You appear to understand the situation. Off the record, I won't deny it - we're together. The circling vultures necessitate desperate tactics. As for the Picasso - well, it's our last asset of any value, and we'll fight to keep it. It's something we both love enormously. It was a marriage present, you understand. It means far more to us than it ever could to any collector. But if we're forced to let it go in order to survive, in spite of the pain, we will.'

'You're aware of the history of the painting?' Ilena asked.

'Of course I am. But then, that's all a part of the mystique, isn't it. A lost masterpiece that can't afford to ever show its face. And what a beautiful face it is. A lot of people make the mistake of thinking that Picasso despised Dora when he painted these works. They confuse the distorted, tortured features with a damaged relationship. But when a dealer once asked Picasso what he meant by the double profile - two eyes looking in impossible directions - Picasso said: 'it's only that I keep my eyes always open...it's simply the face of my sweetheart, Dora Maar, when I kiss her'. How about that? I thought we'd have the pleasure of looking at Dora's face all our lives - but now that's not going to be possible. So we'd like to sell well and see her placed into the right hands. We just have to stay a jump ahead of the scavengers.'

It was a nice speech, movingly delivered and Mitchell might have bought it had it not sounded even less spontaneous than all the others. Ilena was unsure of where to next take the interview. The man had confessed to everything and now sat before her with an almost vacant expression, his hands resting lightly on his knees. She was rescued from embarrassment by a commotion at the front of the house. The Alsatians were barking in a frenzy at an apparent intruder. This was followed by an outburst of aggressive German, and then some good Australian invective. After a few moments the dogs calmed down and then came the sound of the front door closing and a woman's heels clattering on the parquet floor.

'Don't your crazy dogs ever remember anyone?' the woman protested. It was Marlo's voice, Mitchell knew it immediately.

She came to the terrace doors and McGraw stood to kiss her. She looked like no one Mitchell had ever seen before. Her hair was combed back in a smart American traveller's cut. She was dressed in a pale mango-coloured safari shirt over bone calf length slacks and wore a pair of casual rope sandals. Uncharacteristically she also wore a delicate shell choker necklace and an expensive silk scarf. When McGraw wrapped his arm around her waist, and stood with her head to head, they look like they had just stepped off a lugger in Havanna, 1932.

Had he been a smoker, Mitchell might have chosen that moment to slip away and join Todd down in the garden. But there was no way he could possibly escape that encounter. Marlo peered at him quizzically, as though trying to place some forgotten acquaintance. 'Mitchell?...Mitchell Jameson?' She continued with caution; her tone excluding any hint of their former intimacy. 'Didn't we meet once down in Saint-Paul?'

'No, sorry,' he said, hoping his denial would be interpreted as discretion. 'You must have me confused with someone else.'

Marlo took the hint and shifted her attention to Ilena. 'Hi - I'm Marlo,' she said, in her freshest American manner.

Without showing that he sensed a problem, McGraw stepped in and introduced them both. 'This is Ilena Vadas - you must have heard me talk about her, and...' There was a moment's hesitation as he reached for Mitchell's name. 'Miles?...Miles, isn't it? He's the producer, or production manager, or something – but don't ask me what he does.'

Marlo took Mitchell's hand and steered him just enough to seize a moment of private eye contact. 'You sure I haven't met you somewhere before, Miles?'

There was a spark of erotic mischief in her look. Mitchell was relieved that things were going to remain playful, and for a moment he felt a perverse revival of desire. 'It's possible,' he said. 'In our game we get around a lot.'

But Marlo was in an evasive, teasing mood. She immediately turned away and slipped an arm around her husband's waist. 'Work's over for today,' McGraw declared, 'and we have another bottle of Pomerol right here.'

33

August 24 - 25: Toulouse

'You know, I think I might have a programme,' Ilena told Mitchell, as she took up the bottle of 2005 St.-Julian and topped up her own glass. She was already a little drunk, and the bottle was almost empty. They had been seated for an hour and had only now received their entrées. 'I can't get over the eloquence, and the fact that he wants to talk about it all - I mean way beyond the deal he struck.'

They were sitting at an outdoor table of the Restaurant La Fayette in the Place Wilson, up in the chic quarter of Toulouse. It was perfect still Mediterranean night, and the tables out in the Place were all overflowing with high-spirited, affluent young parties. Earlier that evening they had all checked in to the Hôtel des Beaux Arts on Rue de Metz, down near the Garonne. Todd and Brooke had gone off in search of their own dining experiences, and now he was pleased to be sitting alone with Ilena.

She was amazingly buoyant from their afternoon with McGraw, a transformation that Mitchell couldn't quite fathom, since the man had given her little other than a serving of polished mendacity.

'Extraordinary afternoon...just extraordinary,' was all she seemed able to offer.

'It didn't bother you that he lied about almost everything?'

'Well, did he? Of course you can argue against any of it, but what other stance would you expect him to take?'

Mitchell shrugged and drained the remains of the St.-Julian into both their glasses.

'Sure, he's done all those appalling things,' she said. 'But he's been through his own hell as well.'

Mitchell was waiting for some sign that she was merely kidding, but it didn't come. 'He really got to you, didn't he?'

She hesitated just long enough for him to realize that he had struck a nerve.

'Okay, I won't deny it. I think he's incredibly charismatic – beyond the obvious charm.'

'And urbane, and witty, delightfully considerate,' added Mitchell, taking the piss.' Leaving out altogether the fact that he blackmailed you into this charade.'

'No - I'm not forgetting any of that. He's a rogue, a total bastard. And yes, this is probably just a subjective response. But I'm only reacting to what I was getting from him.'

'A load of self serving crap.'

'Whatever - but it's also showing promise of being enormously entertaining. When has anyone ever heard him speak about himself like that?'

'I think it can be safely said you have a special interest in the subject.'

'Well, of course I fucking do - I'm writing a book about the man.'

'I thought the book had been forgotten'

'Temporarily. Nobody writes a book when they have the opportunity to shoot a television special.'

'Just hold your judgement until tomorrow. Wait till you've heard him tell his whole story. A true tale of big dreams, passionate drives, achievement against all odds, envy inspired in all quarters, enemies finally in for the kill, fortune gone, collapsed hopes, exile and personal anguish. It's an amazing saga - best made-for-TV movie ever.'

'Fortunately, I know you're being facetious.'

'Oh, no, I'm not,' she said, enjoying winding him up with her playing the vapid TV huckster. 'Once you've sat at his feet and heard him tell it, you can't possibly see him as an ogre. People are going to be intrigued by him. He's a gambler and a big thinker. He's played for the highest stakes and lost. A great romantic, in a land of accountants. You can't tell me people won't be stirred by that.'

'Or outraged.'

'Who cares whether they love or hate him. They won't be bored.'

'Wedged between all the Toyota commercials, you're probably right. But if they're concerned about truth...'

'For you, Mitchell, it's all very simple, isn't it. It's genuine - or it's fake. It's valuable - or it's worthless. But I like to believe everyone has their reasons, and that most judgements miss the mark.'

'Try thinking that in a bath tub full of party ice.'

'Listen, you - lighten up. And eat your entrée or they won't serve us a main until midnight.'

'Only if we can order a bottle of that same Pomerol McGraw served,' he said, getting onto her wavelength.

'They wouldn't have it here.'

'They might,' Mitchell urged.

A waiter was summoned and the wine list produced for their

inspection. Mitchell burst into laughter when he saw the very wine that McGraw had served that afternoon.

'Oh, my God, they do have it,' she said, 'but look at the price for the ninety-eight.'

'No matter at all. We'll put it on the production account. I'm the producer. I can authorize that sort of thing.'

The bottle of Pomerol arrived and they toasted the McGraw enterprise - regardless of their differing views of its ultimate value. And naturally the wine tasted nothing like the way it had tasted on that terrace earlier that afternoon.

'Something's missing,' Mitchell said, faking bewilderment.

'It's called ambience,' she said.

'Yeah. You'd probably have to be dining with McGraw for that.'

Ilena smiled, then looked away sharply, a troubled expression in her eyes.

'You told me that you'd interviewed him before,' he said, 'back in the days when he was merely rich and famous.'

'Twice.'

'Did you ever get close to him?'

'Close?' she said, sounding defensive, wondering where this was heading. 'Yes, I suppose we became friends for a short time - a year or two.'

'What happened to the relationship?'

'You *are* curious.'

'I think I'm on to something.'

'We became lovers.'

'Oh.' The news hit him like a punch. It was not so much jealousy, more a sudden sense of exclusion.

'Wasn't that what you expected to hear?'

'I suppose it was.'

'But I'm sure I wasn't the only one.'

'I can't believe you wouldn't have been enough,' he said, instantly regretting the remark.

'Please - don't get mushy on me. I was just a kid, trying to make it the male world of financial journalism. I had a desk on the tenth floor alongside the meat pie and horse racing fraternity.'

'And he was the ultimate mentor. The entrepreneur's entrepreneur.'

'Yes - he'd tell me extraordinary things. Secrets about big deals going down that even he shouldn't have known about.'

'He was your mystery source?'

'Some might have wondered. I mean my editor questioned me about it. A few people must have known whom I'd been talking to. But it wasn't out there in the public domain, no.'

'No wonder you still - '

'Sure. I owe him a lot. I suppose he shaped the way I think about business. Maybe he could have taught me how to make millions, too. But that wasn't what the relationship was about. I think he was lonely in his marriage. It was a disaster in the midst of a life where everything else was booming. I was a confidante. He loved teaching me things. And I was - no I wasn't in love. I was deeply infatuated. I mean, to be in bed with the king of the jungle. It was all too much.'

'So you understand him far better than you pretend.'

'I know how he used to think. It was all an extraordinary game back then. I had the impression that he never really cared about the money in itself - I mean, of course he liked a lot of what it bought, but there wasn't much that he couldn't do without - he was far more interested in the game itself. Winning was what he really cared about. And ultimately, winners are cold company,'

'Were you the official mistress or a well kept secret?'

'What do you think? I'd get the phone call - and I'd turn up on the doorstep, take the trip, or whatever was on offer. It became pathetic towards the end. He was the one who had no time, I was the one who waited.'

'So it ended badly?'

'Over the phone. The worst way.'

'Do you still have those feelings for him?'

'No - he's like some dead movie star to me now. It's like having a crush on Cary Grant. You see him up there - all that charm and vitality and charisma, everything you've fantasized about - but none of it's there any more. It's all a mirage.'

They spent another hour at the restaurant, quietly finishing their meals. Mercifully, even Ilena was too exhausted to return the conversation to the subject of McGraw.

Back at the Hôtel des Beaux Arts they hugged goodnight in the lobby and went their separate ways, Ilena to use the fax machine in the office downstairs, and Mitchell to trudge up to his top floor room.

He was far too tired to fathom what any of the day's revelations had meant. All he knew was that Marlo had lied. The simplest explanation had been true all along, and the Picasso was just another piece of property to be sold off and forgotten. Mitchell felt a disgust at his gullability, his readiness to attribute heightened notions of significance to mere possession. Marlo and Mike McGraw were hardly different from Franco Orsini, they just had a little more finesse.

Around midnight he took a long shower. His back ached and the wine had left him with a vague headache. The only comfort came from the feel of the taut, cool bed sheets against his bare skin.

The arrangement with McGraw was for them to show up for the interview at ten the following morning.

The drive out to the Val d'Aveyron was excruciating. Little was said; all of them were absorbed with their own thoughts. The combination of mild hangovers and an all round jaundiced view of their cynical mission had numbed most of the party. Even Ilena, who had tried so hard over two bottles of wine to spin a little enthusiasm and excitement out of the prospect of the interview, appeared to be having second thoughts for the second phase.

They crossed the Aveyron near Cazals and drove along the D137 towards McGraw 's farmhouse. As they neared the property,

Mitchell, who had his passenger side window fully down, heard two sharp cracking sounds that came from somewhere across the river, He was certain that they were rifle shots, but he knew this wasn't the hunting season. Moments later, as they crested the final hill and had their first view of the farm house walls, Mitchell and Todd were both aware of some kind of frantic activity happening just out of clear view behind the iron gates. There were two dark shapes lying on the gravel driveway. Bodies? No - dogs. The Alsatians they had seen previously. A blonde haired man in a tracksuit was crouched over the corpses, looking about wildly, gesticulating towards someone back at the house. He didn't even glance in the direction of their approaching car.

Todd changed down and slowed to a crawl.

'There's something nasty happening here,' Mitchell said. 'Turn around, let's get out.'

Ilena leaned across from the rear seat to get a clearer view. 'Are you crazy?' she protested. 'Pull over, Todd! We're getting the camera out!'

'No, no - I think he's right,' Todd said. 'This is fuckin' weird.'

At that moment several more shots rang out. It was hard to tell from where, but Mitchell thought it sounded like the other side of the house. The blonde man, who still seemed oblivious to their arrival, ran back up the driveway.

'More shots! We should back off! Whatever's going down, we can't afford to walk into it.'

Ilena was furious. 'This is action! This is a fucking *event!* What are we doing running away?'

'Don't you get it?' Mitchell shouted. 'Somebody firing on the house.'

'What if Mike needs help?'

'We're not the ones who can give it,' Todd said, throwing the car into reverse.

Only Brooke seemed to be heeding Ilena's call to action. She had her digital sound recorder on her lap and was poking a boom mike out the window to see if she could pick up any further gunshots - a creative decision that left Mitchell shaking his head in disbelief.

'I can't understand you guys!' Ilena kept wailing. 'I can't believe we're just walking away.'

'Give it a few secs and we won't be walking,' Todd said, at an adrenalin induced pitch. 'We'll be doing one-hundred-and-fifty k's - out of here!'

'Back there - that's where our job is!'

But once it was clear they were doing as Mitchell suggested, she calmed own somewhat and fished out her mobile. On the way back to Cazals she tried to contact McGraw on his land line number as well as his mobile, but although the phone rang normally, nobody picked up.

'Does anyone know how to dial the *gendarmes?'* she asked.

None of them knew.

Cazals was deserted as always. The village didn't even possess a tabac. They parked the car and continued trying to contact McGraw, placing a call every five minutes. Nothing. After an hour they agreed to drive back to the farmhouse, but to turn around immediately at the first sign of danger.

The enterprise had altered from being a cynical exercise to now seeming like an extraordinary story that they were in danger of botching. All four were confused by the opposition of their fear and their professionalism.

34

August 25: Val d'Aveyron

At first light, Eddie and Jacques had driven out to McGraw's hideout in the Val d'Aveyron. They had parked Eddie's dark blue Renault Kangoo van - hired for the purpose on the previous afternoon - in the usual parking space on the D115.

When they stepped out into the gloomy cover of a massive chestnut tree, they saw that the river was obscured by a layer of mist. Fortunately, the contours of the farmhouse on the other bank were just visible. At least it was possible to see that there were no lights in any of the windows and that nothing was moving in the grounds. It was harder to work in the half-light, but Eddie was relieved to have the set-up time.

While Jacques smoked and complained about the cold, Eddie wheeled a bicycle from the rear of the van and checked the equipment in a small knapsack. Jacques was to stay put with his high-powered rifle while Eddie would cycle across the river and pass the gates of the house. Eddie knew he was expecting a lot from Jacques, but he had put in the time painstakingly going over the plan. He had mastered the phrase, *'c'est compris?'* which he repeated at every step, never moving on until he had elicited a confident, *'oui, d'accord'* from Jacques.

By seven Eddie was cycling through the mist across the bridge to Cazals. It occurred to him that there were people who actually did that kind of thing for pleasure. People back home who fantasized about romantic holidays bicycling through the French countryside. But not too many who carried sawn off .30 calibre M2 Winchesters in their knapsacks. Mister-kiss-my-arse was always a comfort.

The village of Cazals was also silent. Eddie turned left onto the D137 and continued cycling in the direction of McGraw's farm house. He hoped McGraw and his minders were all safely tucked up in bed. That way there was a chance that Eddie might walk out with the painting with no one getting hurt. Otherwise, it was going to be a shit fight from start to finish.

The steep roof of the house loomed over the hillside up ahead. He was relieved to see that the tower was still in darkness. As he approached the walls he began to whistle *La Mer,* the only French tune he knew. This was the tricky part of the exercise. It all depended upon the dogs being free to roam within the grounds. And he hoped to Christ that Jacques wouldn't go to water on him. He slowed his cycle speed and made as much as racket as he could with his boots against the pedals.

At the moment he drew level with the iron gates, the dogs appeared, bounding silently down the driveway, bristling with the instinct to kill. They slammed their paws up high against the gates and forced their muzzles between the bars. Still they maintained a stalking silence. Eddie steered his bicycle into a wide circle in front of the gate, hoping to taunt them as much as possible.

Across the river, Jacques adjusted the focus of his telescopic sight and viewed Eddie's antics on the bicycle. The man was a clown. Right then and there Jacques would have enjoyed taking him out in one. The thought of losing his final payment was all that held him back.

It was only when Eddie stepped off his bicycle to toss a few rocks in their direction that the Alsatians were goaded into barking. The ironwork clanged and groaned under the thrusts of their massive bodies. The terrifying rasp of their barking echoed back and forth across the valley. Eddie wheeled the bicycle around in another tight circle. The dogs clamped the bars between their slavering jaws. In the midst of the frenzy, Eddie saw lights come on in the tower. One more circle with the bicycle and he was out of there. This was when it all needed to happen - but what was Jacques up to? He waved his hand in an urgent motion in Jacques' direction, and then took off as fast as he could.

From somewhere across the high wall Eddie heard someone shouting in German. Even though he was pedaling as fast as he could go, the sound chilled him. It was like he was in a stalag break-out from some wartime movie. He was well away from the gates, almost half way along the western wall, when he heard the shots - two distant pops, nothing more. The dogs fell silent instantly. So maybe the man was as good as he had claimed.

Eddie continued pedalling towards the wheat field that adjoined the property, and then rounded the north western corner of the wall. A narrow donkey path ran parallel to the northern wall, separating the farm house from the field. From his first survey he had planned to scale the wall on that side. He had seen that there were no north-facing windows in either the tower or the lower farm house.

Jacques took a long look at the results of his marksmanship. The dogs lay in the gravel, massive as two felled lions. A fit looking young man, a northern type, wearing a gym trousers and a plaid pyjama top was wandering in circles, screaming. The game was on. Monsieur Pike had better know what he was doing.

Eddie dumped his bicycle out of sight in the wheat field and tore the knapsack from his shoulders. He took out a long coil of nylon rope, knotted and looped with handgrips. At one end he had fastened a steel grappling hook. It took him several attempts to hurl the rope and securely snag the hook on the lip of the ten metre high wall. He tested it with his full weight, then, began the climb. If anyone caught him halfway up he was finished. There was no way that he could even get to Mister-kiss-my-arse, let alone heft it accurately enough for a shot. Eddie was suffering. No strength in the arms and hands. Too long without exercise. It took all his determination and both hands to haul himself up. The truth was, he was getting too old for this kind of work.

When he reached the top of the wall he took a good long look around to recover his breath and see what was what before committing himself to going over. Below him there was just a garden of cactus, rosemary and lavender, with more stone paving than lawn. Just the thing for a bone-shattering landing. The inner wall, unfortunately, was covered with climbing roses. There was no way he could avoid getting shredded by briars on the way down. At least the garden afforded an easy way in. Stone steps led up to a terrace from which French doors gave access to the house.

Eddie took his weapon from his knapsack and made the drop. He tried to leap well clear of the wall, but halfway down felt a tangle of thorns tearing at his arm. He was sent spinning off balance. The rocky ground slammed against his boot soles. His body buckled, collapsing him into a patch of tall, spiky cactus. He had the instant image of himself as the hapless Wily Coyote. Ignoring the pain, he staggered upright, his first instinct to recover his weapon from a nearby bush of rosemary. And then he knew. He had done his ankle - twisted it badly, sprained the bastard maybe. 'What a fucking time,' he muttered, as he sagged onto the grass, grasping his suddenly useless ankle with both hands. Tears leaped into his eyes.

But up on the terrace there was a blur or movement. A flash of reflection as the French doors were flung open. A stocky man in red striped boxer shorts and a white corporate T-shirt was waving a gun at him. A police issue Glock, Eddie thought in that brief moment of decision.

'On your feet, mate! Get your fuckin' hands in the air!'

An Australian accent. Eddie couldn't believe it. In one movement, he scooped up Mister-kiss-my-arse and found the trigger. A burst of three cut the silence wide open. The French windows collapsed in a shower of dancing glass. The figure in the shorts and T-shirt was jerked backwards and disappeared.

Eddie limped up the terrace steps, each movement of his twisted ankle an agony. The man was lying face upwards on the tiles, his head wedged into one of the broken panes. One in the face that had removed a wedge of cheek bone. One in the neck that was already making a mess of the terra cotta tiles. And one through the breastbone, with seepage the same colour as the Harvey Norman Discounts T-shirt logo. Nice grouping for first up in the morning, was Eddie's immediate thought, followed by: 'What's another dumb fuckin' Australian doing over here?'

While he listened for sounds of movement in the house, Eddie replaced the three spent shells. If it had to be this way, he preferred to do business with a full clip. He slipped through the French doors and took a good look around before making the next move. It didn't seem to Eddie like the home of a particularly wealthy man - but then, what did he know about decor? Or maybe it meant that McGraw was so desperate these days he couldn't be too choosy about his friends.

At that moment a door slammed down the far end of the house and a man's heavy tread crackled on the parquet. What the fuck was that lunatic doing across the river? He was supposed to be running a little diversionary fire, keeping these minders of McGraw's distracted out the front while Eddie got the job done in the house. Instead it sounded like Jacques had decided to shoot the dogs then call it a day.

Eddie took cover behind the heavy maroon drapes that bordered the French doors. Not exactly cover, but the light in the room was dim enough to give him the advantage. The man entered the room almost before Eddie was settled. From the little Eddie could see of him - muscular, blonde, northern European type, also carrying a Glock and dressed in black track suit pants and a yellow T-shirt - he was another of McGraw's minders. The man was calling for his mate, Gary and muttering encouragement to himself, in what sounded like German. There was no point in trying to tell these guys that he had just come to collect some paintings. He was going to have to take them out one by one.

When the man saw the splash of shattered glass on the floor, and then Gary's blood soaked body, he sagged a little and uttered a tirade of high-pitched curses. Eddie stepped out from behind the curtain and put away a bracket of five. Ugly overkill, he thought at once - but if you were heading down that path it made no sense to lower the odds. The man jackknifed then toppled back into a lounge chair, like some cartoon character receiving bad news. He writhed for a short while, clutching hopelessly at the red mess that was pooling in his stomach, at the same time trying to suck air like a surfacing goldfish. Eddie walked quickly over to the lounge chair and sunk another round behind his left ear. These poor fuckers had no idea of what they had signed on for when they came to work for McGraw. He would have preferred to never have involved them - to have come in clean and slipped out with the paintings under his arm - but this was what they were paid for. This was what you got when you minded the door.

From upstairs Eddie heard what sounded like panicked whispers and a furtive scurrying of footsteps. But he had no intention of committing himself to the stairs until he was certain there was no one else on the ground floor. It took him five minutes to check each of the downstairs rooms and satisfy himself that there was no one about. He didn't expect for a moment that he would be so lucky as to stumble across the Picasso. His swollen ankle was a real distraction, and he would have slipped off his boots if he thought it would ease the pain. All the while he listened for sounds from above, but heard nothing more.

When he finally mounted the stairs, it was with the forlorn

knowledge that he was going to have to shoot McGraw on sight. Too bad there was never going to be the opportunity to talk. The man was probably up there waiting for him, cringing behind the bed covers with a gun in his shaking hand. He'd close his eyes and pull the trigger before he made a call on Eddie's intentions.

Eddie paused at the door of the first room off the landing. There was no advantage in stealth, the creaking floorboards gave away even the slightest movement. With his good foot he gave the door a solid nudge. It was a bedroom. Probably the one used by McGraw, judging from the smell of male toiletries and the slightly askew soft furnishings. From the doorway, Eddie could see that there was nobody behind the bed, and no room for cover beside the wardrobe. But the door to the en suite was slight ajar. Eddie approached it obliquely, Mister-kiss-my-arse at the ready.

He saw a movement in the mirror, heard the sound of a body brushing against the shower curtain. Eddie stepped aside quickly as the figure committed to a confrontation. It was tall, middle-aged man, stumbling over the edge of the free-standing bath tub, getting half tangled in the translucent black shower curtain as he tried to straighten his arm to fire a chrome-plated revolver. Eddie gave him a single clean shot. Knew he couldn't miss at that range. The man bellowed and slipped backwards, bringing the shower curtain down around himself. The revolver shot had blown some oak chips from a beam overhead, and Eddie stepped in quickly to seize the weapon before the man could get away another.

He saw at once that it was McGraw. He was down in the bathtub, cradling himself, clutching at his bloody upper arm and groaning like a man who was sure he was gone. The shower curtain, streaked with his blood, had turned a sickly purple.

Eddie took hold of McGraw's undamaged arm and hauled him upright.

'Calm down,' he said. 'You're not shot bad. It's just your shoulder.'

McGraw was too shocked to register the advice. Eddie tossed

him one of the pristine white fluffy towels from a neat stack near the bathtub.

'Hold that tight against it.'

McGraw obeyed dumbly. After a minute of total absorption with his injury, he looked up at Eddie with an expression of total incomprehension. How was this possible? 'Who are you?' he asked in a voice thick with emotion. 'Who the fuck sent you?'

'Can't tell you,' Eddie said. 'Just come for some paintings.'

'What are you talking about?'

'The Picasso and a couple of others - that's all.'

'There's a lot of people who want my Picasso. Who are you working for? Leon Meyer? That Hollywood fuck Orsini? You working for the Australian Government? This the way it's done now?'

'Can't say. Mister McGraw. Just here to collect.'

'You think you'll ever be able to sell my Picasso? You might as well go steal the Mona Lisa. Listen - a lot of people would like to take me down - but most of them are smart enough to know they couldn't pull it off.'

'I'm not here for the compliments, Mister McGraw. Take me to the paintings.'

Eddie nestled the barrel of the .30 cal Winchester carbine under McGraw's armpit, lined it up with his heart, left it it to him to draw the appropriate conclusion.

'Okay, okay, okay - I'll show you. Just get that fuckin' thing out of my armpit.'

McGraw led Eddie along the central passageway and into another bedroom. This one had the untouched anonymity, the *pot-pourris* smell of a vacant guest room. He indicated a bulky dresser against a bare, stone wall.

'It's behind there,' McGraw said with resignation.

Eddie kept Mister-kiss-my-arse trained loosely on McGraw while with one arm he dragged the chest away from the wall. And there it was: a brown paper package clad in protective bubble wrap. It had the size and shape of what he was looking for, but Eddie needed to be sure. He dragged it from it place of concealment and rested it on the bed cover.

'Packaged and ready to go,' Eddie said with a cool smile of appreciation.

McGraw was too preoccupied with his shoulder wound to pay much attention. 'This bleeding is serious…' he kept repeating. 'This towel isn't working at all.'

Eddie ignored McGraw's complaints and drew a folded hunting knife from his pocket. The blade quickly sliced through the bubble wrap, which he tore away and threw onto the floor.

'Christ's sake, careful!' McGraw warned.

Eddie slit open the package like an envelope, then, peeled the paper back from the surface of the canvas. He took a piece of paper from his pocket and unfolded it flat: it was a digital colour reproduction of the painting, given to him by Gornik and Toop. He had been carrying it in his pocket since Bangkok. He then began a patient comparison of the two images.

'You have a fondness for Picasso?' McGraw said with a sneer. 'Do you know what you're looking at?'

'I better be looking at a genuine Picasso,' Eddie said.

'Oh - you'd know one from the other?'

'I just know what I get paid when I deliver.'

'Then I guess you might as well call 'snap' right now,' McGraw said, trying to take a closer look at the photocopy.

'What?' said Eddie, already preoccupied.

'It's a joke, my friend. Something about this whole fucking fiasco ought to be amusing.'

'So where are the others?'

'What others?'

'I'm told you own four of these Picassos.'

McGraw tried to laugh. 'Sold already. Liquidated. Gone.'

'My friends will be disappointed.'

'Not as much as me.'

'It's just my line of work, Mister McGraw. Sorry about the pain and inconvenience.'

'Are you some kind of stand up comic? This all somebody's sick idea of how to recover what they imagine I owe?'

'That I can't say.' Eddie was too absorbed in repackaging the painting to pay the man much attention. He almost had the bubble wrap reattached when a movement from the doorway caught his eye.

A woman stood glaring at him, both arms extended, her trembling hands training a .38 Sig Sauer right at his head.

'Put that weapon down,' she said, wound so tightly that her lips barely shaped the words.

Eddie judged that although she might make a hash of the first shot, she was too close to miss altogether. Still, Eddie hesitated. The woman responded by taking a lunging step closer. Her eyes were demonic. Her finger was stroking the trigger. She was close enough for Eddie to stare down into the black eternity of the barrel. He calculated that he had no choice, but to toss "Mister-Kiss-My-Arse" onto the bed. McGraw immediately shuffled forward and scooped the weapon up. When it came to a crisis the man's shoulder didn't appear to trouble him at all.

'Thank Christ, Marlo...' McGraw gasped, 'I thought you were gone.'

The woman stood her ground, holding her bead between Eddie's eyes. Now that she had disarmed him she seemed to have no idea of the next move.

'Get him into the study, 'McGraw said, suddenly perking up now that they had the upper hand 'It's got a deadlock.' Eddie saw that the mechanism of the .30 Winchester seemed to perplex McGraw. He gave up and allowed the weapon dangle ineffectually at his side. But the woman was no such stranger to weapons. She took the .30 Winchester from McGraw, and while keeping the Sig trained on Eddie, ran the action as a demonstration.

'Get moving - out the door,' she ordered.

Eddie obeyed, almost curious about her next move. She was an immensely attractive woman and he had no idea who she might be.

The study was a small bedroom that had been appointed like a modern office. There was a row of contemporary office cabinets, a work station with a sophisticated PC set up, a large standing safe, and a desk cluttered with accounting stationery. It was the banker's home office.

Eddie barely had time to scrutinize the security bars on the windows before the door was slammed behind him. They had been too jumpy, and in too much of a hurry to get him locked away, to attempt to truss him up or even frisk him for a concealed weapon. Unfortunately the hunting knife lay forgotten on the bed cover back in the bedroom.

From the moment the lock was turned on the door Eddie could detect their rising panic. He could hear muffled shouting and a lot of frantic running from room to room. He imagined them hastily packing bags, taking what they needed for a long trip. There was going to be no way they could ever explain what had happened in this house. When he heard a loud descending drumming of feet on the stairs, he knew it was safe to make his move.

There was no possible view of the grounds immediately below from either of the windows, but Eddie wasn't concerned. He knew what they were up to, it didn't matter that he couldn't see them drive away. He took a small piece of torn cigarette pack from his pocket and picked up the telephone on the desk. In their hurry to get away, they hadn't even thought to wrench the socket from the wall. He dialed the mobile number written on the cigarette pack.

'Bonjour, Jacques,' he said, *'ça va?'* He smiled to himself while Jacques gave a long-winded, undecipherable explanation in French. Served Eddie right for getting cute with the language. 'So where the fuck are you?' he demanded. That did it. The man understood perfectly.

Eddie knew that he didn't have much time, and he was counting totally on Jacques's co-operation. He knew that Marlo and McGraw must have realized the full extent of their predicament when they arrived downstairs. The bodies of Gary and the German would have made them see for certain that they had no option but to flee the house. Would they dither around in uncertainty, or act immediately?

Eddie almost had the door off its hinges - the wood was seasoned oak, but the iron mongery was crap - by the time he heard the Mercedes start up. To his relief, he found that the hinges couldn't resist the leverage of a steel fire poker.

The Mercedes accelerated in the driveway. He could hear the tyres tearing up the gravel. Maybe it was too late to stop them, but at least he would escape.

The sound of the collapsing door almost obscured the gunshots. Five of them came in rapid succession. Eddie heard the Mercedes rev to screaming point. Someone's foot was jammed on the accelerator. Then came the ugly whump of metal colliding with stone, and the explosive crack of shattering glass.

Eddie hobbled down the stairs and headed towards the front of the building as fast as the pain would allow. He unlatched the heavy oak front door and saw immediately what had happened. The Mercedes had ploughed into one of the massive stone gate pillars.

Eddie took his time walking to the car. He saw that Jacques had shot out a tyre as well as the windscreen. The woman had lost control of the wheel. At that moment, Eddie realized how easy it would be for Jacques to take him out as well.

Eddie stood alongside the coupé and surveyed the damage. McGraw, who had evidently failed to fasten his seat belt - the ultimate irony for a man who had lived his entire life in the fast lane - was wedged beneath the dash. His body had been rammed forward and compacted on impact. From the odd angle at which his head jutted from his contorted body, it looked as though his neck had been broken. There was no movement in his chest. The man was probably already dead. Eddie was amused to see that the blood-soaked bath towel was still wrapped around his shoulder.

The woman was still sitting, dazed in the driver's seat, with one leg provocatively propped out of the open door. Her head was in her hands and she was whimpering between each rasping breath. She didn't hear Eddie's approach. The .38 Sig was lying in her lap. Eddie reached down and took it, then slowly lifted the woman free of the car. A string of mucous trailed from her wet lips. A blue bruise covered most of her forehead.

'I hope you haven't damaged my Picasso,' Eddie said. A callous joke, he knew, but it was too late for restraint now that a boundless malevolence had been unleashed inside him.

'Who are you...you miserable asshole?' she said, as she tried to regain her balance.

Then, while the woman walked in a circle of faltering steps, her face turned towards the sun, as though it might be some source of recovery, Eddie took the keys from the ignition and opened the trunk. The packaged painting was lying on top of a Louis Vuiton travelling case. Eddie tucked it under his arm and returned to the woman. He touched her chin and turned her face towards his.

'Get out of here - now,' he said.

'My husband?...My God...what's happened to my husband?' She had only just noticed that he had been forced beneath the car's dash. Eddie allowed her to rush to the passenger side of the car, where she broke into uncontrollable sobs. Finally, he had to restrain her.

'He's not going to make it - you can see that. And neither are you, unless you get out of here right now.'

He took hold of her face again and rested the barrel of the .38 against her cheek. 'In that study where you locked me up, there are some keys to a BMW. They're lying on the desk. The car's in the driveway. Go back up there and get them, and leave right away. I know you don't feel capable of anything right now, but this you'd better do.'

Why was he offering to let her walk? What was stopping him from pulling the trigger on her? In his entire career he had never done a woman, but that wasn't exactly it. Right now she had as many reasons to run as Eddie; there was no reason to fear her wanting to talk to the *gendarmes*; but that wasn't it, either. It was the effect she'd had on him. The moment he had first seen her, up in that room with the Sig in her hand, something about her had got to him. A beautiful, lean and hungry look that appealed to Eddie. She didn't deserve to die to for a fucking painting.

He guided her to the car trunk and lifted out the travelling case. When he placed it in her hand she allowed it to fall onto the gravel. She stared at him obliquely, not comprehending at all.

'Christ Almighty,' Eddie said. 'Do I have to put you behind the wheel myself?'

'So, please...help me,' she said, with an irresistibly imploring look.

'I don't know who you are, lady. And the truth is, I don't really give a fuck, but you've got a choice. Stay here and talk to the *gendarmes* - they'll be all over the place in an hour or two - or get into that car and drive away.'

The woman wiped her mouth with the back of her hand and held her head upright. 'All right,' she said with stern dignity. 'Help me.'

Eddie walked her to the BMW and then limped back upstairs to the study to get the keys. He stowed the suitcase in the trunk and even opened the driver's side door for her, picturing himself like one of those guys in evening wear who always featured in car commercials. She was an amazing, courageous woman, and he wished there was some way he could see her again, but the thought was ludicrous and he crushed it instantly. She looked far too young to be McGraw's wife, but maybe that's how it was when you lived a multi-million-dollar lifestyle.

'I don't know where you're going, but good luck to you,' he said, not expecting her to believe that he meant it. 'And I regret what happened to your husband. It was nothing personal.'

'Fuck you,' she said with an animal ferocity. 'I hope you die in the dirt the same way.' She slammed the door, almost jamming his fingers, punched the ignition, and then accelerated away.

As he was returning to the Mercedes he heard a car approaching. Expecting the *gendarmes*, Eddie took cover behind the rear end of the Mercedes and ran the unfamiliar action of the .38 Sig. But when the car came to a stop and he heard the sound of two pairs of boots on gravel and a burst of familiar laughter, he stepped away from his cover.

'Eddie, Eddie, Eddie - what a mess!'

It was Didier, accompanied by a poker-faced Jacques, greeting him with a big grin, throwing his hands up in the air in a gesture of comic despair. 'Good thing you hired Jacques,' Didier said, indicating the damaged front end of the Mercedes, ' but you made him earn his money.'

'He'll get paid,' was all Eddie said. He didn't like the sly, satisfied look in Jacques' eyes. Didn't like the way the man was still brandishing his rifle.

Didier pointed to the Picasso under Eddie's arm.

'And you've got your painting. Nice work. So? Everybody happy?'

'Except him,' said Eddie, leading them over to the passenger's side of the Mercedes, where McGraw's blood-speckled buzz-cut was already gathering flies.

'This the man?' Didier asked, with the hushed awe he had always had around death. 'Mister two billion dollars, huh? Look at that - no seat belt.' He was seeing the connection between the bloody smear on the dash and the crushed body wedged low in the seat. 'Lucky I'm not with the *gendarmes* no more. Big fine for no seat belt.'

'Yeah - he's real lucky,' said Eddie, his mind off on his own train of thought, trying to calculate how long it would be before these jackals made their move.

'So we two - we get a bonus?' Didier said, with a cheeky wink and a rapid glance between Jacques and Eddie.

'Afraid not.'

'Well, that's bad news for us, Eddie. We have to help ourselves. Maybe take this painting instead.'

Eddie knew it had been coming. 'Excuse me?' he said.

'Come on, Eddie, don't play fuckin' dumb with me. We want the painting.'

Eddie brought it out from under his arm with a distracting flourish. With his other hand he felt for the Sig in his trouser pocket.

'You're a greedy fuck, Didi, old man...' The Sig came up and Eddie gave Didier three rapid rounds in the chest. 'But you can have half a clip - my compliments.' The man stumbled backwards in shock, gabbling a strangled plea, the fell into a feathery bed of lavender.

Jacques took a few a skittering steps towards the cover of the Mercedes, but he didn't make it. The man raised his rife, but Eddie got there first and emptied three in his direction. Jacques spun around and whacked his head against the bonnet before going down. He lay on the gravel with his eyes wide open, a startled expression on his paralyzed features. One of his boots quivered with an involuntary spasm. Eddie took a good close look at the body. It had been a better placement than he had hoped - one in the gut, one in the chest, and another in the throat.

He took a last look at McGraw's body. The absurd posture, the stupid circumstances, all of it so random and meaningless, nothing to be learned from any of it. He had never wanted it to go that way. He had only come for the painting. Otherwise it would have been fine by Eddie if McGraw had got away clean. The man meant nothing to him. He hardly knew a thing about him, he'd been out of the country when McGraw was making the news. Skimmed a few articles, heard the rumours, that was all he'd picked up. As for what the man had done, Eddie hardly cared. The way business was done everywhere, the winners always fucking over the losers, the rich salting it away, McGraw's greedy run seemed about par.

The poor, miserable fucker - what an ending.

The woman was a different matter. She'd had the sense to get away. She'd pick up her life somewhere else. Maybe he was just a sucker for a woman with a gun, but it did seem to promise something. But not something that Eddie was ever going to get.

On the floor of the Mercedes, tangled up with McGraw's feet, Eddie found Mister-kiss-my-arse, the stock now sticky with dark blood. It felt good to heft it again, not that he could afford keep it for long. Too many bullets sprayed around the landscape.

Eddie took a last look back at the house, then at the bodies of Didier and Jacques. Jacques he'd had no time for from the start. Obtuse Frog - he'd had it coming. But what the hell had happened to Didier's judgement? The man's life must have truly hit the wall for him to try a stunt like that. Did he think Eddie had come all that way to fall for some sucker take-down? And how did the clown think he'd ever unload a stolen Picasso?

Eddie shook his head and looked up at the white-hot sky. For the first time that day he felt the sun's full intensity beating down on his back. He was dehydrated and felt himself succumbing to the dizzy leglessness of the Mediterranean midday. He remembered that the woman had packed a tall bottle of Evian water for the trip. Eddie retrieved it from the Mercedes, drank half and sloshed the rest across his face and hands.

Two dead Alsatians. Five bodies. Rounds from four different guns. Who the hell shot whom? He had no idea what the *gendarmes* would make of the mayhem. All that was missing were the vultures.

The pain in his ankle was excruciating. Before walking out the gate, he snapped a limb from a tall lime tree and shaped a crude crutch. It took him over five minutes to limp back along the pathway that ran beside the wall. He hauled his bicycle up out of the wheat and attached the package to the iron carry-rack. It felt good to saddle up and pedal slowly back along the road to Cazals.

Halfway along the road a car full of peering faces crawled past. Eddie acknowledged them with a nod and kept on pedaling. Maybe it was headed to McGraw's place, but then they didn't exactly look like friends of the family. Thank God he looked like a peasant.

A few minutes later he reached the bridge across the Aveyron. Midway out he dismounted and rested the bike against the stone railing. He took Mister-kiss-my-arse out from under his shirt and fondled the grip one last time. The best piece of instant intimidation he had ever owned. He leaned out and let it drop into the river.

The blue Renault Kangoo was waiting for him in the shade of a big tree on the other side. It was like none of it had ever happened. Nevertheless he spent five minutes looking carefully behind all four wheels and under the chasis before touching anything. There was no telling what skills Jacques might have possessed, and no guessing what he might have had in mind.

He placed the package under a rug in the rear of the van, then drove away. The van would go back to a yard in the centre of Toulouse - he mistrusted airport car hires, they were the first records the police always checked - and he would then take an airline bus out to Blagnac, But first, before leaving the Val d'Aveyron, he would re-visit Albert Laussier at La Serre.

It had been six days since he had left the old man bound and tethered on the floor of his barn. Laussier's strength had been failing even then. Eddie hoped he was not too late.

Once again, he parked the Kangoo near the farm's entrance, and sat with the windows rolled down, listening for any hint of human activity. He heard nothing unusual. After several minutes, he left the vehicle and approached the barn. From the direction of the pigpen he heard the sounds of scurrying creatures. In the semi-darkness he saw several large rats dart across the floor.

He smelled Laussier before he saw him. The stench of putrefaction made him wince. The old man's body was still tethered to the mattress, but now contorted in a rigid foetal huddle. A portion of his cheek had been gnawed away, exposing a grimacing row of yellow teeth, set in a serrated brown gum.

Eddie had known all along that this was what he would discover, but he had tried to put the thought out of mind.

How many deaths was he responsible for? It hardly mattered now. Remorse was pointless. All he could do was keep moving. Stay ahead of the forces that would soon be in pursuit. And there was no telling what they knew already. Had Didier given Eddie's name to anyone? Once news of the killings reached Paris, would Roger Knight remain silent? Eddie thought he could count on nobody.

He left La Serre with all traces of his visit erased and drove towards Toulouse. His thoughts were focused on anonymity and the unexpected.

He felt safe in the Kangoo. He would have preferred to have driven it all the way to Paris, but hanging onto anything was a risk. Along the way he would trade vehicles. He slipped a tape that he'd brought into the deck: *Riding with the King*, Eric Clapton and B.B. King jamming together. Thirty minutes of bliss each side. If only he could feel it.

35

August 25: Val d'Aveyron

They parked their car a hundred metres from the entrance gate to McGraw's hideout and sat for a minute to assess their situation. There was no activity up at the farmhouse - no sign of any cars, and no sound of human presence.

Todd and Brooke prepared their equipment. They would tape Ilena's "courageous" approach to the gates - creating a long take of the kind of pseudo dramatic filler one frequently saw in network investigative documentaries.

Apart from the ominous crunching of their footfalls on the limestone gravel of the entrance road, Mitchell imagined all was silent. Until he picked up the distant whine of small car engines, straining on the hills of the D115 across the river; the solitary thrush, making his territorial claim in song from his perch high up on the tip of the satellite television dish; and then, as he neared the gates, the massed, low frequency droning of bees in the blossoms of the *tilleul* trees.

Ilena was the first to see the two fallen dogs in the driveway. Mitchell saw her face crease with apprehension. She quickened her pace and arrived at the scene of carnage well before the others. Todd had to scramble to keep her in frame.

She stood staring in disbelief at the scene before her: the compacted Mercedes *coupé* with its bonnet rammed into the gate post, its windscreen blown away, and alarming, gouged slew marks behind it in the gravel; the two Alsatian bodies, lying on their sides, feet extended, as dogs do in the sun, giving the illusion that they were simply basking; and the grotesquely arrayed bodies of Didier and Jacques, now leaking dark pools of blood onto the snow bright white gravel, their weapons discarded like children's toys.

Impelled by dread, she hurried to the side of the Mercedes. In the moment of seeing McGraw's crushed body she gave out an anguished cry. Mitchell rushed to her aid. Her tanned face had suddenly turned distressingly pale. Her mouth remained open, frozen in a mute scream as she slid to her knees onto the gravel, both palms pressed against the dusty silver duco of the door.

Mitchell crouched down beside her and wrapped an arm around her shoulders, pressing her close.

'Oh, God! How could this happen?' she moaned. 'Did we cause this?'

'No, no - I don't think so. Not at all.' He had no idea what he meant by such empty reassurance, but he could not withhold it. When he did have a moment to reflect on the scene, he could only imagine that it had been Franco Orsini and his gang who had done the killing when they had at last come to collect their painting.

Todd, almost oblivious to the anguish in front of his lens, continued taping for a few minutes. He was slowly circling the Mercedes in a long, uninterrupted tracking shot, as beautiful as it was cruel. To keep out of the shot, Brooke was forced to shuffle along behind him. Finally, she could take it no more, and nudged him to request that he button off. There was no way that abject footage of Ilena Vadas, on her knees and weeping, no matter how authentic, was ever going to make it into the documentary. But once Ilena had recovered a little and had seen what they had been shooting, she too, couldn't restrain her exploitative instincts.

'Todd! Stop shooting this stuff!' she commanded, brushing away the hot tears that had completely wet her cheeks. 'His body! Up close! All of it!'

Todd, somewhat awed by the situation, walked awkwardly around the Mercedes, attempting to transform his moral confusion into a series of aesthetic decisions.

At last, Ilena too, came to her senses and began to regret her impetuosity. 'Oh, my God - I've touched the car all over the place,' she wailed, distressed by her temporary abandonment of professional standards. 'I've contaminated the bloody crime scene!' Mitchell helped her to her feet and steadied her with an arm around her waist.

'Who were these people?' she said, pointing to the bodies of Didier and Jacques.

'I have no idea,' said Mitchell, 'and it really isn't our job to try to find out.

He took Ilena's mobile phone from her – she made no protest - and began a search for the *gendarmes* emergency number.

'I know we have it somewhere - maybe on the production schedule,' Brooke said, thrusting a piece of folded A4 at him..

Mitchell led Ilena away from the Mercedes, steered her out the gates and back towards their own vehicle. As soon as he had steadied her, he put in the call to the *gendarmes.*

'When we talked yesterday I thought everything was going to be all right for him again,' she said. She was talking about McGraw as though they had been closer than Mitchell had realized. 'He seemed to have such strong belief in himself. I thought he'd survive...I thought he was invincible.'

'But it all caught up with him,' Mitchell said quietly. 'Had to, some time.' It was the kind of anodyne observation one made when feeling such helplessness. 'Who can understand anything?'

For an agonizing thirty minutes, all of them, in their own disoriented and anxious ways, waited for the arrival of the *gendarmes.* Ilena took a solitary walk down towards the river. She wanted to be alone with her grief. Mitchell realized that she had barely been honest about the depth and extent of her relationship with McGraw. As for what had become of Marlo. he had no clear thoughts at all. Could she have been the one who dispatched the two men lying dead in the driveway after they had killed her husband? It was possible, but he seriously doubted it. Franco Orsini was the only suspect who made any sense at all. Marlo had probably fled at the first sign of danger. Whatever happened, she would have escaped. That was her talent, her form, when things got rough. He was pleased that he would never have to see her again.

And as for the portrait of Dora Maar, perhaps it was still in its wrappings, hidden somewhere up in the farmhouse, but he doubted that, too. Maybe Marlo had escaped with it, or maybe it was heading back to its place on the wall of Orsini's boss's *château* in California. The only thing he could be sure of now was that he would never know the truth.

Half an hour passed before the *gendarmes* arrived from Saint-Antonin-Noble-Val. The road was sealed off, and the farmhouse became a secured crime scene. Within an hour a forensic team from Toulouse arrived, and then the television and news crews, all of them as eager as bargain-sale shoppers, turned up soon after. Mitchell and Ilena were questioned at length by the senior homicide detective and told nothing in return. Afterwards, Mitchell held her in his arms for a long time, until she had assured him that she was calm.

Later that evening they were driven back to their hotel in Toulouse, and the following morning they all flew back to Paris.

It would be days before they learned the results of the police investigation. As Mitchell anticipated, the forensic experts admitted to having discovered very little. Apart from the identities of all the dead and their means of death, the police were without answers. The identities and motives of the killers (at least they were certain there had been more than one, although they had offered no evidence for this conclusion) remained a mystery. Franco Orsini's name never appeared on any list of suspects - not then, nor at any time in the future.

36

August 26: Paris

The small, twin-engined plane was parked at the edge of the runway, fueled and ready for take off. Eddie followed his instructions and drove his new hire car, a small grey Peugeot, up alongside the starboard wing. Two men that he hadn't at first seen, stepped from the shadows to meet him. They introduced themselves as Johnny and Maxwell, and shook Eddie's hand in a perfunctory way. But little was said. From their accents, he judged Maxwell to be a Londoner, and Johnny an Australian. They made no pretense of having any interest in Eddie. Their only concern was for the painting.

Eddie unlocked the rear door of the Peugeot and took the package out from under a rug. He handed it to the two men, and then stepped back to allow them unwrap it.

'Only one, huh?' said Maxwell.

'That's it,' said Eddie.

As soon as they had it out in the open, Johnny held a small torch while Maxwell made a close examination of the painting. In the lurid glow of the industrial orange airport lights it was hard to see exactly what they were up to. The man called Maxwell was clearly the authority. He had a copy of the same digital reproduction of the Dora Maar portrait that Eddie had been given, but he took considerably more time to make the comparison. Using a magnifying glass, the man subjected various areas of the canvas to close scrutiny. From the mutterings he occasionally made to Johnny, the judgement was apparently being based on the *'rendering of certain motifs'*, various *'characteristic brush patterns'*, and the *'texture of the pigments employed'*. He took a particularly long time to examine the Picasso signature. The jargon sounded like bullshit to Eddie. If the thing was valuable, it should have been obvious in a flash.

Twenty minutes later, Maxwell told Johnny that he was satisfied. They repackaged the painting in the same materials it had arrived in, and then fitted it into a slim, pine packing crate. Only after they had stowed it away on the aircraft did Eddie come forward and raise the matter of his final payment.

'You boys haven't forgotten my other two hundred thousand euros?'

Johnny and Maxwell looked at one another and grinned.

'Nah, sorry mate,' Johnny drawled, 'We thought you'd be happy to fuck over that bastard McGraw for free.'

Finally Maxwell climbed into the cockpit and returned with a small package, tightly wrapped in plastic. He bounced it from hand to hand, in a provocative gesture of contemplation, before tossing it to Eddie.

'Surely the easiest money you'll ever earn.'

Eddie took a few steps back, opened the blade of his stiletto and slit open the package. He withdrew the wad of notes. Crisp hundred-euro notes. Maybe they had short-changed him. Maybe they were counterfeit. But how was he to tell in this light? It would take half an hour to check them all. He plucked a few notes from the centre of the wad. At least they bore the familiar watermark.

'You're a cautious man, Eddie,' Johnny said.

'It pays,' was all Eddie offered in reply.

'Mr. Gornik and Mr. Toop have asked me to relay their gratitude,' said Maxwell, speaking with menacing formality. 'They hope you'll remember what has to happen next.'

'Nobody ever knows what happens next,' Eddie said with a cold smile.

Eddie tilted his head in farewell and returned to the driver's door of his Peugeot. He stood there for a short while, watching as Johnny and Maxwell secured their cargo and slammed the hatch door. They were still checking their aircraft as Eddie drove away.

Once he was a hundred metres from the plane, out of sight behind the terminal building, Eddie pulled over and abandoned the car. He had done this ever since he had been in France. At every stage, switched vehicles after each transaction. Over in the public parking lot, he had a small Citroën sedan waiting. It had been sitting in readiness since the day before. All these discarded cars. Hire firms from one end of France to the other were going to want his arse.

Minutes later, he was sitting in the darkened Citroën, watching the runway. He could see the lights of the plane as it taxied in preparation for take off.

All at once, the sound of sirens rose to swallow up the roar of the plane's engines. Police cars - three of them - were speeding along the entrance road to the airport. They flashed past the car park in dangerously close convoy. Strobes of blue light played across Eddie's windscreen. But nobody was looking for a man in a hired Citroën.

He had no idea how they had been tipped off. Maybe they had tracked him in the Kangoo all the way from Toulouse. It didn't matter now.

Off in the distance, Eddie could see that one of the police cars had peeled off to investigate his abandoned Peugeot, while the other two continued on towards the runway. They had turned on their searchlights and the darting beams cut a curious pattern in the light mist that lay across the airport.

He would have liked to have continued watching, but needed the cover of the sirens to slip away unheard and unseen. A little later, as he turned onto the freeway that led back to Paris, he was able to get another view of the runway. He could see the aircraft, gathering speed for take off. The police cars, pursuing it, on the road that ran parallel to the strip. The plane, lurching into the air, appearing to lift off prematurely. The angle of take off, impossibly abrupt. A misjudgement. A moment of panic. The starboard wing, suddenly dipping, dropping away. The aircraft losing momentum as it stalled. Tail sagging towards the runway. A brief plummet. And then the fireball. Blossoming out to engulf both plane and one of the cars in an orange inferno.

Dora Maar was never leaving France.

Eddie pulled off the freeway to see the last of it. By now the police car had also been consumed in the conflagration. Thick white smoke drifted across the runway, and for a brief, uncanny interval, all that could be heard was the comforting roar of traffic on the freeway. There was nothing more to be done. In a few minutes the place would be swarming with even more police and emergency vehicles.

He drove in the direction of Paris, and then, turning south, took the E60 towards Tours. A light rain had begun to fall, but that didn't slow down the traffic on the *autoroute.* That suited Eddie, too, who kept his foot to the floor with the needle on 130. Fortunately, he had remembered to throw his bag of tapes into the new car. He fossicked around in it until he found what he was after, slipped the cassette into the player, and up came Al Green's, *Soul Survivor.* Eddie began to sing along, his joyous off-key voice mingling with the slushing thrum of his speeding tyres:

'So I'm taking out a policy,
Gonna get some soul insurance...'

In four hours he would reach Bordeaux. Another one-and-a-half to Toulouse. And by 2:00 a.m. he would be crossing the Spanish border, where, if things became tricky he would present an Irish passport in the name of Nigel Bannerman. He had a booking on an early morning flight from Barcelona to Athens. From that point on, he had no plans at all. He had heard about the Cycladic Islands. A man could wander there, no questions asked. He would buy a ferry ticket and see how he felt. Maybe he would turn up on Mikonos as Nigel Bannerman, or maybe as Eddie Pike. The deal was to stay out of sight for three years, but who was going to call him on that? He would lie low just long enough for the McGraw thing to die down and then drift back to Asia. Make sure he had one more Royal Thai dinner in Bangkok. He could afford it. Two hundred thousand euros was going to last a long time.

37

August 27: Paris

Back in Paris, Mitchell and Ilena reported to the Australian Embassy for a meeting with agents of the Attorney General's Department. They told their story and they presented their videotaped evidence. But it shed no light on the man's death and none of it seemed of any great consequence. Roger Knight, who now appeared strangely distant, shrugged and declared it all very perplexing.

Later, Ilena and Mitchell went for lunch together at a single-starred Michelin restaurant in the sixth. It was her way of saying goodbye. Mitchell had once been told that the food wasn't up to much and that the service was indifferent - but did any of that matter at this late stage in their adventure? Ilena had arranged for a table with an extraordinary view of the city to the south of the Seine. The ambience made up for everything.

She told him that she was going to London on the Eurostar

that evening, then flying back to Australia at ten-fifty the following night. Twelve and a half hours out to Singapore, and another seven or eight down to Sydney. For a few painful moments Mitchell wondered whether he should have been on it himself. But no - he had unfinished business in France.

Her reasons were obvious. Now that McGraw was dead all her plans no longer made sense. The horrific circumstances surrounding McGraw's death had made the story the property of the news services. Her opportunistic network had already aired key segments of *THE FINAL INTERVIEW* in one of their nasty current affairs programmes. His death was already old news. If there was ever to be a documentary about the last years of McGraw the story would have to be rethought entirely.

What would she do in the face of this calamity? Perhaps quit television altogether and finish the book that she had put aside for too long. Or maybe dig in and stick to her plans to deliver a documentary - in spite of the fact that events had moved beyond her comprehension. For the first time in his experience of her, she seemed lost, rudderless. She was depressed and remote, and the poise that had held him in her thrall seemed to have gone missing. He wondered why she had even wanted to have this final lunch. What could it be other than a lingering over something that was already over?

'What will you do now?' she asked.

'Well, tomorrow I'll show up at the Musée. Pick up where I left off. Finish with my obligations. Try to deal with what happened to Luc. And make plans to finish up over here.' He was trying to sound purposeful, but in fact was at that moment contemplating his sadness at the prospect of her leaving Paris. All departures affected him that way, his own no less than hers.

'Oh,' she said distractedly, 'that's not what I meant. I want to know what you'll try to do about the missing Picasso?'

'Oh, that's over – surely. There's nothing I can do. I don't have the resources to trawl around Europe looking for Marlo McGraw. I don't have the heart for it, either.'

'You really believe that's what happened? She took it?'

'It's what I'd like to believe - that she's out there somewhere, travelling incognito with a Picasso in her luggage.'

Ilena put down her wine glass and gave herself over to laughter. It took Mitchell by surprise. He had barely seen a smile from her in ages.

'You liked her a lot, didn't you,' she said.

'I suppose I did.'

'Did it ever go past that?' she asked, pressuring him with a wry smile.

Mitchell hesitated. It would have been simple say no, but after her confession of an affair with McGraw, he believed he owed her an honest answer. 'Yeah...once.'

'Only once?' she said, trying to sound amused. 'Well, I don't think I want to know when.'

Mitchell smiled and shrugged. He didn't want to talk about it either.

She raised her glass, inviting a toast. 'Will I see you again in Australia? Your time here will be up soon.'

'It will – and I hope so.'

She didn't pursue the matter. No empty promises. They were seeing the last of each other for the time being, and the energy for looking past tomorrow was spent.

'To our little caper,' she said, touching her glass against his.

'Our failed caper,' he said gently.

'To Dora Maar.'

'It might have amused her.'

'And to Marlo - whoever she was.'

Mitchell could see that Ilena understood exactly how much she had fascinated him.

'And Mike McGraw.' He didn't really mean it, but it seemed ungenerous not to include him.

'And Picasso,' she said, finally. 'I'm sure you don't want to leave him out.'

He walked her back to her hotel and waited with her in the

lobby for a taxi. Their time together sped by. Every fantasy he'd ever entertained about her was already lost, out of reach.

In the taxi to Gare de Nord a storm burst over the sweltering city. Heavy rain hammered the windows, cocooning them in the cramped rear seats. They looked away from one another, both too desolate to communicate.

He saw young women dodge the rain as they dashed in front of their taxi, faces pale and beautiful in the bruised light. Lovers huddled under a tiny umbrella, laughing, already soaked. A skinny dog, with sopping fur, skulking for cover. The blur of lurid neon and red tail-lights. The city dissolving as they passed.

It was her leaving, but in a way, his too.

He took in the warmly lit, vivid and inviting interiors of passing shops, rendered even more sadly impressionistic by the curtain of rain. People's transactions, offered only in fragments and fleetingly glimpsed, seemed complete and totally comprehensible.

At the station, he dashed across the street with her, heedless of the sluggish traffic, her suitcase balanced on his head. He would remember how it felt, every moment of it, but hang on to nothing.

They kissed at the barrier. He brushed her wet cheek, but she found his lips and pressed herself against him.

And then she was gone.

Tomorrow belonged to Picasso, Dora, and Luc.

www.ingramcontent.com/pod-product-compliance
Lightning Source LLC
Chambersburg PA
CBHW030811310726
48980CB00006B/458/J

9781426906527